Queen Victoria:
DEMON HUNTER

A.E. Moorat weaves a seamlessly lurid tapestry of royal biography, gothic horror and fist-gnawing comedy as he lifts the veil on what really took place on the dark and cobbled streets of 19th-century England.

Queen Victoria:
DEMON HUNTER

A.E. Moorat

HODDER

First published in Great Britain in 2009 by
Hodder & Stoughton
An Hachette UK company

First published in paperback in 2009

1

A CIP catalogue record for this title is available from the British Library.

B format PB ISBN 978 1444 70026 8
A format PB ISBN 978 1444 70034 3

Typeset in Berkeley Book by Palimpsest Book Production Limited,
Grangemouth, Stirlingshire

Printed and bound in Canada by
Webcom

Hodder & Stoughton policy is to use papers that are natural, renewable
and recyclable products and made from wood grown in sustainable forests.
The logging and manufacturing processes are expected to conform to the
environmental regulations of the country of origin.

Hodder & Stoughton Ltd
338 Euston Road
London NW1 3BH

www.hodder.co.uk

To you, brave Bear

Acknowledgments

Firstly thanks so much to Kate Howard and Carolyn Mays at Hodder. Not only were they the book's midwives, but they excelled at being there when needed and not there when not. I hope I've repaid their faith. Also at Hodder I'd like to say thank you to Katie Hall and Katie Davison for their work on this book, but also to Henry and Jocasta and Fenella and Cecilia and Helen for being wonderful and supportive in past lives. A million thanks to my agent Antony Topping for, well, everything. To Justine Taylor for a great copy-edit. To Dave Taylor for overcoming his fear of rats to read on and give me invaluable feedback. To David Granger and Toby Tennant for being inimitable. To families Holmes, Oakley and Harrison for endless, endless help. And lastly to Dylan, for bringing me so much joy, and then more joy.

Part One

'I will be good'

I

Much later, as he watched his manservant, Perkins, eating the dog, Quimby gloomily reflected on the unusual events of the evening.

But oh! It had begun so promisingly! All of the zombies were safely confined to the lower quarters, the prostitutes had arrived and were being served drinks in the library and Quimby was briefing the man about the . . .

'What is Henry calling it, this new technique of his?' he had asked, directing his question at the young man who stood in his study, Henry's assistant.

Quimby had schooled with Henry Fox Talbot at Harrow. The two had since gone their separate ways, of course: Quimby had inherited his father's title and estate and used his leisure and wealth to pursue a life of dissolution, ungodliness and an unholy interest in revenance; Henry, meanwhile, had inherited his father's great intellect and put his time to altogether more worthwhile use, developing something called calotype.

How calotype worked, Quimby wasn't sure and didn't care. He was interested only in the end result, and upon hearing of this invention and seeing its great potential for adding an extra frisson to his debauchery, he had issued a summons. Fortuitously, his knowledge of certain *events* at Harrow had secured him access to Henry's new process, though – somewhat understandably – not Henry himself. Instead Talbot had sent a young apprentice, a snickering fellow named Craven, to do his dirty work for him (and if Quimby had his way, which was after all a foregone conclusion, it would be very dirty work indeed) and it was he who now stood in Quimby's study having set up the contraption for his lordship to inspect.

It looked like nothing more than a box on a tripod, and a rather shabby box at that, but was, apparently, so it was said, capable of doing something most extraordinary.

'It's called photogenic drawing, sir,' said Craven. 'Though in France they're calling it *photographie*.'

Quimby thought about this for a moment.

'Hm,' he said, 'much as I hate to credit our seditious overseas neighbours with anything approaching common sense, it has to be said that *photographie* is certainly less of a mouthful than photogenic drawing, do you not think?'

'Mr Talbot's very keen on photogenic drawing, sir.'

'So be it. And what has Henry *photogenically drawn* so far?'

'He's captured some scenes of the lake of Como, sir, very nice they are too, as well as the Oriel window in the south gallery of Lacock Abbey, a truly beautiful photogenic drawing, sir, if I may say so.'

'Scenery,' snorted Quimby derisively. '*Scenery*. Typical of Henry. No imagination whatsoever.'

'Sir?'

'Craven, listen carefully,' said Quimby, his voice taking on the tone of a conspirator, 'in the library downstairs sit three of London's most debased and degenerate women, and shortly I shall be availing myself of them. One at a time and all at once, though not necessarily in that order. It will be your job, Craven, to document this momentous event, using . . . that,' he indicated the tripod Craven had carried into the study, which now stood in the corner of the room, 'and I can promise you the results will be far more diverting than scenes of the lake of Como.'

'Yes, sir.'

Quimby leaned close. 'It has been said, Craven, that one of these ladies can accommodate an *entire pineapple*.'

'Goodness, sir.'

'Exactly. Not a sight we wish to entrust merely to our memory.'

'No, sir,' beamed Craven, happily.

From outside came the sound of a scream, and Quimby moved to the window in order to push aside his gratifyingly weighty drapes and peer out to the street beneath.

Filthy cobblestones shone dully, the only illumination from weak gaslights positioned at either end of the street or else from his own scullery window. He frowned, squinting, looking for the source of the noise – from the mews behind him, perhaps? But then, as he watched, a man appeared at one end of the street, running for his life, eyes wide in terror.

He wore the cloth cap and leather apron of a working man – a cooper, perhaps – and he appeared to be streaked with some fluid.

Was it tar? Oil? The gas-lamps were flickering wildly, as though affected by something more than the wind.

Flickering off.

Then on.

Off.

On.

No, not tar or oil, Quimby saw, as the man drew nearer, passing beneath his window; it looked like blood.

For a moment the only sound was of his boots on the cobbles. Next, another noise that Quimby took a moment to place. Scuttling.

Then he saw it. The man was being chased by rats, four score of them at least. They seemed to flow along the street after him, thick and viscous like a stream of effluent, black apart from bared teeth. At their head, unmistakably, was a rat that was much larger than the rest.

A rat that had two heads.

The running man glanced desperately behind him then screamed again. In response the pack began to squeal, and for a second or so the sound was so piercing it was all Quimby could do to not cover his ears.

Then the man reached the corner and was turning it just as the pack leader jumped, the teeth of one of its heads slicing deep into his neck, the other head twisting back then striking, almost like that of a cobra. The man was dropping to his knees as he turned the corner out of sight, his hands coming back, flapping at the two-headed rat, trying, failing, to dislodge it, his impetus carrying him forward, around the corner.

Just his feet visible now, kicking on the cobblestones.

Quimby watched as the chasing rats turned the corner, seeing their mass build. A pool of blood spread around the man's boots, still scrabbling but unable to find purchase, the weight of the vermin bearing down on him, preventing him from finding his feet. His screams became muffled, as though something had been forced into his mouth. Then came the sound of wet gagging.

Then silence.

His feet stopped kicking, his whole body jerked by the mass of rats as they ate him alive, the gas lamps flickering on and off.

'Sir?'

Craven spoke from behind him and Quimby turned. How long had he been standing at the window? He rubbed at his eyes. Christ, that was the last time he touched absinthe. The absolute last time . . .

'What was the screaming, sir?' said Craven.

'You heard it, too?'

'Yes, sir. From the road outside.'

'Did you hear . . . squealing?'

'Something very odd, sir, yes.'

Perhaps, thought Quimby, he'd been too hasty in blaming the absinthe. Maybe an unfortunate cooper really *had* been attacked by a two-headed rat right outside his window.

He barked with laughter.

Don't be so bloody ridiculous, Quimby. It was nothing but a hallucination. An old drunk running, who fell and hit his head, that was all.

Could be dead, he mused.

Hm, they were always in need of a cadaver. Messrs Hare and Burke had become so bloody expensive of late; neither were the bodies as fresh as they might be; thought they could charge the earth just because they had the name. Who's to say they really were the sons of *the* Burke and Hare anyway? After all, they could be any old pair of Scotsmen; there were so bloody many of them in London these days . . .

Anyway. Quimby took a deep breath. Clapped his hands briskly.

'Right, my boy,' he told Craven, 'down to business. Bring your contraption and we'll repair to the library for some . . . Hm, I've a mind to christen the process *pornogenic drawing*, what do you think?'

'In France they'll call it *pornographie*, sir,' joked the younger man.

'It'll never catch on, Craven.'

Just then came the noise of an almighty scream, this time from inside the house, and the door to Quimby's study was flung open.

The two men started as into the room burst Quimby's manservant Perkins, red-faced and flustered, reaching for the door and slamming it closed on the unmistakeable sounds of a great commotion from downstairs, then standing with his back to it as though to keep it barred. He stood for a moment, wide-eyed and breathing heavily, his clothes in disarray.

'Really, Perkins,' snapped Quimby, 'what is the meaning of this?'

'Sir, it's the zombies, sir,' Perkins managed, breathing heavily.

There was a crack of lightning from outside, a rumble of thunder.

'Yes?' said Quimby, still irritated. 'What about the zombies?'

'Sir, they're eating the prostitutes.'

II

20 June 1837, twenty-five minutes past two in the morning. A servants' residence in the grounds of Windsor Castle.

All was silent in the small, low room as Clara entered from outside, her brisk knock having gone unheeded. She bent to pass through the miserly frame then turned to close the door behind her, shutting out the night and a summer storm that raged hard and rent the sky: maniac lightning; distant, angry thunder; rain that fell in huge droplets then stopped. Then started again. Then stopped.

She was pleased to escape it; grateful the rain had ceased long enough for her to make the dash across the lawns from the castle to the relative sanctuary of the Browns' cottage.

Which was quiet, the family at rest. In the parlour before the fireplace, even though the fire was not lit, snoozed Margaret Brown in her rocking chair, a shawl pulled over her shoulders. Her husband, John, would be sleeping off the whisky behind the thick, dirty muslin curtain which hung from a rail dividing the room; while not far away was a low cot in which lay her son, John, eleven years old, curled up, sleeping and no doubt dreaming of catching fish on the River Dee in Crathie.

Clara stood before the redoubtable matriarch, smoothed her apron, silently cursed her misfortune – the short straw, *again* – and cleared her throat as loudly as she dared.

Mrs Brown slept on; young John Brown slumbered undisturbed; there was neither sound nor movement from the other side of the tattered muslin curtain.

Clara swallowed, thrust out her chin, clasped her hands in front of her, then, casting her voice loudly and clearly into the room, said, 'Ma'am, I'm very sorry to have to disturb you, but . . . the King is dead, ma'am.'

At that Brown jerked awake in the rocking chair, her eyes wide and her hair, long and black as a winter night, wild and untamed about her visage.

'The King is dead?' croaked Mrs Brown. 'Did you say the King is dead?'

She put her palms to her eyes, pushing the sleep from them.

'Yes, ma'am,' replied Clara, and she crossed herself.

The Royal household had been in a state of preparation for this eventuality since the end of May, when Sir Henry Halford, physician to His Majesty, had reported that King William was 'in a very odd state and decidedly had the hay fever and in such a manner as to preclude his going to bed', which the King had – gone to bed, that is.

Shortly afterwards the foreign secretary, Lord Palmerston, upon visiting the King, had felt it his sad duty to report that the King was in a very precarious state and unlikely to last long. (Privately the foreign secretary had declared that he hoped the King would last longer, 'for there would be no advantage to having a totally inexperienced girl of eighteen, just out of strict guardianship, to govern an empire.') On which note the Royal household had begun to ready itself for this very moment.

And now the King was dead, and Mrs Brown, furious at having let herself fall asleep – quite literally, she thought, caught napping! – stood and reached for her broadsword, which leaned against the brickwork by the side of the fire. Picking it up she shrugged off the shawl to reveal a rough jerkin over which was strapped a leather brigandine.

She wears armour, Clara realised with a start, and it was all the serving girl could do to suppress a laugh. Not of joy, but of shock.

'How long?' barked Mrs Brown

'Ma'am?'

'How long has the King been dead, stupid girl?' she roared.

John stirred slightly at the sound of his mother's raised voice and Maggie Brown cursed herself. He was so sensitive; he had such visions – such visions – he needed protection from all of this . . .

'How long, Clara?' insisted Brown, her voice lower and kinder now. 'How long is it since the King passed over?'

'I was told five minutes ago, ma'am,' replied Clara.

'And have they left?'

'Have who left, ma'am?'

'Lord Conyngham and the Archbishop of Canterbury. Have they set off for Kensington Palace with the news?'

'Yes, ma'am, they have.'

'Then in two hours' time England will have a queen. A new reign will begin.'

And nothing would ever be the same again, she thought.

For too long England had been ruled by tyrants and madmen, womanisers and fools. Europe was wrought by revolution and in France . . . well, it hardly bore thinking about, what had taken place in that godforsaken country, the blood that had flowed in the name of revolution. As a result of it, English eyes were cast in that direction; some nervous, some envious.

Revolution. Bloodshed. Anarchy. It was his work and he chose his moments well.

Brown ceased busying herself then tilted her head slightly so that she appeared to be sniffing the air.

'There is a disturbance tonight,' she said, softly at first; then, her voice rising, 'there is darkness abroad. I must reach the wee lassie before he does.'

'Before Lord Conyngham, ma'am?'

'No, girl, *he*: the lord of misrule. He who would bring war, disease and pestilence to this land. I can sense it, lassie, he's ready; he'll make his move tonight. He's assembled his acolytes, his hellish acquiescents.'

Clara gulped. They spoke of this below stairs; that every so often Mrs Brown took leave of her senses and spoke in tongues; that two hundred years ago Matthew Hopkins would have drowned her for a witch but in these more enlightened and liberal times she found herself in the King's service and from there it was said she was dispatched often for secret, stealthy assignations; that she often rode out at night, caring not a jot for decorum; that her horse was shod in felt and velvet so that she might travel in silence and that she wielded weapons with all the ferocity and power of the best, most highly trained soldier.

They said much, below stairs.

Mrs Brown swept back her glorious hair and pulled on a

tunic, still talking as though she had taken leave of her senses.

'Rank upon rank of them, Clara.' She held out a hand, rubbing forefinger and thumb together like an archaeologist testing dirt he'd scooped from around his boots. 'They're in the air, can you feel them?'

Clara shook her head no, edging back along the flagstones; nevertheless, entranced by the sight of the firebrand in full flight.

'Satraps and viceroys of the night,' said Brown, eyes burning with gypsy fire beneath her coal-black fringe. 'They're on the move . . .'

She reached and tightened her sword belt; she tossed her hair and, standing with her legs slightly wider apart than was proper, she put her hands to her hips.

'How do I look, girl?' she demanded of her visitor.

'You look . . . like a warrior queen, ma'am,' gulped Clara, feeling herself grow hot all of a sudden.

'Do I scare ye?' asked Brown.

'A little ma'am, truth be told.'

'Good. It's the effect I desire. If you, who attends Royalty, is touched by the cold fingers of fear, then what hope the denizens of Hell, eh?'

'Denizens, ma'am?'

'Servants of the fallen and beasts summoned from the infernal regions,' she said as though it were obvious, moving past Clara to the door.

As she did so, the muslin curtain was swept aside and standing there was John Brown in breeches and vest, his long hair unkempt.

He coughed.

Husband and wife stared at one another for some moments.

'Make the wind your minion, Maggie,' he said, at last.

'Aye, John Brown,' she said, the ghost of a smile upon her lips. 'Aye, that I will.'

'And watch your stance,' he added, 'block and parry.'

But if she heard him she didn't respond. She was gone.

III

Princess Alexandrina Victoria, heiress presumptive to the throne, was seated at a generously sized mahogany writing desk in her bedchamber, making a list by flickering candle-light.

Or, to be precise, she was making *lists*, two of them in fact: on one page of her diary, a list of those things she liked; on the other, those that formed the subject of her loathing.

Princess Victoria (it was years since she had last been addressed as Drina, and then only by her closest family) was aged eighteen, having achieved womanhood just one month previously. Young though she may have been, she neverthe-less had much learning behind her: at three years old the Princess could speak English and French in addition to German, her first language, and shortly afterwards developed an excellent knowledge of Latin, Italian and Spanish, all linguistic skills she put to good use: by sixteen she had already read Mr Dryden's translation of *The Aeneid*, Mr Pope's *Iliad* and Mr Voltaire's history of Charles XII (in the original French, *naturellement*). Since then her appetite for education had proved almost insatiable. She had gone on to read Ovid, Virgil and Horace; Messrs Cowper, Shakespeare and Goldsmith; she had pored over vast treatises in business and astronomy; she knew law from Blackstone and had studied geography, natural history and moral teachings, learning many of them off by heart. She had studied Mr Goldsmith's *History of England*, as well as his fascinating histories of Greece and Rome; Mr Clarendon's *History of the Rebellion* and Miss Mangnall's *Historical Questions*.

Indeed, it was whispered that her education, presided over by her governess Baroness Lehzen, quite rivalled that offered by the University of Oxford, an establishment she was, of course, ineligible to enter on account of her gender, future Queen of England or not.

Above and beyond those subjects she had studied, all endeavours conducted within the walls of Kensington Palace, within which she was virtually a captive, there was one thing she knew with the greatest resolution – and that was her own mind.

Which was how she was able to say with absolute certainty that she really and truly, completely and utterly, *despised* turtle soup.

Hated it.

The sound of scratching, her quill upon the page of her diary, was the only noise in the room as she wrote the entry 'turtle soup' in an elegant hand in the right-hand side of her diary.

Just the thought of it. Turtle soup. *Ugh*. Her stomach turned. Her mouth pursed. Just the thought of it was enough to make a pinchpenny of the most generous heart.

The Princess shared her room with her mother, who now looked up from her own reading.

'It's getting late, Victoria,' she said, in German, the language they used while in private.

In fact, noted Victoria, it would soon be getting early, it being almost past midnight. 'A little longer, mother,' she asked.

'A sovereign needs her rest,' admonished the Duchess of Kent, smiling.

Twenty miles away at Windsor Castle, King William IV lay dying of his 'hay fever' and it was no secret that the Duchess would welcome his expiration more than most. '*Hay fever*,' she had snorted derisively upon hearing the diagnosis, 'he is to be pollinated to death. Quick, let us send flowers to wish the King a speedy recovery!'

'Tsk, mother,' chided Victoria then, as she did now, for she loved her uncle. It was certainly true that he and her mother had quarrelled and that he was held in no great affection by the English public, but he had always treated his niece with great kindness and affection.

'You can continue your writing tomorrow, my dear,' insisted the Duchess, and rang the bell. Victoria hid her disappointment. She loved to stay up late.

There was once more silence in the room.

That is, apart from the *scratch, scratch* of Victoria's quill. She had transferred her attention to the left-hand side of her diary and more pleasurable thoughts.

Few were more pleasurable than those featuring her spaniel Dash – her beloved Dash. She dressed him like other young girls dressed their dolls and bathed him every week, regular as clockwork, come rain or shine; she took him everywhere with her and in return he was the most playful and faithful companion she could possibly have hoped for.

As well as being quite the little cupid. Why, only last year,

Victoria had been paid a visit by the rather handsome and dashing Prince Albert of Saxe-Coburg, and Dash had had quite a hand (or should that be 'paw', she thought to herself, inwardly groaning at her own pun) in turning what was at first a rather tiresome encounter into something . . . well, something perhaps a little more.

It was a visit for which she had to thank her uncle Leopold, the King of Belgium, whose name would surely soon be joining Dash in the left-hand page of her diary, for it was he who had arranged that she should meet Albert and his brother Ernest at Kensington Palace on the occasion of her birthday.

It was true that she disliked these carefully engineered introductions intensely; arrangement and connivance hung so heavily over them that it was almost impossible to enjoy them on their own terms, though she tried, of course: there was usually dancing, at least there was that to be said for them. Dancing was another entry for the left-hand side of her diary; she absolutely adored to do it, and took every opportunity to do so. The trouble was, those opportunities came so rarely.

Just then there came a knock at the door.

Victoria glanced over towards where her mother sat, but the Duchess was asleep in her chair, her book hanging from her fingers and her lips vibrating slightly as she snoozed. Looking at her, watching her sleep, Victoria felt a longing for her mother's embrace, her kiss, her understanding and love. It was there, between them, she was sure of it – somewhere – but it had become buried, like diamond in coal, and in place of maternal affection there was something else. *Expectation*. *Ambition*. Not all of it, Victoria was sure, with the very purest of intentions. Now though, asleep, her face devoid of its usual cunning, the Duchess seemed so serene and almost vulnerable.

Victoria found herself wanting to go over there and clasp her mother in her arms.

Another knock at the door. It brought Victoria from her reverie.

'Come,' she said, hearing a croak in her voice, thinking herself silly and weak. She dabbed wet eyes discreetly as the door opened softly and into the room came a lady-in-waiting, one of the eight ladies of the bedchamber, her long skirts rustling. She held a candle, a hand cupped in front of the flame.

Except, Victoria, realised, her eyes adjusting, she wasn't actually one of the ladies of the bedchamber, and neither was she accompanied by two maids of honour, as was the custom . . .

Which was most unusual. Unheard of, in fact . . .

Seeming to acknowledge her confusion, the lady put down the candle then curtsied, casting her eyes downwards to address the Princess. 'Your Royal Highness,' she said, 'the chief butler sends his sincere apologies and begs your pardon, but there has been a measure of uncertainty concerning the rota. He and the housekeeper are seeking to reach a resolution now, your Highness.'

Victoria could well believe it. Uncertainty and confusion were regular guests of the household and it was not unknown for the chief butler and the housekeeper to exchange lively words on such occasions.

'Oh dear,' she said, pleased to hear that her voice had returned to its usual timbre, 'is there a terrible upset?'

'Quite an uproar, yes, your Highness.'

The Princess glanced over at her mother, aware that any uproar was as nothing compared to the potential conflagration should the Duchess be informed. Victoria had lived at Kensington almost all of her life and had never known such a thing happen, so goodness only knows how her mother would react.

'Very well,' said the Princess, 'then we shall do our best not to make matters worse . . .'

She cast a meaningful glance at the sleeping Duchess and touched a finger to her lips.

'You may carry on,' added Victoria.

For a moment her visitor's face was illuminated as she moved to place the candle, and Victoria took the opportunity to study her, though she was still unable to recognise her. A lady in her mother's household, perhaps, a new arrival; after all, they each had complete autonomy when it came to the hiring of staff. She was quite beautiful, that much at least was apparent. Then her face was again in the shadows and she turned her back and began busying herself turning down the beds, preparing the chamber for sleep.

From outside came a distant rumble. A summer storm? Victoria fancied that the room was lit more brightly all of a sudden, as though illuminated by lightning, then, as if to confirm it, there was a second crack of thunder.

Pleased to be indoors, she turned in her chair, her back to the lady-in-waiting, her thoughts returning to Albert.

She had to admit, she had not been immediately bowled over by the Prince's charms, though charms he most definitely possessed. He was undoubtedly the better-looking of the two; she noted his beautiful nose and mouth in particular. She had decided many years previously that she liked to watch a person's mouth in conversation. Others said it was eye contact one should endeavour to establish but, as usual,

Victoria had her own feelings on the matter and for her it was most definitely the mouth. Albert's was full and sweet; she loved his moustache. Oh, his eyes were lovely, too, clear and bright. What's more, he was musical and could draw well.

But, on the other hand, something of a bore.

For a start, Albert had arrived suffering from terrible, almost debilitating seasickness. Well, that wasn't a very good start, was it? He was a little shy, to tell the truth. Now, Victoria detested men who were too confident (one in particular sprang to mind and she pursed her lips at the thought of him) but there was such a thing as being *painfully* shy. In that respect, Albert was quite unlike Ernest, who also displayed greater enthusiasm for those pursuits Victoria enjoyed: the receptions, dinners and balls, and the late nights that went with them. At one point on his first evening at court, Albert had even fallen asleep, causing great hilarity, while on the evening of her seventeenth birthday ball he'd had to excuse himself and go home early, 'as pale as ashes' as she later wrote in her diary. Almost a week later and he still hadn't sufficiently rallied to enjoy the Grand Ball held at Kensington Palace, when she twirled and danced into the early hours of the morning. Once again, Albert had retired early.

Yes, it was nice enough to spend time with him during the daytime, when they would sing and play piano, go riding and draw, but his habit of disappearing at night-time was really rather a bore and to be honest, she thought now, only half-hearing the sounds of the lady-in-waiting behind her as she bustled about the room, she might well have ended the visit much preferring Ernest, even though he was not nearly so pleasing to the eye.

It was Albert's treatment of Dash that played the greatest

part in turning her affection towards him. He played with Dash and fussed all over him and was most attentive; in return Dash seemed to like him back, taking every opportunity to lick the young Prince's face. The two liked each other, they *palpably* liked each other.

Well, that had sealed it. She had gone back to her diary the night Albert and his brother had left, telling it how she would miss her two cousins, 'whom, I *do* love so *very, very* dearly, *much more dearly* than any other cousins in the *world*.'

She was always so fond of stressing certain words when she wrote, it gave her writing a great vitality, she felt.

She glanced over to her mother, who slept on. She should wake her by rights, but then again, Mother would only make her close her diary and she was enjoying her list-making, and anyway, the lady-in-waiting was still working behind her, moving between the beds. No, she would let mother sleep a little longer.

There was another rumble of thunder from outside, the swish and rustle of the lady-in-waiting's skirts. Candlelight cast her shadow on the wall above Victoria's desk and she watched it for a moment or so. How very strange, she thought, the shadow makes her fingernails look abnormally long.

Then she turned her attention back to her book and the list of pleasurable things.

Scratch scratch.

Victoria wrote that she very much enjoyed the music of Mr Mendelssohn, cream cakes and trifle, her 132 dolls (for which she was a little too old, chided Lehzen, but which the Princess secretly still adored) and staying up late dancing and ale and Lehzen and Uncle Leopold and poor Uncle William, so desperately ill with the hay fever at Windsor Castle.

Then she turned her attention back to the right-hand side of her diary and those things she disliked.

Under turtle soup she wrote the word 'bishops'.

It was the wigs. The powder that choked and the cloying perfume. She hated wigs.

Whigs, on the other hand, she liked. Tories, though. Hm, she had a rank distrust of Tories. She knew she wasn't supposed to, of course, with her being in the position of soon-to-be-Queen, and that if (well, when) that happened she would be duty-bound to be scrupulously even-handed in all matters of state and internal politics, but still, this was *her* diary and she had no need to hide her true feelings from it. So she wrote it down.

Now, though, she had left the best of the worst to last, and she steeled herself to inscribe it now.

Scratch scratch.

She wrote: Sir John Conroy.

IV

The rain and thunder didn't stop her hearing the drum-beat of their hooves on the ground. To tell the truth Maggie Brown had been half expecting them ever since leaving Windsor: *Acheriders*, the dread horsemen who served the Prince of Darkness.

They would have but one purpose: to stop her reaching the Palace. They would die rather than fail in that mission.

Which meant there were plans afoot to kill the wee lassie.

The thought spurred her on. She leaned forward to whisper in the ear of her mount, Helfer, echoing John Brown's words to her as she left (his last words to her? Her sweet John Brown? Her rock? She prayed not), 'Make the wind your minion, Helfer,' she breathed, 'ride hard.'

She released the reins, holding the horse by his mane, pressing herself hard to his body so that she could feel the muscle and sinew working beneath her. She felt him increase speed. 'God speed you, Helfer,' she whispered, holding him close. Breath billowed from his nostrils.

Now, what did she know about the Acheriders? That they were half-entity, half-horse, usually hunted in packs of three and only ever under the cover of darkness; that they fought using swords forged from the reconstituted and hardened bones of their victims, and that each subsequent kill only increased the strength of their weapon, which could literally suck the life from your bones; that she had never met one in battle, but had heard it told that there were only a handful of mortals who had done so and lived. Those that had survived spoke of great swordsmanship, cruelty and low cunning and that the only way to defeat an Acherider was to stay on your horse. To sacrifice your seat was to die.

And there was one other thing that she knew about Acheriders, God help her.

That they were fast.

In Royal horsemanship circles, Helfer had a reputation for speed that was second to none – why else would Brown have chosen him but for his swiftness? But was he as fast as an Acherider? Three of them? She pressed her face to her mount, breathed in his scent, made herself one with him, her beloved horse.

Behind her the hellish thunder of the hooves. She daren't look back. Even to gaze upon an Acherider is to hasten your own death, she had been told . . .

On the other hand, perhaps it was the followers of Astaroth that one should never gaze upon? No, they had terrible breath; you should never inhale, for fear of making their breath your last. Then was it the Nephilim? She grinned despite herself, thinking of her old teacher burying his head in his hands, exasperated, ancient demonology texts tossed to the wall in frustration. Then the moment was gone as from behind she heard the whinny of something that was neither human nor horse.

They were gaining. She urged Helfer forward, tearing into the night, bringing Kensington Palace closer. Behind her, the cacophony of hooves closing in; ahead of her open space.

How far now? A couple of miles? It must be, she estimated. Once there she would be safe; they couldn't follow her inside.

But they would surely be upon her soon. Helfer had given her everything he had but it wasn't enough – he couldn't out-run an Acherider. It had been madness to believe otherwise.

Then – salvation!

Perhaps. She dared hope so anyway. For ahead of her, appearing slowly from the gloom like a defeated, retreating army, she saw a treeline, trees crowded together colouring the grey night black.

Here she might have a chance in combat. The Acheriders would be denied the room to manoeuvre. It was true that she faced the same problem, but then she was Maggie Brown and she was used to fighting in such conditions. It was what she did. (There had been no exasperation from her combat tutor, oh no. Just praise, admiration, then stolen kisses, love, marriage: 'Block and parry, Maggie, block and parry.')

Now her lips came to the ear of Helfer, who altered direction at her command. Behind her it was as though her pursuers perceived her intentions and their efforts to catch up with her redoubled. There was no other sound apart from that of the galloping hooves, her hair out behind her, as she clutched Helfer hard, urging him on, on. *Make the wind your minion.*

She felt something. As though her hair had become entangled in a branch, though there was none. Something reaching for her, grabbing at her. She pulled away and in doing so looked behind herself.

And saw it. An Acherider.

It was a man – no, not a man, a *thing* – that was somehow joined with beast – a beast that most resembled a horse – so that they were one, and it seemed to quiver and ripple like a mollusc as though constantly forming and reforming.

At first she thought it had no features, then realised it was a trick of the darkness. Features it had, but they were black, a smooth, oily black: eyes, eyelids, everything. Black lips were pulled back in a snarl to reveal ebony, pointed teeth, rows and rows of them like fangs, behind them a void for a mouth. Then came its shoulders and arms, but it had no legs. Instead its body, ribbed like that of a whale, seemed to spread at the hips with the consistency of mucus, as though resolving itself into its mount.

One hand was outstretched toward her, nails like talons. With a lurch of disgust she saw strands of her hair stuck to its fingers; in its other hand it held its sword, the only thing about it that was not black. Instead it was bleached white, gleaming and sharp, the blade smooth and razor sharp and not at all like bone, though she fancied she saw knuckle joints at the hilt.

It took but a second to drink in the sight of the Acherider then she was facing front again. 'Go, Helfer, go,' she gasped, 'they're close now, breathing down our necks!'

Perhaps it was the note of panic in her voice that spurred him on, for their speed seemed to increase and from behind them came a squeal of displeasure that was as music to Maggie Brown's ears. But even that was not as gratifying as the sound of the hooves receding a little as she and Helfer pulled forward, faster and faster now, tearing across the plain towards the trees.

Lightning split the sky and there was a clap of thunder. She felt droplets of rain splat onto her bare arms. *Good*. Let it rain. The conditions would suit her. She didn't suppose they had the rain where they came from.

She dared another glance back and saw the three of them riding in a line some forty feet behind, their swords drawn, almost in a salute. She grinned and returned the gesture with one of her own, a two-fingered salute, eliciting another squeal of frustration from her pursuers.

Now they crashed into the trees and Helfer was pulling up, slowing down but not enough, so that for an instant she feared he might impale himself on a branch and she sat up in the saddle taking the reins.

She needn't have been too concerned, however; Helfer was nimble, their adventures together having taken them across similar terrain, and behind them she could hear the Devil's riders coping less well. How sweet it was, the sound, and as they crashed forward she allowed herself to hope: 'Hang tight, there, wee lassie,' she murmured to herself, 'we're on our way.' There were enemies already resident at the Palace, she knew, one in particular; however, there were friends, also, and she offered up a prayer that it should be the latter who was the first to act.

They came upon a clearing and she allowed herself another glance behind, grinning again to see two of them thumping forward messily, ungainly in the undergrowth and losing ground.

The third, though.

She tensed. Her smile faded. Where was the third?

Another squeal. This one triumphant.

Stupid Maggie. Lazy, arrogant Maggie, she realised. She reached across herself, fingers seeking out the grip of her broadsword, but too late . . .

The third rider appeared on her blindside, streaking into the clearing with its sword raised before she'd had a chance to react.

She saw the sword sink deep into her shoulder, and saw it withdraw from the wound, a chunk missing from its blade.

She tumbled backwards from Helfer, and as she fell and hit the soft forest floor, scrambling to her feet in one fluid movement, she saw him rear up, hooves kicking and nostrils flaring.

The Acherider reared up also, the two facing one another for battle. Dimly realising what was going to happen Maggie Brown screamed a warning '*Helfer*' as the remaining two Acheriders thundered into the clearing from behind her, coming upon her brave horse from behind, and they hacked him down.

She saw all of this before she felt the pain.

Agony, white-hot, shot through her. Her hand went to her shoulder and she spun back into a tree, feeling her fingertips brush something hard and jagged in the wound left by the Acherider.

Bone from the sword blade, draining the life from her.

She dropped to her knees, incapacitated by the pain, wet hair falling in front of her eyes. She heard her horse whinny and scream in agony, its feet kicking as the Acheriders slashed at him. Their bodies slid to the side of their mounts like globules of aspic, so that they were able to reach Helfer now that he lay dying in the dirt.

The rain fell, hard.

After some time, Helfer's cries stopped, though the Acheriders continued working on him with their swords, a dull, wet sound, like men tenderising meat. She tried to control the pain, tried to focus. Her fingers went to the shard of blade lodged in the wound, to the fire there. As she touched it she felt it grind against her collarbone and the pain intensified.

The Acheriders finished their business and resolved themselves, drawing up to their full height and forming a line on the opposite side of the clearing. They regarded her, defeated and dying, on her knees, the life leeching from her. Blood dripped from their swords. Helfer's blood.

Through her soaking wet hair, through tears of pain and grief, she saw the mutilated body of her horse, then looked at the Acheriders. She saw their lips pull back from their teeth, their laughter dry in the watery night.

Her fingers gripped the shard of bone and with a shout of pain she pulled it from her shoulder. And flicked it toward the hell riders.

The laughter died.

She drew her broadsword, held it two-handed, hardly able to lift it, the tip of it digging into the wet mulch and dirt of the forest floor.

'Not going down that easily,' she managed. 'I'll be taking at least one of you with me. Which is it to be, eh?'

They charged.

V

With the beds prepared, the lady-in-waiting departed. She would return when the Princess and the Duchess had retired, when the candles would need extinguishing and removing (the stubs distributed amongst the servants), ready for fresh ones to be placed there in the morning.

Victoria watched her go, deciding she must find out the lady's name, and thanking all their lucky stars that the Duchess had not been roused from her slumber; there would no doubt have been an outcry at the breach in protocol and her mother would have summoned her comptroller and private secretary, her confidante and conspirator, the dreaded Sir John Conroy.

Her mother spoke often of how she would be lost without him. Sir John, she said, had been a dear and devoted friend of Victoria's father, her late husband, the Duke.

Victoria had never known her father. She had been just eight months old when, during a reinvigorating holiday to bracing Sidmouth, he had caught a chill, contracted pneumonia and died, leaving the Duchess and her daughter penniless, without the funds even to return to London. It was then that Conroy had offered his services as organiser, and the Duchess had gratefully accepted: she was desperately short of money, she spoke no English and felt she lacked allies in a country that was not her own.

All of which, Victoria now knew, were circumstances exploited by Sir John Conroy in order to further his position way beyond that of his birthright and put him in a position to plan a most audacious attempt at gaining Royal influence. Musing upon it now, she knew she had nothing to thank him for save that: a lesson in the cunning of men who see an opportunity to seize power and would exploit others to do so. Hers was a baptism of fire in that sense.

As though in response to her thoughts, the room was lit with lightning for a second. Victoria glanced over at her mother, watching her sleep, her figure illuminated by the flash of the lightning.

'How could you have been taken in?' she murmured.

Oh, much as she disliked him, she had to admit that he gave off a certain air of confidence. She could at least see the qualities in him that were admired by her mother. He was handsome. She would very much liked to have denied the fact, but it was true. He wore his hair long, very much against the fashion; he had sharply defined cheekbones that were the envy of many a lady-in-waiting and his eyes could appear quite black at times, seductively so.

These were traits he knew how to use, and Victoria felt as if it was only her who saw through the man: to the fact that he was manipulative, devious and that his temper was not born of romantic *passion*, but rather spoke of a petulant and tyrannical nature, and it was this aspect of his personality that had allowed him to so completely dominate the Duchess.

For dominate her he did.

His reason to do so? Victoria. The death of King George III (Poor, mad Grandpa, she thought, they said he had spoken nonsense for fifty-eight hours before his death!) had made her third in line to the throne, behind two men well into their middle age, neither of whom were likely to produce an heir. Victoria, of course, was but a child. Should her accession take place before the occasion of her eighteenth birthday, a Regency would be established, making the Duchess the proxy ruler.

And who would be advisor to the Duchess?

Who would be the 'power behind the throne'?

Why, her loyal comptroller and private secretary, of course.

Conroy was able to dominate others, too. It was said that he had acquired his rank by such means. However, the one person he had never managed to charm, win over, or otherwise influence, was the Princess Alexandrina Victoria.

Not that he hadn't tried, of course, but his gifts, such as they were – and one had to admit that he had a certain charm and could exude a definite charisma – did not extend to the beguiling of children. Thus he had tried to win the affection of the young Victoria with teasing and cruel practical jokes that not only failed to impress her much, but had the opposite effect. She grew to despise him and he never gained her trust – something he had obviously hoped to do while she was still an impressionable young girl – before she was aware of her destiny.

That day came when she was aged eleven, when the Baroness Lehzen had placed a family tree in one of her books. Reading it, she saw that after George IV and the Duke of Clarence (who would, of course, go on to become King William

IV who now lay so desperately ill with hay fever at Windsor Castle) she was next in line for the throne.

She would be Queen.

Victoria remembered the moment well, how she was suddenly suffused with a great sense of duty (she had to admit, also, of *importance*, but then she was only human and after all it was *mainly* duty) and of a desire to do the right thing – by her country and by God.

'I will be good,' she told Lehzen, and never had she meant any words as much as she meant them then.

Still, to her great vexation this momentous knowledge did little to change the monotony of her daily life, a routine made so much harder and vastly more dull by the rigorous application of the Kensington System, for which (who else but) Sir John Conroy was an enthusiastic advocate.

These rules dictated that she should never travel anywhere in the palace alone, nor even ascend or descend stairs without accompaniment. At nights she was to sleep with her mother and during the days she was supervised and monitored at all times; the Duchess was continually present, and she was not permitted to converse with anybody except in the presence of a third party, that person preferably being her mother.

Worse, under this system she was prevented from playing with children her own age and was instead surrounded by adults. Many of whom, she now knew, used the rules as an excuse to sequester her from the world. To segregate her from outside influences.

The room went suddenly a little darker and looking over to the fireplace she realised that one of the candles had snuffed out. Should she call the maid for another? Perhaps, but on the other hand, she could manage with four, and if they were still having staffing problems she wasn't sure she wanted to add to them. She decided against, her mind going back to Conroy.

As Victoria's eighteenth birthday drew near, he made repeated attempts to have her ratify documents appointing him her private secretary. She had demurred, repeatedly. Even when she had been ill and feverish he had tried to take advantage of her reduced health to try and persuade her to sign, but Lehzen had intervened. Lately, since she had come of age, there had been further attempts. How could Mother have allowed them to happen?

How?

Because he was the 'demon incarnate'. Or so she told her diary.

Shortly afterwards, she wrote, 'Today is my eighteenth birthday! How old! And yet how far I am from being what I should be.'

Hm.

Maybe she had, without consciously intending to do so, invested in the idea promoted so enthusiastically by Conroy and her mother, that she was not ready for the monarchy. 'You are still very young,' her mother had written to her, and Victoria wondered if he had been standing looking over her shoulder during the composition of that particular missive. Thinking back to that diary entry, perhaps his strategy had been a successful one.

No. She would show him, she thought. And she cast her mind back to that day when she was eleven years old and she had thrust out her chin and told Lehzen, 'I will be good.'

She was resolved then, as she was now. When it happened, she would be ready.

Ready to rule.

She turned to a new page in her diary because it was time to put away childish thoughts of hating turtle soup and perfumed wigs. No doubt both were to figure in her future, so she had better get used to them. It was time to think like a sovereign.

She closed her eyes a moment, in order to better compose the first entry on the page . . .

Then awoke, suddenly.

To wetness . . .

Blood?

She reached a hand to rub her eyes and it was wet, both on her hand and on her face.

Oh God, had she inadvertently cut herself?

She stood from her seat, a little shaky and panicked, instinctively wanting to cry out for her mother but checking herself in time. Nothing was hurting, she told herself. Don't be so silly now. Whither all that talk of putting away childish things? It was probably a nosebleed, that was all. Certainly nothing serious.

The room was much darker than it had been when she . . .

Of course. She'd fallen asleep. For how long? All but one of the candles had burned themselves out. Goodness only knows the time. She moved to the fireplace and reached up to take the one candlestick, bringing it down and in the process casting light on her fingers. She saw now that it was not blood on her hands, nor indeed was there much of it – it was ink.

She laughed and moved to the mirror where she held up the candle close to the glass and confirmed that it was indeed ink; she had a spot of it on her cheek.

The room was lit by lightning and that was followed by an

explosion of thunder. In the sudden brightness she saw the mark clearly. Quite a beauty spot, she mused, and walked back to the writing desk to confirm that she had indeed knocked over the inkpot while she slept. Thank goodness she had been so prodigious with her words this evening, there was so little of it to spill.

Now, for how long had she slept? She offered up her candle to the clockface. Goodness, it was *three o'clock in the morning*. There she was, covered in ink; her mother still asleep in her chair, and just one candle left to light her preparations for bed. There was nothing for it: as much as she hated to do so she would have to summon the maids. She only hoped the chief butler and the housekeeper had been able to resolve the rota issue.

They had not, as it turned out. For after she had rung the bell – mere moments later, in fact – there was a knock at the door and a lady-in-waiting entered. Just one. The same one, thought Victoria, though she couldn't be certain, the light being so dim in the room now, and oh, what a silly girl! She brought no light with her!

Silently, the lady-in-waiting closed the door behind her and moved into the chamber, staying towards the back of the room. The only sound was the rustle of her skirts.

'I'm afraid, I fell asleep . . .' said Victoria, all at once feeling a little unnerved. It was the storm, she told herself. That was all it was. Waking so suddenly. Knocking over the inkpot.

Even so, she could not help but wish the lady-in-waiting would move forward a little and out of the shadows, so that she could see her better.

'That's quite all right,' said the woman, a different tone to her voice, deeper and darker than Victoria had noticed on their previous encounter. And there was something about the way she said it . . .

'Quite,' said Victoria, bringing a regality to bear, or trying to. 'Well, I shall need your help.'

The lady said, 'How can I serve you – *Your Majesty*?'

Victoria felt herself go cold.

'I beg your pardon?' she said. 'What did you just call me?'

A flash of lightning lit the room and for a second she saw the lady-in-waiting in full. Yes, it was the same one; what struck her again was the woman's beauty, so beautiful, she was, it was almost hypnotic, it was as if she cast a spell . . .

The second thing that struck Victoria was the woman's posture, her expression. She no longer carried herself like a lady-in-waiting. She stood with her arms spread, her palms forward, almost as though attempting to channel something . . .

(A crack of thunder.)

And she was smiling.

Victoria scrambled to her feet. Her nightdress became snagged on the back of the chair and she snatched it free.

'Come forward,' she commanded.

Once again the woman was in darkness. All Victoria could see of her was the outline. The skirts, the arms. Then she spoke.

'The King is dead, your Majesty,' came the voice from the deep and dark shadows. 'Long live the Queen.'

The King is dead?

There was another crack of lightning, this one more prolonged than the last and once again the woman was illuminated. Victoria grabbed the edge of the desk for support. As she watched, the woman's hands seemed to grow, her fingernails became elongated, evolving from human fingers into something approaching claws or talons; her stature increased so that she seemed to rise above the fireplace next to which she stood. Then, candles, long since burnt to stubs suddenly burst into life; the fire, dormant some two months now, roared into flame. She began to move forward, her eyes red and gleaming; her mouth, still beautiful, tilted back and open wide to reveal rows and rows of razor-sharp teeth.

'Come, Your Majesty,' she hissed. 'Come to me.'

There was a low grumble of thunder.

The woman glided towards her; one clawed hand reached out.

And Victoria knew what to do.

(Later she would have time to ask herself: *how*? How did she know what to do? Was it intuition or conditioning? And how did she know what it was, the thing in her bedchamber; that it was a succubus?

But that was later, not then. Then she did not stop to think. She acted.)

From her writing desk, she snatched a letter opener with her right hand, tossing it across to her left, then taking up a stance, the knife held forward, her right arm behind her for balance.

The succubus hissed, taking a step back. A rustle of skirts. Her eyes, red and gleaming, dimmed somewhat. Her mouth closed. Her face became wary and she crouched in response to the Princess, slowly bringing one hand behind her, taking up a position that most resembled the fighting stance of a scorpion, so it seemed to Victoria. Her other hand came forward, talons upwards; bending her knees, she brought her centre of gravity low.

The two women faced one another.

Neither blinked.

From the other side of the room, the Duchess stirred a little in her chair. She let out a great breath and she smacked her lips like an obese monarch enjoying his evening banquet. She said something incomprehensible that might have been 'her-be-kum' but was probably not.

The succubus smiled.

Victoria smiled in return.

The Duchess slumbered on.

Then, from behind the succubus, the door to the bedchamber opened and into the room came a figure that Victoria did not recognise.

The eyes of the succubus flickered, but she did not turn. With her balancing hand she raised a finger as though to acknowledge the new arrival.

'You have taught her well, Protektor,' she said.

'Well, here's the thing,' said Maggie Brown, striding into the room. She had three bloodstained boneswords tucked into her belt and her brigandine armour was stained black with blood. 'I've taught her nothing. In matter of fact, we've not had the pleasure, have we, lassie?'

Victoria, somewhat bewildered, shook her head no.

With a hiss the succubus whirled to meet Brown, who in one movement drew two of the boneswords.

'Time to die, succubus,' she said, 'time to die.'

Then there was a knock at the door, and all three women froze, their attention going from the Duchess to the door and back to the Duchess as she stirred, her eyelids fluttering.

With no immediate reply from inside the room, there came a second knock.

'Your Grace,' came a voice in a state of excitement, 'the Lord Chamberlain and the Archbishop of Canterbury wish to see her Royal Highness Princess Victoria. They wish to see her at once.'

The Duchess's eyes sprang open.

VI

Earlier
A carriage, west of Kensington Palace

While sitting in a carriage in the main forecourt at Windsor Castle awaiting a driver, Lord Conyngham the Lord Chamberlain and the Archbishop of Canterbury had each availed themselves of a glass of sherry offered to them on a silver tray by a footman, who wore a white wig tied with a black bow.

As was the custom, they had thanked the man, swiftly drained their glasses and replaced them to the tray, at which point the footman had made a short bow and turned on his heel and departed, the gravel crunching beneath his black, polished shoes.

The two men waited, hands folded across their laps. Every now and then one would glance at the other and receive a smile in reply. At one point the Archbishop of Canterbury coughed rather heavily and the Lord Chamberlain offered him his handkerchief, though it was politely rejected, and once again silence was their uneasy companion.

In truth, the Lord Chamberlain thought the Archbishop of Canterbury rather tiresome company, finding he was always pressed into discussing matters ecclesiastical, and thus tended to avoid encounters with the man whenever possible. There was no avoiding such an engagement tonight, however. They were on a mission of the utmost importance to the monarchy: to Kensington Palace, to meet with the Princess Alexandrina Victoria and inform her Royal Highness of her accession to the throne, they were to leave at once and *don't spare the horses*.

They waited.

The driver did not appear.

Shortly, the footman appeared with his silver tray bearing two more glasses of sherry, and the Lord Chamberlain and the Archbishop of Canterbury had each availed themselves of one.

As was the custom, they had thanked the man, drained their glasses and replaced them to the tray, at which point the footman had made a short bow, turned on his heel, and departed.

Not long later, they had a third sherry, which at least heralded the arrival of the driver who walked unsteadily to his mount, paying no mind to the loud berating delivered by the two gentlemen in the carriage who wished to be delivered with paramount urgency to Kensington Palace, and good Lord, what on earth was the hold-up?

But first, they agreed, another sherry before they embarked on their vital mission.

Duly, a further fortification was brought by the footman and the two men drained their glasses with a loud smacking of lips, placing them firmly back on the silver tray and thanking the footman more effusively than was necessary.

Now they were on the road the Lord Chamberlain found

that the Archbishop of Canterbury's company wasn't quite so vexatious after all; indeed, the man seemed most jovial, and as they shuddered past hedgerows the two men traded news of the Royal household, being most candid, some might say indiscreet, in their views, and doing little to hide their glee that it would be they who broke the news to Victoria, which was a state of affairs sure to infuriate the Prime Minister, Lord Melbourne, until talk, naturally, turned to the young Princess.

'A child,' said the Lord Chamberlain, breaking wind and trusting that his companion would either forgive the exclamation or hold accountable the rugged surface of the road.

'A *child*,' echoed the Archbishop, who, it seemed, was too busy holding onto his mitre to even notice Lord Conyngham's transgression (for which, later, reviewing events with a heavy head, Lord Conyngham would be most grateful).

'She is the captive of her mother,' declaimed the Lord Chamberlain at great volume. 'She and that man Conroy. Tell me, Archbishop, what possible good can come of that? England is set on a course to ruin, you mark my words.'

The Archbishop leaned forward, all the better to make his point, which he was about to commence with a great exaggeration of the ecclesiastical finger, when the carriage traversed a particularly uneven section of road and he was pitched from his seat, crumpling to the floor of the carriage. For a moment the Archbishop lay in the well in a most undignified manner, his mitre at right angles, and both men were silent, each of them considering the protocol of such a situation. Then they were both laughing, Lord Conyngham offering his hand to the Archbishop of Canterbury, the two of them guffawing so hard they were not aware of the felt-shod horse that overtook the carriage at that very moment, the rider's jet-black hair flowing behind her, her broadsword at her hip.

No, the occupants of the carriage did not see her; instead, they were telling each other jokes.

'I have one,' said the Lord Chamberlain, 'are you ready, sir?'

'Indeed, I am, sir,' replied the Archbishop.

'Then I shall commence and tell you the tale of a new servant who was told by the mistress that a maid prior to her employ was let go owing to the revelation of a follower in the kitchen . . .'

At this, the Archbishop's cheeks puffed in anticipation of great hilarity.

'Well,' continued the Lord Chamberlain, 'the new maid stated that she never had followers, and so was employed. Well, a few short nights later, the mistress of the house, having scented tobacco smoke, arrived below stairs and found a soldier in the coal cellar. Now, the maid . . .' he laughed in anticipation of the punchline, 'the maid denied all knowledge of the soldier . . . and said that *it must be one left by the last maid.*'

For some time, the two men laughed uproariously at that joke, then told others and were reduced to such a state of hilarity that they were actually clinging on to one another for support, until, upon hearing a discreet cough from the platform above where they sat, they realised they had passed through the gates at Kensington Palace, (the driver had acknowledged the porter and jerked a thumb back at the two men, and the porter had recognised the import of their vestments and waved them through), and they each sat formally upright, arranging their clothes, before the door to the carriage was opened and they were led across the forecourt and into the Palace.

There in the great hall, which was decidedly shabby in comparison to Windsor, noted the Lord Chamberlain with a sniff, they were met.

'Please acquaint the Princess Victoria that we are here to see her,' said Lord Conyngham, whose voice boomed within the great architecture of the Palace.

'My lords,' said the servant, dismayed, 'but she is sleeping.'

Lord Conyngham drew himself up to his full height and said, 'Will you please do me the service of telling the Princess that the Lord Chamberlain and the Archbishop of Canterbury are here to see her, and it is a matter of great import,' and with that he looked across at the Archbishop, who nodded agreement.

The maidservant was dispatched upstairs, wondering why none of the ladies were present (a mystery that would, tragically, be solved the next morning upon discovery of a body on the scullery steps), and the Lord Chamberlain and Archbishop paced the black and white tiles of the vast, wood-panelled hall as they waited.

And waited.

'Good Lord,' exclaimed the Lord Chamberlain. 'How long are we expected to—'

But he was cut off by the appearance of the Duchess, who came down the stairs towards them, her nightgown flowing.

They each took a bow.

'Pardon, your Grace,' said the Archbishop, 'but it is her Royal Highness we need to see.'

The Duchess raised her chin and told the two visitors in no uncertain terms that her *daughter* – lest they forget – was asleep and not to be disturbed.

'Your Grace,' said the Lord Chamberlain, coming to his

colleague's aid, 'we come on business of state, and wish to see the *Queen*.'

The Duchess pursed her lips, motioned to the maid-servant and the two of them ascended the stairs. The Lord Chamberlain and the Archbishop looked at one another.

'A captive of her mother, you see,' said Conyngham, and the two men burst into a most inappropriate fit of the giggles.

VII

The same time
The Queen's bedchamber

As the door closed behind the Duchess, Maggie Brown emerged from beneath the writing table and the succubus from behind a dressing screen, while Victoria threw back her covers and leapt out of bed.

'A wise decision, succubus,' said Brown. 'It would not do to have your Regent babbling of having seen demons now, would it?'

The succubus scoffed, throwing back her head and exposing her teeth. 'You flatter yourself, Protektor, to think you know anything of my motives or those of my masters. Why, even the lowliest acquiescents and acolytes operate outside the sphere of your knowledge.'

In reply Maggie Brown smiled, intending her response to appear unknowable, though secretly she thought there was much truth to what the succubus said.

'She'll be back in a moment, the Duchess will be,' she said. 'Time has run out for you, succubus. He'll not be best pleased at you. What's the punishment for failure?'

With a frustrated scream, the succubus lunged forward,

but was feinting and as Maggie Brown went to parry, she whirled, slashing outward with her talons and catching Maggie Brown across the cheek as she ducked.

Maggie shouted, in pain and frustration, swinging a little wildly with her sword but using it as a cover to dart nimbly out of range, cross the room and step onto Victoria's chair, then up to her desk.

She crouched, the two swords crossed, ready to meet the succubus should she strike. In turn, the succubus stayed at the rear of the room, pacing in front of the fireplace, regarding them, a low hiss escaping her lips, occasionally spitting, which was her habit.

Watching her carefully, Maggie wiped her bleeding cheek on her sleeve. She addressed Victoria. 'We haven't been properly introduced, Your Majesty, my name is Maggie Brown. I'm a Demon Hunter, the Royal Protektor.'

Victoria felt somewhat giddy. She had heard of such things as demons, of course, The Rev George Davys had often spoken of them. Mr Dante's *Divine Comedy* was full of vivid descriptions and Mr Milton had also spoken of demons in his poem, *Paradise Lost*, but she had to admit to wondering whether they were in fact a fantastic concoction and had never dreamed of meeting one. That there should be such a thing as a Royal Demon Hunter also came as a surprise, though not an outright shock; after all, there were many staff at Kensington, fulfilling many roles – the palace had a resident rat catcher, another whose job it was to sweep the chimneys. That there should be a Demon Hunter did not unduly surprise her.

Or, perhaps, any incredulity she may have felt about demons and their hunters was at a minimum, not because of the revelation, but because of the company it kept.

'Then it really is true, is it?' she said.

'Your Majesty?'

'That the King is dead, that I am Queen?'

'Aye, Your Majesty.'

'And this?' She indicated the pacing succubus, still hissing.

'This, Your Majesty, is your first assassination attempt.'

The succubus spat, then came at them. Victoria sidestepped, bringing the knife forward ready to defend. Maggie Brown, an impressed expression crossing her face, also dodged the whirling claws of the succubus, her boneswords meeting the talons and drawing sparks. In one movement the succubus turned and kicked, her long skirts rustling, and Maggie Brown was somersaulting from the table to avoid the blow, landing on the floor in time to meet the succubus as she came head on, using her talons like swords. For a moment the two were locked in combat, and Victoria watched, crouching and ready should the succubus come her way, but fascinated also, transfixed by the noise and speed, the sparks, the grunts the two women made, neither willing to give headway.

Then, one sound cut through the noise of combat, and it was the voice of the Duchess from the corridor outside.

'*Victoria.*'

The room froze.

The succubus was the first to react. She spun round, bringing her claws up and across, dragging them across Maggie Brown's stomach, opening the armour and drawing blood. As Brown stepped back into a defensive stance, the succubus crossed the room, seeming almost to float, and with one hand she raised the sash window, using the other to point at Maggie Brown.

'Next time, Protektor,' she hissed.

'I'll be ready, bitch,' replied Brown, one arm across her stomach, already making her way across to the writing desk and slithering beneath it as the succubus cast one final glance at Victoria and was gone. How or to where, Victoria had no idea. All she knew was that she now stood alone in the middle of the room just as the door opened and in walked the Duchess.

'Ah, Victoria,' she said, 'you are awake, and already busy opening your correspondence I see. Well, there's no time for that now, we have visitors.'

So it was that in something of a daze she repaired to the reception hall, where the Lord Chamberlain and Archbishop of Canterbury, red of face and wreathed in smiles, greeted her as Queen and she offered them her ring to kiss, which they did, bending low.

'Your Majesty,' said the Lord Chamberlain, standing. 'I trust you are not hurt. You have what appears to be blood on your face.'

'Oh no, Your Grace,' she said, smiling, 'nothing quite so exciting, it is only ink.'

When she returned to her bedchamber in order to dress for meeting the Prime Minister, Lord Melbourne, she checked beneath her writing desk.

Maggie Brown, of course, was gone.

VIII

The home of Lord Quimby

Lord Quimby dropped the bloodied axe, which, just moments ago he had wrenched from the wall. It had been hung there as decoration, but had now been pressed into service decapitating zombies – in which function it had served admirably. Breathing heavily, Quimby surveyed the devastation in his library.

For devastation it was – truly it had been a night to dismember. There had been a long and bloody battle. In fact, he thought, it had been more like a massacre, and in the manner of such events there was a good deal of restorative work to be done in its wake. The library looked as though someone had taken the decision to redecorate it, and in place of paint and wallpaper, used offal instead, accessorising the colour scheme with severed limbs, strings of glistening entrails and decapitated torsos. Moreover, thanks to the exposure of so much internal workings, including the inevitable rupture of bowels and vacation of bladders, the room also bore a most unpleasant odour, that of a latrine.

In all, it was a stinking, bloody mess.

Quimby was now the only living person in the house. The

photogenic drawer, Craven, had made his escape; the three prostitutes had not been so lucky. Surprised by the five zombies, who had boasted greater numbers and enhanced strength, it was they who accounted for much of the viscera currently decorating the library.

The butchery had been in full swing when Quimby, Perkins and Craven burst into the room; the sight before them, that of a charnel house.

The first thing Quimby saw was Rosa – such a talented girl, he had been led to understand – on her knees screaming and clutching at her stomach as she was attacked by a zombie named Jones – his only male – who was tugging her insides from a gash in her belly as though they were a string of sausages, then pushing them into his mouth and munching upon them with the kind of gusto usually reserved for the consumption of a fine steak.

They are, Quimby thought, they actually are *eating* the prostitutes.

This was incredible. For a mad moment he considered conferring with Perkins, for they were witnessing an entirely unexpected side effect of the process. They had of course been expecting decomposition (and by the looks of the zombies, the degradation had already begun), but this . . . *taste for human flesh.*

There was no time to ruminate upon the finding, however. The other two prostitutes were in a similar state of siege. Fanny lay on the floor, dead it seemed, while two of the creatures, Miss Corwent and Miss Stanley, knelt over her, devouring her with great ferocity. As he watched, horrified yet fascinated, Miss Corwent wrenched one of Fanny's arms from its socket and sank her teeth into it, just as though it were a chicken leg she was enjoying during a leisurely picnic out of doors; while opposite her, Miss Stanley tore a significant chunk of flesh from Fanny's throat and sat back on her haunches with her chin aloft, all the better to gulp down the still-warm meat, which she did with evident gratification, greedily licking the blood from her fingers as the last strip of skin disappeared between her lips.

The prostitute called Sugar, meanwhile, a girl Quimby had been most eager to sample, stood with her back to a bookcase attempting to ward off Miss Pearce and a zombie he knew only as Jacqueline. Sugar was wielding a bust of Quimby's father as a weapon and at the same time screaming at the three men for their assistance, having seen them enter the room. For a moment, Quimby wondered if she might make good her escape, such was the spirit of her defence. Then she made a connection, striking Miss Pearce with the bust and knocking her sideways in a move he would have applauded had it not left her so exposed. Indeed, Jacqueline used the moment to strike, driving her fist into Sugar's face and into her mouth, Sugar's jaw breaking with a snap. With a low, gurgling moan, Sugar dropped to her knees and Jacqueline moved to stand over her, ramming her fist further down the poor woman's throat until it was immersed fully to the elbow. She seemed almost to be rummaging for something, an expression on her face like that of a child rooting about in the sawdust of a lucky dip barrel. Then her gore-streaked arm emerged, her hand clutching an assortment of innards that she pushed greedily into her own mouth as, behind her, Sugar fell forward to the library floor, blood pouring from her mouth which gaped loosely open.

Quimby barely registered the library door open and close,

knowing only that Craven had left the room shortly after a bright magnesium flash that had the effect of alerting the five zombies to their presence. And they all looked in the direction of the library door where Quimby and Perkins stood.

'Oh dear,' said Quimby.

His Lordship's first instinct was to run. There was nothing to be gained by staying here, he reasoned, save to be eaten as dessert. The best course of action would be to let the zombies escape, sate their appetite on the streets and then, with any luck, the army would deal with them. There was nothing to lead them back to Quimby, not unless the brutes had suddenly learned to think as well.

'What shall we do, sir?' asked Perkins.

'Run, Perkins,' said Quimby.

'But what if they get out, sir? They'll eat the public, sir.'

Quimby looked in disbelief at his manservant.

'Well, would you prefer it if they ate—'

However, he never finished his sentence. As they were deliberating, Jones, who was nearest, had stood from the corpse of Rosa and was walking over, his mouth coated in coagulating blood, which slid down the front of his neck. As he came closer he lurched forward, heading straight for Quimby.

Who grabbed Perkins and used him as a shield.

'*Sir*,' protested Perkins, caught off-balance, his arms flailing, unprepared to meet Jones who came with teeth bared, sinking them into Perkins' shoulder.

Perkins screamed. 'Sir,' he squealed, staggering backwards, thumping back against the door and blocking it just as Quimby whirled round to make his escape.

'Get out of the way, you fool!' shouted Quimby, trying to kick Perkins out of his path. But by now Jones had brought his full weight to bear and the two men were firmly lodged against the door. Jones's teeth were embedded deeply in Perkins' shoulder as he shook his head trying to worry free a chunk of flesh and Quimby fancied that he must have torn through an artery in the neck, for all of a sudden Perkins' terrified face was obscured by a spray of blood.

'*Sir*,' wailed Perkins as he sank to the floor, ineffectually beating at the creature with his hands.

From behind him Quimby heard a low growl and turned to see Jacqueline shambling towards him, one arm out-stretched, black with Sugar's viscera. Forgetting about kicking Perkins away from the door, he dodged behind Jacqueline. Good, she was heading towards Perkins. He watched as she bent down and grasped one of his legs, lifting it, then biting into it, at which Perkins' screams increased in intensity, if such a thing were possible. Now Miss Pearce had joined the gathering. She bent forward, almost as though to offer Perkins the variety of sexual excitement Quimby had in mind when he had first conceived of the night. In fact, she was nuzzling further upwards, at Perkins' stomach, where she no doubt hoped to find meat of a rather more succulent nature, and his screams as she sank her teeth into his belly indicated that she had been successful in this regard.

Quimby was not off the menu, though, and was very much aware of the fact. Miss Corwent and Miss Stanley both regarded him with an expression of blank hunger that sent him tearing over to the wall near the window, where he spotted the axe, an artefact he had never paid much mind before, save to provide vague and wholly concocted explanations for its presence should a visitor ask. Many years ago, prior to bedding her, he had told Lady Caroline Lamb that the axe had belonged to his ancestor who had stood alongside Queen Elizabeth when she gave her famous speech at Tilbury and that she must not touch it (which she seemed about to ask to do) as it was razor sharp. The knowledge had certainly increased her ardour; the Prime Minister's wife had been no disappointment in that area, and Quimby's comments post-coitus, though made in the manner of his usual fabrication, had in fact been genuine on that occasion.

Now, he thought, scrambling up to the desk in order to reach the axe, were his comments about the blade also genuine?

There was only one way to find out.

He stepped down from the desk and to the side, drawing Miss Corwent towards him. He took a step backwards to balance himself.

Perkins was still screaming. For pity's sake, man, keep it down, thought Quimby, crossly.

And he swung the weapon around himself in the manner of a competitor at the Highland games.

There was more to this axe-wielding than met the eye, he thought, as he braced a leg against the library desk, working to remove the blade from the wood in which it had become lodged, having missed Miss Corwent.

The blade was keen, at least there was that, he thought.

Christ, how on earth could he concentrate with Perkins screaming like that? With a grunt it was free, and he danced to the side once more, to give himself a little room. Abruptly, Perkins ceased his screaming. Quimby, grateful for the reduction in noise, once again took up position, Miss Corwent still shambling towards him. Once again he swung, but this time he took no chances. Rather than swinging from side to side, he chopped downwards, his intention being to strike Miss Corwent at the crown and cleave her from head to toe. His aim was true and Miss Corwent was opened almost to the hip, the two parts of her body dividing like a split tree-stump, depositing her insides to the floor as they did so, then hanging there, as . . .

She kept on coming.

Amazed, Quimby looked at her, then gazed at her internal organs quivering on the boards. She had the body of a weak and feeble woman, he thought, distractedly, but she had the heart and stomach of, well, a seemingly invincible zombie. Curse the woman!

Then from his side came a low groan and Miss Stanley was almost upon him. He dodged to the side, raised the axe and swiped wildly, smashing the blade into Miss Stanley's skull, which sprayed grey brain matter as it opened and she slid to the floor, eyes rolling up.

The head, he thought. You have to sever the head.

Turning back to Miss Corwent, he swung underarm, twice, in order to achieve the same effect and was relieved to see her sink downwards, her seemingly inexorable progress halted at last.

Jacqueline was moving towards him but he was now becoming accustomed to his new role as executioner and he took her head off at the neck. Now covered in gore, he bared his teeth and chopped at Miss Pearce until she, too, was dead, the top of her head rolling to the middle of the library floor where it joined a gruesome collection of entrails.

Finally, Quimby went to Jones, who was kneeling, oblivious to the carnage around him, spooning Perkins' stomach into his mouth with a cupped hand. Revolted, Quimby stood over him and brought the axe down upon his neck with every ounce of his strength. So hard was the blow that it severed the head of Jones and continued its journey forth, amputating Perkins' leg just above the knee.

Now, Quimby stood, letting the axe drop from his fingers and surveyed the scene.

Not for long did he tarry, though. Whirling, he pulled open the library door and dashed to the stairs, descending them two at a time until he reached a large, thick curtain in the main hall that he swept aside to reveal a huge oak door. He felt along the top of the doorframe to locate the key, opened the door, then was breathing in stale, damp air (though it was still a great deal more pleasant than the faecal aroma of his library) as he ran down the stone steps to his laboratory.

Once in the cellar he lit a burner with shaking hands then raced along the workbench, collecting to himself silver-stoppered jars boasting labels such as jimson weed, belladonna, monkshood; others, smuggled into the country by Perkins from Haiti, marked only with symbols.

Hands shaking, Quimby mixed ingredients into a round-bottom flask, placing it above the burner to heat it until it began to bubble and smoke, holding it aloft and swirling it to further mix the ingredients. Good. It was Perkins who usually mixed the potions but this looked perfect. Then, holding the jar carefully he raced back upstairs. Their theory had always been the closer to death the more brain function should be retained. Now to test that theory.

Back in the library and Quimby, gagging at the smell and rank atmosphere in the room, pushed the headless corpse of Jones aside and knelt to Perkins. Placing a hand beneath his head, he lifted his lips to the warm beaker and poured the smallest amount of potion into his servant's mouth, thought about it for a second, shrugged, then poured the entire contents of the beaker inside.

Now Quimby picked up the axe and retreated to the centre of the room, his shoes squelching in blood and body parts as he did so, and stood to watch. For a few seconds there was no reaction, and Quimby feared he had been too hasty when measuring out the quantities. But then Perkins' lips moved, and he coughed, spitting a mix of potion and blood onto his own chin; his eyes opened and rolled about his head and he jerked, very suddenly, so that he moved from lying on his back to lying on his side. The parts of his lower intestine that had not been devoured slithered out of him, but this seemed in no way a barrier to his recovery, which continued apace, for now he was coughing and spluttering, expelling much foul-looking fluid, his whole body jerking and shuddering in very much the same manner as their previous reanimations, so that Quimby allowed himself to believe that it had worked. Thank God, he thought, thank God Perkins was alive. How else was this mess to be cleared up?

On the other hand . . .

Would the reanimated Perkins retain his memory?

Quimby increased his grip on the axe and took some tentative steps forward. Probably better to be closer should he need to strike.

'Perkins,' he said, carefully, 'Perkins, are you all right?'

Perkins, whose leg had been severed just above the knee, whose stomach had been opened and emptied like a melon stripped of its fruit, who had a gaping hole in his neck and shoulder exposing white bone, red tissue and cartilage, said, 'Yes, sir, I think so, sir.'

'Good man,' said Quimby, hefting the axe. Have to be careful, he thought, don't let your guard down. What if Perkins was shamming?

'And do you . . . *remember* anything?' he asked, cautiously.

'No, sir,' said Perkins, 'nothing. Did I lose consciousness, sir?'

Quimby snorted a laugh. 'No, you fool, you died. You were eaten. Look at yourself.'

For several moments there was the sound of screaming and anguish; Perkins, now sitting upright, desperately trying to gather his intestine and replace it in the stomach cavity, only to discover parts of it missing, or severed, then giving up and flinging it away from himself like a petulant child. Then he placed his hands to the floor in order to pull himself to his feet. Or, foot. And there was renewed distress as, too late, he discovered the loss of his leg and came crashing back to the floor, sobbing and wailing, until Quimby began to become quite irritated and wished the man would bloody hurry up and pull himself together.

Once Perkins had recovered composure and was sufficiently reconciled to his situation, Quimby went to him, explaining how he had done all he could to help, but that the zombies had beaten him back. How he had tried to prevent Jones from biting into Perkins' leg, and how his failure ailed him so, and his horror at seeing Perkins' leg bitten clean through by one of the creatures; but how Perkins really must get to work before the staff returned in just a few short hours when there would be some very searching questions to answer: why there were the remains of eight dead bodies in the library for one thing.

'And *then* we have a couple of matters demanding our attention,' added Quimby.

'Sir?'

'Firstly, I thought the whole bloody point of raising miscreants from the dead was that they would then be miscreants *under my control*. Correct me if I'm wrong but they weren't very under my control this evening, were they?'

'No, sir.'

'And secondly, our friend Mr Craven.'

'What about him, sir?'

'Before he left he made a photogenic drawing of the scene.'

'Sir?'

Quimby sighed, then spoke as though addressing a child. 'Perkins, you are aware, of course, of the crime of blackmail?'

'Yes, sir.'

'Well it occurs to me that, along with the making of erotic images, our friend Craven's device might be most useful in this regard. Most useful. I would, of course, have hoped to benefit from its application thus, but alas, I find myself in a position where I may well be on the receiving end. Unless Craven is as guileless as you, Perkins, which having taken his measure, I sincerely doubt. No, there's only one thing for it. We need to find this Mr Craven, and waste no time in doing so.'

'Yes, sir. And, sir?'

'Yes, Perkins.'

Perkins looked a little abashed. 'I'm hungry, sir.'

Quimby bent to pick up the axe, putting a distance between him and his manservant. 'How hungry?' he snapped.

'It's like nothing I've ever experienced, sir,' said Perkins, who was looking about the room, 'it's overwhelming.'

Quimby gestured about the room. 'Well, isn't there sufficient here, man?' he said, his face betraying his irritation and disgust.

'Good Lord, this must a banquet for a man in your . . . *state*, surely?'

'We don't have anything a little more . . . *fresh* do we, sir?'

'You needn't look at me, Perkins.'

'The hunger really is quite irrepressible, sir. It would surely be a tragedy were it to render me ungovernable, if you get my meaning. And what with my enhanced strength, sir . . .'

'Do not forget I have an axe, man,' roared Quimby in reply, his colour rising. 'This evening has found me well practised in dispatching the living dead back whence they came, one more should not unduly concern me!'

'Then who would clear up in my stead, sir?' asked Perkins in reply, a sweet smile playing about his lips.

There was silence in the room. Then, mollified, Quimby said, 'Very well, I shall see what I can do.'

Thus, a short time later, Quimby sat, disgusted and disconsolate as Perkins ate his beloved Irish water spaniel, Barmaid, Perkins not even having the decency to look apologetic about the matter.

The cries of a newsboy from outside in the street drew Quimby to the window and he peered out into the street to find out what the day's big story was, then came back to his chair to muse upon it. Well, at least in all likelihood the missing prostitutes would go unreported, he thought. Instead the papers would be full of the news that the King was dead.

IX

Later that morning
A drawing room, Kensington Palace

'One of my staff, a very capable man named Nobo, has assembled this for me,' announced the Prime Minister, struggling with a contraption boasting three legs and some form of easel at its head. 'Though not quite as fully as I might have hoped,' he continued, with a self-deprecating smile, 'for I'll be blowed if I can get the accursed thing to stand up straight . . . Please, if Your Majesty will bear with me, I feel sure that against all evidence to the contrary it will prove a most useful accessory in my presentation, in which I hope to cast some light on the most unfortunate events of last night. Or, to be more precise, earlier this morning . . .'

Victoria paid it no mind, the sight of the Prime Minister grappling with his unusual easel being most beguiling. Plus, it allowed her the opportunity to study the famous Lord Melbourne, subject of much rumour and survivor of many a scandal, up close. What had struck her first about him were his eyes. He had amused eyes; his mouth, also, was often pursed, as though he were trying not to break into a broad grin; he wore his sideburns long, his hair was just a little unkempt and the white necktie at his throat somewhat skewwhiff. He lacked a woman's touch, she thought. As for his manner, he was charming, that much was obvious, and handsome, too, though several decades her senior. Certainly on the strength of the time they had so far spent in each other's company – she as his sovereign; he as her Prime Minister and, as he had explained, her private secretary into the bargain – it seemed certain that they were going to be great friends.

The Prime Minister had started by introducing himself, familiarising the new Queen with the workings of the government and preparing her for the speech she was shortly to make to the Privy Council; in short, easing her, with the very gentlest of guiding hands, into her new role. For her part, she had given all matters her attention, doing her best to ignore the one nagging thought that had plagued her throughout the preliminary stages of their encounter, which was, *Is Lord Melbourne aware of the events of last night?*

Presently, she had her answer when he had clasped together his hands and held her gaze.

'There is something else we need to discuss,' he said, his voice serious and lacking the slightly satirical edge it took when he explained matters of Parliament and the workings of court, 'an issue of the utmost importance, a national secret to which very few are party, which is this: the subject of the war in which we are involved; the war in whose front line you found yourself this morning. The war between man and demon.'

At this, he had reached for his contraption, which was now, finally, installed. Onto it he placed some large sheets of paper then stood to one side, fixing her with a hard stare and inclining his head slightly, which was something she was to learn he only did when he was addressing particularly serious matters, saying, 'Your Majesty, the creature you met last night, was—'

'A demon, Prime Minister, yes, we were introduced.' Having kept a multitude of thoughts and questions to herself since the attack in her chamber, Victoria found her thoughts emerging in a rush. 'I also made the acquaintance of a *Demon Hunter*. I owe her a great debt, of course, but the fact remains that her presence in my chamber came as something of a surprise. For I must admit that prior to the events of a few hours ago I had never considered the threat of demonic activity to be quite so . . . well, quite so *imminent*. In fact, I must confess, at the risk of committing blasphemy, that I had wondered whether stories of demons were primarily fictions, aimed at frightening small children and ensuring the continued virtue of ardent churchgoers. Yet now it transpires that not only do demons walk among us, they are predisposed to paying visits to my chamber at night and attempting to kill me. Thank goodness for Mrs Brown, for I would surely be dead otherwise, but her presence leads me to believe that she, and therefore I must infer *you*, had some notion of this attack and thus *could have warned me*.'

Her colour had risen during the speech, as had her voice, and Melbourne had a moment of profound sympathy for this poor young girl, thrust into an unknowable destiny.

'Your Majesty,' he said instead, 'if I might just beg a moment I can explain. What transpired was most unfortunate and we owe a great deal to Maggie Brown, but predicting the intentions of the forces of darkness is a difficult enterprise at the best of times. Warning you was quite out of the question, I'm afraid, for this and other operational reasons.'

She seemed about to protest but left it, saying instead, 'But there *are* such things as demons, though, and they move among us?'

'Ah,' said Melbourne, 'here is where my flipping chart shall prove its worth. For I have some illustrations. Tell me, ma'am, what have you read of them in the past?'

'Very little, Lord Melbourne,' she replied, 'the works of Milton and Dante, of course, but if I'm honest, as a young girl I found it all a little terrifying and probably did not pay as much attention as I should have done . . .'

'Very well,' said Lord Melbourne, 'then let us begin with the fall of Satan, expelled from Heaven by God.'

He lifted the first piece of paper, tucking it behind the easel to reveal an illustration beneath: Satan, with the wings of a bat, falling.

'"*How art thou fallen from Heaven, O Lucifer, son of the morning?*"' quoted Melbourne.

'Please, Lord Melbourne, put my mind at rest. You are not about to tell me that Satan himself walks among us.'

Melbourne laughed. 'Absolutely not, ma'am. This event dates to the time of the creation. We can be sure that Lucifer exists, just as we can be sure that God exists. But God is up there,' he pointed, 'and Satan below, in the ninth and lowest circle of hell, eternally feasting upon the mutilated body of Judas Iscariot. He left earth and took with him the majority of his followers, those angels who were also expelled from Heaven and cast down, but,' Melbourne held up a finger, 'the dark one decreed that a force be left on earth, here to do his work, which was to spread darkness, death and destruction among us, and which for centuries they have done, like a slowly growing cancer, killing us with war, plague and famine, with anger and hatred, ignorance and jealousy.'

As he had been talking, Melbourne had been flicking back pages, revealing images: a Walpurgis Night procession, an evil female spirit casting a spell on a woodcutter, a goblin bewitching a ploughman, a witch burning at the stake, a man torn asunder by sprites, a nun, her head at a grotesque angle, tongue lolling from her mouth, eyes upturned, habit stained dark with blood . . .

The colour had slowly drained from the Queen's face. 'Are you saying that demons are responsible for all of the evil in our world?'

'Oh good heavens, no. Not even most of it. Think of them more as crusaders, the midwives of our evil. No, they are not responsible for all the evil in the world, but they are at its root. Sometimes I think of them as being our dark mirror image, only instead of being good, with evil buried deep, they are the opposite.'

'So there is good in them?'

'Perhaps, Your Majesty, perhaps,' he said doubtfully.

'How? How do they do they carry out this work?' asked Victoria.

'Oh, a variety of methods. The abominations are much like us in many ways. Just as in our society, there are different ranks, from the very lowest sprite and hobgoblin to the highest demon, and just as in our society the havoc that they wreak is concordant with their rank, so that at the lowest level, say, a werewolf might spread fear and suspicion among a small rural community; at the summit, a deviant of high birth can insinuate himself into a position of power and wreak a more terrible devastation, a war, a massacre, a holocaust.'

'Of high birth?'

'Indeed, ma'am. All those centuries ago, the dark lord left high-ranking clans in charge, there to rule over their minions; needless to say it is these that are the most dangerous, who were no doubt responsible for the events of last night; against whom we need to be most vigilant.'

'Who are they?'

'Those who concern us most are the descendants of Baal, a demon who was Lucifer's right-hand man, who, it is said, was furious at having been left behind on earth; who wanted his rightful place in hell but was denied it – and with it his immortality – and as a result vents his fury on mankind.'

'He is their king?'

'No. He's been dead for centuries, ma'am. With the obvious exception of vampires – the cockroaches in the demon nest – deviants are bound by earthly laws of mortality and will age, just as we do. They do so much more slowly, of course, but eventually they will grow weak and die. Thus, just as we do, they have a need to continue the bloodline, and rank is determined by lineage, so that those master demons we find ourselves at war with today are the descendants of Baal and of his wife, Astharoth. Just as in our society, it is *primarily*,' he deferred to the Queen as he said this, 'male heirs who lead; indeed, from what we know of them, the male blood-line is far stronger than that of a female.'

'And you say these are the demons who orchestrated the attack of last night?'

'We think the Baal were behind it, yes.'

'The succubus. Was she of the Baal?'

'No. A follower. Not as high-ranking as Baal.'

'She was quite beautiful. Do they always appear as humans?'

'How they manifest themselves varies according to the individual demon, but it seems they very, very rarely show themselves as they really are, for they are so disgusting to look at. Obviously if they are moving among us, it is best that they adopt the guise of—'

'Human beings,' finished Victoria.

'Exactly,' said Melbourne, 'even ladies-in-waiting.'

'Was it really her aim to kill me, Lord Melbourne?'

'We believe so, ma'am.'

'To what purpose?'

'We believe that what we witnessed last night was nothing less than an unsuccessful demonic coup, with the attempt on your life at its very epicentre.'

'Then is it likely to happen again?'

'Almost certainly. We believe not for some time, though.'

'What makes you say this?'

'We gain our information in a number of ways, Your Majesty. From the experiences of our forefathers in the struggle; from intelligence gathered in the field, from closely observing patterns of behaviour, and from prophecies handed down to us through the ages. We have academics at the major universities – their identities a closely guarded secret – who pore over these manuscripts night and day; who observe and analyse demonic activity. They tell us that these prophecies speak of the Baal bringing untold sorrow to earth in our time; that there will be a great calm followed by a storm. Last night certainly marked the end of a period of great calm: Maggie Brown tells me that there were supernatural beings abroad last night – indeed she was very nearly their victim; plus, we have had reports of, and I hesitate to tell you this so fantastic does it seem, of vermin boasting two heads attacking members of the public; of dogs turning on their owners, mothers killing babies and husbands killing wives. Definitely, Your Majesty, evil was active last night. Yet even so, it was not quite the offensive our experts predict. They feel there will be another gathering of the forces; they speak of a building impatience within the Baal, that they grow tired of their place in the world – that they wish to rule over us.'

'So what do we do now, Lord Melbourne?'

'We wait, we watch, we remain vigilant.'

'We?'

'The Protektorate, ma'am.'

'Ah yes,' she said, 'the Protektorate. Perhaps you could tell me about Maggie Brown.'

So he did, and she learned about her and the Protektorate, the tiny force of Demon Hunters led by the redoubtable Maggie Brown. The Queen was told that only a handful of people were even aware of the threat, such as it was, though it had repercussions for many hundreds of thousands.

'These demons,' she said, 'if they are able to maintain human form, could they be among us, talking to us, behaving like those we know, but in fact with hidden motives?'

'Most certainly, Your Majesty,' said Melbourne, more guarded all of a sudden.

'Sir John?' she said.

'Ah.' He paused. 'Your Majesty, you must understand there is only a certain amount I can afford to tell you about these matters—'

'He is my mother's private secretary, Lord Melbourne. If you have information regarding Sir John Conroy I must insist you tell me at once.'

'In that case, ma'am, no, we have no evidence nor even any suspicion that Sir John is in any way employed against Your Majesty.'

'How would we know?' she asked. 'How would we know whether or not he was a demon?'

Melbourne took on a pained expression. 'The truth, Your Majesty, is that we wouldn't. There is no unique feature we know of; no test we can perform. Unfortunately, we have to rely on our wits, our intuition and our intelligence sources. The sad fact of the matter ma'am, is you must trust no one.'

'Thank you, Lord Melbourne,' she said, and with that she summoned her ladies, ready to repair to her chamber in preparation for the speech she was due to give to the Privy Council. Once they were assembled, they departed, their skirts swishing. Melbourne stood and watched her leave, admiring her grace, in awe of how well she seemed to have adapted to her role.

As the door closed behind the Queen's party there came a disembodied voice in the room.

'Somewhat economical with the truth there, Prime Minister.'

As always, though he knew full well she was present, Melbourne jumped.

'Maggie,' he said, looking around him as he usually did, wondering where in the room she was. She was another who seemed to have adapted swiftly to the new system. 'Shouldn't you be recovering in bed?'

'Aye, no doubt, but I'm needed more than ever. More to the point, I wanted to hear you initiate the lassie – if you can call it that.'

'You think I should have told her everything?'

The silence spoke volumes. Confound the woman!

'Maggie,' he said at last, 'it is our job to guide this young woman through the early days of her reign, to see that she blossoms into the ruler this country needs and deserves. I don't think the most expeditious means of achieving that is to scare the poor thing to death with talk of the Antichrist now, do you?'

Part Two

'*I do*'

X

Greek Street, Soho

McKenzie stood outside the Pillars of Hercules awaiting his contact, a man he knew only as Egg. His top hat was pulled down low over his face so that his eyes were only just visible below the brim; his cloak was done up almost to his whiskers against the chill and, as he watched his icy breath plume in the air before him and stamped his feet, he cursed the man for being late. He tapped his cane impatiently against the cobbles and stared about him, making unsuccessful attempts to peer through a mist that seemed to hang permanently in the air, curtains of it, floating like ghosts.

Each drunk that passed, he scrutinised carefully, at one point even saying, 'Egg? Is that Egg?' in an exploratory manner, to which the fellow had just laughed and coughed, doing both with such force that he was compelled to hold on to a wall for support (and McKenzie wondered briefly if the man might simply die there in the street, and what a bloody funny thing that would be: killing somebody with the word 'egg') then finally wiping his mouth and moving on.

More people passed. McKenzie spat. A carriage drew up

and the driver, his face hidden by a three-cornered hat and a scarf about his mouth so that he resembled a highwayman, stared down at him, eyes like granite. McKenzie stared back before a movement caught his eye and he glanced at the body of the carriage just in time to see a curtain drop back into place. There was the knock-knock of a signal. The driver shook the reins. The carriage moved on.

McKenzie watched it go, frowning, then returned his thoughts to the late arrival. Where was he? The damn, infernal man – this . . . *Egg*?

McKenzie was no stranger to Soho. For a man of his profession it was a rich source of material, but he very much disliked being kept waiting. He swept aside his cloak, took his pocket watch from his waistcoat and resolved to give Egg another five minutes then move on, whatever it was the bugger had to say, he could—

'Psst,' came a sound and he looked around expecting yet another nightwalker leering sloppily at him and inviting him into an alley, a request he would have to most regretfully decline as he was happy to avail himself of this pleasure whenever he could – those ailments affecting his genitalia allowing. But there was nobody there.

'Psst,' it came again. By now McKenzie was looking left and right, furiously.

'Don't look up, sor, but I'm above you,' came the voice, the accent not of town, but of the country.

McKenzie looked up.

'Don't look, I did say, sor,' whispered the voice, urgently.

'Well then, what am I to do, my friend?' growled McKenzie peevishly, 'stand here as though I'm talking to myself on the street like an escapee from Bedlam?'

'You can start by identifying yourself that you're the gentaman I'm s'posed to be seeing,' rejoined the voice.

'You contacted me, if I recall?' sighed McKenzie.

'That's my first question answered correctly, sor.'

McKenzie placed both hands to the top of his cane and leaned forward, resting his weight upon it. Bloody Nora. He had a right one here. And he looked upwards to where the buildings met the sky, looking for a sign of his contact.

'Don't look, I said,' whispered the voice from above.

'Oh for the love of God, can't we get on with this?' snapped McKenzie. 'Do I look like I've got all night?'

'No, sor, first I need to know . . .'

'No, "sor", you don't,' snapped McKenzie, 'I've had enough of you wasting my bloody time. Good day to you, my friend,' and he turned and started walking along Greek Street in the direction of Old Compton Street.

Above him there was the sound of scuttling as Egg made his way along the rooftops after him, hissing, 'Sor, sor, please stop, I meant no offence. Only that the lady on whose behalf I have agreed to meet with you has asked me to be most careful regarding matters of both confidentiality and security.'

A man and a woman walked past McKenzie arm in arm, giving him an odd look as they did so, having heard him talking to himself in the street like a lunatic, no doubt! He touched a hand to the brim of his top hat in return; then, once they were gone, stopped.

Above him the sound of movement also ceased, and for a moment the street was quite still: the hubbub of Soho in the background, receding laughter from somewhere as a pub deposited more drunks into the street. Then, silence. Just the sound of dripping water hitting brickwork that ran slick with rain and condensation, shining in the dark.

'Who is it then, this lady?' he called, casting his voice up, above the mist and smoke, above the waste both human and animal and above the running water, to the roofs above him. He had a poetic soul, McKenzie did, though nobody he would meet in his short life should ever suspect as such, and in that moment he imagined his voice travelling upwards, flying high, high and as free as a bird.

To the stars.

'I'm sorry, sor?'

'This lady who has you in her employ. Who is it?'

There was a pause, during which McKenzie imagined Egg looking up and down Greek Street. What a vantage point he must have up there. Able to see all around, no doubt.

When no answer came, nor was there any evidence of a reason why an answer might not be forthcoming, McKenzie continued his walk along Greek Street.

'Sor,' came the harried voice from above, to the accompaniment of more sudden scrambling as he negotiated his way across the roofs in pursuit of McKenzie. 'I can give you nothing save her first name, sir, which is Flora,' came the reply, 'and that she works at one of our great country's most prestigious houses, and that in fact she divides her time between homes of equal prestige in service of her employer.'

'I take it, my friend, that it's her employer who provides the interest?'

'There is no doubt at all, sir, that if she were in the employ of a lady belonging to the new middle classes, then, how shall I say it?, the subject under discussion might well be of less interest to a man in your profession. Indeed it is the exalted stature of her employer that leads us to believe you might be willing to pay for the information . . . sir.'

'Pay for the inform—' McKenzie stopped and brought his cane to the street surface, making a sound like that of a short explosion. 'What on earth makes you think that I will pay for the information?'

From above him came the sound of a stop as though done under emergency circumstances and there was a crash of an upset. A moment passed and a window somewhere was shoved open.

'Oi,' came the screech of an uncouth woman, 'fuck off or I'll whistle for the peelers.'

Both men kept their counsel. Just the sound of dripping water. Soho alive. Shouting, screaming and the smashing of glass; the banging of doors and a dog howling.

'Go on, then,' screeched the harridan, when no reply came, her voice rising above the din, 'fuck off.'

McKenzie looked up and for the first time he saw who it was he was speaking to, an outline at least. Quickly the man drew back from the edge.

McKenzie kept on walking.

'Sor,' said Egg, whispering now, sounding almost hoarse with it. 'Sor, the reason we need payment is that my lady will be forced to leave her employ before divulging the information, for the information is of such a sensitive nature. She tells me that she fears for her life should it be known that the plans to discuss these matters with a man in your profession, sor. Any payments made to her would be necessary to ensure her safety and continued well-being.'

'So the lady would be requiring a lot of money,' said McKenzie. 'How much money would she be requiring, exactly?'

Egg named the price.

McKenzie coughed theatrically, even though the price was what he had been expecting. 'Out of the question,' he said, 'I'm afraid you'll have to tell your mistress to approach another newspaper.'

'Yours is the best reputation in London.'

'Tell her to lower her price and we'll talk.'

'I'm afraid she will not agree to place a lower value on the information she has.'

'Tell me the information and I can be the judge of its worth.'

'I'm afraid I cannot do that, sor.'

'Then I shall have to bid you good night.'

'Very well. Here is how to contact me should you change your mind.'

A stone dropped to the ground at his side, wrapped in a piece of paper, surprising him.

'Egg?'

But there was no reply. The man had gone. McKenzie frowned, picking up the stone and taking from it the piece of paper, which bore the name of a hostelry.

Perhaps he had bluffed too hard, frightened Egg off.

Then again, no. If he held his nerve there was every likelihood Egg would return to him with his price lowered.

McKenzie hoped so. For if there was something in it, the story could potentially be big; certainly if, as McKenzie suspected, 'Flora' was Lady Flora Hastings, one of the Queen's ladies-in-waiting.

XI

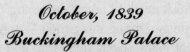

October, 1839
Buckingham Palace

The Duchess of Sutherland, Harriet Leveson-Gower (such a beautiful, dignified and graceful lady and a perfect choice for her Mistress of the Robes) was selecting Victoria's attire for the day, talking to the Queen as she did so. The main news of the morning, she said, was that several of the palace windows had been broken during the night and that the Lord Steward and the Lord Chamberlain were most aggravated and suspected vandals of the damage.

It was because of me, thought Victoria.

She sat at her dresser, her tea in a Spode china cup before her, regarding herself in the mirror, and she wondered: had vandals hurled rocks at the palace windows in order to register their fury at their Queen? Was she failing them already, her people?

'They really have taken you to their hearts, Your Majesty,' Lord Melbourne used to tell her (in fact, he was regularly telling her this during the first year of her reign, as she had many moments of self-doubt, often believing herself to be too young for the role she was being asked to fulfil). 'You are *their* Queen.'

She had to admit, however, she had something of a head start when it came to courting the affections of the public, as she was under no illusions as to the esteem in which her predecessors had been held. Determined not to squander that goodwill, she nightly repeated to herself her pledge that she swore to serve and respect her people. During her years at Kensington Palace her mother the Duchess and Sir John Conroy had insisted on instigating a series of what they called progresses, which involved taking the young Victoria on tours across the country. During this period Victoria had been the guest at a great many stately homes up and down the land, and been introduced to what seemed like vast numbers of noble men and dignitaries. She had, during that time, attended her fair share of balls and admired a great many feathered hats. And though she liked nothing better than a ball and was even partial to a combination of plumage and millinery, she found herself increasingly aware that life in the country she was soon to rule over was sharply divided: there were those who were very rich and those who were very poor. As she passed through the Midlands and into the north of England, through her carriage window she would see the poor of the rural areas, dirty and downtrodden, scraping a living in the fields, walking solemnly along roads, their backs bent beneath their load.

She had heard talk of the squalor in London, of course, but here it was in the provinces, too. She told herself then, and repeated to herself the pledge, that as Queen she would make it part of her duties to help those less fortunate than herself.

But in order to help them she needed their trust and now she wondered whether it had already been forfeited through her own silly, selfish actions.

Or, perhaps that wasn't it.

Maybe the damage was the work of these dark forces Lord Melbourne had spoken of, and her mind went back to that very first day of her sovereignty, when she had met her Prime Minister, specifically to something he had told her: *'In that case Your Majesty, no, we have no evidence nor even any suspicion that Sir John is in any way employed against Your Majesty.'*

Over the last two years she had grown to love and trust her Prime Minister. She now referred to him in private as 'Lord M', so the bond was undoubtedly strong, but her thoughts often went back to that moment during their first meeting and what she thought, quite simply, was this: *Lord M lied to me then.*

'You must trust nobody, ma'am,' he had told her.

Not even you, dear Lord M, she reflected ruefully.

She took her thoughts with her as she dressed, then, as had become her custom, went for a walk in the grounds of the palace.

Though she walked with the Baroness Lehzen the pair were silent, leaving Victoria alone with her thoughts, her breath blooming in the air in front of her.

Why had she allowed Melbourne his lie? she wondered. Perhaps it was because she was happy to have her sovereignty shield her from some of the more unpleasant aspects of the Empire's struggle. Her one encounter with a demon had convinced her that she would rather leave such matters to the Prime Minister and the Protektorate.

Then again, it was a double-edged sword, she supposed. After all, there was nobody more shielded from the secret war between the forces of good and the forces of darkness than the common man. What was the expression? Ignorant bliss, wasn't it? As she walked she wondered if she really did benefit from such a state of affairs. Instead of simply believing that the broken windows had been the work of vandals, which was no doubt the conclusion reached by the majority of those who lived and worked at the Palace, she, with her connections, her ministerial advisers and Royal Protektors, found herself beset by fear and paranoia. Not only that, but it was a strange sort of impotent fear and paranoia. After all, what could she, young Victoria, she with 'the weak and feeble body of a woman' do against demons?

There was at least one consolation, however: there had been no demonic activity in the last two years, certainly none to speak of anyway. Something had to happen soon, though, warned Lord Melbourne. When periods of quiet ended, they often did so with devastating consequences. In the meantime, there were the occasional findings of more than usually suspicious body parts on the banks of the Thames, suspected attacks by hell-hounds or other hellish acquiescents, but whether or not it was the work of inhumans was hard to say.

'Sometimes, Your Majesty,' he said to her once sadly, having reported to her the discovery of an horrific baby farm, 'I wonder if humankind really needs a great deal of help from the underworld in order to do itself damage.'

Not that life at court had been dull in the absence of the demonic hordes. Indeed, there was another secret war being waged, that between her and her mother.

Victoria, unwilling to forgive her mother for her friendship with Sir John Conroy, had, when they moved the household from Kensington to Buckingham Palace, arranged for the Duchess to occupy apartments some way from those of her own. This infuriated her mother, who, it was clear, still hoped for a measure of influence in Royal affairs. The Duchess would try and contact Victoria, scribbling furious notes requesting permission for an audience. In return, Victoria would scribble notes in reply, bearing but one word: 'busy'.

The Duchess had been at the Coronation, of course, where the ceremony was long and muddled and, if Victoria were honest, erring on the side of dull, until something happened.

Something she would mull over later. The speed. How it was pure instinct.

Because as the ageing Lord Rolle approached the Queen in order to pay homage, he lost his footing, and in the same instant Victoria was reaching forward, her hand shooting out to save him. Then, she stopped herself, with a cry, turning the movement into something else, as poor Lord Rolle, in a manner befitting his name, returned to the bottom of the steps.

There was a gasp. Those assembled thought of protocol. Then the Queen rose to her feet, very quickly ran down the steps, sending her ladies-in-waiting into a minor panic, and bent down in order to help up the Lord, a gesture that was accompanied by a spontaneous round of applause led by Lord Melbourne.

Westminster Abbey had never witnessed anything quite like it.

Victoria thought only of how she had been able to stop Rolle – *she had been quick enough to do it* – but hadn't, because . . .

Why?

Because some other instinct told her not to.

Then came the moment when a new Queen was crowned, and it was as though the Abbey seemed to shimmer when those assembled put on their coronets. Trumpets were sounded and from outside came the salute of booming cannons to signal the fact that England had its new Queen.

At that moment she looked up into the gallery of Westminster Abbey, and saw her mother, her hands clasped in front of her, held to her face.

And beside her mother was Sir John Conroy, who stood with his hands behind his back, his hair in a ponytail, cheekbones casting dark shadows, his eyes black.

Victoria was bestowed her crown, her orb, her sceptre and, with absolute composure and dignity, she returned to her carriage, passing back through the streets of London, lined with her subjects, still smiling and waving, and back to Buckingham Palace.

There she gave Dash his bath.

Some tasks were sacred, Queen or not.

There had been times, during the difficult year that followed, when she had looked back on the day of her Coronation as being the last time she was truly happy. Not least of the scandals that had rocked the court in her first year of sovereignty was the business with Lady Flora Hastings. And who should be at the centre of that?

Conroy.

The Queen had dismissed him from her own life, but he remained involved with her mother, and was still her comptroller. He had taken Hastings as a mistress, and when she was thought to be pregnant a scandal broke out within the court. However the poor woman was not pregnant; she had an abdominal growth, which had turned out to be an advanced, cancerous tumour, and she had died.

Victoria had not been *kind* to Hastings, she knew. Nor about her.

But she paid the price for her unkindness when newspapers picked up on the story and shortly afterwards, travelling through London in her carriage one day, Victoria had waved at some members of the public and they had not returned her wave; worse, they had hissed at her, as a mob might do to a criminal.

She was shocked and hurt. Somehow she had not expected the public to *know* there was another side to the story, and she had pushed herself back into the seat of her carriage, attempting a smile for the Baroness (who saw through it, of course), and felt a mixture of feelings: frustration, grief and sorrow.

She looked back on that incident now. There had been wrong done, she knew that. She had not been as diplomatic or as sympathetic as she would have liked to have been; she had allowed her feelings for Sir John Conroy – and therefore Lady Flora – to influence her judgement.

She had promised herself not to make such a mistake again.

And she had tried to keep that promise.

Throughout the year there had been little time for Victoria's mind to wander and consider matters of the heart; she had to admit that on occasion it had. And on such occasions, it wandered across the sea, to Germany, to the house of Saxe-Coburg. And Albert.

They had parted on good terms. She thought now of his very handsome countenance, not forgetting the immediate friendship that had sprung up between he and Dash. And, oh, there was something else, too, for not only was he handsome but there was something about him so upright, so moral and principled. It was difficult to imagine Albert enmeshed in the squabbles and petty politics that seemed to infect life at court like a dose of the flu. She imagined him above all that and what a support such a figure could be: his impartiality a wonderful asset; his wisdom a great strength, both qualities she longed to have at her side. Of course Lord M was a wonderful confidante and mentor, and there was no doubt his advocacy had been most beneficial during these early days of her reign, but, friend though he was, he was also a politician and she was under no illusions about that.

Would Albert have allowed her to make the mistakes she did during the Lady Flora Hastings affair? Undoubtedly with a greater measure of sagacity than the advice she was given.

He could be an asset to the crown, she knew – an asset to her: handsome, kind and fair.

But did he feel the same way? After all, she had heard whispers of his reluctance; that her love of music and dancing was not to his taste; in addition it had reached her ears that he had once described her as 'stubborn', the cheek of him.

Would he want her?

As Queen it was up to her to make any marriage proposal; the idea of that proposal being rejected was out of the question. To do so would create a rift between the two houses. Uncle Leopold, pressing so hard for the liaison that he had organised another visit, would never allow it.

She couldn't help but grieve the process, though. Like anybody, she hoped to marry for love first, duty second. Like any woman she wanted to be romanced by a suitor who placed her on a pedestal. How would she know how Albert felt if the time came?

So, she had been quite clear about this, writing to Leopold, telling him that Albert must understand that 'there was no engagement between us'. She had never given any indication that she would promise to marry him, she said, and did not propose to do so now. She added, with a little wry under-statement, that from what she had seen of Albert, she very much liked him, and indeed thought he made a most agreeable friend and relation, but there was to be no more to it than that. Even if there was, she continued, she 'could make no final promise this year for, at the very earliest, any such event could not take place till two or three years hence.'

Reluctant, she had thought, smiling, applying her wax seal. We shall see who is reluctant.

In the weeks leading up to the visit, those around Victoria noticed a change in her temperament; she was sharp and impatient, not only with her staff but also with her ministers. She knew she was this way, but chose not to admit the reason why, which was, simply, this: butterflies. Nerves that increased with each passing week, day and hour as she awaited confirmation of her guests' expected arrival time.

Thus, on this particular day, with the added worry of the smashed palace windows, she found herself in rather dark humour during the walk with Baroness Lehzen, and may have been less than courteous to the unfortunate page who approached her on the Palace perimeter path, bowing quickly before her companion, then doing the same to Victoria, though more deeply, and passing her a letter bearing the seal of her uncle, King Leopold of Belgium.

The very news she had been waiting for.

He was excused before Victoria prised open the letter, in her heart knowing its contents already.

'It is just as I expected, Lehzen,' she told the Baroness, 'they are to arrive imminently.'

The baroness, who, in private, did not especially approve of the liaison, smiled thinly.

'When, Your Majesty?' she said.

Victoria looked at her. 'Tonight,' she said. 'They are coming here tonight, Lehzen.'

As they continued their walk, she looked upwards, to the windows of the palace, those of her mother's apartments.

There, watching her, stood her mother, the Duchess; even from the distance her expression of maternal reproach was clearly visible.

Next to her mother stood Conroy, staring down at her, eyes black, his expression indecipherable.

XII

Victoria would never forget the moment that she fell in love. She would never forget where she was, what she was wearing and how she felt – a honeyed sensation quite unlike anything she had ever experienced before.

'Your Majesty,' came the booming announcement. She swallowed and smoothed her dress, standing on the steps of Buckingham Palace waiting to receive her guests with Lehzen at her side. 'Their serene highnesses, Ernest, Duke of Saxe-Coburg and Gotha, and Prince Albert of Saxe-Coburg and Gotha.'

The sound of their footsteps preceded them. She remembered to raise her head and point her chin in a queenly manner, while trying desperately to quell the butterflies in her stomach.

And there he was.

Suddenly she found herself completely overcome. For a moment she even thought she might have to reach out and grasp the Baroness for support in order to prevent herself from sinking to her knees on the steps.

Because he was beautiful. As he climbed the steps, resplendent in his uniform, wearing red leather-top boots and with his sword at his hip, she drank in every detail of him: his striking blue eyes; his physique – the last time they had met, she had thought of him as being somewhat portly. Now, though, he boasted broad shoulders and a fine, tapered waist – the sight of him quite taking her breath away; his moustache so delicate, his mouth so pretty, his nose exquisite . . .

Victoria remained outwardly composed, the only sign that betrayed the sudden high emotion she felt was when she turned her head slightly to address the Baroness: 'Why, Lehzen, my heart is quite going.'

Ernest came forward first, dropping to one knee, and kissing her proffered hand. Then it was Albert. His boots creaked as he knelt to the stone. Their eyes met and his gaze melted her heart.

'Your Majesty,' he said.

And that was it. That was the moment.

'Oh, Lehzen, do you think he will love me too!' she said later, in her chambers, as the Baroness prepared her for the evening's dinner.

'I'm sure he will, Your Majesty,' said the Baroness, some-what more curtly than was necessary, and Victoria shot her an admonishing look before continuing her expressions of joy.

'Then we must make sure of it,' she said, 'I shall be sure to look so entirely fetching that he won't be able to resist me, and he'll *twirl* me around the hall.' With this she did a demon-stration of exactly what she meant, clasping an imaginary Albert to her bosom.

So, to say it was something of a disappointment when Albert failed to appear for dinner was to commit the sin of understatement. The two boys had arrived having crossed the Channel in a paddle steamer. Their trunks had not yet been delivered to the Palace and so it was that they sent a messenger to say they felt 'incorrectly attired to attend a dinner'. Lord

Melbourne had a word or two to say about that, she noticed, yet they did indeed grace them with their presence after dinner when Victoria was first able to waltz with Albert, who held himself so well and was in no way a disappointment.

Later in the visit she discovered that not only had he acquired a liking for Byron, but that he played piano as well as he danced, and she listened to him playing Haydn symphonies. They chased one another in the great maze at Windsor. They went riding together and sheltered beneath a tree when it rained, giggling as they became soaked. They walked and talked and for the first time in her life she felt as though she was conversing with someone who understood her totally. Who addressed her as though she were an equal, without subservience or obsequiousness or servility. He spoke so eloquently of reform, and the ways in which the monarchy might be instrumental in helping the common man through improvements in housing. He had such an earnest, soulful way about him. He would place his hands very carefully in his lap and hold her gaze as he talked with great passion and intellect.

'What does housing have to do with the Queen, Albert?' she asked him, half-teasing him, but wanting to see more of that reforming zeal.

'Well,' he said, in the measured, Germanic tones she had grown to adore, 'if you forgive me the impertinence,' she nodded, smiling, 'but in my view it is the obligation of the monarch to give a voice to the underdog, the disaffected, the working man, because if he – or she – does not, then who will?'

'Well, quite,' she agreed.

'In England, the industry is changing and workers are moving to escape the dreadful conditions in the countryside,' she nodded again, no longer teasing; instead, fascinated, 'and they are moving to the towns, but there they are finding that conditions are as bad if not worse because nobody is building them the places to live . . .'

He tailed off.

'Yes?' she prompted.

'Your Majesty,' he said.

'Please, Albert, you can call me Victoria.'

'Thank you,' he nodded slightly. 'Victoria, we must build these people places to live, or they will continue to live in squalor. If they live this way, and we live . . .' he indicated the grounds of the Palace, 'this way, then soon, perhaps, it will be more than a couple of stones that are thrown at the windows of the palace.'

Yes, she had used to think him a stuffy bones, but she was just a girl then. Now she was a woman, a Queen. 'I will be good,' she had promised, a long, long time ago. And if perhaps she was too young and inexperienced to be as good as she would sometimes like, here was someone who could help her: a good man. 'I will be good,' she thought. I *can* be good with you by my side.

Victoria would always remember the moment she decided she would ask Albert to be her consort. Her companion for life. Her one true love. It was that moment.

XIII

A safe house, London

'Prince Albert is in place,' said the demon, the one known to the dark kingdom as Førse, the descendant of Baal, 'this is excellent.'

To humans he was known as King Leopold I, the king of Belgium.

Førse sat at the head of the table, before him a small saucer on which were the last vestiges of his favoured snack of fishbones. He enjoyed them fried and crispy; it gave them a tremendous texture, he thought, scooping up a handful and throwing them to the back of his throat.

Crunch, crunch, crunch.

As he ate, his teeth seemed to move, subtly shifting into points; his whole face, in fact, morphed and changed, rippling, so that it looked like an optical effect: his human self in one moment; the next, his true self. By his side sat Baron Stockmar, a mortal who had been his faithful servant for some ten years now; even so, Stockmar was still fascinated to see the inhuman that lay so close to the surface of the being most knew simply as Leopold – genial, benevolent King Leopold, the head of the house of Saxe-Coburg. Who was, in fact, the leader of the

most powerful demonic clan still on Earth's plane: the descendant of Baal, he who had been instructed by the dark one to
remain on earth and spread evil.

Over the centuries the great demon's scions had done just
that, gradually inveigling themselves into Europe's Royal
families.

'I'm sorry, Stockmar, does it bother you to gaze upon my
real self?' he said, ever mindful of the mortal's feelings.
Stockmar was used to it, of course, but even so. Mortals were
not meant to look upon demons. It drove them mad.

'It is quite all right, my Lord,' Stockmar reassured him.

'It *hurts* to maintain this human face, Stockmar,' complained
Leopold, chewing, then removing something from his teeth
and placing it in the saucer. 'I envy the half-breeds. They have
no such problem. No need to indulge *appetites*,' he indicated
the saucer of fishbones, 'they can simply move about among
humans. Their face is their own.'

'They have *other* problems, my Lord,' warned the Baron.

'That they are half human,' chuckled Leopold, relaxing into
his own face for a second, so that Stockmar was able to behold
it in full: the sallow, grey hide, the red glinting eyes, hooked
nose, sharp pointed teeth. 'But humans are so easily corrupted,
Baron – you yourself are proof of that, and your blood is
mortal. And Conroy, too, of course, whose conversion is so
complete he becomes something of a worry to us.'

'Not all humans though, perhaps,' warned the Baron, 'not
even all half-breeds. There is, after all, a significant question
mark regarding the Prince – and whether he is able to face
his destiny.'

'His destiny is to provide a male heir to the throne, that
is all,' said Leopold, 'one who carries the bloodline of Baal.

As long as he can do that his inner conflict must remain his own predicament.'

'As long as it does,' said Stockmar.

'Time will tell,' replied Leopold.

At that moment the door to the chamber opened admitting two more, who came into the room and took their seats: the Duchess of Kent, mother to the Queen, sister to Leopold, once a powerful demon like her brother but now much reduced and reliant upon her comptroller, the other new entrant into the room, Sir John Conroy.

Arrogant human. Leopold couldn't stand him.

'I hear that things are going well concerning the Royal romance,' said Leopold, after greetings had been made.

Conroy answered for the Duchess. 'The Royal lovebirds are getting on famously,' he said. 'Victoria's diaries are full of amorous sentiments regarding the Prince. He has her in his thrall.'

'Good, very good,' nodded Leopold. 'When might we expect a proposal?'

'Sooner rather than later,' said Conroy, smiling, 'for it is surely her intention to do so. The only barrier might be . . .'

'Melbourne?'

'Quite.'

Conroy recoiled a little, as Leopold in his displeasure took his demon form for a second, but thrilling to the sight also.

'Does Melbourne suspect?' asked Leopold.

'If Melbourne suspects anything, then it is that *I* am the inhuman at court,' said Conroy. 'An admirable piece of misdirection, I'm sure you'll agree.'

'Not really,' scowled Stockmar. There was no love lost between the two mortal servants. 'The admirable course of action would have resulted in the Protektorate suspecting nothing. It was your woefully mishandled attempts to gain influence that alerted them to our presence in their midst.'

'We judged it best not to wait,' said Conroy, 'the Duchess and I. We saw an opportunity.'

The Duchess nodded, and was about to speak in support of the comptroller when Leopold snapped, '*You* judged it best not to wait, Conroy. *You* did. *We* have waited centuries. You prove vexatious to me, Conroy. First that; then the affair involving Hastings. On which note: you've taken care of her, but there is a leak, is there not? This stable boy.'

'Yes, my Lord . . .'

'And you have not been able to resolve it, though months have passed, and this creates a situation that requires my intervention.' Leopold shook with rage. 'And this displeases me. Do not disobey me again, Conroy.'

He became Førse, glowering at Conroy, who swallowed, but said nothing.

Leopold resolved into his human self.

'I hope for your sake,' he said, 'that Victoria soon makes her proposal.'

When Conroy and the Duchess had left, Stockmar turned to Leopold.

'Conroy is a problem to us,' he said starkly. 'He is too impulsive and too greedy.'

'Yes,' agreed Leopold nodding gravely, 'indeed. Conroy wants to hold the torch that burns humanity, and that worries me. He does not understand the true nature of evil, which is that it is insidious and must be allowed to grow slowly, for only then can it triumph.'

XIV

The next day

Victoria stood in a corridor overlooking a courtyard, which rang to the sound of hooves on cobblestones as Albert and his brother returned from their morning ride. Stable hands rushed to meet them, wiping hands on aprons, reaching to take the reins. Instinctively she stepped back from the glass as Albert glanced up to the surrounding walls, even though he did not look in her direction. Then she drew forward again as the page she had summoned approached Albert.

Her hand went to her mouth, where she felt it shake slightly, so that she took it away again and clasped it with the other in front of her, chewing her lip instead.

She wanted to see Albert's face when the page passed on the message.

She watched, carefully as Albert bent forward in the saddle to hear the page. She did not hear, but knew what was being said: '*Her Majesty would like to see you in the Blue Closet, sir.*'

Seated in the horse beside him, Ernest heard too, and as Albert straightened the two of them shared a look.

There was nothing on his face to betray an emotion either way, even though it should be perfectly obvious why the

Queen wanted to see him – in the Blue Closet, no less – that she was to request his hand; he was this close to beginning life as the consort to the most powerful woman in the world. *This close*. And how did he react? Nothing. *Nichts*.

Curse him, she thought. Curse his German reserve!

Frustrated, she picked up her skirts and hurried down the corridor, the Duchess of Sutherland and Lehzen scuttling in her wake.

'I am to wear my heart on my sleeve,' she snapped back over her shoulder, 'am I to be given no indication how he will meet my proposal?'

'He will say yes, ma'am,' replied Lehzen, a touch of ice in her voice. 'What else would he say?'

Victoria stopped suddenly, her skirts swishing on the polished boards as she whirled to address the Baroness, doing so at a speed that surprised them all, not least herself. 'Lehzen,' she snapped, 'you have been too long at court, for your heart has become like the stone that surrounds us. Of course Albert will say yes. He will say yes because that is what I desire him to do. However, there is one thing I want more with all my heart.'

'And what is that, ma'am?'

'For him to *mean it*, Lehzen.'

She whirled to face front, picked up her skirts and strode off. Behind her, the two women exchanged a look then hurried on.

Moments later, Victoria stood in the room, gathering herself, waiting for the knock, which, when it came, made her jump slightly.

She cleared her throat, 'Come,' she said, her voice sounding small, engulfed by the wood panelling in the room. She had

had it prepared, the curtains partly closed. A fire crackled in the hearth and she stood near to it, in order that she should look prettier bathed in its orange glow.

The door opened and Albert entered, turned to close the door behind him, bowed slightly, then walked to the middle of the room where he stood, face impassive, still betraying nothing!

'Your Majesty,' he said in greeting.

'Victoria, Albert. You're to call me Victoria. Whatever . . . happens.'

His eyes flickered. If he had harboured any doubts on his journey to the room then surely now they were laid to rest.

'You no doubt know which issue I have asked you here to discuss,' she said.

He said nothing. She allowed the silence to build until at last he nodded his head slowly.

'Well, of course,' she continued, 'all of court is abuzz. Indeed I shouldn't wonder that if I were to open that door now, the entire staff would tumble into the room, my mother among them.'

Albert smiled thinly.

She continued: 'You realise of course, that as a monarch, it is I who has to make any marriage proposal, should marriage be my intent.'

'I am aware of this custom,' said Albert, flatly.

'Good. We two, more than any other, know of the pressures brought upon us to enter into marriage together. There are those who wish to see us married, just as there are those who would prefer it if our two houses were never joined.'

Albert nodded.

'But it is my belief that only two people enter into a marriage and therefore they are the two best qualified to decide upon the suitability of the union.' She took a deep breath. 'Albert, we both know that if I were to make a marriage proposal you would have no choice in the matter but to accede to it. To do otherwise would be to cause me great embarrassment and incur the wrath of Uncle Leopold, causing great damage to the two nations.'

Again, Albert nodded. Now, though, she could see the first signs of uncertainty in his eyes.

'So, dear Albert, I have decided to spare us both the indignity of such a situation. I do not want to put you in a position where you feel it is your duty to give your assent to a union your heart does not desire. Therefore, there will be no marriage proposal.'

Albert and Victoria looked at one another. She noticed his hand on the hilt of his sword. Was it shaking slightly?

'Then . . .' said Albert, his voice low, 'this is a situation that causes me great sorrow. For my heart . . .'

'Yes, Albert?'

He looked at her, looked deep into her eyes. 'My heart wishes more than anything to be with yours. My heart has wished for nothing more since the moment I arrived to see that the Princess I met three years ago has in the meantime become a Queen, and a woman. A woman with whom I have fallen deeply and unashamedly in love, in a way that has nothing to do with our two countries, or duty. However,' and here he bowed once more, 'I do of course understand your decision and will honour it.'

He turned to go.

'Albert,' said Victoria.

He stopped and turned to face her.

'Yes, Victoria,' he said.

'Albert, it would really make me happy – *too happy* – if you would consent to marry me.'

He looked at her.

'Victoria,' he said, 'I thought you would never ask.'

They came together in an embrace, the passion of which caught them both by surprise such was its intensity. For the first time in her life, Victoria felt . . .

. . . *safe*.

XV

That night
Westminster

The drums were so loud it was as though the air about him was vibrating. The hot stench hit him at once.

'Roll up, roll up . . .' McKenzie heard as he made his way blindly down steep wooden steps so wet they seemed to squelch underfoot. He hugged the streaming, slippery wall for support.

'Roll up, roll up!'

At length he descended to a large underground cellar – the result, no doubt, of two cellars knocked together – and he was here, inside the famed Cockpit of Westminster, home to Raticide.

'Roll up, roll up, for . . . *Raticide*.'

It was the monthly rat-baiting event, where one might expect to witness in action the city's most legendary dog, Turpin, a bull terrier that had once killed one hundred and two rats in five-and-a-half minutes. Two or three in the jaws at once. A fearsome beast indeed.

McKenzie's mission was not to see Turpin tear into a hundred rats, however.

No.

Here at Raticide, he'd been told, he'd find Egg – finally. Egg, who had disappeared since the Hastings scandal. Egg: the man he had spent months trying to track down.

Who, so his contact said, would be here this very night.

This had better be worth it, he thought.

Inside the cellar was a sea of bobbing top hats worn by gentlemen come to bet on the games, some with handkerchiefs held to their noses. Smoke hung in the air in thick grey layers, doing little to mask the stench of stale beer, dirt, body odour and dogs, but, above all, of rats. Those rats destined for the pit had not yet been brought forward but still their stink was all-pervading. Those used were caught in sewers and drains and emitted a stench that, when he had first smelled it, had almost caused McKenzie to vomit. He supposed he was used to it now, but even so, the aroma almost sent him staggering as he entered the cellar, reaching into his pocket for a handkerchief and pressing it to his nose, eyes scanning the room in search of his contact, instinctively hunched against the noise of the drums, which were so loud they seemed to push the breath from his chest, a rhythmic, tribal sound there to whip up the fervour of the crowd and of the dogs. The source of it was a team of negroes who wore white shirts and caps and were hunched, grim-faced and sweating over their drums, faces slick with sweat, hands a blur, not so much playing the drums as channelling them. A dark, furious noise.

The sides and corner of the room were in virtual darkness. Instead, flickering gaslights lit the centre, where the arena had been set up, enclosed by wooden barriers. In the ring was a dog – Turpin, he took it to be – and Turpin stood with his front paws against the side of the ring, barking, though McKenzie could barely hear it over the din of the drums and the ring-master and the rising sound of the voices as bets were placed.

The clamour increased, if that were possible, as a boy made his way through the crowd holding aloft a basket, like that in which you might keep chickens. Inside it were not chickens, though, but rats. The basket seethed with them so that they seemed to move as one. Behind this first boy came another boy, also carrying a basket. McKenzie was transfixed for a moment or so by the sight of the rats moving about in the baskets. For a brief second he felt that one caught his gaze and that it bared its teeth, and its eyes glittered.

He was so transfixed that he failed to see a gentleman who was waving at him from the other side of the arena, until at last the constant motion caught his eye and he waved to acknowledge his contact, then shoved his way through the crowd to reach him, an action made even more difficult by the increased excitement in the cellar.

'Hello, Mr McKenzie,' shouted the man, Cuddy, a name he always fervently denied was Cuthbert shortened. He stood at the side of the arena and McKenzie wriggled in next to him, incurring the displeasure of a drunken toff who was silenced with a glare from McKenzie.

'And good day to you, Cuddy,' he shouted. 'Is our friend Mr Egg in the vicinity?'

Cuddy grinned and pointed towards the second of the two boys who had appeared with the rat baskets, on the opposite side of the arena.

'There he is, Mr McKenzie,' said Cuddy, voice like a rusty saw, 'that's your boy Egg.'

'Good work,' said McKenzie. Money changed hands. 'What do you know of him?' he asked, watching as Egg and the other boy clambered into the ring placing the baskets on the wooden boards. At the other side the ringmaster held Turpin back by the collar. No easy task, by the looks of things, the dog barking and slathering, veins taut at its neck.

'Not much, sir,' rasped Cuddy, 'save to say that he wears a hunted look on his face, and they do tell that when he's taken too much ale he talks of a mistress he's lost, and that it was an employer very dear to him.'

'Aye, it all makes sense,' said McKenzie, but not loud enough for Cuddy to hear, who was pointing again.

'Something else.'

'Yes?'

'Once, they say, having drunk a little too much, he talked of dark forces occupying the very highest echelons of society.'

'I beg your pardon. Did you just say dark forces?'

'That I did, sir, that I did.'

'Was he specific?'

'Sir?'

'Did he mention any particular incarnation of these dark forces? For example, revenants?'

'Revenants?'

'Zombies. The undead.'

Cuddy looked askance at McKenzie. 'Well . . . now you come to mention it . . .'

'He did?'

'No, he bloody didn't, sir, excuse my bloody French.' He shook his head in bemused disbelief. 'The living dead, I ask you.'

Might not be as far-fetched as you think, Cuddy, thought McKenzie, his mind going to an object he had in his possession. Then Cuddy was indicating Egg.

'Don't think you're going to get to speak to him before the contest begins, Mr McKenzie,' he bellowed. 'You fancy a flutter on old Turpin? He's been known to do . . .'

'. . . one hundred and two rats in five-and-a-half minutes, Cuddy, I know.'

'A most impressive tally, sir,' Cuddy said with a grin. 'I'm proud to say that I was there when he set that record, sir. Up to three rats at once he was killing. By the time he'd finished the arena looked as though it had been pelted with strawberry jam, hair and meat.'

Now it was McKenzie's turn to look askance at Cuddy, who winked in return.

'He's getting on now, though, lost an eye an' all, they can be pretty vicious when cornered I can tell you, them rats, they sell their life pretty dear and it cost old Turpin one of his eyes.'

'So what's your bet?' asked McKenzie.

'Fifty in five, sir. Fancy joining me?'

'It's very kind of you, Cuddy, but I'm here on business – that business being young Mr Egg over there.'

Then the sound of the drums was rising, becoming even more frenzied. Some of the crowd put their hands over their ears but even so they were grinning, knowing what the increase in volume signalled: that the rat-baiting was about to begin. Reaching a crescendo the drums stopped, the cacophony replaced by noise of another kind as the crowd began shouting and gesticulating, money changing hands. Egg and the other boy opened the chicken baskets, then scrambled to escape. McKenzie was careful to keep an eye on Egg, noticing how the boy's eyes darted about the room. The rats now set free swarmed to one side of the arena, a black, oily mound of them piling up against the wall, desperately trying to escape the slavering jaws of Turpin who was straining at the leash, the ringmaster's teeth bared with the effort of holding him back.

Then the ringmaster straightened as best he could, the look on his face indicating that he was relishing the moment.

'London, are you ready for *Raticide*?' he called.

The crowd screamed in approval. McKenzie, caught up in the delirium of the moment found himself doing the same.

'I can't hear you,' taunted the ringmaster. 'I said. "*Are. You. Ready . . . For Raticide?*"'

A great cheer went up.

'*Five . . .*' he began.

The rats, all hundred of them, squealed, claws scratching the wood, each of them trying and failing to claw its way to the top of the stinking mass and escape.

'*Four . . .*' The entire crowd joining in the countdown now. '*Three . . . two . . .*'

The ringmaster reached to unclip the leash.

'*One!*'

The ringmaster vaulted out of the pit. Turpin tore forward, making straight for the centre of the pile of vermin. Immediately he came up with a rodent in his jaws, chomping down hard on its neck then flinging it to the side, where it dashed against the wood, leaving a smear of blood, Turpin already delving into the panicking pile of rats for another victim.

Then the dog yelped. A high-pitched anguished yowl that for just a second silenced the baying crowd.

Turpin appeared from within the roiling mound of rats, but not as had been expected, with one or even two rats between his jaws. Instead he had rats hanging from him, their pink, fleshy tails swishing so that in one hallucinatory moment, McKenzie imagined him to be wearing a tasselled jacket. But the dog was in pain. There were rats at his muzzle. Rats at his belly. Rats clinging to his body, holding fast with their snouts, legs scrabbling, tearing into its hide as the dog screeched, shaking to try and rid itself of the terrible biting teeth and lacerating claws. And in the next moment, poor Turpin's fate was sealed as those vermin that had been forming a pile at the far wall seemed somehow to realise that the tide of combat had turned in their favour and suddenly there was a pile no more as instead they swarmed across the floor to join those who had attached themselves to Turpin. Then the dog disappeared beneath bulbous, bristling bodies and all that remained of it was its dying yelps followed by one last agonised scream that tore into the crowd, leaving a shocked silence behind it. It took McKenzie a second or so to realise that the rats had stopped their noise, too. No longer panicking and squealing, almost eerily silent now, they seemed to slide away from their victim, leaving Turpin a bloodied mess on the floor.

'Cuddy?' said McKenzie no longer having to shout.

'Yes, sir,' replied Cuddy, his voice empty as though attempting to make sense of this turn of events.

'Isn't the dog supposed to kill the rats, not the other way around?'

'I've never seen its like, to be honest wiv you, sir. Never seen its like.'

The rats were still moving around on the wooden floorboards, but now McKenzie noticed something else. Many of the rodents seemed to be looking at something outside of the arena. More of their number were doing the same. Then more. Until most, it seemed, had their attention taken by the same thing and had affixed it with a watchful gaze, sniffing, snouts and whiskers quivering.

They were staring at Egg.

At the same time that McKenzie noticed so did Egg, the rest of the crowd oblivious, too involved with arguing over the bets or watching the ringmaster, who had broken down and was howling and screaming at the side of the arena, two men in top hats restraining him from clambering into the ring to retrieve the mauled corpse of his dog. Egg's eyes widened. McKenzie began pushing his way through the crowd, sensing that Egg might be about to take flight. The rats, too, began to move, scuttling as one to the wall of the pit, a great accumulation forming, becoming higher and higher. McKenzie saw it as he skirted the arena, shoving his way through arguing, hollering men, on his way towards Egg, who was now standing stock still as though terrified into immobility. He saw how the rats no longer scratched and scrabbled with panic, but rather moved with purpose, an organisation almost, and that they seemed to be building upwards towards the lip of the wooden boards surrounding the arena, soon to spill over it.

And that if they achieved their objective then it was Egg who was their quarry.

Incredible as it seemed the rats were after Egg, and were getting closer, were seconds away from escaping the arena.

When into the pit blundered the grief-blind ringmaster.

'Raticide,' he screeched, his war cry lacking its previous vigour, sounding somewhat plaintive now, as he waded into the heaving mass of rats with his boots stamping, his arms pin-wheeling and anguish etched deep into his face that was streaked with tears.

Instantly the pile of rats was in disarray. The spell was

broken. Egg had taken steps backward, lost his footing and fell and McKenzie was almost close enough to touch him when he regained his feet and was making for the wooden stairs to ground level. McKenzie went to follow but there was a scream, a scream of such agony the like of which he had never heard before (and would only ever hear once again) and he found himself looking over to the arena where the crowd was parting as the ringmaster tried to climb over the boards to escape, unsuccessfully.

He had stopped trying to stamp on the rats in revenge for the death of Turpin. Now he was fighting for his life.

'Raticide,' he screeched as though he had forgotten all other words but that one. '*Raticide.*'

He had them hanging from him.

From his body.

From his face.

Which gushed blood, and as McKenzie watched he grabbed one round, bristling body and yanked it away from himself, the rat coming free with a slurping tearing sound that was clearly audible in the cellar. From its mouth dangled the ringmaster's eyeball, hanging by the optic nerve clamped firmly between the rodent's teeth.

The ringmaster screamed, dropped to his knees and was immediately set upon by scores more of the creatures, one of them pushing itself into the eye socket, almost all of its body disappearing as it burrowed deeper into his skull, the pink, scaly tail protruding and waving about the ringmaster's face as he pawed at it ineffectually, more rats jumping to his body until he was writhing beneath them, sharing the fate of his beloved dog.

There was a moment of collective horror in the room, and

then the crowd were stampeding for the stairs. McKenzie, already halfway there in pursuit of Egg, was one of the first to reach the steps and bounded up them, aware that behind him the sheer number of bodies was creating a horrific crush made worse by what was an obvious splintering sound. The steps were buckling, unable to cope with the weight of people.

For an instant he hesitated at the top, the sound of screaming behind him giving him pause to consider stopping and helping those who were in pain.

But no – the story. What could he do anyway?

'Egg,' he shouted, bursting out of the Cockpit and into Westminster, almost immediately seeing the boy, who had stopped at the mention of his name, then, when he saw McKenzie, turned to flee.

McKenzie, though no athlete, was nimble on his feet. Plus he carried a cane and knew how to use it, thrusting it forward to catch the boy between his ankles and send him sprawling to the ground. McKenzie was upon him almost immediately, dragging Egg up, taking him by the collar.

'I want to have a word with you, son,' he hissed.

'I can't, sor,' whimpered Egg in reply.

'Why were the rats after you?' demanded McKenzie.

'I don't know, I can't say that I know.'

'You know. And it's not because you're made of cheese. Why is it? It's because of your mistress, isn't it? Who was your mistress, Egg? Was she a lady-in-waiting at the palace?'

Egg whimpered and tried to turn his head away.

'Was she?' pressed McKenzie. 'Was her name Lady Flora Hastings, the Queen's lady-in-waiting?'

Egg squeezed his eyes tight shut as though trying to wish

himself away but McKenzie simply bunched his hands tighter, pushing his face closer to Egg.

'Was it?' he pressed, shaking the boy. 'Was she your mistress?'

At last he nodded yes and McKenzie relaxed his grip upon the young man.

'The last time we met,' he said, 'you said she feared for her life and she's dead now. Either it's a ghastly coincidence or she was right to show caution. Which is it?'

'I never found out, sor, I read it in the newspaper like yourself. They say it was a tumour but I think differently.'

McKenzie dragged Egg to his feet. 'Why?' he asked, casting a look about them, 'what makes you say that?'

'My employer had been a follower of the Duchess's comptroller, sir.'

'Wait, don't couch your information – don't prettify it for my ears. You mean Lady Flora Hastings and the Duchess's comptroller—' he struggled to remember the name. Sir John something? '—they were lovers?'

Sir John Conroy. That was it.

'Yes, sor. By holding that position she discovered such things about the monarchy, sor, that I think may have killed her, sor, especially those that had much to lose in the light of revelations she may or may not have made.'

'Yes. Yes. Such as . . . ?'

Around them people were running, either to the Cockpit or away from it.

'Like what, man?' snapped McKenzie. 'Like what? These dark forces, you speak of when you're drunk?'

'That's right, sor. At the palace, sor. She spoke of demons there.'

XVI

The grounds of Buckingham Palace

B last! Since the engagement had been announced, Lord
Melbourne seemed more than usually prone to gaffes
involving Germans. Now, for example, he found himself
apologising for an off-the-cuff remark in which he had stated
that all Germans smoked, and that they rarely washed.

It was to the Queen's credit, and a measure of the happiness that the engagement had brought her, that she dismissed
these improprieties with the lightness of air.

'Don't worry, Lord M,' she smiled, walking on clouds that
took her through the grounds of the Palace. 'Even if it were
true, I would not believe it of Albert. Not of *my* Albert.'

'Ah,' said the Prime Minister, his hands clasped behind his
back, 'he has truly captured your heart, has he not?'

'You had notions otherwise? That I might have agreed to
a marriage of convenience?'

'Perhaps not,' he demurred, 'knowing Your Majesty as I do.'

'And Albert also,' she reminded him. 'He is certainly a man
who knows his own mind.'

'And how pleased I am to hear of it, ma'am.'

'He has been explaining to me some of his ideas on reform.'

'Ah.'

They walked in silence. She sensed the unease pouring from Lord Melbourne. He and Lehzen, though hardly the best of friends, did at least have common ground in their distrust of Saxe-Coburg, though possibly for different reasons: Lehzen she wasn't sure about, though she felt it had more to do with a fear of being replaced in the young Queen's affections than practical matters or those of state. The Prime Minister, on the other hand: in the weeks leading up to the visit, not only had he been complaining about German habits of toilet, but had voiced reservations about the family. 'The Coburgs are not popular abroad,' he had told her, warningly.

Now, this crisp October morning, she could sense his resistance still. Neither was he being especially discreet when it came to expressing his reservations. Anybody else and she would have dismissed them with a curt rebuke for their impertinence. But this was Lord M. *Dear* Lord M. So she indulged him. For now.

'Ma'am,' he said, 'on the subject of Germans I have heard it said that when visiting a spa, our Teutonic cousins use somewhat underhand methods when it comes to reserving a place at the water's edge by placing a towel on a seat prior to partaking of breakfast. The latterday Germans I'm talking about, of course, not those of Your Majesty's ancestry.'

'Come, come now, Lord M, you hardly expect me to believe such outlandish falsehoods.'

'I fear it is true, ma'am.'

The two of them laughed.

'But on to more serious matters, ma'am. Is it not your concern that the Prince will side with your mother on certain issues; thus that you may inadvertently be in danger of handing the reins of power to our friend, Sir John Conroy?'

'If the Prince should side with my mother and her comptroller, then he would find himself literally side by side with them – sharing apartments with Sir John,' she laughed.

'Yet again I make the mistake of underestimating Your Majesty's resolve.'

'Indeed you do, Lord Melbourne, if you think I would place matters of the heart before my duty to my country.'

'Even if the country disapproved of the union?'

'Why should they do so?'

He spread his hands. 'Prince Albert, though undoubtedly a man of fine character is nevertheless . . . a foreigner, ma'am.'

She sighed. 'Oh, Lord M, this really is below you. Albert is a perfectly delightful gentleman, whatever his nationality. I have every faith that the people will see this.'

'Alas that we cannot introduce him to each and every one of them, ma'am,' he noted.

'They will learn to love him,' she said.

'Perhaps. Nevertheless, by making that request you set them a test,' he said darkly.

'A test I believe they will pass.'

'And if they don't?'

'More talk of revolution, Lord Melbourne?'

'The memories of what happened in France, though now some four decades gone, are still fresh. There is unrest in Europe, ma'am. On the home front we've seen Chartist unrest. There are those who say we were a hair's breadth from national revolution after the Newport Rising. Had that uprising been successful, Your Majesty, who knows what might happen?'

'Our heads might be decorating pikes, Lord Melbourne?' she laughed.

Melbourne coughed in surprise. 'Possibly, ma'am. One dreads to think. The fact of the matter is, however, that there are those who would wish to question the established order. Dangerous revolutionaries.'

'What if these people are not dangerous revolutionaries as you claim, Lord M, but merely "people" – those who need and deserve a change?'

'Ma'am . . .' he sounded doubtful.

'Lord M, Albert talks very eloquently of reform. It seems to me that reform is exactly what the people need. Ergo, Prince Albert is what the people need. Do you not agree?'

'That, ma'am, is open to debate.'

'You don't have a very high opinion of ordinary people, do you, Lord Melbourne?' she said.

'I . . . I wouldn't quite say that, ma'am,' he protested.

'You call them rabble.'

'Well . . . they can be . . . it's true, somewhat . . .'

'The hoi polloi?'

He squirmed. 'Perhaps, once or twice, I have been known to . . .'

'The great unwashed, the riff raff, the lower classes, the proles, the plebs? Sometimes, Lord Melbourne, it strikes me that you have a great many synonyms for those lower in rank than yourself. Far more than you employ to describe the nobility.'

He coughed. What she supposed he intended as an embarrassed, chastened cough.

'Perhaps it is because I believe that the people need to trust in their Queen, and that their Queen needs to win that trust. That marrying a German may not be the most expeditious way in which to achieve that trust.'

'Lord Melbourne, we might as well be in the maze for you are beating about the bush to such a degree. If in your official capacity as my Prime Minister and private secretary it is your advice that I should not marry Prince Albert, then say so and keep your own counsel while I reach my decision.'

'Before I do, ma'am, I think there is somebody you should meet.'

She had not realised it, having been so deep in conversation, but their walk had led them off the usual path, Lord Melbourne having steered them across the grounds. In fact, Victoria realised with a slight lurch that she was not fully aware of exactly where she was in relation to the Palace, which she could no longer see. The only building was the one they now stood before. A low, stone cottage with a sloping roof, a thick, gnarled wooden door inset into the stone, upon which Lord Melbourne rapped hard, twice.

From inside came a voice. 'Melbourne?'

'The very same. With me I have Her Majesty the Queen.'

'Code word?'

Melbourne furrowed his brow, looking at Victoria as though she might know, to which silent enquiry she shrugged, feeling thoroughly offset by the turn of events.

Melbourne seemed to remember.

'The code word is sasquatch,' he said into the door.

From the other side came a sound of great unlocking of bolts and the door swung open. Melbourne ushered Victoria through and she picked up her skirts to descend a short flight of stone steps that deposited her into a room, which, with the exception of a WC, was quite the smallest accommodation she had ever entered, and certainly the lowest ceiling. In the room were two beds, a food preparation area, a fire in the grate, an old rug, and very little else. This one room, it seemed, comprised the entire cottage. Some kind of gardener's quarters, perhaps? She felt very grateful for the presence of Lord Melbourne as he closed the door behind him then came to join her.

Already in the cottage were two people standing to attention; both had taken up position at the other side of a large wooden table that dominated the room: a young boy, perhaps in his early teens, and by his side an older man, who looked like the boy's father, sporting a beard and long, untamed hair through which he passed a hand now, attempting to neaten it, unsuccessfully. Melbourne cleared his throat meaningfully, and the older man remembered himself, bowing low then administering a clip round his son's ear to do the same. In return, Victoria smiled, looking to Melbourne for the introductions.

'Your Majesty, may I present John Brown, and his son, John Brown.'

'It's an honour to make your acquaintance, Your Majesty,' said the older Brown and she immediately warmed to him, being so fond of the Scottish accent.

The boy, who stood with his hat screwed up in his hands, did a short, low bow.

Victoria smiled in return. 'Brown?' she said. 'Am I to assume, then, that you are . . .'

Just then there came another knock at the door.

'What's the code word?' called John Brown.

The door opened. Down the stairs came a figure wearing a cloak, who reached the bottom before sweeping back the hood.

'The code word is sasquatch,' snapped Maggie Brown, shaking out her long, dark hair, 'but it might help to lock the bloody door, don't you think?'

'We had guests,' protested Brown the elder.

'Aye, we will have guests if you leave the door unlocked. Plenty of them and all.' She addressed Victoria, voice softening and curtsying slightly, her eyes bright, 'It's an honour to meet you again, Your Majesty.'

Victoria looked from her to the door. 'You come from outside? Did you know . . . ? Were you following . . . ?'

'Was I following you? Aye, Your Majesty, always. I wouldn't be much of a Royal Protektor if I sat on my arse in here all day, now, would I?'

Victoria looked sharply at Melbourne. 'Is this true?'

Melbourne, still visibly recovering from Maggie Brown's 'arse', managed, 'Indeed, ma'am, your protection is assured around the clock.'

'But I've never . . .'

'Seen us?' finished Maggie Brown. 'Well, no, we offer a fast, professional but above all discreet service. I have to say, I thought there was a moment the other day when you spotted me, you seemed to look right at me during your talk with the Privy Council, but I think it must have been a trick of the light.'

'Sorry,' said Victoria, who was having much difficulty taking in so much information at one time, 'did you say "*we* offer . . ."?'

'Aye, ma'am, and they should be along any minute now.'

Right on cue there came another rap at the door.

'Come in,' barked Maggie Brown, 'it's open.' At that John Brown senior made an exasperated sound to which Maggie responded by shooting him a look and poking out her tongue.

Down the stairs came three more hooded figures. Like Maggie Brown, they each swept back their hoods as they reached the bottom. Victoria, gently ushered by Lord Melbourne, moved around the table to make way for the new arrivals, the room suddenly even more uncomfortably small than before.

'This here is Hudson,' said Maggie Brown and one of the men stepped forward. He bowed, murmuring, 'Your Majesty.' A rather handsome man, Victoria could not help but notice.

'Hicks.' Maggie Brown introduced the second of them, who did the same.

'They are two legendary swordsmen,' said Maggie Brown, in a rather arch, ironic manner, then nodded towards Hudson, who took a step away and swept back his robe to reveal a sword which he drew then twirled for all to see. It was like no sword Victoria had ever seen. Thick and curved. One edge seemed to boast an orthodox blade, the other side bristled with what looked like barbed hooks. It was quite the most evil-looking thing Victoria had ever seen and it was all she could do not to recoil in horror. Hicks replaced his sword in its scabbard and Hudson was about to step forward to demonstrate his own blade when Melbourne, perhaps sensing his Queen's discomfiture, stopped him with an upraised hand.

'Their weapons are designed especially for them by the Quartermaster, ma'am,' he said, 'and have been most effective in battle. To the layman, of course, they might appear a little unsettling.' This last comment he directed with a frown at Maggie, who moved on to the last of her introductions, a woman with long flaxen hair, about Victoria's age, very pretty.

'And this is our archer, Vasquez,' said Maggie Brown.

Vasquez curtsied and Victoria nodded in reply.

'And you four are my bodyguards?' asked Victoria.

'Aye, though from what I saw in your chamber two years ago, you're scarcely in need of one,' said Maggie Brown. She addressed the other three Protektors. 'I dare say there's a thing or two she could teach you about close-quarters combat,' she said, 'this wee lassie is a natural.' She turned back to Victoria. 'Have you thought about training, Your Majesty?'

Victoria bridled. *Wee lassie?* 'No,' she snapped, 'I most certainly have not. I am the Queen. Queens do not wield swords nor do battle with demons. Any prowess you detected in that situation was entirely as a result of the extraordinary situation in which I found myself.' She caught herself, her voice becoming more gentle. 'For which, Mrs Brown, I don't believe I have ever had the opportunity to thank you.'

'That's quite all right, ma'am,' said Maggie Brown, with a wry smile, 'all in a morning's work.'

'I recall the . . . monster pledging to meet you again. Was there ever such an encounter?'

Maggie Brown rubbed a hand across her stomach at the memory of the encounter. 'I would very much like to have met that particular demon again, ma'am, believe me, I would. Sadly, she's yet to show her face. In fact, our friends from the other side have been a bit quiet of late, truth be told. Activity: zero. I think they're waiting for us to get fat, actually.'

'Or,' said Lord Melbourne, 'there is another reason for their inactivity. That there is another conspiracy in the offing, yet more sophisticated than ever before.' He looked at Victoria. 'Your Majesty, I think there's something you should hear.'

Victoria nodded.

'Mrs Brown,' said Melbourne, 'over to you.'

Maggie Brown looked to the end of the table. 'John?'

The boy stepped forward.

Then, everybody in the tiny cottage was shuffling around. 'Perhaps you'd like to take a seat, Your Majesty,' Maggie Brown was attempting to direct operations, seven adults and a child in a space barely big enough to swing a cat.

'Hudson, you go there, next to Vasquez. Hicks, you go . . . no, not there. If you stand there, then Her Majesty can talk to John. *John.* No, not you, the big John, what are you doing standing there? Make way for the Prime Minister, man. John. No, not you, little *John*, take a seat here opposite Her Majesty . . .'

Until, at long last, after what felt like many minutes of shuffling and arrangement, John Brown the younger sat at one end of the large table and Victoria at the other end, facing him. Around them crowded the others, all but Maggie and Vasquez having to bend their heads beneath the eaves of the low ceiling.

'Right, little John,' commanded Maggie, 'do you want to tell Her Majesty what you saw?'

The young John Brown began to speak, then stopped, his fingers twisting the cap he still held in his hand. Victoria looked at him, trying to smile encouragingly.

'It's . . .' he looked over at his mother, who nodded, urging him on, 'it's these visions I have, miss . . .'

From the corner of her eye, Victoria could see Melbourne about to interject, to give the boy a swift lesson on how to address his sovereign, but she held up a hand to stop him.

'They are visions I have when I'm asleep, and sometimes when I'm awake,' continued the young John Brown.

'Clairvoyance, ma'am,' said Maggie Brown. 'John has certain psychic abilities that we are aware of . . .'

Somebody standing about the table huffed disbelievingly but Victoria did not see who was responsible. Not Maggie Brown or Lord Melbourne, that much was for certain. For when she looked at them their faces were set gravely, and for their sakes at least she suppressed a smile and determined to take the boy seriously.

'What,' she leaned forward, 'what do you see, John?'

The colour drained from his face.

'Death, miss.'

'I see,' said Victoria slowly, choosing her words carefully, 'Who, young John? Who do you see dying?'

'Many, many people, miss. Men. I see fire and I hear explosions.'

'Ma'am,' said Lord M, leaning forward, 'we think that what young John is seeing is revolution.'

'Is it, John? Is it an uprising in England?'

'I'm not sure, miss,' said John in reply.

'Tell Her Majesty about the voices, John,' prompted the Prime Minister.

'Some of the men spoke in a foreign tongue, miss.'

Victoria looked sharply at Melbourne, who nodded, his face as grave as she had ever seen it.

'The language they speak?' she asked John now. 'Do you know what it is?'

'I have been told, miss, that it is . . .'

'No,' she said, holding a finger up to silence him, 'John. *Ist es die deutsche Sprache, die Sie hören? Sprechen die Männer Deutsch?*'

'That was how they spoke, miss,' said John, 'just like that.'

Victoria sat back in her chair and cast a glance at Melbourne who met her gaze. Then she turned her attention back to the young John Brown.

'And this was happening here was it, John?' she asked, 'This was happening in England?'

'I don't know, miss, I'm afraid. I think so.' His face was ashen.

'Thank you, John,' said Victoria. 'You've been very brave.' She looked to Melbourne, nodded to indicate the meeting was at an end and went to stand up.

Melbourne stepped forward, 'Before we take our leave, Your Majesty, there is one more thing young Brown has seen.' He addressed the boy, 'Go ahead, John.'

'I see you grieving miss, underneath a tree inside your castle.'

Victoria caught her breath, shocked suddenly, feeling as though her privacy had somehow been invaded. She heard the frost in her voice as she said, very slowly, 'There is no tree in my castle, John.'

'It's what I see, miss. I see great sadness.'

'Lord Melbourne,' said Victoria, not taking her eyes from John Brown.

'Yes, Your Majesty?'

'Kindly escort me back to the palace, *at once.*'

XVII

Sir George Kraft MP, his manservant, Frederick, and Lord Fawcett had commandeered one of the upper corridors of The Reform Club on Pall Mall and were, with great dedication and serious intent, constructing a new parlour game. It was a variation on bowls or *boules*. At one end of the corridor sat a heavy medicine ball awaiting use. At the other end, along polished boards chosen for the very reason that they provided a smooth uninterrupted passage, was standing a series of pegs, or pins, that had been carefully painted, each numbered to indicate a score, then placed with infinite caution in an arrangement meticulously worked out beforehand.

Other members were invited to make their way along the corridor carefully, for fear of upsetting the apparatus the three men had so carefully laid out, and they were, in the main, good tempered regarding the unorthodox use of the area, most stopping to arch an eyebrow and enquire after the studied activity taking place, before moving past the pins, carefully and with their backs to the wall save the arrangement was upset, and onward to one of the club's legendary rooms.

'Gentlemen,' said a prominent Whig, somewhat put out at having to pass along the corridor thus, 'might I ask the rules of this distraction?'

'My Lord, it is very simple,' said Lord Fawcett. 'This heavy medicine ball, here, is rolled slowly and carefully along the floor, to here . . .'

He, his manservant, the prominent Whig and Sir George Kraft all turned to inspect the pins.

'The object being,' he continued, 'to gently touch one or more pins, those pins on the outside being the lower scoring pins. Any pins knocked down will . . .'

'*Gentleman, gangway please,*' came a shout from the other end of the passage and all looked in its direction to see Lord Quimby, having taken up the medicine ball, adopt a low stance and swing it back behind him with all the prowess of an Olympian athlete.

'*No, sir . . .*' exclaimed Lord Fawcett, too late because Quimby had released the ball and was springing into a standing position as it barrelled at great speed down the corridor and struck the cluster of pins, bringing each and every one crashing to the floor.

'Excellent variation on skittles, gentlemen,' roared Quimby with a grin as he strode down the corridor towards where they stood, speechless. 'Have you thought about some fingerholes for the ball, perhaps? Give it a bit of extra grip? Otherwise, wonderful stuff. Mine's the score to beat, looks like.'

And with that he stepped over the fallen pins and beyond them as they watched him go, none of them yet able to articulate a response.

For Quimby's part, it was quite the diversion he needed, as he strode along the passages of the club: a welcome respite from the serious matters to which he must attend, this assignation, for example.

First he went to the library where he glanced left and right, then sat at a seat, looked at the shelves and selected a suitably positioned book, *Memoirs of a Madman* by Gustave Flaubert, from the shelves and opened it. He took a knife from his pocket and used it to cut out a large section of pages creating a gap between the covers in which he might secrete the knife. With that done he replaced *Memoirs of a Madman* on the shelf, threw the sheaf of removed pages on the fire and exited the room, happy that he was adequately prepared for his meeting with – and oh, how it irked him to think of it – his blackmailer, an assignation that found him ruefully reflecting on the events of the last couple of years, the cumulative effect of which threatened to ruin him.

Blackmailed! To think of it. Here he was, yet again, pocket weighed down by a small leather drawstring purse intended for his *nemesis*.

Though, he mused, darkly, not for much longer, perhaps.

What cheered him up was to see the Prime Minister, Lord Melbourne, sitting alone in the news room where members habitually spent time alone with a copy of *The Times*.

It pleased Quimby greatly to make implications regarding the affair he had once had with the Prime Minister's wife, Lady Caroline Ponsonby, now deceased. In fact, it was an almost unlimited source of entertainment to him, as it was well known in social circles that Quimby had introduced the Prime Minister's wife to the delights of cunnilingus. It was well known, of course, because Quimby had been characteristically indiscreet about the fact; indeed, had made imitation of the Prime Minister's wife in the throes of orally induced passion his party piece (and ensured that there was no shortage of willing society ladies ready to assume the dear departed Lady Caroline's position in Quimby's bed. Whatever position that might be).

Added to Quimby's merriment was the fact that prior to being bedded by him Lady Caroline had enjoyed a very public affair with Lord Byron, an episode during which she had coined the enduring description of Byron as being 'mad, bad and dangerous to know'.

Poor Lord Melbourne. The catchphrase cuckold.

Sometimes, reflected Quimby, it was difficult to know when to start when it came to the business of ridiculing the Prime Minister. A hard task indeed.

Nevertheless, someone had to do it.

'Gracious,' he said, approaching the leather armchair from behind, 'Lord Melbourne. It is you. The way you were holding your paper, why, it almost looked as though you were wearing a pair of horns.'

He dropped into the armchair opposite Melbourne and revelled in the baleful stare of the Prime Minister. Melbourne was no doubt more used to being fawned over in court where his scandal lent him a certain romantic notoriety. Yet this was a character facet entirely indiscernible to anybody who knew the tawdry truth, which was simply this: that Melbourne was a man who loved his wife who had humiliated him, and who in death continued to do so. His tragedy was that he loved her then; that he never stopped loving her, and that he loved her still.

'Quimby,' said Melbourne icily, 'I rather thought you had been blackballed from The Reform.'

'Oh no, Prime Minister. The Athenaeum, the Travellers, Brooks', the Houses of Lords and Commons. From all of these I have been blackballed, but not yet The Reform, I'm pleased to say.'

'Ah well,' said the Prime Minister, deciding on the spot to

carry on along Pall Mall to the Travellers Club in future, where he could be assured of never having to bump into Quimby, 'I'm sure there's plenty of time for you to be blackballed here, too.'

'Let's hope, eh, Prime Minister?'

'In the meantime, what brings you here?'

'Oh, a meeting,' said Quimby airily. 'I'm blackmailed. Undone!'

Melbourne smiled thinly. 'Nothing too trivial, one hopes.'

'As the custard-covered kitchen staff might say, it is but a trifle. Are you aware of a new technique called photogenic drawing?'

'I must confess not,' sighed Melbourne, singularly unamused.

'Photogenic drawing is a process by which one can capture a still image of an individual involved in all manner of indiscretions,' said Quimby, adding impishly, 'One's spouse, even . . .'

Melbourne said nothing, refusing to give Quimby the satisfaction.

'As you can imagine, my Lord, it can be employed in a most unfortunate application for a gentleman of my proclivities.'

'Well, Quimby,' sighed Melbourne, 'I can but hope there is not so much as a sliver of truth to what you say. Oh, how it would truly pain me to see you either bankrupt or at the gallows.'

'Quite, quite.'

The two men were interrupted for a moment as a waiter bearing a tray and two glasses of port approached, bending to allow them to take one each, which they did, in frosty silence. Taking advantage of the interruption, Quimby's eyes raked the room: the leather chairs, tasselled gaslight shades, bookshelves. There was yet no sign of the man inveigling himself into the surroundings. His membership had been one of the many conditions of the extended extortion, and there were times Quimby wasn't sure what irked him more: the fact that the blackguard took his money, or the fact that he had used Quimby as a passport to the higher echelons.

The waiter backed away, bowing low. Melbourne rustled his *Times* as though to signal his resumption of reading and raised the paper to obscure his face entirely.

Quimby leaned forward and placed his hand in the fold, drawing down the paper to reveal the Prime Minister's resentful gaze.

'What now, man?' said Lord Melbourne testily.

'I wondered, what news of the Queen, Melbourne? How is Her Majesty?'

'She adapts to sovereignty with great fortitude,' sighed Melbourne, with the self-satisfied air of a man regurgitating a well-worn soundbite, the telling of which nevertheless reflected well upon him.

'Under your tutelage no doubt,' rejoined Quimby. 'I'm certain you wield quite the silver tongue?'

Melbourne shot Quimby a withering look then raised his newspaper, shaking it to register both disgust and finality.

Behind it he sighed, thinking, indeed, of the Queen, and of her walking angrily ahead of him as they exited the Browns' cottage in the grounds of Buckingham Palace. She had left him in her wake, hurrying to catch her up and feeling every day of his fifty-eight years.

'The feverish visions of a boy,' she had raged, her arms working as she moved swiftly across the lawn, 'you ask me to sacrifice it all for the ravings of a schoolboy. My love for Albert, the approval of my family, the joining of the two houses.'

'Please, Your Majesty, I pray you stop so that we may discuss this.'

She did so, spinning on her heel, one hand at her bonnet as though it were in danger of being torn off by the speed her fury generated.

'Lord Melbourne,' she said as he came skidding to a halt, 'you have placed before me every conceivable reason why I might not marry Albert. That I'm too young. That *he's* too young, that he is interested only in my wealth, that he is too lowly. And now . . . *this*. This tactic I cannot even dignify with a name.'

'Your Majesty, young John's visions have in the past proved very—'

'You tell me he can see the future?'

'Well, yes, ma'am, he has in the past—'

'Really? Then why are the family not rich on their winnings?'

'I don't think it works quite like that, ma'am.'

'Did he predict your defeat by Sir Robert Peel?'

'No ma'am, he didn't . . .'

'No, he didn't. Has he any other sage words of wisdom for his country or monarch save a sense of discord involving men who speak the German language? How very convenient, Lord Melbourne, that it should be German. *Ja, es ist sehr günstig.*'

'Ma'am, not for the first time you have me in awe of your linguistic skills. Neither can I fault your logic which, as usual, you wield with the skilled precision of a surgeon, but—'

'Pretty words, Melbourne,' she snapped.

The air was very still about them.

'Perhaps,' she added, taking a step forward that forced him to move back, 'what concerns you is not a matter of age or station, nor even of politics or international diplomacy; rather you fear Albert shall replace you as my mentor; that in future my counsel will be delivered with a German accent. Is that it, Melbourne, do you think? '

'Ma'am—'

She held up a hand to silence him.

'That is all, Lord Melbourne,' she said, curtly. 'Now kindly point me in the direction of the Palace.'

'It's that way, ma'am,' he said, pointing in the opposite direction to the one in which she was making for.

She harumphed and brushed past him as she began walking, very swiftly, back to the Palace, leaving him chastened and pondering in her wake.

Silver tongue? Not that Quimby's innuendo was lost on him, of course. Indeed, he was most sensitive to almost any remark pertaining to oral activity, and was known to flinch at the very mention of the name Byron, never mind repetition of that dreadful epithet. But silver tongue? Not then. Perhaps she was right, the Queen. Perhaps he revelled in his position as her advisor; perhaps he enjoyed their . . . intimacy? Was that it? Whatever it was, it was an intimacy afforded ever more rarely to him. Perhaps he enjoyed it too much.

Opposite him, Quimby jerked upright and the Prime Minister noticed a flicker of displeasure across his previously amused features. Melbourne found himself wanting to turn around in his chair to see who it was that had caused Quimby such vexation but preferred that Quimby should think he took no interest in his affairs, so remained as he was.

'Your meeting is here, it seems,' he said, instead.

'Indeed,' said Quimby, who stood. 'Another time, Prime Minster,' he said.

'I shall look forward to it,' said Melbourne.

By the time he thought it safe to turn and look, Quimby and his guest were nowhere to be seen.

As Quimby and his blackmailer made their way to the library, Quimby reflected that he had been right all along about the possible uses for the photogenic drawing equipment, man of great prescience that he was. Not that he had any call to congratulate himself, though. Absolutely not. The situation had brought him nothing but heartache.

It had not been long after the gruesome events of that evening that Talbot's accursed assistant, Craven, had paid him a visit at the house. Perkins had let him in clad, as he always was then, in a large scarf wrapped around his neck to obscure the wound left by the zombie's bite. It was not the correct attire for a manservant indoors, even during winter, as it was now, and it had raised questions with other members of staff, who had noticed a difference in Perkins and at first begun avoiding him, then, one by one, leaving Quimby's employ, much to his chagrin.

In addition, Perkins now walked with a pronounced limp. He and Quimby had tried to effect some emergency maintenance on his severed leg; his own had, unfortunately, been too severely chewed for use as a prosthetic, so instead they had sawn off Sugar's leg and used that in its place, affixing it by hammering wooden staples into it then tying it with bandages, and when hidden by his trousers, socks and shoes, there was no way of telling that one of Perkins' legs had had a previous owner, aside from the limp.

Quimby knew, however. As he'd watched Perkins sawing off Sugar's leg, he had noted with a mixture of gratification, regret and no small measure of sexual excitement that Sugar had followed his somewhat unorthodox pre-orgy instructions to the letter by painting her toenails bright red and that, just as he had predicted, the painted toenails did indeed cast the foot in a most erotic light.

A *most* erotic light.

However, the leg was now attached to Perkins, and this Quimby found most confusing since he still found himself luxuriating in the sight of the leg and its brazen painted toenails, even though it was no longer attached to Sugar and her promise of musky nights, but to Perkins, his manservant. Indeed, often, and on the pretext of 'giving the leg some air', Quimby had his manservant remove his shoe and sock, and would cast furtive, charged glances at the foot.

Together they had realised that the only way to arrest the decaying process, which applied to both physical and mental faculties, was to see to it that Perkins had a constant supply of fresh meat. Messrs Burke and Hare junior had been reassigned to ensure that new corpses were regularly admitted to the house. No doubt the two of them were privately dismayed that his Lordship somehow detected corpses that were older than a day or so, little knowing that he now had in his household a personage of refined tastebuds when it came to human flesh and the decomposition thereof. Indeed, Perkins' palate in this regard was so sophisticated that he and Quimby had devised a most amusing game in which Perkins was blindfolded and took the 'taste test' wherein he was usually able to determine the gender of the meat's source as well as the area of the body from whence it had been sliced.

Throughout all of this, however, Perkins had remained in excellent spirits, and at no point had he neglected his duties as a manservant, including showing guests to his Lordship's study, which he had done that evening, guiding Craven to a seat in front of the fire, opposite where Quimby sat.

Quimby had thanked Perkins and watched him leave, knowing that he would be pressed up to the door listening in, as was the plan should this set of circumstances arise.

'Is your manservant suffering from a cold, sir?' asked Craven, as the door shut, arranging himself in his seat. 'He lacks colour, and I notice that he is wearing a scarf.'

'Indeed,' said Quimby. 'Poor old Perkins is a martyr to his chest.'

'An accident to the foot also, sir?' enquired Craven.

'Quite. Poor fellow. Most clumsy of him.'

'May I ask, was this wound sustained during the conflict of the other evening?'

'Why, I really don't know what you're talking about, man,' said Quimby crossly. He'd already decided to call the man's bluff.

'I have in my possession a photogenic drawing that might aid your memory, sir.'

'Do you indeed? Do you . . . have it with you?'

'I do, sir.'

'Come on then, let's see it.'

Quimby stood and came around to the front of the desk.

Craven produced a large metal plate on which there was an image. He handed it to Quimby, who murmured a thank you, pretending to study it carefully as he moved to stand behind Craven.

The image showed Quimby – from the side, although it

was recognisably him – surveying the carnage in the library. Clearly visible in the foreground was Miss Corwent, who was sitting on her haunches with Fanny's dismembered arm up to her mouth. In the background Jacqueline was feasting on Sugar's entrails.

It was, indeed, a most incriminating image.

Which was why, in one uninterrupted movement, Quimby tossed it into the fire, snatched from the fireplace a thick, heavy candlestick holder and raised it ready to bring it down as hard as was possible on the back of Craven's head.

'That, Lord Quimby, was a copy,' said Craven calmly, unmoved by the destruction of his photogenic drawing, which blazed in the fire grate.

Quimby hesitated.

'A copy?' he said.

'Yes, my lord,' said Craven, 'It was a photogenic drawing of the original photogenic drawing.'

'I see,' said Quimby. He lowered the candlestick holder. 'And where is the original now?'

'No need for your concern, your Lordship, it's in a very safe place. Nobody could possibly find it if they didn't know where to look.'

'Excellent.'

Quimby raised the candlestick.

'Your Lordship,' said Craven, 'I must tell you that you have neglected to close your curtains. I can quite clearly see you reflected in the window.'

Quimby looked up to see the mirror image of Craven, seated, with him standing behind him, the candlestick raised. Infuriatingly, Craven waved at him.

Quimby lowered the candlestick once more.

'Nobody can find it, the original photogenic drawing?' he asked Craven's reflection.

'No, sir,' smiled Craven.

'Then I don't need to worry about it, do I?' said Quimby.

'Well, actually, yes, sir, because . . .'

But he never finished his sentence because behind him Quimby had raised the candlestick once more, and now brought it down with a heavy thud, the blow tearing a flap from the back of Craven's skull and sent him smashing forward to the desk, blood and stinking grey brain matter splashing to the table surface with a wet slap.

His body jerked and writhed. He made a quiet moaning sound. Quimby stepped forward and dealt him a second blow, at the same time shouting, '*Perkins!*'

Immediately the study door opened and Perkins came hobbling in.

'Eat up, man,' urged Quimby, stepping to the side, his hand to his nose. The smell of brain was already heavy in the room, a disgustingly sour scent. 'The bugger's still flapping about here. '

'That's very kind of you, sir, thank you,' said Perkins, reaching to drag Craven from the desk and to the floor, then kneeling beside him. Quimby fancied that in his very last moments Craven was somehow aware of what was happening to him; that he felt Perkins pulling open his shirt with a popping of buttons then nuzzling deep into his stomach; that the sensation might for a moment have felt warm and with the promise of pleasure, until Perkins' teeth sank into the flesh, tearing at the soft, tender meat that was there. Quimby smiled indulgently. He'd known that was where Perkins would go, having learnt of his manservant's fondness for the chest meat over the past few days. How peculiar; he seemed to have grown so much closer to Perkins since he'd died.

'I'm going to leave you to it, Perkins, if you don't mind,' he said then, his hand still to his nose. 'It's the smell of the brains. I find it most off-putting. Perhaps you could join me in the library presently.'

Perkins sat back on his haunches, mouth slick with gore. Beneath him, Craven was open from neck to groin, his insides out, shimmering and pulsing.

'Certainly sir, thank you sir, I'll just finish up here and be with you, sir.'

Shortly afterwards, they had sat in near silence in the library. Perkins, sated, had taken off his shoe and sock to give his leg some air. After a long pause, during which Quimby affected a faraway look in his eyes, though was in fact gazing at Perkins' foot, Perkins cleared his throat.

'Sir, I do wonder if you should have let him finish his sentence before you killed him, sir.'

Quimby, dragged from his erotic reverie, harumphed. 'Really, Perkins. I struck when the time was right, when the blackguard was least expecting it. What on earth could he have been about to say that was of any import?'

The answer, of course, was soon to come to them. It came in the form of a letter from a gutter newspaper journalist named McKenzie to whom, it transpired, Craven had given a copy of the photogenic drawing for insurance purposes.

It was a most tiresome development, especially as McKenzie had proved more adept in the art of blackmail. For two years now he had extorted from Quimby a great sum of money, as well as utilising his Lordship's connections in society, such as they were.

Quimby had, however, decided to put McKenzie out of his misery. Downstairs, in the club's basement, Perkins was waiting. In all likelihood he would be sitting alone in the servants' quarters; when he arrived other staff were apt to leave. Perkins had that effect on people these days. They tended to give him a wide berth. He bore a most unusual scent and he brought with him singularly unappetising packed lunches. Quimby dearly hoped that Perkins would be ready.

'Your Lordship,' said McKenzie, 'if you don't mind.'

Quimby glanced about the otherwise empty library. McKenzie did the same before quickly frisking Quimby for weapons. Satisfied his Lordship was not armed he indicated the chair and Quimby sat, smiling, thinking of the Flaubert a short distance away, Perkins below stairs, the wheels of the plan in motion.

McKenzie had a slightly abrasive manner and had thick whiskers. Nevertheless, the two men seemed to intuit that in different circumstances they might well have liked one another.

'Are you getting me a port, your Lordship?' asked McKenzie. 'Just to help keep out the chill.'

'Of course,' smiled Quimby, picturing his knife wafting back and forth on McKenzie's face, carving chunks of flesh from his stupid, fat, gloating visage.

After the port had been served and the waiter had withdrawn, McKenzie settled back.

'Before we get down to business, my Lord, perhaps I could prevail upon you for a little help? Some information if I may?'

Quimby frowned. Was it not enough that he was being blackmailed by this vagabond? Not enough that he had secured the blackguard membership to the club in the first place? What now? Pumped for information like a common *source*.

He sighed long and hard, indicating his displeasure, at which McKenzie smiled, indicating in return that his Lordship's displeasure was a particularly impotent weapon in the circumstances, pressing on with, 'What do you know of Sir John Conroy, your Lordship?'

'Very little. That he is the Queen mother's comptroller. That the Queen hates him.'

McKenzie leaned forward. 'Because . . .'

'Because he has made little secret of his desire to be the power behind the throne. It is said that when the young Princess was very ill he tried to force her to sign him up as her private secretary. Terribly underhand, don't you think?'

'How did Conroy come to be in their lives?' asked McKenzie.

'Ah, well he began by serving as equerry to the late Duke of Kent, some three years before the Duke died, and a couple of years before the future Queen was born.'

'And she has grown up despising him?'

'Oh, absolutely. She habitually refers to him as "the demon incarnate".'

'Why does she do that?'

'Perhaps she sees within him a darkness.'

'That's not the first time I've heard Conroy and demon in the same sentence, though I have a feeling that in the first instance it was meant rather more literally. It would seem, in fact, that of late there has been an unusually high instance of apocrypha involving supernatural events, would you say so, my Lord?'

Quimby squirmed in his seat.

McKenzie leaned forward. 'That night,' he said, 'it was no party that got out of hand was it, your Lordship?'

Quimby said nothing.

'It was the night of the accession, wasn't it?'

Quimby studied his fingernails. 'It might have been. I really don't remember the details . . .'

'Why?'

'I beg your pardon?'

'Why should it be that evening? Why that night that your revenants attacked?'

'I really don't know what you're talking about.'

'That same night there were reports of similarly hellish scenes through the city, did you know?'

Quimby shook his head no. 'I read nothing about it in the papers. As far as I recall you were all doing special supplements on the King's death.'

'There was talk of a two-headed hound, perhaps you heard of it?'

'A two-headed hound? No, but . . .'

'Yes?'

'Well, I did see a two-headed rat.'

'A rat?'

'Absolutely. It ran right past my window.'

McKenzie leaned back in his chair, as did Quimby. Both were wondering if the other was joking.

'I think there was something abroad that night,' said McKenzie. 'I witnessed something the other night that makes me wonder if it is still abroad. And furthermore, your Lordship, I can't help but wonder if it involves Sir John Conroy and, perhaps, even you.'

'I see,' said Quimby. 'You think I'm in league with the forces of darkness.' He smirked. 'Hadn't you better re-think blackmail as a strategy, that being the case?'

McKenzie leaned back. 'If I were frightened, your Lordship,

I would reserve my fear for the organ grinder, not his monkey. Now, I'll take my money, if I may,' said McKenzie.

Quimby, seething, palmed the purse then passed it across to McKenzie who placed it in his pocket.

'Actually,' said Quimby, 'I'd like the little leather purse back if I may. It's one thing giving you the money, I really don't see why I should have to keep you in little leather drawstring purses, too.'

McKenzie frowned, reached into the pocket of his coat and withdrew the purse . . .

In the library was a dumb waiter, on which the staff received plates and drinks, and a hidden passageway, known only to a very select few. It was that secret passageway Quimby planned to use, using the knife hidden in the Flaubert to direct McKenzie down the stairs and to the lower floor, where, joined by Perkins, they would march McKenzie to their carriage. They would then take him back to Quimby's home, there to install him in the cellar, which nowadays carried the reek of putrefaction thanks to the many corpses that had been deposited there by Messrs Burke and Hare junior, but was nevertheless an ideal venue for the manner of questioning Quimby had in mind. For there, McKenzie would be tortured. Quimby planned to brave the stench, perhaps with the aid of a face mask, purely so that he could watch and enjoy the sight of Perkins consuming parts of his nemesis until such time as the man, who would by then be experiencing almost unimaginable pain, would reveal the location of the photogenic drawing, after which Quimby would proceed to the location of the incriminating image and, having taken possession of it, return home and instruct Perkins to finish the job.

It was an almost perfect plan. It left virtually no margin for error.

Except that Quimby, affecting nonchalance, reached and plucked the Flaubert from the shelf, only to discover too late, that it was not *Memoirs of a Madman*, the English translation of Flaubert's autobiographical work, but *Mémoires d'un fou* in the original French. Panicking somewhat he then tried to return the original French Flaubert to the shelf, only to fumble and drop the book, by which time McKenzie was already standing, dropping the small leather sac, now empty, to the table between them, saying, 'Good evening to you, Lord Quimby, I shall be in touch regarding the date and time of next month's meeting,' and exiting the library. Damn the man!

With McKenzie now gone, Quimby rushed to the dumb waiter, thrust his head into it and bawled down the shaft, 'Look sharp, Perkins, he has outfoxed me. He's coming down the stairs. We'll get him in the street, by God!'

He retrieved the knife and snatched up his top hat, then was moving over to one of the bookcases, getting his shoulder to it and pushing it open to reveal a flight of winding stone steps down which he hurried, taking them two at a time, to find Perkins at the bottom. Good. By taking the shortcut he would have arrived at the bottom at the same time as McKenzie and he and Perkins peered from the barred window of a tradesman's entrance below street level just in time to see McKenzie pass by overhead, his cane disturbing the thick fog, which swirled resentfully about his knees.

Quimby and Perkins looked at one another. Quimby grinned. Perkins did the same. Quimby looked at Perkins and touched a hand to his top hat, a signal that Perkins responded to by touching a hand to his deerstalker. It was to be silence from thereon as they ascended the steps to street level and hurried along the cobbles, trying to locate McKenzie in the fog that billowed about them, so thick they could barely see in front of themselves. Very quickly Quimby began to see the flaws in his latest scheme, because McKenzie was already out of sight; the only sign of him was the sound of his footsteps and the *tap-tap-tap* of his cane as he made his way along Pall Mall.

Quimby touched a hand to his top hat and motioned to Perkins to spread out, which he did, limping out into the dirt and effluent of the highway. They each moved quickly, bent low and struggling to see through the fog, desperate not to allow their quarry to escape.

He had his knife at the ready. The curved blade seemed to glow, hungry.

The footsteps and the *tap-tap-tap* ceased. Quimby whirled a finger in the air to signal a halt and Perkins stopped, his bad leg – Sugar's leg – dragging behind him a little.

Quimby sensed, rather than saw, that they had passed the first entrance to St James's Square. Where did McKenzie live? He had no idea. It was, of course, wholly possible that he lived off the Square and had already turned off.

Then: 'Who's there?' came a voice from inside the fog.

Quimby and Perkins bent lower, each of them tensing.

Silence.

The footsteps resumed. The *tap-tap-tap*. Quimby looked across, touched a hand to his hat and pointed forward. In response Perkins gave a faithful, toothy grin, nodding, and together they inched forward.

The tapping stopped.

Quimby whirled a finger to signal a halt, glanced over to

see that Perkins had stopped, only just able to make out the figure of his manservant, despite the fact that he was just a few feet away.

There was silence. Quimby and Perkins hardly dared to breathe. From somewhere behind them came a clop-clop of horse's hooves, moving away in the direction of Trafalgar Square.

Then the fog directly in front of McKenzie seemed to eddy and part, and before he had a chance to react, McKenzie was upon him. From the mist came the flash of something that he only later realised was McKenzie's cane and he was sent sprawling to the ground with a shout.

A foot stamped down on his knife hand and he screeched in pain. Then McKenzie was over him, reaching down, taking the knife from his hand. For a second or so Quimby's thoughts were of his own death; how there were so many things he had yet to achieve, such as watching three women pleasure one another. But of course, McKenzie had no desire to do him lasting harm. He had no doubt read the fairy tale of the simpleton who slew the golden goose and McKenzie was no simpleton. Instead he silently disarmed Quimby and tossed the knife away into the fog.

'Sir!' called Perkins. On the ground Quimby heard Perkins dragging his way over to them.

McKenzie glanced up and Quimby used the opportunity to roll over, too late realising he had rolled into horse dung. McKenzie, meanwhile, had raised his cane. 'Perkins,' warned Quimby, but again too late and McKenzie swung his cane. The man must have noted Perkins' gait for he swung low, the swine. The crack as he connected was not that of cane with bone, but rather something else, and twisting his head to see,

Quimby witnessed Perkins' false leg simply swept from beneath him with a splintering sound that he knew to be the wooden staples broken, and Perkins crumpled to the ground.

A face came close to his. McKenzie.

From close by an animalistic growling, the sound of Perkins, hungry and thwarted, all of that strength and violence and instinct going to waste. Quimby writhed with the frustration of it all.

McKenzie's breath was warming his face, the aroma rank with tobacco and alcohol.

'The price has just gone up, Quimby,' he hissed, then was gone.

XVIII

Buckingham Palace

Lord Melbourne sat in the sumptuous Blue Drawing Room, awaiting his daily audience with Her Majesty. Alone, he allowed himself to slouch a little, stretching his legs beneath the table at which they were due to sit and discuss matters of state, his elbow on the arm of the chair, chin in hand, thinking, a study in reflection. He thought, as he always did in such moments, of Caroline.

From somewhere in the room came the sound of a throat being cleared.

Melbourne jumped a little, an almost imperceptible amount, but a jump nonetheless and he rolled his eyes heavenward, sighing a little.

'Maggie,' he said.

'Aye, sir,' came the disembodied voice. Not for the first time, he wondered where in the room was her secret hiding place. Not information he was ever privy to, of course, but wherever she hid was confoundedly clever. Or did the woman possess some secret powers he knew nothing of? Invisibility? He stifled a smile. He wouldn't put it past her. The redoubtable Maggie Brown.

'If you're here,' he said, 'pray tell who guards the Queen?'

'Hicks and Hudson, sir.'

'You know I prefer it for you to watch over her personally. These are . . . uncertain times.'

'You're telling me, Prime Minister.'

'Oh? You have news.'

'Indeed.'

'And what nature of news is it?'

'Good news . . . for those enthusiasts of bad news.'

Melbourne sighed. 'Go on.'

'We've made some further investigations into events at the Cockpit. It seems the rats were targeting the boy, Hastings' stable lad, Egg.'

'Rats,' Melbourne shuddered. He hated rats. Not that he had ever met anybody that claimed to like them, but he strongly suspected there were very few who disliked them quite as much as he. 'You feel that these rats were in his thrall, Maggie?' he asked.

'It would seem to have been an attempt on the boy's life, aye. And who do we think might like to see the boy dead?'

Conroy, thought Melbourne, who walked the galleries and halls of the Palace a free man, the keeper of the Queen mother's confidence.

The Queen mother who was, of course, the aunt of Prince Albert, who had so thoroughly captured the Queen's heart.

Some days previously, Lord Melbourne and Sir John Conroy had passed one another in the courtyard and Conroy had smiled a greeting, his eyes alive. Perhaps he thought he had every reason to smile, mused Melbourne, because he felt fortune was once again in his favour.

Melbourne didn't like it. He didn't like it at all.

'Anything else?' he asked, glancing at the grandfather clock. The Queen was due to arrive at any moment. For a few seconds he looked hard at the grandfather clock, wondering whether it contained Maggie Brown and she was at this very moment regarding him through means of a peephole at two o'clock.

'Aye, the boy.'

'What about him?'

'He remains lost.'

There were occasions during these conversations when her invisibility allowed him to express his disappointment more profoundly than had she been sitting with him. This was one of them. 'Oh, Maggie.'

'We've been doing our best,' she said, defensively, 'this boy does not want to be found.'

'Is he with the journalist?'

'Not as far as we know.'

Melbourne sighed. Egg had been seen speaking to the journalist moments before he fled. Vasquez, the team's lip reader, had not been able to see much of the conversation, but had reported Egg using a certain word.

Demon.

After that, said Vasquez, Egg had told the journalist McKenzie more, but she had been unable to interpret it. Whatever it was, it had sent McKenzie rocking back on his heels and Egg had used the opportunity to escape.

Melbourne threw up his arms in frustration. 'Couldn't he have been stopped?' he said, for what must have been the hundredth time. To add to their displeasure they believed Conroy was also aware of Egg talking to the journalist. Vasquez had seen his carriage nearby.

'We need to find this Egg, Maggie, for his sake more than ours.'

'We're on it.'

'This is most unfortunate, Maggie. Good Lord, the last thing we want is tongues wagging with talk of demons at the palace.'

'It was to be expected, Prime Minister, as soon as she went to the papers. God only knows we anticipated it sooner than this.'

'True. Whatever Lady Flora Hastings had to say about Conroy of interest to the newspapers, it was never going to involve his prowess between the sheets.'

'Demons at the palace, though, Prime Minister, nobody will believe it.'

'No, true. At the moment it's little more than a tall tale, paranoia, a wild imagination and coincidence. But there's every possibility this McKenzie will continue turning over stones until he discovers something with a little more substance . . .'

'Should we tell the lassie?'

'Tell her what? The truth?'

'A version of it, aye.'

'And remind me how we came by our intelligence, Maggie?'

'Because of a vision, Prime Minister.'

'Precisely. Young Brown's precognition of the bloodline of Baal ruling the world's greatest empire.' Melbourne still bore the mental scars of the last time he had tried to use one of young John's visions to warn her of impending danger. 'I fear it won't be enough to convince her,' he said. 'We shall keep quiet for the time being, Maggie.'

At that moment there was a knock to signal the entrance

of the Queen and Lord Melbourne was scrambling to his feet as the door to the drawing room was opened by a footman and the Queen entered, the Duchess of Sutherland in her wake.

'Lord M,' she smiled.

'Your Majesty,' he bowed low.

Victoria dismissed the Duchess and took her place opposite Lord Melbourne at the table. Ever since that day in the Brown's cottage there was always one question to which she wanted the answer when they were together.

'Is she here? Maggie Brown? Is she in the room, somewhere?'

Lord Melbourne smiled at her as sweetly as he could manage. 'I really wouldn't know, Your Majesty,' he said, 'but just in case, we should refrain from intimacies, don't you think?'

She threw back her head and guffawed. For his part, Lord Melbourne was sure he heard the sound of a smothered laugh from the direction of the grandfather clock.

XIX

He always did make her laugh, she thought. Refrain from intimacies!

So, yes, she had made it up with Lord Melbourne. How could she do otherwise? He was, after all, her mentor, her private secretary and Prime Minister. He charmed her. He brought laughter to her day.

However, the days of him fulfilling the role of best friend were at an end.

Now she had Albert.

Lord M had apologised for what he described as the rather tactless manner in which he had raised the issue of his doubts concerning the Royal wedding. He had nothing against Albert, he was most keen to emphasise. His concerns lay with the continued prosperity of England. It was true, he was forced to admit, that young John Brown's visions hardly constituted firm evidence of discord arriving from overseas, and were not enough on which to base policy of any kind, not least of it that which concerned the Queen's marriage. However, he said, he was still of the opinion – as was the Protektorate – that an uprising remained a distinct possibility. Worse, that it would be an uprising conceived of and masterminded by the forces of darkness; that unrest, chaos and disorder were the fertile soil from which evil was grown – which was something he told her often.

'Sir John Conroy? What of him? Have you established any

links between Sir John and this possible uprising?' she had asked him next – something she asked him often.

'Ma'am,' he demurred, as ever, 'any information we have involving Sir John is based purely on conjecture and guess-work in much the same way as, I dare say, your own opinion is formed.'

'Then set your agents upon him,' she insisted, 'see to it that his movements are traced; that his confidantes and contacts are monitored.'

'Ma'am,' said Lord M wearily, 'all of these things we have done in the past. There has been not one shred of evidence linking Sir John to demonic activity. He is your mother's comptroller. This fact makes him more dangerous than almost any other man in the Empire. Do you think we would have allowed him access to you if we thought he was somehow involved in plans to overthrow you?'

'He virtually was,' she reminded him, sharply, 'he tried to force me into appointing him my private secretary.'

'And he was repelled, ma'am. Your Majesty, it pains me to say it, but there is evil and darkness in this world, and not all of it associated with the minions of hell. Much of the time it is simply greed and vanity and a lust for power that can explain away acts we think of as evil. Sometimes I wonder if these forces really are as pernicious and as clever and manipulative as we give them credit for.'

As usual, she paid great attention to his wise words (although as usual she wondered how much of the truth was hidden from her), but noted that these days he tended to deploy them with a note of regret, as though already in mourning for that day when it would be Albert to whom she turned for support and advice.

Which was very soon to arrive. She and Albert had been inseparable since the engagement, time they had spent by singing duets together, going for long rides and taking walks. They had exchanged rings and locks of hair, and were often to be seen, whispering and laughing together. She wrote tirelessly of him in her diary. When she reviewed the troops in Hyde Park, he accompanied her, wearing, she wrote that night, 'a pair of white cashmere breeches with *nothing under them*' and she wrote often of his beauty, the happiness he had brought to her. For the first time in her life she felt truly loved, not for her rank – Queen Victoria – which was, after all, an accident of birth, but for herself.

She went before the Privy Council to announce her engagement and had any privy councillors been in any doubt as to the nature of Her Majesty's relationship with Prince Albert, then they were no longer. For on a bracelet at her wrist she wore a miniature of him, as though to give her the strength that she always felt she needed whenever she addressed the assembly; as though she could not bear to be anywhere without him.

XX

So it was that she awoke on Monday, 10 February 1840 to the sound of her bedchamber windows under attack from the weather, and her heart sank. Looking out of the window she was greeted with her wedding-day weather: wind and rain.

'If the weather refuses to acknowledge wedding-day traditions,' she declared, 'then so will I,' and so she visited Prince Albert in his chamber despite the protestations of her maids of honour and ladies-in-waiting, who threw up their hands in horror. 'It's unlucky, Your Majesty!' 'Ma'am, I beg you not to!'

'Nonsense!' she said. 'No force on earth will keep me from him today,' and bid a maid of honour pass her a tiny box which had sat on her dressing table before repairing to his chamber, showering the surprised bridegroom with kisses, taking his cheeks in her hands and gazing deeply and gladly into his eyes.

'Ready?' she asked him.

He looked at her. 'I was never so ready as I am now, my darling,' he said. 'Victoria, today you make me the happiest man in all of the world, for I have captured the heart of an angel.'

She came to him with her arms open, and they embraced, stiffly, all too aware that even meeting in this way they were in breach of tradition. However, they could not help themselves, could not prevent their lips meeting, and for a longer moment she luxuriated in his arms, bringing her hands to the back of his head, pushing her fingers into his hair. In that moment time stood still for Victoria. It was as though every single sense and nerve ending was concentrated on that kiss.

At last they came apart, and she cast her eyes downwards, quite taken aback by the force of passion surging throughout her body. She too breathed heavily, the only sound in the room, apart from the rain spraying against the window.

'Albert,' she said, 'I have something for you,' and she gave him a ring, which he accepted, his eyes shining.

'Albert,' she said, 'I want there never to be a secret that we do not share.'

He took her face in his hands. 'We are together now, Victoria,' he said. 'Now we will share everything.'

Later, her hair was parted and curled over her ears and she was wearing her dress, white satin trimmed with Honiton lace, and on it she wore a diamond necklace and a sapphire brooch set with diamonds that had been given to her as a gift by her beloved Albert.

'Do you think I am right to wear white, Lehzen?' she asked her governess, 'I'm only wearing white to go with the lace and I do so worry that it is an unpopular colour.'

'You look beautiful, ma'am,' replied the Baroness, 'you are sure to begin a trend for it.'

I'm more likely to provoke a mad stampede for green, thought the Queen, for she feared that her people might not have forgiven her for her earlier mistakes; moreover that her wedding might go unremarked and that she might find herself driving in her carriage to St James's Palace through empty and indifferent streets.

She could not have been more wrong. Just as it had been on the day of her Coronation, the crowds lining the streets were smiling and waving and she found herself choking back tears of happiness and gratitude as she returned their waves and goodwill, her diamonds twinkling in the sun which seemed to have appeared in honour of the occasion, chasing away the wind, burning off the rain, bathing them all in its warm glow. This was the Queen's weather.

The ceremony was followed by the ride back to the Palace for the wedding breakfast where they had some moments together – their first alone as man and wife – then they travelled to Windsor Castle, through streets still lined with well-wishers, until, finally, much, much later, they were alone and he drew up a foot stool to be close to the sofa and clasped her in his arms, the two of them kissing. The next morning, she awoke (having had very little sleep) and looked over to see Albert, finding herself quite overcome. Later, she wrote in her diary, 'he does look so beautiful in the shirt only, with his beautiful throat seen.'

In short, they were blissfully happy, and had they lived an island – population two – they might never have had a cross word.

Victoria's duty beckoned, however. It loomed over them. Theirs was such a short honeymoon, just three days, and at its end duty called – and problems within the union became apparent.

For example, she knew that it vexed Prince Albert not to fully share her confidence as monarch. When she met with Lord Melbourne to discuss affairs of state with him, Prince Albert was not invited to join them, nor was he allowed to see the state papers which occupied so much of her time, while, needless to say, she had been advised not to apprise him of the demon threat.

They would argue, sometimes, about this. 'My darling, my beloved,' said Victoria on one such occasion, attempting to pacify her husband, who, to add to his sense of superfluity, felt homesick, 'the English can be very jealous of any foreigner they perceive as interfering in the government of the country.' (And, once or twice, she thought of the young John Brown's vision.)

Even so, these were minor niggles and Victoria, young though she was, an inexperienced monarch she may have been, knew better than to ascribe greater significance to them than was warranted. They were merely teething problems; they would soon be sorted out and anyway, they were minor in comparison to the great love that continued to blossom between them. Sometimes it was as though when she closed the door to their chamber and rested her head on his chest she was no longer Queen Victoria, ruler of the British Empire, but just Victoria, Albert's wife, and she felt that there was nothing in the world that gave her greater pleasure. Those moments were the happiest of her life, and for them she would be forever thankful. Nothing, she thought, could besmirch that happiness.

Sadly, events in her future would do exactly that.

XXI

The Queen was in a most dreadful turmoil.

'I have no wish to be pregnant,' she exclaimed. 'No wish whatsoever.' She glared at Albert, the look leaving him in no doubt that she regarded him the architect of this new woe.

'It really is too dreadful,' she raged, 'I could not be more unhappy. This pregnancy has been sent to spoil my happiness. Oh, how I longed to least enjoy six months with you, my love. But to fall pregnant within just a few short weeks of blissful marriage, it really is *too* dreadful. How can any woman wish for such a thing?'

Even though they had been married but a short time, Albert knew better than to interrupt his wife while in full flight or offer words of condolence. Like a fire, he knew, her anger would burn herself out – although rarely did he see a conflagration of quite this magnitude. 'What if my plagues are to be rewarded only by a nasty girl?' she raged further. 'Why, I shall drown the thing!'

At this, Albert bridled. 'Come, come now Victoria,' he said, moving to her and placing his hands on her shoulders, bringing this most animated Queen to a standstill at last, 'that is not an appropriate sentiment for a mother-to-be.'

'Oh, Albert,' She pulled angrily away from him. 'You and your *appropriate*. Albert, I do declare that your ideas of what is and what is not appropriate matter more to you than the health and well-being of your own wife.'

'No, no, my dear,' he said, protesting, 'merely that usually it is – how can I say this . . . *commonplace* for a woman expecting a baby to greet the news with some semblance of joy.'

Now she was very angry. 'I, Albert,' she said, the blood rising prettily in her cheeks, 'am not *usual*. If you wished for a usual wife then I dare say you should have stayed in Germany.'

She glared at him, daring him to protest, which he, exercising restraint, diplomacy, and not a little self-preservation, did not.

Perhaps he thought he should make amends. For it was largely thanks to him that she remained fit, strong and healthy in both body and mind throughout that accursed pregnancy and, on 21 November 1840, when the day was dark and grey (a rainswept, windy day, it was, the air thick and choked with smoke from the chimneys), after a labour of some twelve hours, during which Victoria suffered great pain but bore it, so Albert was to tell her later, so stoically, she gave birth to their first born.

A girl.

After it was over, sitting by her bed, Albert waved away the maids of honour who came to wipe the sweat from her brow, preferring to do it himself, gently dabbing at her reddened cheeks, whispering to her. 'My darling,' he said, 'you have to promise not to drown her.'

Even in all her pain and trauma, and, yes, for there was no getting around the fact, disappointment, Victoria found a moment to laugh.

'No,' she said, gazing up at him, 'I promise not to drown her.'

'Good.'

'I'm going to expose her instead.'

Now it was his turn to laugh.

'You were with me,' she said to him, when he had finished, 'you were with me throughout it all.'

'Always, my love, always. If I could have taken from you all of your suffering I would have.'

'All of it?'

He pretended to think. 'Well . . . perhaps not all of it. Most of it. Some of it. A *bit* of it.'

She laughed. 'Did I use unsavoury language in my pain, Albert?'

'I'm afraid so, my darling.'

She blushed. 'Really? In front of the doctor?'

'You used the word . . .' and he leaned in low, to whisper into her ear, ' . . . "blazes".'

'Oh.'

'That is not all, Victoria,' he shook his head with mock-sadness. 'Not at all, I'm afraid. For other expletives also escaped your lips, such as,' he leaned in to whisper once more, '"damn" . . .'

Now she was beginning to giggle.

'. . . and "cockchafer". Plus you did at one stage declare that you didn't give – and I quote – "a beggar's fart" about the baby, you just wanted the "bloody" thing out.'

'Oh, *Albert*.'

'I'm teasing you, my darling,' he said. 'You were, of course, the picture of propriety at all times.'

'Thank you,' she whispered. 'Thank you for everything.'

She reached to draw his fringe from his eyes and they shared a moment. Then she raised her voice slightly, addressing her mother who sat by the door engrossed in needlework, 'and thank you, Mama,' she called.

The Duchess rose to her feet, placed her needlework on the seat behind her and made a short bow. 'Your Majesty,' she said.

'Are you disappointed it is not a boy, Mama?' asked Victoria.

Her mother's eyes flickered. 'My only concern is for you, my little one,' she said.

Victoria smiled. The Duchess regained her seat.

Next door, ministers and dignitaries awaited the news in a smoke-filled room into which the newborn was carried for their inspection.

These included Lord Melbourne, the Archbishop of Canterbury (who had partaken of a little drink, or so Victoria was later to hear), the Bishop of London and the Lord Steward of the household. Distinguished gentlemen all, in front of whom the baby was placed stark naked upon a table, and they crowded forward to see, swift to express their relief that Victoria had survived her ordeal, but nevertheless disappointed that it was a princess, not a prince.

Victoria remained in bed for a fortnight to recover from the birth of Victoria Adelaide Mary Louisa, who would be known in the family as Pussy. During this time Albert nursed her back to full health: he sat with her in her darkened room, he read to her, he wrote letters for her. He allowed no one but himself to move her from her bed to the sofa, and whenever she was required to move around the Palace he insisted on being called upon to wheel her along the corridors, whatever his current duties. These, of course, included behaving as her proxy. He represented her at Privy Council meetings; and he took care of all Cabinet business and reported back to her, he busied himself with his causes and political life. In the evening he dined with the Duchess then tended to Victoria in her chamber. He was a man who was content and in love, and this made him so much happier in the home, something that was never so apparent as during his enthusiastic preparations for Christmas.

Their daughter's first Christmas should be an event to remember for ever, he declared, and he set about organising Windsor Castle. His first task was to import what he said was a German custom: a special Christmas decoration. German fashion, he told her, proudly, was to have a fir tree as tall as could be obtained, in pride of place, decorated all over with tapers, with smaller wax dolls placed all over and strings of almonds and raisins hanging between the branches.

They were there to see its arrival, having relocated to Windsor for Christmas, with Victoria now out of convalescence, and she gasped to see its size as it was carried into the drawing room by no less than five bewigged footmen, then was the subject of much head-scratching, debate and puzzlement among the gardeners, with the head gardener finally deciding that it should be placed in a bucket, while the housekeeper grumbled about the fact that the tree was certain to 'shed its pine needles all over the rug', but at a glance from Albert added, that it was 'most assuredly a festive addition to the drawing room'.

When they had departed, Albert reached to take her hand and for a few moments she enjoyed the feeling of his touch.

So much so that she hardly noticed a footman arrive, who whispered something to the Duchess of Sutherland, who replied in a whisper then excused herself and followed him out of the room. She was far too engrossed in the sheer scale of this grand addition to the drawing room to pay the exchange much mind.

'It is really quite imposing, Albert,' she said. 'Perhaps, my love, *too* imposing?'

'I asked for the largest one that could be found,' he said, 'but I'm not sure that I expected my words to be taken quite so literally. I fear that somewhere in Europe is missing a treasured landmark.'

She laughed, and was still laughing when the Duchess of Sutherland returned to the room and moved to stand in front of her. Her face was grave and she stood with her hands clasped in front of her, curtsying slightly.

'Yes, Harriet,' said Victoria.

Behind the Duchess was the fir.

('*A tree inside your castle . . .*')

Victoria froze.

'I have some most upsetting news, Your Majesty,' said the Duchess fretfully.

'Yes?' she said, her voice small, hardly daring to ask. 'What is it?'

('*I see you grieving, miss.*')

'It's Dash, ma'am,' said the Duchess. 'I'm so sorry, ma'am – but your faithful Spaniel has succumbed to old age at last. Dash is dead, ma'am.'

XXII

'The code word is sasquatch,' came the voice at the door and everybody crammed into the Browns' tiny cottage was so startled that there was for a moment much confusion and scraping of chairs, followed by cursing and rubbing of craniums, especially from Hudson and Hicks, who had leapt from their seats and, being taller then the others assembled, hit their heads on the low ceiling.

And the reason for this moment of consternation and great upset?

An unexpected visit from the Queen.

Having provided the code word, though it had not been elicited, she opened the door to the cottage (provoking a series of recriminatory looks between Maggie and John Brown the elder, each blaming the other for leaving the front door unlocked) and down the stairs she came, the only word to describe her descent being 'angry', for 'angry' it was, even her crinoline seemed to rustle with apoplexy as she stood facing them all: Hudson, Hicks and Vasquez, Maggie Brown and husband John, Lord Melbourne (upon whom she fixed a most reproachful glare) and young John Brown, who stood with a steaming kettle about to attend to the making of tea.

'Your Majesty,' said Melbourne, leading a great show of bowing and curtsying and touching of forelocks and casting of eyes to the flagstones by all those present, 'what a truly unexpected pleasure, ma'am. To what do we owe . . .'

Victoria was looking past them all, to young John, who stood staring at her as though rooted to the spot, his eyes wide, the kettle in his hand.

'It was Dash,' she said finally. 'You saw Dash dying. You saw me cry for him.'

John Brown nodded mutely. His eyes shone.

'Ma'am, I'm so very sorry,' said Melbourne, 'this must have come as a terrible shock to you; your fondness for Dash was legendary and a thing of joy for all who witnessed it.'

'Thank you, Lord M,' said Victoria, 'those are very kind sentiments and indeed I shall be mourning Dash, but my immediate concern is for my country. For with this accurate vision of Dash's passing, young John has more than convinced me of his gift. John,' she addressed the boy, her voice soft, 'sit down, please. I need to know more. The vision you had before. That of violence. The men speaking German. Have you had it since?'

There was much shuffling and rearrangement as those assembled made space for John and the Queen to sit, Victoria opposite John.

'I have had the vision since, miss,' he said, 'but with no extra information to add. I'm given very little detail.'

From within her sleeve, Victoria produced a piece of fabric, offering it to Lord Melbourne and indicating that she wished it given to young John Brown, who accepted it.

'Do you know who this belongs to, John?' said the Queen, 'whose handkerchief are you holding?'

'It belongs to your husband, miss. It belongs to Prince Albert.'

Victoria touched a hand to her mouth. It was true that the death of Dash had given her a new appreciation of John's gift and that she had been moved from her previously unassailable position of sceptic to something approximating belief, but that did not prevent her feeling shock, surprise, admiration when she saw that gift in action. For how could he know, if not via some psychic power?

A lucky guess? said a little voice – a little voice that could have been Albert, for she felt sure she knew how he would have reacted.

But the tree in her castle? Grieving beneath the tree in her castle? How could John Brown have known?

'Tell me, John,' she said, 'tell me what you pick up from the handkerchief.'

Taking the handkerchief, he pulled it through his fingers, as if to test it for quality. His eyes closed.

'There's great conflict within him, miss,' said John. His voice was small within the cottage, but his audience were rapt.

Victoria found she was holding her breath and let it out. 'Tell me more, John,' she said.

'Your Majesty,' interrupted Melbourne, pushing a hand through his hair then putting his fists to the table in order to have her ear. 'Is this wise?' he said, his voice low. 'Just as the eavesdropper hears no good of themselves, so the psychic tourist . . .'

She looked at him sharply.

'Possibly,' he amended.

'I need to know, Lord M,' she said, 'I need to know my Albert is all the man my heart tells me he is.'

'He loves you, miss,' said John. 'His love is like a force

that he feels within his chest and sometimes he feels it with such ferocity, why, it is like a pain to him sometimes, miss.'

Victoria shot a triumphant look at Lord M, who held up his hands and backed away from the table, pointedly casting his attention towards John, who was oblivious to anything else but that which was in his head, continuing now, 'but there is great conflict within him, miss. I sense a great fear . . .'

His hands were fretting with the handkerchief. Victoria found herself wondering whether or not Albert would miss it. '. . . great fear and . . . doubt. He feels doubt, miss, as though he were being torn in many different ways at once.'

But we are! she thought. That is our destiny; to be torn between our duty to ourselves, our duty to our family our duty to our country, to God. Of course we are torn . . .

'He thinks of destiny. He fears it. He feels the pain of it with the same passion and strength that he feels for you and his children.'

'His child,' corrected Victoria.

'No, miss, his children.'

Victoria was confused. Her eyes went to Maggie Brown, who addressed John. 'John, love,' said Maggie, 'Her Majesty and the Prince only have one child, a little girl.'

John shook his head no. 'There is another baby,' he said and now he pointed towards the Queen. 'It's inside you, miss.'

All of a sudden Victoria felt frozen somehow. It was as though the world about her receded until there was only her and, at the end of a long tunnel, the young John Brown, his eyes closed as his hands worked at the handkerchief.

'It can't be,' she heard herself say. Her hands went to her belly and in that moment she knew that the boy spoke the truth. So soon! Her heart sank.

'It's a little boy, miss,' said John Brown.

Somebody in the room said, 'Oh my goodness,' and Victoria realised that it was her and that she was having difficulty in catching her breath.

'Are you sure, John?' she heard Maggie Brown say and was grateful for it, the question puncturing the shock that had descended over her in a black cloud.

'Aye, I'm sure, mother,' said John Brown. 'It's a boy, an heir to the throne of England, and it's what he fears most.'

'What *who* fears most, John?' asked Maggie.

Victoria felt unsteady. Her hands gripped the table edge.

'Prince Albert. I sense that he fears a male heir. He fears it more than anything. For he knows that it is the road to darkness – to death.'

XXIII

Nine months later
A safe house, London

The cabal had met to wet the baby's head, Stockmar and Conroy drinking whisky, Leopold raising a glass of offal and casting a sideways glance at his sister, who preferred tea.

Once, she, too, would have drank offal with gusto, he thought, now she preferred tea. *Tea.* He felt a moment of contempt. For over a century she had been fearsome and feared. Now she crawled towards her twilight years, with shame surrounding her. She felt shame because she had been unable to provide a male half-breed of the Baal. Instead she had given them Victoria and their plans to ascend to the throne had to wait a generation, until such time as they had their male heir. Instead of fighting the shame, though, the Duchess allowed it to consume her, and as a result she was little more than a husk – a *tea-drinking husk* – barely able to maintain her human self. And she had placed too much faith in her ambitious, impatient comptroller.

Even so. This day was not for lamenting the failures of the past; instead they were assembled to toast the success of the future.

'At long last our kind will sit at the very apex of power,' announced Leopold, banging down his empty goblet of offal, 'A son is born to Victoria and the Baal has its heir: Albert Edward, next in line for the throne of the greatest empire in the world. A half-breed. A child who will be tutored and coached in the ways of the Baal, and will understand and embrace his destiny, who will put in motion the wheels of mankind's greatest catastrophes. Men will suffer and our kind will *thrive*.'

'Hear, hear,' said Conroy.

Stockmar placed his glass to the table. 'May I ask,' he said, 'to whom the task of mentoring the boy will fall? In most cases one might expect the father – but in this instance . . .'

'Albert is a good man,' said the Duchess. The room froze. Not only was it rare these days for her to speak. But to say such a thing . . . !

Conroy sneered.

'My dear, this isn't quite what we want to hear,' said Leopold, humouring her.

'I have spent much time with Albert of late,' said the Duchess, 'and his talk is never of his destiny, or of his lineage. It is of love, and change. These subjects have become dear to Victoria's heart also. Your half-breeds have a conscience, my lord,' she smiled.

'*My* half-breeds,' exploded Førse. 'Victoria was *your* issue. You and your useless, philandering Duke.'

'A female, isn't that right?' said the Duchess, 'lacking the power of the male? Yet in Albert we see no evidence of that power. Is the Prince's father, your brother, Ernest, forced into shame as am I?'

'*He* is not *weak*.'

'Nor is he strong.' The Duchess became her demon self, and brother and sister glowered at one another for a long moment, then the Duchess lowered her eyes and once more withdrew.

Leopold resolved into his human shape.

'This being the case that Albert seems resistant to his calling, he must be reminded of his duty. Conroy, Stockmar and I shall see to this.'

'What if he is strong – if he cannot be persuaded?.'

'Then with regret, we would have to kill him; Victoria too. It is the only way we can sure that those closest to the Heir serve our interests.'

'You would not!' snapped the Duchess.

'My dear,' said Leopold, coldly, 'I will kill anything – human, half-breed or demon – that goes against the interests of the Baal. Do I make myself plain?'

For a moment, she seemed about to say something, then once again withdrew.

'Before we plan Albert's fate, two more orders of business. Baron . . .'

'Yes, my Lord,' said Stockmar.

'You are to contact the succubi. Once again they are to be tasked with eliminating the Protektor, Brown. Inform them that they are fortunate to be entrusted with a second chance, and that they must not fail this time. They should be informed that Melbourne is a problem for us also . . .'

'Yes, my Lord.'

'Now,' Leopold addressed Conroy, 'your task.'

Conroy bristled a little. 'Perhaps, first,' he said, 'we should talk about what I am owed. The powers you spoke of bestowing upon me, so that, I, too, may become one of you.'

'Indeed that was my undertaking,' said Leopold, 'and it shall be so. But, first, this business that must be taken care of.'

Stockmar smiled a little and Conroy regarded him with contempt. *Stockmar,* he thought, content to be a mere lapdog. Wishing nothing more than to serve. He was pathetic.

He turned to Leopold. 'Then tell me,' he said, 'what is it you would have me do?'

'The Baal needs control of Parliament. As we gain control of the monarchy we need to see to it that the monarchy remains in control. All this will be for nothing if the monarchy were to be weakened by reform. You are to see to it that Parliament becomes sympathetic to our needs and remains in that position.'

Conroy smiled and said, 'And do you have a plan for how this might be achieved? Blackmail? Financial inducements?'

'Both of which are methods that appeal, but neither are as fool-proof as I would like,' said Leopold. 'I have in mind another procedure.'

'And what might that be, my lord?' asked Conroy.

'Revenants, Conroy. You shall be using revenants.'

XXIV

Five weeks later,
the grounds of Windsor Castle

Late December, the night was cold and their breath billowed before them as they walked together, arm in arm: Albert, in his top hat, his leather boots, his tunic buttoned up tight; Victoria wearing her black bombazine dress, over it a long woollen coat buttoned up tight, her bonnet keeping the cold from her head; behind, a respectable distance away, followed two footmen in black leather shoes, white stockings, frock coats and white wigs; in all, the four of them looked like ghostly figures haunting the lawns of Windsor Castle, upon which a low fog had settled, that rippled on the ground like an expanse of foaming water.

Victoria was fully recovered after the birth of her second child, which had arrived on 9 November 1841, born at Buckingham Palace.

'It is a boy, Your Majesty,' Dr Locock, had said solemnly, and he'd proffered the slimy infant for the Queen to see, so that she might inspect that which determined his gender, before turning him slightly and holding him so that the Duchess should also bear witness.

'Oh, Victoria,' said the Duchess. Her hand went to her mouth and her eyes were wet with tears of joy, 'a boy. You have given us an heir.'

'Yes, Mama,' said Victoria, who had expected nothing less; indeed, had been certain of a male since that day in the cottage when John Brown informed her of the impending birth. Or, at the very least, when she discovered that she was indeed pregnant, for it was at that moment that any lingering doubts she had about young John Brown's psychic talents were for ever dispelled.

Which left her expecting to give birth to a son.

While, with a terrible sense of foreboding, simultaneously dreading it. For she had reached for the hand of Albert and she wondered about other things John had said – that for Albert the birth of a male heir would change everything; that he dreaded it above all.

Why?

Because there he was: the male heir, the future king of England. Albert Edward they called him, though he would always be known to them as Bertie.

'How was I this time?' she had asked Albert.

'This time,' he said, 'you were far better behaved. The room was only briefly scandalised by your language. Two arsecheeks and a cocksnot, wasn't it, Duchess?'

'Albert,' chided Victoria's mother, laughing and blushing at the same time, 'I do believe you are a caution.'

Albert took both of Victoria's hands, leant in to kiss her and she inhaled the smell of him. 'And you, Victoria,' he whispered, 'you are a caution, too. For I do not believe that any woman was ever braver or suffered with greater fortitude than that which I have just witnessed.'

He always knew just what to say, she reflected now, strolling with him. She breathed in the crisp air gratefully, enjoying the cold of which she was so fond. Indeed, it was a point of much frustration among the staff, she knew, that she insisted on open windows in her residence and though her ladies never gave voice to their discomfort, she was aware that they begrudged entering the Queen's icy chambers, even colder than the remainder of the Castle – which was saying much.

Meanwhile, Albert, of course, bless him, was far less enamoured of the cold and not so shy when it came to venting his frustration. He was prone to illness, he said, which was true (though Victoria secretly felt the fresh air would do him the world of good), thus preferred the comfort afforded by windows shut firm against the weather and a fire burning in the grate. How frustrated he had been when he first came to live in the household, she remembered, with a secret smile to herself, and had discovered that the simple making of a fire was a far more complicated procedure than he had been used to. In common with many of the domestic systems at court the preparation of the fire was handled by different departments within the house: the Lord Steward's staff were tasked with laying it, while it was the duty of the Lord Chamberlain to light it. Thus, as Albert discovered, much to his chagrin, if the two departments were not operating in harmony – and they never did – the fire might well remain at its ashes, and the Prince Consort would shiver and curse. As a result, he had taken it upon himself to 'bring some order to the house', and had done just that, consolidating the duties of the three departments as well as seeing to it that wastage and needless expenditure was avoided. Needless to say, none of this had won him additional friends at court. Certain of Albert's improvements had involved the cessation of long-held traditions while others had meant stopping privileges and benefits that the staff enjoyed: the distribution of 'used' candles, for example, when the candles were not used at all, but were simply replaced because it was the practice to do so. Not any more. Not under Prince Albert's steely gaze.

Victoria, who had grown up with the old systems and had neither cause nor desire to question them, had watched his progress in this area with concern – she was unhappy to see her staff disconsolate, even if, as Albert assured her, it was for the greater good – but also admiration and a feeling of having the great love she felt for him justified. She watched him and, she hoped, she learnt from him. She loved him, but she also felt for him a great respect, an admiration for the clear-eyed, determined manner in which he dealt with those problems that either vexed him, or for which he cared very much.

Having taken matters at the household in hand, Albert had turned his attention to another situation, that of the family's finances and it was this, he'd told Victoria earlier, that he wished to speak to her about. Quite out of character, he had suggested they go outside to talk, joking about the walls having ears, even though he would usually have gladly avoided a perambulation in the cold.

'It is refreshing, though, Albert, don't you think?' said Victoria, holding his arm with both of hers and putting her head to it, snuggling into him. The footmen might raise an eyebrow at such intimacy, she knew, but she didn't care. She wanted his closeness. This, for her, was like a walk in the park on a summer's day.

'It is most bracing, Victoria,' said Albert. 'I'm sure those parts of my body not suffering frostbite are finding it most rejuvenating.'

Normally a staunch advocate of that which was proper, he allowed her to burrow into his arm, she was delighted to note, making her happiness complete.

She laughed. 'I love the cold, you crave heat. I could spend all night listing our differences. What is it that brings us together, Albert?'

'Neither of us like turtle soup,' he said. 'Perhaps it is our shared distaste for this broth that provides the glue in our union.'

'Ah,' she laughed, 'yes, that could be it. Who on earth would want to eat a turtle anyway?'

'Quite,' said Albert, 'one always thinks of the head of a turtle and is put in mind of something most unsavoury.'

'Albert,' she admonished him with a clap on the arm, 'I do believe you are being vulgar.' She looked behind them to check on the proximity of the footmen, whose faces remained impassive. Some way behind them she saw a third footman, moving as if to join them. Further away, on the roadway leading to the Castle were two carriages, and she briefly wondered their purpose; indeed, thought about raising the matter with Albert, but had second thoughts, not wishing to spoil the moment.

'I am truly sorry, Victoria,' he laughed, 'sometimes I forget myself.'

They strolled on, in the direction of the maze. Victoria was thrilled to see that it had a dusting of frost, so that the bushes seemed to shimmer with light, that and the fog on the ground created something most beautiful to behold, as though the maze were a white castle, suspended in the night air.

'Victoria,' said Albert, most grave, 'there is something I need to discuss with you.'

'Yes, Albert,' she said, worried all of a sudden by the change in his demeanour, but she knew the moment was inevitable; she'd been expecting it since he suggested they take a walk.

They had reached the entranceway to the maze and went inside, the beautifully manicured hedges rising high above them, their layers of ice glinting. The fog swirled about their feet, higher in here than outside, thicker, compressed as it was by the corridors of giant topiary.

'As you know, I've been looking into your mother's finances,' said Albert.

'Yes, Albert?' They had reached the first corner and she stole a look behind her, seeing the two footmen. Distantly she wondered about the whereabouts of the third. She heard the sound of a horse and carriage, drawing nearer, perhaps returning from the Castle. And she ignored a tiny, gnawing nagging feeling she had that all was not right.

'There are many . . .' he was choosing his words carefully, '. . . irregularities.'

'I'm sure I don't know what you mean, Albert,' said Victoria, confused.

'Victoria,' he said, 'it appears as though there is money missing from your mother's funds. A not inconsiderable amount. Enough, in fact, to suggest that money has been going missing from the account for some time now.'

She caught her breath, stopped; she looked back to see the two footmen stop also.

'*Conroy*,' she gasped.

'Yes, Victoria,' said Albert, looking into her eyes, 'it would seem that Sir John is the person responsible for the removal of the funds.'

She felt a mixture of disgust, anger and elation, the latter because this development could mean only one thing. 'He must be dismissed,' she said fervently. 'He must be dismissed from the household at once.'

At that moment, there was a howl, a bloodcurdling animal howl such as Victoria had never in her life heard before, that ripped through her and chilled the blood.

She gripped Albert, who tensed, looking up as though something might have appeared at the summit of the hedge, then he looked into her eyes, said, quickly, 'There is something else I must tell you, Victoria. Something I have been keeping from you – that it has been my duty and destiny to keep from you, yet I find that I no longer can, for I love you too much to harbour this secret a moment longer . . .'

There was another howl. From where it came Victoria was not sure.

'What is it, Albert?' she said. Her hands went to his cheeks, and she found herself wanting but not wanting to know – because she knew that what he had to say would change things she wanted left alone; could destroy her happiness. But even so. 'What is it, my love?'

But before he could answer there came a high-pitched scream from behind them, then the sound of tearing, like a dead tree branch wrenched from the trunk. And Victoria and Albert turned – just in time to see the werewolf tear off the second of the footman's arms.

The beast had transformed from footman into wolf. He still wore his white breeches, which had split during his metamorphosis to reveal the muscled, hairbound legs beneath; his feet had burst the leather shoes and were paws now, tipped with deadly claws, as were his hands, the whole of his upper body bulging beneath the frock coat; his face was now a snout, teeth bared in a low growl, above it his wig remained in place.

The beast held the writhing torso of the other footman, whose last moments were, no doubt, spent first in shock as his colleague transformed from human into slavering wolf, then in pain as the wolf ripped his arms from him. The footman now dropped to the ground and fell forward, the fog billowing up around him. The wolf stood over him, put one foot to his back and dragged it back in the manner of a bull pawing at the ground – and tore the man's spine from him.

The wolf looked at Victoria and Albert. It snarled.

Then, it charged.

'Run!' shouted Albert, pushing Victoria ahead of him and shielding her, but too late, for the wolf had covered the distance between them in moments and just feet away, leapt, its legs pulled up, one paw thrown back poised to slice through Albert.

But it didn't reach the Prince.

It met Hudson instead.

Hudson, who at that moment had dropped into the maze, having jumped from the top of the hedge – a second early enough to save the Prince from certain death, a second too late to formulate an attack. For instead of besting the wolf with the advantage of surprise, he was able only to knock it off balance and the two of them went sprawling.

'Go, Your Majesty,' shouted Hudson. 'Run!'

Then, as they obeyed, Hudson scrambled upright and drew his sword, facing the wolf, which had regained its feet and now regarded him, snarling, flexing its claws, just the two of them on the pathway now.

'Good boy,' said Hudson, 'good doggie.' In his hand he twirled his sword so that it caught the moonlight, which reflected from its razor-sharp blade and barbed hooks. 'Got a tasty bone here for you,' he goaded the wolf, 'here, doggy, come and get it. Din dins.'

The wolf smiled.

'Fuck you, Protektor,' it said.

And leapt.

In one fluid motion, Hudson twisted, turning side on to the wolf so the target was small and slicing horizontally with the sword in a move that should have opened the chest of the wolf. But it had anticipated the action – just – and reached one paw to the ground, to pivot, coming in low, leading with its hind legs.

It made contact and Hudson felt the breath leave him, caught off balance and staggering back a few feet before regaining his stability, facing the wolf once more, which stood, glaring at him, then smiling as, without breaking its stare, it reached to pick off something from one of its hind paws – something that was snagged there.

Something that shone wetly in the dark. That led back from his hand – Hudson followed it with eyes – into Hudson's lower stomach, which gaped open, his intestine stretched taut from within it like a grotesque, bulging umbilical cord.

'Oh, God' said Hudson, staggering a little. He dropped his sword. His hands went to his stomach, to his intestine, which he grasped as though to try and reel it back into himself, and for a moment it seemed as if Hudson and the wolf might be about to enjoy a game of tug of war, Hudson's innards as rope. Then the wolf was winding in his end and Hudson was pulled towards him, moaning in pain, unable to prevent himself being dragged towards the jaws of the wolf.

'Here, doggy,' said the wolf as it pulled, 'time for din dins.'

Victoria and Albert heard Hudson's scream and clasped

one another in shock. They had been running, blindly, but now stopped, Albert took Victoria by the shoulders. 'Victoria, listen,' he said, 'we must take a hold of ourselves. The many hours we have spent in this maze, we know it better than anybody at Windsor, better than any wolf. He can track us if we make noise, but if we are quiet we can use our knowledge of the maze to our advantage and find our way to the exit.'

'No,' she said. 'They'll know that. It'll be just what they're expecting. There is another one, Albert, a third footman. I saw him talking to the man who transformed but have not seen him since. He'll be at the exit.'

'What makes you say that?' he said.

She looked at him, bemused, 'It stands to reason, Albert,' she said. 'If I was trying to catch us that is what I would do. Come. We need to use our greater knowledge of the maze, that's true. But not to find the way out. To outsmart our pursuer and double back to the entrance.'

'Victoria,' said Albert, grinning despite it all, 'you never fail to surprise, did you know that?'

She smiled and touched his cheek. 'I shall never forget your bravery back there, my dear. Ever,' she said. 'If it had not been for Hudson you would have met the wolf's claws that were meant for me. You were prepared to die for me.'

'Always,' he said.

'But not tonight, though,' she said, 'not here.'

She touched a finger to her lips, listening, hearing the thump of feet, the sound of the wolf slashing at the hedge. The wolf, she reasoned, having finished poor Hudson, would be moving through the maze making as much noise as possible in order to keep them moving towards the exit, where the second beast would strike. She assumed that it had many of the attributes of the wolf, which would include heightened sense of smell. However, it wasn't tracking them – his role was bush beater, nothing more – so had no need to use it. Even so, she untied her bonnet, took it off, then reached and removed Albert's top hat from his head.

'What?' he said.

'For the scent,' she said, tossing them to the ground, 'it might buy us some time. Come on.'

Listening carefully they made their way noiselessly along the pathway. From over to the right they could hear the wolf, noisy as before, but seeming closer now. Crouching low, they reached a junction and Victoria concentrated for a moment, conjuring the image of the maze in her head. Left. They needed to go left. She hesitated, trying to place the wolf in the maze but finding she was unable to do so. She looked at Albert. He nodded: take the risk. They scuttled quickly left, then right, then stopped in a new pathway, listening. Now they stood but stayed low, and then began to move more quickly, Victoria realising with a surge of relief that the crashing of the wolf was more distant, allowing herself to believe that they were going to reach the entrance and that the next howls they heard would be of frustration.

They went right. Then left. Still walking as fast they dared, Victoria with one hand holding her skirts, the other holding Albert's hand as he led the way, until they reached a pathway parallel to that which led to the entranceway.

Almost there. Almost there.

Then the hedgerow in front of them exploded, and they were covering their faces to protect themselves from a shower of leaves and branches, thrown off-balance as the first wolf burst through a hole in the hedge, its paws whirling like mechanical clippers, and was standing before them.

The wig, now, was somewhat skewwhiff on its head. It reached up to straighten it then pointed a finger at Victoria.

'Clever girl,' it said.

'Go, Victoria,' managed Albert.

But then the wolf was attacking, streaking forward, arms flailing and both Albert and Victoria were knocked backwards, Victoria, in particular, was flung several feet back, landing badly in a tangle of bombazine and woollen coat, the breath knocked out of her. For perhaps half a second she lay dazed, and in that moment steeled herself for the swipe of the assassin's claw.

But it didn't come. And then she was scrambling to her knees to see the wolf standing over Albert, who lay bleeding, half propped up against the hedge. As she watched, Albert twisted his head, saw Victoria on her knees and cried, 'Run!'

The wolf bent to Albert

'*No*,' screamed Victoria.

But then instead of striking Albert the wolf placed a paw to his neck, finding a pressure point, and instantly Albert's head lolled as he lost consciousness. Next the wolf was picking him up and tossing him over one shoulder.

It wasn't her they wanted, she realised with a sick lurch. It was him. It was Albert.

And she threw back her shoulders and with all her might screamed into the sky.

'*Maggie Brown!*'

XXV

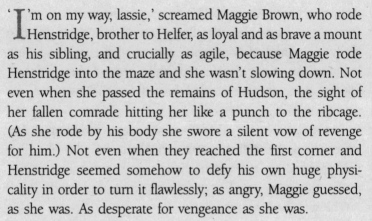

'I'm on my way, lassie,' screamed Maggie Brown, who rode Henstridge, brother to Helfer, as loyal and as brave a mount as his sibling, and crucially as agile, because Maggie rode Henstridge into the maze and she wasn't slowing down. Not even when she passed the remains of Hudson, the sight of her fallen comrade hitting her like a punch to the ribcage. (As she rode by his body she swore a silent vow of revenge for him.) Not even when they reached the first corner and Henstridge seemed somehow to defy his own huge physicality in order to turn it flawlessly; as angry, Maggie guessed, as she was. As desperate for vengeance as she was.

'I'm on my way!'

Maggie was cursing herself. Cursing Conroy for creating the diversion. Where was Hicks, she wondered? He would be inconsolable, she knew. She thundered along the pathway, around another corner. Here, the hedge had been destroyed.

'Maggie Brown,' came the second scream. The lassie. She was on the move. God, what was she up to? Was she trying to get herself killed?

'Where are you, Your Majesty?' shouted Maggie, urging Henstridge on. She knew the maze well. Heaven knows she'd tracked the two lovebirds through it enough times. Even so, she was wary of taking the wrong turn, leading Henstridge into a dead end, wasting precious seconds.

'Maggie,' came the shout in reply, 'I'm here. I'm here.'

'Well stay there, then,' Maggie called.

'They've taken Albert,' came the response, so desperate and so impassioned that Maggie Brown thought she would take it to her grave.

Above her appeared Vasquez, bow in hand, quiver at her back, making her way across the top of the maze by leaping across the pathways from one hedgetop to the next, neither losing her footing nor breaking stride, fitting an arrow into her bow as she ran, the ice detonating beneath her feet.

'Vasquez,' called Maggie, passing beneath the archer who leapt over the top of her, 'can you see her? Can you see the Queen?'

'I'm on it, sir,' said Vasquez, running the length of a hedgetop then, without pause, jumping to the next.

'I see her,' she called triumphant, 'I see the Queen.' Next, darting along the top of this hedge, she was addressing Victoria, 'Your Majesty, I have your back.'

'No,' screamed Victoria, out of sight, seen only by Vasquez, 'not me. Save Albert.'

'Yes, ma'am,' and Vasquez was on the move again, now in pursuit of the werewolf, leaping across the dividing hedges until she stopped suddenly having found her man.

In a blur of movement she snatched an arrow from the quiver and fitted it to the bow, which she raised, drew back the sinew with which it was strung then took aim, tracking her quarry.

'I have him, sir,' she called, 'permission to fire.'

'Do you have a clear shot?' called Maggie.

Vasquez paused. 'Negative,' she said.

Vasquez used arrows tipped with strychnine. If one of them

even grazed the Prince he would be dead within seconds. But the wolf was big.

And Vasquez was good.

The best.

'Take the shot,' commanded Maggie Brown.

Vasquez tensed.

'*No*,' screamed Victoria. Then Vasquez was unsteady on the hedgetop, it having been shaken from below, by the Queen no doubt. Her aim spoiled, Vasquez was throwing up her arms in a gesture of annoyance, turning to shoot a look of frustration and disbelief at Maggie Brown, who – at last – and with every muscle in her body screaming from having clung so hard to Henstridge as he'd taken them through the maze fast and strong and sure, came bursting from the exit and onto the lawns of Windsor Castle.

For a second she thanked their lucky stars that the huge maze shielded them from the windows of the Castle, although on second thoughts it hardly mattered. Anyone peering out would surely have kept quiet about what they saw for fear of dismissal on the grounds of being a drunkard or, worse, shipped straight to Bedlam as a madman.

For what they would have seen was the Queen, sprinting across the lawn with her skirt held in one hand, the other pumping as she ran – and by God the lassie was fast – in pursuit of a werewolf wearing a footman's wig.

It ran on all fours, and would no doubt have been even further ahead were it not for the burden it carried – the Prince consort – taking him towards one of two carriages waiting on the roadway. The one in front was a larger Clarence, while in the rear was an open, six-seater wagonette but each of them, Maggie saw now, was manned by a werewolf in a footman's wig. The driver of the Clarence was readying his horses, at the same time shouting encouragement to the wolf that bore the Prince, urging it to hurry.

As this was happening another wolf was clambering onto the wagonette behind, exchanging words with the driver, which pointed, drawing its comrade's attention to something approaching.

Hicks.

He was running from the direction of the other side of the maze, sword drawn. From his expression Maggie guessed he had stumbled upon the body of Hudson and instantly she was concerned. They were not brothers – not by blood – but they were blood brothers and Hicks could be reckless at the best of times.

The wolf on the wagonette reached for a bow.

Hicks, out in the open, blind with rage and grief.

Behind Maggie, Vasquez dropped from the hedgetop to the ground, landing badly, rolling.

Maggie reaching the Queen now.

'Your Majesty,' she called, and Victoria turned to see Henstridge bearing down upon her, the breath billowing from his nostrils, and she was just in time to ready herself for Maggie Brown, who in one smooth and fluid movement, scooped her up and deposited her behind her. Henstridge never broke stride.

'We must reach him, Maggie,' said the Queen, out of breath from running.

'We'll reach him, Your Majesty,' said Maggie Brown and she spurred Henstridge on.

The wolf on the wagonette fitted an arrow, drew back the string; in his sights, Hicks, still running.

'*Vasquez*,' screamed Maggie Brown but Vasquez must have been ahead of her because they heard the fizz of an arrow that cut through the sky past them, Vasquez firing at speed but without accuracy as the arrow missed its target, thunking into the side of the carriage instead. However, the archer swung towards them, sensing the new threat, and let off his own arrow in haste. It missed but grazed Henstridge at the flank, opening a wound there, neither fatal nor crippling, but painful enough that Henstridge rose up, whinnying and Maggie and Victoria were both thrown as Henstridge's legs buckled beneath him and he pitched to the grass where he lay, snorting in frustration.

The first wolf had reached the Clarence and bundled Albert inside. Victoria saw and scrambled to her feet.

'*No*,' she screamed.

And began running, sprinting across the lawn, her skirts held. Good lord, the lassie had guts to spare, marvelled Maggie Brown, regaining her own feet, drawing her two swords and taking off in pursuit of Victoria.

'*Go*,' she heard from the wolf at the first carriage, Albert safely aboard now.

'Yar,' roared the driver in response, whipping his horses into action. The carriage began to move.

'Albert,' screamed the Queen and her free hand was outstretched as she ran but she had no hope of reaching it now and instead she changed direction, heading for the second carriage. Maggie did the same.

Maggie had never before seen a werewolf bearing an expression of surprise, but that was precisely the look worn by the bowman on the wagonette which realised there were three people now bearing down upon his carriage. I'm a werewolf with a bow and arrow, his expression seemed to say, you're supposed to be petrified of *me*.

'*Go*,' he commanded the driver.

'Yar,' came the gee-up in response and the wagonette shot forward catching the werewolf off balance and sending him tumbling to the well of it.

Which gave Hicks just enough time to board, reaching the rear of the carriage and pulling himself up to it with barely a pause. Already the wolf was there to meet him, though, claws swinging and Hicks found himself adopting a defensive stance.

The carriage was picking up speed but Victoria reached it, arriving from the side and grasping one of the seat uprights. For a few seconds she was running at its side, the carriage moving too fast for her legs and Maggie feared she might let go and be pulled beneath the wagon wheels, but then she was, with great athleticism, swinging herself up and into the carriage, able to arrive unimpeded as a result of the battle that already raged on the wagon. Maggie, now, reached the carriage. She grabbed Victoria's outstretched hand and was pulled aboard.

In short succession, the driver screamed something at the bowman just as the bowman sliced Hicks across the chest, eliciting a scream of agony from the Protektor, who tumbled from the carriage and into the road in the same moment as the wagonette burst from the gates of Windsor Castle, moving at such a speed now that it tilted on to two wheels as it skidded out on to the highway.

'Hicks,' screamed Maggie Brown, who had seen enough Protektors die for one day, but as the wagonette moved out of sight she saw him scramble to his feet. Thank the Lord.

Then: '*Maggie.*' Behind her the Queen was screaming as the wolf moved towards her, teeth bared.

'Catch,' called Maggie, and she tossed a sword to the monarch, who caught it, span out of reach of the wolf's scything claws, and with her back to the beast struck back and upwards, spearing it through the belly so that the blade exited through the shoulder.

The wolf screamed.

In the Clarence up ahead the first wolf had been travelling with his head hanging out of the window, seemingly enjoying the sensation of the wind in its face. But at the sound of the scream it twisted around to stare back at the wagonette and what it saw made it howl in frustration.

Back on the wagonette the archer sank to its knees, and it howled a second time, a howl that rent the sky but that was cut short as Victoria took the broadsword in two hands and sliced off its head.

'*Bitch*,' screamed the driver, and it dropped the reins, twisting in its seat about to attack, when Maggie Brown opened its throat.

'That, my son,' she said, as it grasped its throat and gurgled, pitching forward off the carriage and into the highway, 'is no way to speak to the sovereign.'

For an instant the driverless carriage slowed. Then Maggie was in the driving seat, geeing up the horses and they were once again in pursuit, Victoria by her side.

'I prefer these odds, don't you, Your Majesty?' shouted Maggie Brown over the noise of the carriage wheels. 'Two against two. Plus, we have an advantage.'

'What's that, Maggie?' asked the Queen.

'We won't need to stop to do a wee up a lamp post.'

The Queen's laugh was dry and humourless, her focus on one thing only: getting Albert back.

'What are they?' she asked, 'these things?'

'This lot of hairy bastards go by the name Arcadians. Shape-changing deviants with a limited imagination, as they are only able to become wolves. Ever wondered where the werewolf myth came from, Your Majesty?'

Victoria shook her head no.

'Well if you had then you'd know. There are plenty of them about as it happens. Lots of them remained on earth plane rather than go home after the fall, being partial to the meat here.'

'Humans?'

'No, livestock. Many is the fox that has been blamed for an Arcadian attack. They only kill humans if a human gets in their way or, as is the case here, if they're employed to do so.'

Now the two carriages thundered along a straight stretch of highway, trees lining either side. Victoria saw the driver of the Clarence checking behind itself, then urging on his horses, wielding the buggy whip viciously.

'Can you catch the Clarence, Maggie?' asked Victoria, 'allow me to board it?'

Maggie Brown shook her head no. 'You've seen enough action for one day, Your Majesty. Now I have you safe you needn't think I'm letting you out of my sight. You can drive. I'll board.'

'Sorry, Maggie,' said the Queen, 'I never learned to drive. It's not a skill considered essential for a monarch. I'm going.'

'You are joking,' said Maggie. 'I mean, please, ma'am, put my mind at rest as to your intentions. Making the leap from one carriage to another is danger enough, without having to battle two of the creatures when once you've done it. You'll be killed for sure.'

Victoria shrugged. 'I'm not losing him, Maggie. Do you understand that?'

'Aye,' sighed Maggie Brown. 'Aye, I do.'

'Good. Now, do you have a small, sharp knife about your person?'

Maggie produced one that the Queen used to slice off the bottom of her skirts, leaving a ragged hem around the knees.

Maggie looked at the Queen, who grinned.

'Bloody thing was slowing me down,' she said.

They hurtled on. The wagonette, being so much more light-weight, was gaining, just a matter of yards between them now, and when the driver of the Clarence looked back its eyes widened in panic.

'Yar,' it screamed. 'Yar.' The buggy whip a blur in the air.

'Leave those horses alone,' screamed Maggie Brown, 'or I swear you'll be sorry.'

But if the driver heard he paid no attention; indeed, the first wolf had now put its head from the open window and was screaming at it to go faster, it, too having noted the proximity of the carriage behind.

They raced on, now reaching the great banks that surrounded the castle, and Maggie directed them onto the slope, coming up behind the Clarence.

'Bring me to its side, Maggie,' called the Queen, crabbing behind Maggie and bracing herself, ready to make the leap from the wagonette. Maggie shook her head in disbelief, for she knew two things, and the first was that she had vowed to *protect* the Queen from danger, not place her in even more peril, and that Lord Melbourne would most undoubtedly have kittens if he could see them now; and the second thing she knew was that the Queen was not to be dissuaded.

Now the wagonette was on the bank, above the Clarence, the two carriages almost side by side. The driver looked to its right and saw the Queen just feet away, ready to jump, and it howled in frustration, the buggy whip raised to administer another crack.

Victoria jumped.

She landed on the plate beside the driver, one hand snatching the buggy whip from him, swinging the broadsword with the other, catching the wolf on the side as it twisted to avoid the blow then rolled back on to the roof of the carriage. Where it crouched on all fours, about to pounce.

Maggie saw the muscles of its hind legs bunch. Saw the snout pulled back, brown teeth, red gums like flayed meat.

The Queen still off-balance on the driver's plate, sword down, a sitting duck.

The wolf sprang.

Just as Maggie rammed the Clarence with the wagonette, and the Clarence tipped on the slope, crashed to the ground and with a terrible pained cry from the horses, rolled on to its back. The wagonette barrelled on, Maggie pulling hard on the reins, saying, 'Oh God, oh God, oh God, oh Christ, oh God, oh Christ,' grabbing her broadsword, jumping down from the wagonette and sprinting back to the crashed Clarence, which lay capsized on the highway, its wheels still spinning, the two carriage horses tangled and thrashing at their restraints.

As she came upon it she saw the driver trapped beneath the roof, either dead or unconscious; Victoria, meanwhile, her face scraped but otherwise unhurt – oh thank the heavens –

was at the door of the carriage, screaming for her husband, yanking at the door, her broadsword on the ground beside her.

'Your Majesty,' said Maggie Brown breathlessly, arriving at the scene.

'Help me, Maggie, I can't open it,' said the Queen, still heaving desperately at the door and Maggie bent to lend her strength to the enterprise.

Just then there came a sound from the other side of the upturned carriage. A noise made by the far door opening then coming off its hinges and clunking to the ground. As one, Victoria and Maggie collected their swords and darted to the back of the wagonette in time to see the first wolf straightening, with Albert, still unconscious, held in front of it like a shield, one paw at Albert's throat, pressed hard.

'Stop,' it said, 'or I'll open his throat.' The fur on its leg was matted black with blood and as it edged backwards it limped a little.

Victoria stopped dead, face ashen.

Maggie sauntered over to stand by the side of the Queen.

'He won't do it, Your Majesty,' said Maggie. 'If he wanted to kill the prince he would have done it by now. They want Albert alive. We can take him. He won't harm your husband.'

The wolf smiled. 'Come on, then,' it said, 'take me, what are you waiting for?' It pretended to think. 'Oh? Is it because if you attack me you know that my last act on this plane will be to kill the Prince? Could that be it, I wonder?'

'You won't,' said Maggie.

'What would I have to lose, pray tell? Mrs Brown, your reputation precedes you. I'm hurt and weary from the chase. You would best me in battle.'

'I could let you live.'

The wolf snorted. 'I'm a demon. You've a duty to exterminate me, and that is what you will do.'

'I could make an exception in your case,' offered Maggie.

'And see to it that I live out my life in the depths of the Tower? No, I don't think so, Protektor. I would rather die here, with dignity and with the blood of the Prince on my talons.'

'What if we let you go?' said Victoria, 'here and now. Unhand the Prince and you may disappear into the night. You have my word on it.'

'As a marked Arcadian,' said the wolf, 'covered in disgrace, a price on my head for my failure? No, Your Majesty, I'm sorry. No, my answer still stands, I opt for attack.'

Maggie tensed, thinking: the wolf won't kill the Prince. He would take his chances in battle with Maggie and Victoria.

But then . . .

Maybe not.

'Your Majesty?' said Maggie Brown. 'I think he's bluffing. I think I can take him.'

'Uh, uh,' said mister wolf and he dug his claws into Albert's neck. In response, Albert's eyelids fluttered. Victoria let out a gasp.

'No,' she said, and her sword dropped.

'That's the spirit,' said the wolf. He grinned at Maggie, wolfishly.

Maggie's eyes narrowed. Could she have taken him? Really? Maybe so; maybe not.

So they watched, helplessly, as the wolf dragged Albert back to the wagonette bundled him in and climbed on to the driver's plate.

'I'll leave you to clear up the mess,' it said, and with a shake of the reins, was pelting away from them.

Victoria dropped to her knees, sobbing. Maggie bent down to her, clasping her by the shoulders. For some moments they remained that way.

'I want him back, Maggie,' said Victoria.

'Don't lose heart, Your Majesty,' replied Maggie. 'Whoever has him doesn't want to kill him, that much is clear. A ransom demand is my guess. Hicks and Vasquez and me. We'll find him. We three are the best there is.'

'Four,' said the Queen.

'Ma'am?'

'You've just gained a new member,' said Victoria. She stood, brushing herself down.

'Ah, Your Majesty,' said Maggie, 'I don't think—'

'You asked *me*, remember, at the cottage?'

'Aye, but not seriously . . .'

'I'm going after Albert, Maggie. I'd rather do it with you than on my own. You want to protect me – then *teach* me.'

'I'd need *a year* to train you as a Protektor.'

'You have a day,' she said. 'Oh, and Maggie?'

'Yes, Your Majesty?'

'I'm going to need weapons. Very, very sharp weapons.'

Part Three

'I, Demon Hunter'

XXVI

The General Cemetery, Kensal Green

It was dusk and an urchin sat on a low wall beside the imposing monument at the gates of the General Cemetery, swinging his feet and disturbing the mist that swirled about his tattered trouser legs and bare feet.

'Look sharp, Perkins,' murmured Quimby, *sotto voce,* as they approached the entranceway, the monolithic arch of Portland Stone that loomed over them in the fading light. 'He'll be wanting to extort money from us, the pint-sized blackguard.'

He recalled the last time he'd seen one of these little scruffs. This was in Pembridge Villas in Notting Hill. *Right outside his home*. 'Penny to look after your carriage, mister?' the child had said impertinently.

'A penny to look after my carriage?' Quimby had repeated, quite mystified. 'Why on earth would I give you any money to look after my carriage?' He really could not see what the deuce was to be gained from this exchange – the very definition of fruitless, or so it seemed – and so he added, 'Now be off with you . . . or I shall set my manservant on you and believe you me, if I do, it'll be the rock you perish on.'

The lad seemed to slink away. But the next day Quimby had learned exactly what he meant by looking after the carriage, which now bore a long scratch along its side.

Which was why, now, Quimby regarded the young boy with such suspicion. 'It's the latest thing among the young.'

But he was wrong. The lad, his clothes filthy, his cheeks black with soot, simply watched them pass through the spiked gates, under the arch and into the huge cemetery. There they found themselves on a wide path that seemed to bisect the graveyard, dotted as it was with stones and mausoleums. For some moments they walked in silence, comfortable in each other's company, just the shuffling, dragging sound of Perkins' prosthetic leg.

They had been able to arrest the leg's decomposition by means of adding to it drops of their potion and this was – from whatever angle you chose to regard the matter – a significant breakthrough for Quimby, Perkins and, indeed, the sum of man's medical knowledge (the discoveries he had made in service of his libido! marvelled Quimby on occasion). However, they had not yet achieved an effective means of securing Sugar's leg to Perkins' thigh, which meant the limb had a habit of dropping off at inopportune moments, such as the last occasion on which they had tried to turn the tables on McKenzie. On top of which there had been other occurrences, too; one recently where Perkins had been serving drinks to Quimby and a female guest of low birth and his leg had fallen off. Of course this had deposited poor Perkins rather rudely to the floor, eliciting a laugh from Quimby's guest. Furious at having his manservant ridiculed in this way, he had forcibly ejected her; then, as a special treat, allowed Perkins to take her into the basement to eat the impudent woman alive. That would be the last time *she* mocked the afflicted.

'What do you think, Perkins?' asked Quimby at last. He had been gazing around the cemetery as they walked, wondering how he might be guaranteed of a place here when he turned up his toes. Brunel had bagged a spot, apparently; Babbage, too. Was there a waiting list, he wondered, as with Blacks? Then again, Highgate had just been opened and there was talk of it being a *most* salubrious setting for one's interment . . .

'What do I think of what, sir?' said Perkins. There was an edge to his voice that Quimby had learnt to recognise was hunger. Perkins was liable to become most disagreeable when he was hungry.

Most disagreeable.

'The cemetery?' prompted Quimby, 'quite a construct, do you not agree?'

'Oh, very nice, sir.'

'Better than Père-Lachaise in Paris?' asked Quimby. 'It's modelled on Père-Lachaise, you see, so one would have thought they would have taken the trouble to improve upon their inspiration in the process . . .'

'Well, sir, I couldn't say, sir,' said Perkins, 'not having been to Père-Lachaise, sir.'

Quimby started. 'You've not been to . . . ? Have you even been to Paris, Perkins?'

'No, sir.'

'Oh,' said Quimby, then, thinking about it, supposed not. Why, after all, would Perkins have been to Paris?

They walked along for a distance. The leg brushing.

'Perkins?'

'Yes, sir?'

'I was wondering. Perhaps when we've killed the journalist and retrieved the photogenic drawing and discovered a way of affixing your prosthetic leg on a more permanent basis and perfected a formula that will finally cure you of your craving for human flesh . . . Then, well . . .'

'Yes, sir?'

'Well, perhaps we could take a trip to Paris, just you and me. How would that be?'

There was a pause. Quimby thought he heard a snuffle and decided he best ignore it. 'That would be grand, sir,' said Perkins at last. 'Thank you very much.'

'Of course. Wonderful. Little holiday for us both. Probably what we deserve, isn't it?'

'Yes, sir.'

Drag, drag, drag.

As they walked, Quimby caught sight of a young boy to his left, walking between the graves, drifting in and out of darkness like a wraith, so that Quimby at first wondered if he had imagined him but no, there he was again. Like the boy at the gate he seemed covered in soot. His clothes ragged.

There was a long moment of silence then they were close to the centre of the cemetery. Dusk had become gloom had become dark, and though their eyes had been adjusting neither of them were able to see very well. However at the entrance to the catacombs were, as had been arranged, torches, though the flame was absent and they were required to light them, which Quimby did, with some difficulty and cursing, until he and Perkins stood at the stone entrance, each with a flaming torch, ready to enter.

'It's for your benefit that we're here, Perkins,' whispered Quimby, 'I hope you know that.'

'Yes, sir,' whispered Perkins back.

'We don't have any of this palaver when I need food, do we? When I need to eat I just . . . what do I do when I need food, Perkins?'

'You call for me, sir?'

'Exactly,' still whispering. 'There's none of this creeping about in catacombs. So I hope you appreciate the sacrifice I'm making here. Now, listen, when we meet these low-downs, I want you to look as though you mean business. We need to raise some question about the supply of the product they may find unpalatable and refuse to answer. Our aim here is to drive down the price. Is that clear?'

'Yes, sir.'

'Good. Let's go.'

As he moved aside the wooden gate and took a step into the catacomb tunnel he looked to his left and saw a third urchin, this one sitting atop a gravestone, the heels of his bare feet tapping a drum beat on the stone, the mist seeming to bulge and blossom around him. But then Quimby and Perkins were out of sight, stepping into the catacombs where Quimby found himself inhaling a smell he had never previously encountered – he, a man who had watched his manservant eat human brains from his writing desk! – but no, this was a different nature of aroma – of earth, moist and dank and cloying, it seemed to lodge in the throat as they moved forward carefully along the low-ceilinged tunnel, moving underground.

There was the sound of scuttling ahead. Quimby glanced up and saw areas of the tunnel wall that seemed to be broken, as though for holes, and it occurred to him that the catacombs ran deeper and were more complicated than he could ever have imagined, and not for the first time he was most glad of Perkins' company.

The scuttling.

The flickering.

More than once, he called, 'Hello?'

For this, he thought – for this most unorthodox meeting place – the price was going down. It better had be.

Then they were upon it, the clearing, a circular area as though built in anticipation of some revitalised Hellfire Club gathering, with grey, dank stone rising up, up and away from the circle, portholes and window in the stone.

'Hello there, your Lordship.'

The voice seemed to echo from within the folds of shadow. Quimby wheeled within the circle, as did Perkins, both trying to locate the sound of the voice, chins raised, heads jerking this way and that.

'Burke?' said Quimby.

'No, it's Hare, sir,' came the voice, 'Burke's over there.'

'You have a companion, I see,' came a second voice.

'Good Lord,' said Quimby, thoroughly exasperated, 'show yourselves y'two blackguards, it's not as though your faces are mysteries to me.'

From one of the walls he saw a pair of legs appear. The torchlight danced and moved and he was afforded a glance of a man, Burke, he thought, sitting in one of the cubby holes, his legs dangling down into the pit, his arms folded in front of him.

'We need to negotiate,' said Quimby, uncertainly. Hare – where was Hare? He hoped Perkins had his wits about him.

He had a bad feeling about this. A very bad feeling indeed. He had come here hoping to negotiate better terms for the fresh corpses they needed to keep Perkins fed while they worked on a cure, but it was clear that Burke and Hare had something else in mind.

'We need to negotiate,' came the mocking echo from one of them, and there was a laugh in return. Shadows formed and reformed, the walls seeming to shift and move with them. Quimby, tired of the games, walked over to the wall where Burke had sat but when he reached it the man was no longer there.

'Your Lordship.'

He wheeled around, went again to the centre of the room where he joined Perkins, the pair of them holding their torches aloft to squint into the darkness, occasionally tensing when they saw a shadow shift, a movement in the darkness.

'I'm afraid, your Lordliness,' came the voice, startling Quimby a little, 'that Mr Hare and I will no longer be supplying you with corpses. Isn't that right, Mr Hare?'

The second voice came from the other side of the room.

'That is so right, Mr Burke. Rightily-right, indeed it is.'

'I see,' said Quimby, trying to assert his authority, 'then this meeting is at an end, and we shall take our leave. Quite why this information could not have been conveyed over a glass in the The Plough I fail to understand.'

'Because the meeting is not at an end,' came the second voice, Hare, 'we have further requirements . . .'

Good Lord Jesus Christ. For Quimby knew exactly what was coming. Blackmailed! *Again*.

'. . . for though we wish to discontinue the provision of cadavers for yourself and your . . . *man* . . .'

There was something about the way he'd said 'man'. Oh God. Did that mean . . . ?

'. . . we will be requiring the payment of funds to continue, lest we lose all sense of direction making our home from the hostelry one night and blunder quite by accident into a police station whereby, the ale having loosened our tongues, we reveal some of the gruesome goings-on at Pembridge Villas, Notting Hill, home to the estimable Lord Quimby.'

'And find yourselves equally culpable, man,' snapped Quimby.

'My Lord, don't take us so literal like,' mocked Burke, 'I dare say we might formulate a more sophisticated plan – one not quite so incriminating for us, that is – come the right time. The point, however, is this: either you pay, or you will find yourself opening the door to find Sir Robert Peel's men on your step. Am I right, Mr Hare?'

'Rightily-right, Mr Burke.'

Quimby held his flaming torch away from himself at arm's length, in the hope that neither of them could see him lean towards Perkins and from the side of his mouth whisper, 'Can you see either of them, Perkins?'

'No, sir.'

'Soon as you can, grab one.'

'Wouldn't do you any good, your honour,' said one of the voices.

Blast.

'Now,' came the other voice, 'there's one more thing, and then we can all be on our way.'

'What's that?' seethed Quimby.

'The revenant, your worshipfulness.'

Beside him there was a sharp intake of breath from Perkins.

'I don't know what you mean. What revenant?'

'The one standing by your side, my Lord.'

'It is clear to me that you have taken leave of your senses, man,' roared Quimby, 'for I don't have the faintest idea what point it is you're trying to make.'

'Your Lordship, we may be grave robbers . . .'

'The best . . .'

'. . . but we are not stupid, we have seen that which appears on the bench in your basement: jimson weed, belladonna, monkshood. A little bit of investigation and putting together of two and two to make four and well, it seems, your man-servant is a zombie, sir, a member of the living dead—'

'Yes, he is,' roared Quimby warningly, 'and dangerous, too.'

'Exactly, which is why we're taking him. Having been availed of the fact of his added strength, not to mention, obviously, his invulnerability, we feel he would be a most valuable addition to our operation.'

'I beg your pardon,' said Quimby indignantly.

There was a scuttling sound in the blackness.

The reply was steely. 'You heard, my Lord.'

'Sir?' said Perkins beside him, worried.

'You must be out of your mind, my friend,' said Quimby. 'I do not agree to this request.'

'It is not a request, sire,' said Burke, 'it is a *condition*. Either we leave with the revenant or we leave alone and head straight to the peelers . . .'

'. . . or at the very least to formulate a plan on how best to approach them,' corrected Hare.

'Is that clear, your Lordship? We'd like him now, please.'

'Sir?' said Perkins.

Quimby ignored him. 'And if I refuse?'

'Refusal's not an option.'

Quimby snorted. 'Refusal is indeed an option. Answer the

question, man. What is your course of action should I reject your demands?'

'I mean to say, sir,' came the voice from the darkness, 'that refusal is not an option should you wish to avoid the gallows . . .'

Quimby swallowed.

'. . . for either we leave here with your manservant or leave on our way to the peelers. Your choice, sir.'

'You must think me a fool,' said Quimby, 'if you do that you have nothing. No revenant. No income. Nothing but the glee of seeing me hang.'

There was a chuckle in the shadows. 'I should imagine that might well be pleasure enough,' said the other voice, 'isn't that right, Mr Burke?'

'Certainly, Mr Hare, his Lordship's lack of grace concerning some of our more recent cadavers has been most irksome to behold and I must admit I have found myself wondering whether a lesson in manners might be in order.'

'This is what it boils down to, is it?'

'Your Lordship's disposition towards us leads us to believe that you may not honour our agreement; indeed, that you might attempt to employ the revenant against us. Therefore we're of the belief that we need the revenant to continue with the scheme. If you follow me.'

'I'm to give you my manservant in order that you should feel more secure when you're blackmailing me?'

'In the absence of collateral, sir, yes. What is it to be?'

'This beggars belief,' sighed Quimby almost to himself. He looked at Perkins who looked imploring in return.

'They leave me no choice, Perkins,' he said.

'Sir?'

Quimby's shoulders dropped. They had him over a barrel. Either he give up Perkins or face an appointment with the hangman.

There was a long pause.

'I shan't go, sir,' said Perkins, trying to sound firm.

'We don't have any choice.'

'Sir.'

'Look, it may only be for a short time, until I can get this sorted out.'

'Hurry it up, Mr Quimby, we don't have all night,' urged Burke.

Quimby sighed hard, unable to meet Perkins' eye.

'We grow weary of the wait, sir,' said Burke – or was it Hare? – warningly. 'Either you hand over the gimp now or we go to the peelers straight away.'

Quimby decided. He took a deep breath. He wondered what on earth had possessed him, because instead of handing Perkins over to the men, as all reason and logic dictated that he should do, he said, 'Firstly, you're not taking my manservant. He stays with me.'

Beside him, Perkins let out a gasp of relief.

'And secondly,' added Quimby, 'don't you ever call him a gimp again.'

There came a dry laugh in reply.

'Then you leave us no choice, your Lordship. Mr Burke, let us repair to the peeler house at once.'

There was a scraping, dragging sound as Burke and Hare extricated themselves from within whatever hiding places they had been lurking.

'Look . . .' started Quimby, 'can't we talk . . . ?'

His words echoed in the circle.

'Hello?'

Then he was dashing to the sides, holding the torch up to the cubby holes. But there was no sign of Burke. No sign of Hare.

'Blackguards. Just like their fathers,' raged Quimby, moments later, as he and Perkins trudged, with great despondency, back through the catacombs in search of the exit.

'Not a shred of loyalty between them,' he added, then lapsed into baleful introspection.

They walked, their torchlight describing black patterns on the walls, the only sound that made by the dragging of Perkins' leg.

'Why does this happen to me?' wailed Quimby a few moments later, breaking the silence. 'I really do have the most confounded luck. Blackmailed by a guttersnipe journalist and now this.'

'Do you think they'll make good on their threat, sir?' asked Perkins.

'It's not a chance I intend to take, Perkins,' said Quimby, sadly, 'All I want around my neck is a silken scarf or the long, shapely legs of an athletic lady of high birth and low morals. I have no desire to try the hangman's noose for size. I can't possibly risk it.'

'So what are we going to do?'

'I am going to pack up and leave Pembridge Villas. Percy's widow is travelling on the continent. I can find her, I suppose, and she's apt to welcome me with open arms. Or open something at least.'

'Leave Pembridge Villas, sir?' said Perkins incredulously.

'I see no other option.'

'And what of me, sir?'

'You, Perkins, may do as you please.'

'Then it pleases me to stay with your Lordship.'

'Oh,' said Quimby. 'Oh, that really is rather kind of you, Perkins, it is most appreciated.'

They lapsed once more in wordlessness – the comfortable silence of two friends.

'Perkins,' said Quimby after some moments, 'one of these days we're going to catch those two, I promise it, and you may feast upon them while I lurk in the background chuckling maniacally.' He warmed to the thought.

They had reached the exit.

'I would certainly enjoying seeing them as foodstuffs, sir,' said Perkins. 'In fact, I was just thinking about baking one of them in pastry to make . . .'

'Perkins,' interrupted Quimby, 'if you're about to tell a joke about making Hare pie then I strongly suggest you think again before I change my mind and hand you over to them gladly.'

The door pushed open with a screech like that of a mating fox.

'Sorry, sir, just trying to lighten the mood.'

'Yes, well, don't, because right now I'm—'

They stopped dead.

In front of them in the cemetery, lit by a full moon, stood a group of children numbering about twenty: urchins, chimney sweeps, waifs and strays, a dirty and ragged bunch. They stood in silence and were stock still, most with their arms by their sides as though standing to attention. Each wore the same expression: a blank, glassy stare, a disquieting half-smile.

One of them stepped forward, holding something that he threw – something that landed with a thump at Quimby's feet.

He looked down.

Burke would have been staring back at him if his eyes hadn't been rolled back into his head. He would have been smiling if his mouth wasn't wide in a final scream, his tongue lolling from his mouth. Crusted blood covered his mouth and chin, and the skin of his neck was tattered and torn where the head had been hacked off.

There was a giggle from the children. Quimby looked up in time to see another urchin step forward. This one held a second head by the hair and, like the first, tossed it forward.

Hare. Eyes half closed, mouth full of dirt as though in his final agony he had taken a bite of the sod.

'Oh dear,' said Quimby.

XXVII

'At last,' managed McKenzie, struggling to capture his breath, 'at bloody last.'

Egg, his comportment very much that of a beleaguered man, dropped his shoulders and sighed, having finished running, there was nowhere else to go. He had reached the end of an alleyway off Dean Street, inside which the scent was stomach-churning, rubbish and excrement strewn about it, and was almost dark.

Neither man paid the aroma much heed, however, both of them recovering from the exertion, a chase that had taken them halfway across the city, or so it seemed. Egg, the much younger man, had nevertheless been unpleasantly surprised and thus caught unawares by the endurance and tenacity of his pursuer and now the two of them stood as equals in exhaustion, both of them catching their breath, their hands on their knees.

McKenzie, looking up, saw an urchin at the alley entrance, watching them. He waved the boy away, then turned his attention to Egg.

'You've led me a merry dance, lad,' he said, sweeping his hat from his head and wiping perspiration from his brow with the back of his hand. His whiskers dripped wet; his thick winter coat felt heavy with it. Damn the boy.

'I've not wanted to be found, sor,' said Egg, still breathing heavily. He was as unfit as McKenzie or so it seemed. The reporter made a mental note to report this fact to the fellow drinkers at the Quill & Pen on Fleet Street the next time he paid that particular hostelry a visit.

'Well, it grieves me to say you've no choice in the matter, boy, you've set the ball rolling. I wouldn't be much of a journalist if I wasn't to try and follow this story now, would I?'

Egg looked up at the back wall of the alley. It loomed over him, streaked with something he took to be human effluent: too sheer to climb, too high to jump up to, making escape nigh on impossible – using that route at least. Then his eye was caught by something else. For high up on the wall sat a young boy, cheeks black with coal dust, staring impassively down at him.

Egg wondered how the boy had reached so high. He must be a child belonging to one of the adjoining houses, he thought, who had crawled out of a window.

Glancing back at McKenzie, who stood with his hands to his knees, near doubled over as he caught his breath, Egg then turned his attention back to the little boy. 'You must be careful up there, my child,' he called to the waif, whose expression did not change in response. 'That's a very high wall to be sitting on, you know.'

The poor child probably cleaned chimneys for pennies, thought Egg. Indeed, he had heard of some of the cruelties visited upon these urchins; that they were apt to fall asleep up a chimney, they were worked so hard; or that, worse, they would become stuck in the chimney, unable to move up or down, and that in these situations it was common practice for the owner of the sweep to light a fire beneath the poor mite, which would, of course, do for him, nine times out of ten. Looking at it like that, supposed Egg, well perhaps the young 'un was better off at the top of the wall and certainly in no more danger than he might have been at street level and, what's more, was probably far more used to heights than Egg himself.

'Your concern for the lad does you credit,' rasped McKenzie, who had drawn closer, 'now how about you and I talk?'

'I've nothing more to say, sor. They've already tried to kill me once.'

'Yes, and your continued silence plays right into their hands.'

'Why is that, sor?'

'Because you haven't gone public yet. They want to get to you before you tell other people. The only way to stop them is to come with me. I can protect you. Help me with this, because if we can verify some of this information you've so far imparted, we have a huge story on our hands. A huge story, Egg. Have you any idea how big this could be?'

Egg was now flattened against the back wall, intimidated by McKenzie's greater physical presence. With his back to the brick he looked upwards as though the geography of the barrier might have changed and steps might have magically appeared.

They had not. What Egg did see, however, was that the first urchin had been joined by a second. Over McKenzie's shoulder he saw two more of the children at the mouth of the alley. As he watched, two more appeared. Then more.

'Egg,' continued McKenzie, 'if what you've told me about the Queen is true this could be the biggest story of the age, with me its author and you its source. We'd be rich men, Egg, and famous. The talk of the town, the toast of society. Don't you want that? Or do you want to live out your life mopping the entrails of vermin from rat pits?'

'Sor?'

'Yes.'

'I think you'd better look behind you, sor.'

Something in Egg's voice, the man's eyes, convinced McKenzie he was not the intended victim of a ruse and he turned.

Behind him, in the width of the alley, stood a number of urchins. More of them, he could see, were entering the alley. They moved in a mechanical, robotic manner.

Beside Egg, feet slapped to the cobbles as sweeps dropped from the wall beside him. One, two, three, four of them.

Until Egg and McKenzie were surrounded.

XXVIII

'Perkins?'

'Yes, sir?'

'You have my permission to eat these chimney sweeps.'

'Sir?'

'Go ahead, man. Fill your boots.'

'But sir – they are but children.'

Quimby looked at him, disbelief on his face. '*So?*'

'We cannot kill children, sir.'

'Perkins,' said Quimby from the side of his mouth, deciding now that diplomacy might be the best way to deal with his reluctant manservant, and keeping his voice down, 'these are feral children, obviously, and little better than animals. I know full well that you are hungry . . .'

'Famished, sir.'

'Quite. Thus, here is your chance to kill two birds with one stone. Sate your appetite and get us out of this most unfortunate situation.'

The children, stood, motionless, looking almost cherubic at, though Quimby was struck by the proximity of angelic to diabolic – how their smiles, that had at first seemed so benign, were in fact blank and pitiless.

'I cannot eat a child, sir.'

Quimby wondered whether or not this was the best time to tell Perkins about the provenance of some of the more tender meat he had been enjoying of late. There had been a particular batch that Perkins had praised for its distinctive 'smoked' taste – a consignment Burke and Hare had called the 'Lazy Sweeps'. No, decided Quimby, it was not the best time to reveal that to Perkins. Perhaps that could wait until later.

If there *was* a later.

'I'm not sure these are actual children,' argued Quimby, 'after all what normal child could do *that* to a man?'

To illustrate he put his toe to the head of Hare, which rolled slightly on the grass, earth spilling from its mouth.

'But they are children all the same, sir, and children under a spell or so it seems.'

Quimby took a deep breath, ready to tell his manservant in no uncertain terms that if he did not neutralise the youthful threat – preferably by tearing at least one of them limb from bloody limb to teach the rest of them a lesson – then he had better start looking for employment elsewhere, speaking of which, did he know of any other members of the nobility likely to welcome the walking dead into their home? No. So plenty of luck finding suitable employment elsewhere. Now kill one of these children before I lose my bloody temper . . .

And Quimby was on the point of saying all this, when there came a voice.

'Gentlemen,' it said. 'Do not be alarmed.'

A figure moved forward. A man who wore a three-cornered

hat and whose mouth was covered by a black scarf. He had long hair, Quimby saw, that hung in a ponytail from beneath his hat.

'These delightful children mean you no harm,' said the man, 'and neither do I. Quite the opposite, in fact. We all have your best interests at heart. I had rather hoped our gifts to you might have convinced you of that.' He indicated the severed heads of Burke and Hare. 'A little offering,' he added, 'a gesture of goodwill in the hope of gaining your trust, or at the very least taking the first step towards doing so – towards what I hope may well be the beginning of a fruitful relation-ship. For I am hoping that we may be able to help one another, you and I.'

Relieved that his own head was not about to join those on the ground, and able to savour the fact that Burke and Hare had very much been put out of his misery, still Quimby was nevertheless wary, saying, 'Whatever manner of help it is you require, I suggest an introduction might be a good start to the relationship.'

'Indeed,' and the man reached to pull down the scarf that covered his face. 'Please allow me to introduce myself,' he said. 'My name is Sir John Conroy.'

XXIX

'Conroy's "*gone*"? What do you mean, "*gone*"?'

Queen Victoria glowered at Maggie Brown and Lord M, both of whom were afraid, very afraid. For without having slept since the terrible events of the night, stopping only to be seen by Dr Locock, to whom she'd offered the excuse that she had fallen out of bed, and who did not, of course, question her explanation, Victoria was already on the warpath.

It was her first day at work, and life in the Protektorate was never going to be quite the same again.

The Prime Minister and Maggie Brown had been summoned to the Green Drawing Room first thing. If asked, Lord Melbourne might have said that he expected to see the Queen in a state of shock, worrying and fretting, with occasional outbursts of temper; in short, it was the handkerchief queen that he expected to see in the drawing room that morning.

Maggie Brown, of course, had a better idea of how to expect Her Majesty, having been given a glimpse of her resolve at the roadside, just a few hours earlier. Yet even she, had it been enquired of her, would have admitted that she had anticipated the sovereign to be a little more compliant and acquiescent in the cold light of day. In fact: 'I think we can probably talk her out of it,' she had told Melbourne as they made their way to the drawing room that morning, 'she was determined last night, all right. Matter of fact, I've rarely seen anyone so resolved, but even so, I think we can appeal to her sense of duty. She has a country to run after all.'

Melbourne was more concerned with Maggie's attire. For in order to explain her presence at court she was required to look as though she belonged there, as though she spent long hours alone with the Queen, in fact, and so after considering and discarding several suggestions as to an alias, among them gardener, cook, cleaner and hairdresser, they were eventually forced to alight on Maggie's least favourite option, nevertheless, the most sensible one: lady-in-waiting.

So it was that for the first time in living memory – perhaps even in her life – that Maggie Brown, needless to say not without much cursing and resentment, wore skirts.

'You look a delight, Maggie,' Melbourne had said as they walked.

'Fuck off,' glowered Maggie in reply.

'Mrs Brown, such language! And hardly becoming of one of the Queen's trusted ladies-in-waiting. Really, if you're to pass as one you must act as one.'

'I'll must act a dagger into your ribs if you keep this up, Melbourne,' she growled.

He smiled. 'At least you have a head start in matter of behaviour,' he said. 'It occurs to me that you must be quite an expert in Royal etiquette, having spent so much time watching over the Queen.'

'Well, I know how to pour a cup of tea, and I can talk like I've got something lodged in my rectum, if that's what you mean,' said Maggie.

'Correct me if I'm wrong, Maggie, but I happen to think there's a *little* bit more to it than tea and rectums. And if you're to be a convincing lady-in-waiting you'll need to behave in the correct way at all times.'

'Shove it up your jacksy, Prime Minister.'

'Starting with your gait, Maggie. Really, you know, this is court, not the heathen colonies and correct me if I'm wrong but is that a broadsword in your skirts or are you just jolly pleased to see me?'

'You didn't expect me to come unarmed, for God's sakes,' she hissed, 'there was an attempt on the lassie's life last night.'

'Was there?' Melbourne became serious. 'Do you think so?'

'Well, no, as it happens, I don't. You ask me, those beasts were after Albert and Albert only.'

'And you think a ransom demand is their objective?'

'Aye, in the first instance, but more to the point that's what we should let the lassie believe.'

'For what reason, Maggie?'

'Because there's likely to be more to it than meets the eye.'

'And what might that be?' said the Prime Minister.

'Misdirection. So that we're looking in the direction of the burning stable while he's ransacking the house behind us.'

'Quite, quite,' said Melbourne, deep in thought. 'There would seem to be more expeditious ways of achieving the same effect. How about this? The Prince is a great reformer – a great reformer with the monarch's ear. He has the plight of the workers at heart and the ability to influence the monarchy – which is not such a good combination for those who would like to see an uprising.'

'Remove Albert, remove the likelihood of pacifying the masses . . .'

'Quite.'

'Increase the likelihood of revolt.'

'Exactly. And in the case of a revolution, who should be installed as leader? Why, he who orchestrated the rebellion, of course. Our very own Sir John Conroy.'

And then they were being admitted to the drawing room, where they awaited the Queen. And Hicks, who was installed somewhere in the room unbeknownst to Melbourne, made remarks about Maggie's attire for which he would no doubt pay dearly later on – and then the Queen was entering.

And talking to them.

No, in fact, she was talking *at* them.

And Melbourne began to understand quite what Maggie Brown had meant when she spoke of the Queen's determination and resolve, while beside him Maggie Brown realised she had rather underestimated the Queen's determination and resolve and now felt a little silly for not having predicted that it would have increased in the time since Albert's disappearance, rather than diminished.

And the two of them were having to face up to the answer to the Queen's opening questions, which had been, 'Where is he? Where is Conroy?'

Lord Melbourne had cleared his throat. 'I'm afraid we don't know, ma'am,' he said, 'He's gone.'

'What do you mean, he's gone?'

'Ma'am, it would be insulting your intelligence were I to express it any more euphemistically than that. All we can say at this stage is that it appears Sir John has disappeared for good. Clearly his preparations for departure were intended to partly distract the Protektorate, then he used the cover of the kidnap to flee.'

Queen Victoria stared at Lord Melbourne for a long time. 'You were watching Conroy?'

'Yes ma'am.'

'And why was that?'

Maggie and the PM shuffled uncomfortably, neither replying.

'Lord M,' pressed the Queen, 'why was Sir John Conroy under surveillance?'

'Well, Your Majesty—'

'*When*,' she held up a finger to stop him, 'you specifically told me that you had no reason to believe Conroy was a threat. Why was he under surveillance?'

'Well, Your Majesty—'

'*Stop*, Lord Melbourne. I want you to consider your next words very carefully. For you and I have met at least once a day for some time now, and it may surprise you to learn this, but I know when you are lying to me, Lord Melbourne. Your nostrils flare slightly, did you know that?'

'I can't say that I did, Your Majesty,' replied Melbourne, his nostrils flaring somewhat.

'Then you had better ponder on your next words,' ordered the Queen, 'and I shall give you time to do so, for . . . Maggie.'

'Yes, ma'am.'

Victoria's voice softened. 'Firstly, let me say again, Maggie, how grateful I am for the actions of the Protektorate last night. How sad I am that it resulted in the loss of Hudson, who behaved with such bravery I can hardly relate. The condolences of the Queen go out to his family and I trust you shall see this sentiment relayed. I am placing Lord Melbourne in charge of seeing to it that his family are most generously provided for. Can I be sure my wishes will be carried out, Lord M?'

'Yes, ma'am,' said Melbourne, whose nostrils did not flare on this occasion.

'Secondly, Maggie, I would like to compliment you on your attire, which I think suits you.'

'Thank you, ma'am.'

'Though I think in order to carry off the subterfuge success-fully, you should perhaps be more discreet with the sword.'

'Yes, ma'am.'

'Thirdly, Maggie, now is the time to make good on your assurances of last night. Please, if you will, take me to the Quartermaster.'

They began to walk, first along the cavernous galleries of the palace, then moving into the smaller corridors, where there were fewer portraits and the light was less generous, and then deeper into the bowels of the castle, where there were no portraits, just grey, rough stone walls, and there was even less light, until they were walking along passages below ground, and there was no light apart from what which was provided by flaming torches placed at irregular intervals along the route. Maggie led the way, somewhat erratically. Unused to movement in the long crinoline skirts, especially at this pace, she found herself constantly in danger of tripping forward until Victoria, spotting her discomfort gave her a surreptitious lesson in skirt-hitching.

As they travelled down, deep down into the recesses of the palace, Victoria bade Melbourne speak (and stopped him, more than once, to assess the diameter of his nostrils), commanding that he apprise her of all that was known about activities of the demons, and, most importantly, what he knew of Sir John Conroy.

Which he did, in a fashion. In the sense that he told her that they suspected Conroy of being an inhuman; that they thought he might try to wrest power, perhaps by providing the spark to a revolution.

'And you allowed this man to stay in close proximity to my family? To live under my roof?' she said, curtly. 'When you suspected him not only of being a demon, but of plotting to overthrow the monarchy?'

'Your Majesty, there is an old military aphorism that contends one should keep one's allies close, but one's enemies even closer.'

'I see. So what you're telling me is that it is thanks to the rigorous application of an aphorism that my husband is now missing?'

'Not quite, Your Majesty. You see, Sir John was, after all, your mother's comptroller and private secretary. There was little we could do save to see to it that his influence was kept to a minimum.'

'And my mother? How is she?'

'As far as we know she is well, Your Majesty. Naturally she is concerned as to the whereabouts of Sir John.'

'Who, as far as we know, now has Albert?'

'We would have to assume so, ma'am, yes.'

'Why Albert?' she wailed. 'What is his role in all this?'

'We don't know for sure, ma'am,' said Melbourne, 'only that your husband was an enthusiastic supporter of those causes which might have undermined Conroy's scheme.'

Victoria stopped and wheeled around so that Melbourne almost bumped into her.

'Not *was*, Prime Minister,' she said, then turned and continued, following Maggie Brown, who tripped on, oblivious. 'Is. He *is* an enthusiastic supporter of reform. You, of course, are not. Perhaps you might feel a certain vindication that it may have been these tendencies responsible for his capture?'

'Ma'am, please,' protested Melbourne, 'I find that a most distressing implication.'

She caught herself.

'Then you must forgive me, Lord M, my emotions are high.'

Lord M bowed his head, placing the moment in the past.

They stopped.

'Maggie,' said the Queen, 'I do believe you must have led us down a dead end.' She indicated the stone in front of them.

Maggie tapped the side of her nose. 'The Quartermaster's work is highly secret, ma'am,' she said, reaching to a flaming torch upon the wall and pulling it, at which the stone wall began to move, revealing a flight of steps descending into blackness. 'Now, if you'd like to follow me.'

XXX

Old Nichol Rookery, the East End

None of them spoke as they moved along the streets, which became more and more filthy the deeper into the labyrinth they ventured: Quimby, Perkins, Conroy, the urchins – all making their way through the night, which seemed to close in on them. As did the streets, which became more and more narrow the further they travelled, malevolent buildings rising up either side of them, blocking out the moonlight, a thick, suffocating fug in its place.

Night air. The smog of the slum after sunset. Conroy, his eyes gleaming as he spoke, had warned them of it, covering his mouth with his scarf once more and telling them of how the night air might suffocate entire families, adults and children alike, their lungs screaming fruitlessly for oxygen amidst the poison that had crept into their room in lieu of air. Gulping, Quimby had found a handkerchief with which to cover his own mouth as they made their way through the ever-narrowing streets, to each side of them filthy black buildings and steps sluiced with running water that ascended to doorways and doors, which were closed like the windows – a miserly barrier to the deadly atmosphere that hung about the slum.

As they walked the only sound they heard was that of the slum dwellers behind their doors, arguing, fighting and screaming the night away – this night the same as any other – waiting for daytime to burn the noxious fumes and chimney smoke away. They listened to the hubbub and they kept their own counsel. All with their mind on other things: Quimby on his salvation; Perkins on eating; Conroy on . . . well, it beggared belief what that man had on his mind; and the chimney sweeps no doubt dreaming of warm soup and bread rolls and, going on recent evidence at least, perhaps the odd decapitation. They walked in what appeared to be a formation, surrounding Conroy, who towered above them in his three-cornered hat, nimbly picking his way through the ordure of the streets, comfortable and at home in the squalor. As though he were the landlord of it all.

'All of these children work in factories, or are sweeps, I take it?' asked Quimby, who had caught up with him, pushing through the urchins who formed his protective circle to be at his side for a moment.

'Absolutely not, no,' said Conroy. He took great, long strides, his cane rising up and down as he walked.

'Ah.'

'No, some of them harvest cesspits.'

'I'm sorry?' said Quimby, 'they harvest what?'

'Cesspits, my lord. On hands and knees they must crawl in order to bring the stools to the surface of cesspits so that they might be sold as fertiliser. Human stools make wonderful fertiliser.'

'Does it?'

'Oh, indeed.'

'And what of the children?'

'Drownings are common, of course; disease, also.'

'I see.' Quimby's stomach turned to think of things, and he found his mind unwillingly straying to the steak and kidney pie Perkins had prepared for him that evening.

'I wouldn't have thought it will last much longer, though,' said Conroy.

'Because of reform?'

'Reform?' Conroy's laugh rang about the street, and an old crone sitting asleep on a step, as though living out her last moments, raised her head momentarily to proffer a begging hand – slapped viciously away by one of the urchins.

'My dear Quimby, I should expect not. How else are we to keep the masses under control if not through repression and poverty, disease and starvation? Reform? Goodness gracious no, such a thing would go very much against our wishes, don't you think? Indeed, one of the objects of our stratagem is to ensure this incipient talk of reform goes no further. Indeed, this is where you come in . . .'

'Quite,' said Quimby, with a sizable amount more certainty than he felt. For there was – how should he describe it, this insect in the unguent? – an *issue* concerning the proposal which was clearly unknown to Sir John, and Quimby was yet to avail him of it; in fact, had decided not to bring it up, certainly not at this very moment, his hope being to resolve the problem in private.

'No,' added Conroy, 'the reason that the cesspit harvest will soon cease is that our crops are in need of a finite amount of fertilisation, whereas those who dwell in the city are producing an infinite amount of fertiliser. Here in the bowels of the city they are short of housing, of medicine and sanitation – those aspects of life I dare say you, my lord, consider essential to existence in a civilised society. What they are not short of, however, is shit. Shit is in plentiful supply here.' He laughed. 'This isn't life, really, is it?' he said, waving his cane at the dwellings crowding in on them, 'it's hell.'

'It is certainly most distasteful,' said Quimby.

'Thank God it's them instead of you,' added Conroy, 'thank God you are on the side of the victors.'

Quite, thought Quimby, dropping back behind Conroy and his miniature guards and returning his thoughts to happier matters. For it was the case that Sir John Conroy, had, on their carriage journey from Kensal Green into the city, regaled them of his course of action, and of their function within it. Furthermore he had informed them of how they would profit once the scheme was a success, which of course it would be – it *had* to be, he'd said with a smile that Quimby had found mildly discomfiting.

However, that what he'd had to say was but music to Quimby's ears. Sweet, sweet music.

'This could be the end of all our troubles, Perkins,' he said, when he felt they were out of earshot.

'What about the flesh eating, sir?' whispered his man-servant, giving voice to that issue which also troubled Quimby.

'We can work on that, Perkins.'

'Sir, we have had three years to formulate a solution and been unable to do so.'

'Matters are more pressing now, Perkins,' said Quimby. 'This arrangement will grant me power and influence beyond that I could ever have imagined. In short, we must try harder.'

As they walked on, Quimby mulled over his words, which, he realised, may have given Perkins the impression that he cared more for his own fortune than for curing this flesh-eating affliction.

'I had no idea it was so bad, Perkins, did you?' said Quimby after a moment's reflection. 'The poverty, I mean.'

'My mother spoke of such living conditions, before she went into service sir,' said Perkins. 'I had hoped never to witness them first-hand.'

'I hope never to witness them again,' said Quimby, at a whisper.

'A sentiment known as upper-class apathy, sir,' said Perkins.

Quimby opened his mouth to reprimand his servant but his words never came, for now they had reached a wide gulley, where the stench was particularly high. Peering through the layers of smog, Quimby could see the gulley overflowing with something he took at first to be mud but quickly realised was not. It was 'night soil' as they referred to it in the slums: human ordure that had overflowed from cesspits below homes. Into it, residents had thrown bricks in order to make stepping stones across but thanks to the intestinal activities of the evening, the gulley had filled sufficiently to cover many of the stones. As a result Conroy's young helpers were briefly employed adding more brickwork to the open sewer in order that the men might pass, which they did, emerging from the street into a courtyard that, despite the presence of the malodorous night air, teemed with life.

'Gentlemen,' said Conroy, sweeping his hat from his head and performing an introductory bow for the building in front of which they now stood, 'welcome to the workhouse.'

There before them, was a site built of foreboding: the work-house, in front of it crowds of people: residents or would-be residents. Either way the party moved forward among them, to the door, the urchins pushing the slow and feeble out of the way to allow them passage. They reached the door upon which Conroy knocked and then they were being admitted, urchins scuttling inside followed by Conroy, Quimby and Perkins, the door begrudgingly held open then closed behind them to keep out the evil swirling air crowding their backs.

Conroy thanked a toothless hag, clacking money into her outstretched palm then said something to her to which she replied with a coarse, dry laugh and a grunt in the affirmative. He turned and bade them move through.

Inside the workhouse Quimby saw doors that he knew led to segregated dormitories in which slept those who lived here. Those who had fallen on such hard times they were obliged to present themselves at the workhouse door: men in one room, women in another, children in yet another. Quimby had heard it said that mothers in the poorhouse were separated from their babies and the anguished screams of the young seemed to bear out the rumour. Adults, he presumed were forbidden to talk – indeed, it was like a prison! – so the only noise was that of the babies, and it was all Quimby could do not to put his hands to his ears to block out the noise.

Conroy led them along a central corridor, talking as he went, saying, 'I'm between homes at the moment, gentlemen. Would you believe I have been made most unwelcome at the Palace?'

'Why would that be sir?' asked Quimby, tremulously.

Conroy laughed. 'Never you mind, my Lord, nothing to worry yourself about, merely that I am . . . flitting at the moment. Here is preferable. The other place, well, you wouldn't believe the noise, gentlemen.' He grinned. 'It's bedlam.'

By now they had reached a door into which he inserted a large iron key, ushering in the waifs then turning to Quimby and Perkins.

'Shall we meet our mutual friend?' he said.

The room was large, with a rough stone floor on which had been spread straw at some point many moons ago. High up on a back wall was one tiny window, barred and too black with dirt to admit light – not that the admittance of light was in any way a possibility. This, Quimby realised, was a punishment room. The wall to his left was inset with steel rings. Hanging, his hands bound to the rings with rope, was a man.

McKenzie.

Minus his hat, his head hung down, a patchwork of blood and bruises, plastered with his wet hair. Blood oozed from his mouth.

The room was silent apart from the low groaning sound made by McKenzie and similar sounds emitted by a second, younger man; this one, tied to a chair, lolled against his ropes, threads of blood and mucus hanging from his face. Smiling cherubically, one of the smiling sweeps grabbed his hair and yanked his head back for Quimby to inspect him and for a second or so his Lordship regarded the man, almost feeling pity for him, for the state he was in: his face seemed to have ballooned around his features, which was now purple and yellow and red. His eyes stared back at Quimby, devoid of emotion. He was in shock, probably, thought Quimby, the pain had caused his conscious mind to shut down.

'What do you think of our humble abode?' said Conroy, ironically. 'Oh, I know it's a bit basic and there are those who might say it's something of a comedown after life at Buckingham Palace, but I think it has a certain bijou charm, don't you think? Plus I think you're going to love the neighbours. Over here, Mr McKenzie, with whom I believe you are familiar. Over here the man we know simply as Egg. I know, I know – you're expecting me to make a pun about how Egg has been beaten, but I assure you I'm not – I'm sure Egg has had enough of my little yolks.'

'I don't know him,' said Quimby carefully, wondering what it was that the youth had done to deserve such punishment. Something terrible, no doubt. At the same time he was aware that he was being shown something, he was being given a message, and that message was this: a punishment awaits those who cross me. *Do not do so, lest the next occupant of the chair be you.*

'No,' said Conroy, 'of course not, it's Mr McKenzie that you're acquainted with. In point of fact we have no more need of Egg, since his only function is to be provide me with a joke, at which you didn't even laugh.'

At his nod, one of the boys moved forward and grabbed Egg's hair, holding back his lolling head as Conroy stepped forward, pulled from his coat a knife and swept it across Egg's exposed throat with a backhand movement, sending an arc of blood splattering to the floor.

His head held firm, Egg's eyes widened. He struggled at the bindings. His body shook the chair into which he was tied; the feet of it rattled on the stone floor. Blood soaked his front. From him came an unearthly gurgling sound as his lifeblood poured from him.

For several moments they watched him die until the room was once again silent. That is, apart from an unusual noise that it took Quimby a few seconds to recognise.

'Perkins,' he said, 'is that your stomach rumbling?'

'Yes, sir, sorry, sir.'

Perkins was staring at the dying Egg, on his face such a famished look that Quimby almost took pity on him.

Conroy also took note, addressing Perkins, 'Oh, I'm sorry,' he said, 'where on earth are my manners? Do tuck in, old chap.'

Perkins was moving forward, all but licking his lips, when there came an anguished shout from the other side of the room and all turned their attention to McKenzie, who regarded them through hate-filled, bloodshot eyes.

'You bastards,' he repeated, 'you'll hang for this.'

Conroy moved towards him and arched an eyebrows. 'Isn't that rather the pot calling the kettle black?' he said to McKenzie. 'I mean, for a man in your particular position.'

McKenzie tried to spit at them but was unable to muster much range. Instead, pathetically, he spat upon himself, blood and saliva that slipped down his jacket.

'Oh that's good,' said Conroy, 'it is so very bothersome having to wipe your victim's phlegm from your face. So much more civilised to have one who can't quite manage it.'

McKenzie turned his head towards Quimby.

'Quimby,' he managed.

'All yours, your Lordship,' said Conroy. 'Consider me the matchmaker. A cupid, bringing men and blackmailers together.'

'Of course,' said Quimby, trying very hard to keep his voice steady.

This is what you wanted, he reminded himself, moving to stand in front of McKenzie, who gazed at him with eyes gummed up by blood.

'Where's the photogenic drawing?' said Quimby.

'Help me and I'll tell you,' managed McKenzie.

Quimby looked over towards Conroy who smiled benevolently, nevertheless shaking his head no. 'I am sorry, Mr McKenzie, it is not possible, I'm afraid. There is no help now. You will die here in this none-too-fragrant room.' He turned to the urchins and theatrically held his nose at which the urchins fell about laughing, Conroy further exciting their hilarity by lifting the tails of his coat and wafting imaginary fumes from his backside as though having gifted an enormous fart to the assembled company.

Christ, thought Quimby, watching him in action. What kind of man is it with whom I have become involved?

(And a thought made its way into his head, uninvited. A memory of McKenzie at The Reform club, his comment about fearing not the monkey but the organ grinder. And he wondered if this was it: here be the organ grinder.)

When the hilarity was at an end, Conroy turned his attention back to McKenzie. 'No, as I say, Mr McKenzie,' he continued, almost sadly, 'it really is a case, not of whether or not you die, which you will, here, tonight, in this room, but of how you die and at what speed. I hope that I'm not treading on his Lordship's toes by suggesting this, but I dare say that if you tell Mr Quimby here all he needs to know, then I'm sure he'll be sporting enough to allow his manservant to finish you quickly. If you refuse to do so, however, I will let my boys at you again, and goodness, as you've already discovered, they do so take a pleasure in their work, don't they?'

At this, there was, again, much excitement among the boys in question.

'Are we clear, Mr McKenzie?'

In lieu of a gesture to the affirmative, McKenzie groaned.

'Thank you,' and he turned to talk to the boys, crouching to them and talking in a low murmur.

'Quimby,' whispered McKenzie, his voice low, his gaze darting over Quimby's shoulder – to Conroy presumably, urging, 'come close.' His voice barely audible.

He means to take a bite out of my ear, the swine, thought Quimby.

'I can't bite you,' managed McKenzie, 'look. All gone.' And he opened his mouth pulling back his lips to reveal a mouthful of bloodied stumps. Nothing, just the odd tooth left.

Technically, of course, not all of his incisors were absent, but Quimby decided not to quibble, the man being in such obvious pain, and he leant forward to hear what he had to say.

'The boy Conroy just killed,' whispered McKenzie, 'he worked for one of the Queen's ladies-in-waiting. Hastings. She was in love with Conroy and had his confidence. She learnt things.'

'Yes?' whispered Quimby.

'Help me escape and the information is yours.'

'How can I be sure of its value?'

'It involves the Queen,' managed McKenzie. 'Something terrible . . .'

Quimby looked doubtful. 'My good man, I just need to know the whereabouts of the photogenic drawing.'

'Conroy had other affairs,' whispered McKenzie. 'He'd had an affair with—'

Then his mouth was full of knife.

Conroy had crossed the room, and was there before either of them were aware that he had moved, the knife in his hand.

There was a couple of moments as McKenzie struggled,

tried to bite down on Conroy's hand with teeth that were not there. Then Conroy was extricating his hand from McKenzie's mouth, a torrent of blood in its wake, and he was tossing the severed tongue to the feral children, who used it to begin a game of piggy in the middle.

McKenzie thrashed on the wall, making a strange mewling sound. Conroy looked at Quimby, a dark warning in those eyes – a look that required nothing supplementary to be said.

'I tire of this,' said Conroy darkly. 'We shall find your photogenic drawing. We'll burn down his abode if needs be. Instruct your revenant to feed.'

McKenzie thumped his body against the wall, mute, his mouth foaming blood, eyes wide in terror as he faced his final moments.

Perkins, needing no more encouragement, came running over with the urgency of a man suffering from a severe case of dysentery.

'Make it quick, Perkins,' said Quimby as his manservant streaked past him, 'put the man out of his misery – not that he deserves it.'

'Sir, yes, sir,' said Perkins and began to feed.

And then there was just a ghastly silence, McKenzie unable to voice his agony as Perkins tore his insides from him to eat, while they were still nice and warm – just the way he liked them.

XXXI

'Would you like to take a seat, Your Majesty?' the dwarf croaked, after they had descended the stone steps to a secret area of the Palace, there to be greeted by the Quartermaster's pint-sized assistant, 'and I will tell the Quartermaster that you're here,' at which he bowed, indicating chairs that had been set out along one wall of what looked like an antechamber, and left the room, walking in that distinctive lop-sided gait peculiar to little people.

Maggie Brown, glad of the chance to sit down, picked up her skirts and settled back in a chair, regarding her feet at the hem of her skirts.

'Why, that's about the longest I've ever gone without seeing my toes,' she remarked. 'Do you never miss seeing your feet, ma'am, having them hidden within all that crinoline?'

Melbourne glared at her, correctly guessing that the Queen was in no mood for jocularity; indeed she was not, and as the Prime Minister took a seat beside Maggie Brown, Victoria remained standing, pacing about the small, bare room.

'Why must he keep us waiting?' she asked, testily.

'He is the Quartermaster,' explained Maggie.

'And I am the Queen of England, and the Queen does not like to be kept waiting, especially when her husband currently languishes in the clutches of his arch-enemy. Go and fetch him at once.'

'Ma'am, with the greatest of respect, it might not be the wisest course of action.'

'Why ever not?'

'He's a genius.'

'He's a quartermaster.'

'Ah, no, Your Majesty. He's *the* Quartermaster. He who forges weapons solely for the Protektorate.'

'That's all he does? There is a smith tasked with forging weapons for but a handful of warriors?'

'Aye, ma'am, affirmative.'

The Queen looked in the direction of the thick curtain that separated the waiting area from the workshop. 'Goodness, do we pay him?' she whispered to Lord Melbourne.

'Most certainly, Your Majesty,' he said, 'handsomely. Or else risk losing him to a foreign power.'

Victoria allowed herself a smile, appearing to relax a little. 'Then God help us if Albert were here,' she said, 'he would think it an example of utmost profligacy – of utmost *English* profligacy. He didn't know, I take it? But he's usually so knowledgeable about such things.'

'I dare say not, ma'am, no,' replied Maggie Brown, as Melbourne sank a little deeper into his seat, 'The Quartermaster's wages are paid in such a way as to avoid scrutiny.'

'How?'

'Lord Melbourne claims him as an expense.'

'Is this right, Lord M?'

'Yes, Your Majesty.'

'And do you use the privilege of your expenses for any other shadowy financial dealings we should know about?'

'Certainly not, ma'am.'

Lord M's nostrils were flaring so much so as to resemble

a hat worn by a wizard, when the dwarf reappeared, standing at the curtain and holding it up so that they might pass through, saying, 'The Quartermaster will see you now.'

The first thing that struck Victoria as they passed into the workroom was the heat; the second, the smell: of oil; the third that there were weapons and armour everywhere. All over the walls and in every corner: dirks, daggers, bows, cross-bows, gauntlets, shields, muskets, pistols, warhammers, clubs, maces, hatchets, axes, pikes and rapiers.

Some were what she thought of as being 'traditional' weapons; others . . . well, she had never seen the like. As with the sword used by poor Hudson, which no doubt had been forged in this very workshop, many were subject to modifi-cation, and she found herself both fascinated and repulsed at some of the additions made to the orthodox shape, their express purpose being to inflict as much damage and pain as was possible on those unlucky enough to feel their bite. For a moment Victoria found herself fighting the urge to simply flee – to leave this place so redolent of death and of pain.

But no. She stood her ground, let herself become accus-tomed to the weaponry. The next sight she was struck by was the Quartermaster, an elderly man, with white hair and a long white beard who wore half-moon spectacles, and who had been sitting behind a workbench crowded with instruments and sections of metal. At his side was what looked like a tailor's dummy, dressed in leather armour.

He now stood, as was the protocol, and the Queen was expecting a nod of the head, such as she was used to receiving when meeting members of the lower orders, and felt herself bridle a little, when instead of addressing her, the Quarter-master instead moved over to Maggie Brown, placing his hands on her shoulders and inclining his head a little so as to peer at her over his spectacles.

'I am so terribly, terribly sorry to hear about Hudson.'

'Thank you, Quartermaster,' replied Brown, 'I will avenge him before I shed my tears for him.'

'A good man,' said the Quartermaster, nodding, 'and oh, what a swordsman. Bested by an Arcadian, I hear.'

'Indeed.'

He sighed. 'They can be tricksy, Arcadians. Footsoldiers, of course – there to do the dirty work for the level one demons. But even so, good fighters.'

'Aye, we'll see,' said Maggie Brown. 'We'll see.'

The Quartermaster looked awkward. 'Did you, um, recover his weapon all right?' he said, with an obvious twinge of discomfort at having to ask.

'Aye, we did.'

He nodded his head, relieved. 'Oh good, jolly good. Not something we want falling into the hands of the enemy.'

'Aye.'

'Now,' and at this he turned his attention to the Queen, 'this is our youngest recruit is it?'

Which, for Victoria, was most assuredly the last straw. The impudence of him! 'In fact,' she snapped, 'I am the Queen, your employer and, it would seem, landlady.'

'Oh?' said the Quartermaster, bemused, 'should we be packing our bags and moving on?'

'No, Quartermaster,' said Melbourne, quick to interject, 'Her Majesty is vexed and merely requires perhaps a little more haste in this enterprise, for Prince Albert remains missing. Isn't that right, ma'am?'

Victoria, furious at having to mollify the man yet also aware of the need to maintain good relations, threw Melbourne a peevish look, but submitted; instead she pointed out an item on the wall.

'What's this?' she asked, indicating at a curved sword.

'That,' the Quartermaster said with a smile, 'is a katana, a sword used by Samurai warriors in Japan.'

'It's extremely beautiful,' she said.

He raised his eyebrows, as though to say, 'But of course.'

'Would you like to try it?' he asked, and before she could reply had moved across and with his index finger taken the sword from the wall, holding it perched on his finger. 'Perfect weight and balance,' he pointed out, before flicking it into the air, catching it and snapping it back, holding it with the scabbard along his arm and the hilt held out for her to take.

She did so, sliding it from the scabbard, catching her breath to see the blade, gleaming.

'Suits you, Your Majesty,' said the Quartermaster, as she stood with it, only just resisting the impulse to try it out – which would no doubt have been a disastrous thing to attempt in the cramped workspace.

'May I keep it?' she asked.

'Well, you can borrow it—'

'Er, Quartermaster,' warned Melbourne, 'there is a limit, man.'

The Quartermaster twinkled. 'Of course you may have it, Your Majesty. The scabbard also. If you'll allow me . . .'

From the scabbard he unfurled some leather straps and then Victoria was gasping as he came around behind her and proceeded to strap the sheath to her back.

The impudence of the man. To touch the Queen in this way. How dare he . . .

She caught Maggie Brown's expression, a pained plea to please indulge the Quartermaster, and said nothing.

With the sheath strapped to the Queen's back, the Quartermaster returned to face her, oblivious to the high colour in her cheeks, saying, 'However I am told that you have shown great promise in close-quarter combat.' Here he looked over at Maggie, who nodded enthusiastically, her demeanour that of a proud parent.

'In that case,' said the Quartermaster, 'you will also need weapons for this purpose and I think I might have just the thing.' He walked slowly to his workbench and behind it, placing a hand to his back and wincing as he bent to reach down, saying, 'I've been working on a version of the halbert, cutting the handle down to the size we might ordinarily expect to see on an axe, retaining the hook, but replacing the axe blade with a circular saw – a spinning circular saw.'

'A spinning saw? You're joking,' said Victoria.

He straightened and regarded her over the top of his spectacles. 'I never joke about my work, Your Majesty,' he said, and with that he brought the weapon from out of sight and placed it on the bench.

It was as he had described. The saw, boasting evil-looking curved blades, was at one face; at the other, a longer blade like that of a pick-axe.

'It has within it, a mechanism,' he said, 'made especially for me in Switzerland by a young watchmaker named Antoni Patek.'

He demonstrated with a finger, giving the blade the lightest of prods, at which it began spinning fiercely, with a low ticking sound.

'That's incredible,' said Melbourne.

'Yes,' agreed the Quartermaster. 'Used in battle the saw will begin to spin at an even faster rate, meaning that the weapon's efficiency is increased as it is used.'

He picked up the weapon quickly, dextrously flipping it so that it described a figure of eight, looked at them to see that they were impressed, which they duly were, then handed it to Victoria, indicating the tailor's dummy.

'Your Majesty,' he said, 'would you like to give it a test run?'

Hiding her uncertainty, Victoria took the weapon, holding it like an axe, then stepped to the tailor's dummy and swiped downwards. The blade already spinning faster, then faster as she struck again and then a third time. She stopped. The leather armour slid from the tailor's dummy, split apart. 'Sharp, too, obviously,' said the Quartermaster, taking it from her and replacing it on the tabletop.

'Does it have a companion?' queried Maggie Brown.

'Ah, the melee master speaks,' smiled the Quartermaster, 'why, of course, it does, Maggie Brown, for the close-quarter combatant is best served by a short-handled weapon in both hands, one for bludgeoning and chopping – the blunter of the two instruments; another for more finer, more detailed work, a penetrating weapon such as this . . .'

Now he brought forth what Victoria saw was a knife, though slightly longer than was usual, and which had been fashioned in the style of a sword. One longer, two-sided blade was complemented by two shorter blades, which curved down over the handle, itself sharpened to a point at its base, so that it might be used to stab backwards as well as forwards.

'Aye,' said Maggie Brown, 'I'd say that looks just the ticket, wouldn't you, Your Majesty?'

Queen Victoria, sword in scabbard, took the spinsaw and shortsword from the bench and held them, weighing them up.

'Yes,' she said, 'we think these will suffice.'

XXXII

From outside came the sound of a carriage coming to a halt and Quimby darted to the library window, pulling aside his gratifyingly weighty drape and peering into the street. Below, Sir Montague Tales, the Whig MP for somewhere or other, was alighting from the carriage, placing his top hat upon his head, turning and addressing his driver, using his cane to emphasise whatever it was he had to say. The carriage departed and Sir Montague turned to face Lord Quimby's abode, then climbed the steps to the front door.

There came the sound of knocking.

'Right,' said Quimby, to Perkins and Egg, 'I shall get the door. You two remain out of sight until you hear me call. Then you, Egg, come to the library and do exactly as we have discussed. Perkins, you be ready with the potion. We need him fresh, gentlemen, is that clear? For that may be the key to controlling this desire for flesh.'

With that he hurried from the library and to the main stairs, unconsciously biting his lip; he was nervous, for their experiments in altering the chemistry of the potion had so far been unsuccessful.

Egg being proof of that.

Leaving the workhouse that day, Quimby had said to Perkins, 'Right, Perkins, there are three issues we must address at once, and they are: firstly, we need to prevent the zombies craving flesh.'

'Yes, sir.'

'Secondly, we need to ensure that revenants will always submit to my will.'

'A difficult one to measure, sir.'

'Yes. Yes, I suppose it is.'

They had walked on.

'What about you, Perkins? Do you submit to my will because you want to, or because as my revenant you're compelled to?'

'I couldn't say, sir.'

'Exactly. Damn and blast it. This is what is so darned difficult about this whole business. It really is so very imprecise. I tried to tell our friend Mr Conroy that it really is a most inexact science, but he wasn't having it, I'm afraid. He seems to think we shall have a legion of obedient revenants all subject to my command and therefore, by extension, his.'

'I must say, sir, I didn't hear you express any doubts you might have had.'

'Well, no, perhaps I didn't. They were certainly uppermost in my mind, but you're quite correct, no, I didn't express them, not in actual words, insofar as saying them . . . out loud.'

'Perhaps, sir, it might have been wise to disavow him of his false notions?'

'And find ourselves surplus to requirements? Kicked to death by those ghoulish miniature hooligans he keeps at his beck and call? You are strong, Perkins, I know that, but against such numbers . . . No, the only thing for it is to work on our elixir in order that its efficacy might be improved.'

They had walked on.

'What was the third thing, sir?'

'What third thing?'

'You mentioned that there were three things to which we must attend with the utmost urgency. What is the third?'

Quimby looked left and right, then pulled Perkins into a side alley. 'The third thing,' he said, 'requires us to return to the workhouse . . .'

Conroy, fortunately, had paid little attention to the disposal of the bodies of McKenzie and Egg – he was moving his centre of operations anyway, he said – directing that they should be left out in the street, there to appear as victims of frost, any trauma to the bodies blamed on vermin. Thus it was no great matter for Quimby and Perkins to return, collect the corpse of Egg, supporting it between them as though Egg were a drunken friend, and bring it to Pembridge Villas.

What Quimby wanted, of course, was the secret the man harboured, and as they laid him on the operations table in the basement he prayed that Egg might retain most or all of his cognitive functions. God, how he wished now that they had been more thorough when conducting these experiments. Egg had been dead – how long was it now? – four hours. That give him two hours more freshness than a prostitute Burke and Hare had brought him once, and aside from some memory issues – which did, at the time, of course, suit Quimby down to the ground – she had been fine. Quite good company, in fact.

So, once safely back at home, they had administered the concoction to Egg and stood back, observing what was now a familiar sight to them: that of the dead returning to life. After many minutes of seeing him cough and splutter and the usual period of adjusting to the sensation of having regained life, Quimby went to Egg.

'It's all right,' he said, 'you're safe. Do you know your name?'

'Yes, sor, my name is Egg, but beyond that I couldn't say, sor.'

'Blast, he's brain damaged!' exclaimed Quimby.

'No, sir,' said Perkins, 'I think it's just his accent, sir, which is of the countryside.'

'Really?' Quimby returned from the gates of despair with the same speed at which he had entered them. 'Just his accent, eh? Is that right, Egg, are you man of the soil?'

'By birth, sor, from the Fens of Lincolnshire.'

'That's in this country, is it?'

'Yes, sir,' confirmed Perkins.

'Excellent. Now . . .' he leaned in towards Egg, 'what do you know about the Queen?'

Egg screwed his eyes up as though concentrating hard. 'I can't say that I quite recall, sor.'

Neither had he been able to recall since. Privately, Perkins and Quimby wondered if Egg was telling them the whole truth regarding this situation. Perhaps he was withholding the information in the belief that once he had revealed it, they would destroy him.

This was exactly what they intended to do, of course. They had long ago learnt to be ruthless when it came to the disposal of revenants – that debacle in the library had taught them that – and Quimby was often reminding Perkins that there was no room for sentiment. Egg, possibly not as backward as his accent suggested, might have come to the right conclusion. Thus, Perkins and Quimby did their very best to make

Egg feel at home; indeed, Perkins had very much taken him under his wing. Why, Quimby almost felt excluded at times.

Still, however, Egg had been unable to recall the great secret he supposedly knew about the Queen and they had no time to wait to find out what it was. The plan for which Conroy had engaged them needed implementing and the first stage was now. Sir Montague Tales had been invited to Pembridge Villas for dinner, that dinner consisting of a glass of port as an entrée, for the main course a glass of port. Then, for dessert, a young man.

Characteristically, Sir Montague raced through the first two courses of his meal, pacing about the library in a state of barely concealed sexual excitement, his britches, at times, jutting, rather disgustingly.

'What on earth is this, Quimmers?' he remarked at one point, red-faced and sweating.

'That, sir, is a photogenic drawing,' said Quimby, who thought it made a fine addition to the mantelpiece. 'Are you aware of this new process at, all, by which you can capture an image of real life?'

'Real life, you say?'

'Absolutely, sir.'

But Sir Montague was not listening. 'Just what is going on in this particular scene, Quimmers?' he asked, impressed. 'It looks bloody depraved.'

'A mere fancy, sir,' said Quimby. 'A concoction. A little amusement involving some actors.'

'And some sausages by the looks of things.'

'Quite,' said Quimby, 'now, how about we skip to dessert, sir?'

Sir Montague grinned, moving over to the chair where

Quimby sat and taking a seat. Quimby moved over to his writing desk, took from it a dagger that he concealed in his sleeve, and went to join Sir Montague, taking a seat by his side and calling for dessert.

Sir Montague, agog, watched the door, keenly awaiting the arrival of the lithe young fellow he imagined to be on offer, given the implications provided to him by Quimby, who had promised 'an innocent of the country'.

The door opened and in limped Perkins.

'Hello, sir,' he said.

There was a somewhat shocked silence in the wake of his arrival, just the sound of Perkins' leg dragging on the boards as the manservant stepped in, closing the door behind him.

Sir Montague looked at Quimby.

Quimby stared at Perkins.

'Ah, Quimby,' said Montague, 'without wishing to cause offence to this gentleman here, I had rather thought the entertainment might be on the, ah, younger side.'

Quimby ignored him. 'Perkins, what's going on?' he snapped. 'Where is Egg?'

'Egg is indisposed, sir.'

'What do you mean, Egg is indisposed?' roared Quimby, 'He is not to be indisposed. He can bloody well un-indispose himself and get himself here.'

'He's had second thoughts, sir, regarding the enterprise,' said Perkins. 'We were hoping that I might suffice.'

Quimby was apoplectic. 'You! Christ you're older than I am. *And you're dead*. Sir Montague is a pederast, not a grave robber!'

'I say sir,' protested Sir Montague, 'I would hardly describe myself as a . . .'

'*Shut up*,' raged Quimby and jammed the dagger into Sir Montague's chest, jumping from his seat to confront his manservant. 'Perkins, what the hell is Egg doing? He should be here, seducing that pig over there. The fact that's he's not leads me to believe that he is not quite as under my command as you and I were hoping.'

'Sir . . .' said Perkins.

'And as for you! What the hell did you think you were doing limping in here like some kind of lame, ageing rent boy? *When* – when did I say, Perkins, that if Egg should perhaps be of a mind not to participate then why don't you come instead?'

'Sir,' insisted Perkins, pointing over Quimby's shoulder, his eyes widening, 'Sir Montague, sir, I think he's dead.'

Quimby span and the two of them looked at the MP, who sat, now quite dead. On his face was a look of surprise, while at his nose was a bubble of blood, which hung from his nostril, then, as they watched – popped.

'*Blast*,' ejaculated Quimby, 'the bugger's dead. Perkins, quick, the elixir, where is it?'

Perkins had stored it alongside his Lordship's collection of exotic liqueurs, on a sideboard, and he hobbled over to it, snatching it up, calling for his Lordship and tossing over the stoppered bottle to Quimby, who caught it deftly, tore the cork from the bottle with his teeth, spat it out then straddled Sir Montague, pouring the potion down his throat.

'I honestly don't know why we're bothering to hurry in this instance, Perkins,' said Quimby, as the MP for Gloucester began to thrash, foam and writhe, his resurrection beginning, 'I actually think a bit of brain damage might have done Monty the world of good.'

XXXIII

Weapons training had begun and Victoria was yet to recover from the surprise of who was to be her tutor.

'I don't wish to cause offence,' she said, 'but . . . are you sure?'

John Brown senior ran a hand through unkempt hair and grinned blearily. 'I'm afraid so, Your Majesty,' he said, 'it's old Brown – in the flesh.' And he did a little jig to emphasise his point.

'I know how it must appear, ma'am,' said Maggie, who was tucking Brown's vest into his trousers for him. 'He looks like he couldn't train a dog, I know he does, but really, despite all appearances to the contrary, he is an exceptional swordsman.'

'Why, then, is he not a member of the Protektorate?' asked Victoria.

There was a moment of awkwardness.

'He was, ma'am,' said Maggie, 'until about ten years ago. My husband fought bravely but was overcome by numbers. They were Arcadians, ma'am, and they took a terrible toll on him. He has never recovered his nerve, ma'am, I'm afraid to say.'

John Brown smiled sheepishly.

'I'm sorry to hear that,' said Victoria.

'Oh, it's all right. He has since discovered his metier, isn't that right, love?' cajoled Maggie, punching her husband.

'That's right, Your Majesty,' said Brown, the male Brown, 'I have found within myself a remarkable talent for the imbibing of alcoholic drinks.'

For which he received yet another punch from Maggie. 'He's jesting, ma'am,' she said, through gritted teeth, 'his talent is for teaching others swordplay.'

Now the training had begun, with Brown male senior given instructions not to treat the Queen kindly on account of her rank, but to push her hard, time being of the essence, Lord Melbourne and Maggie taking seats to watch them.

'How do the ladies sit in these skirts?' mithered Maggie after they had sat in silence for some time, watching John instruct the Queen in her stance and the correct way in which to hold the katana.

'Not like that,' said Lord Melbourne, frowning at her posture. She sat as she was used to doing, with her legs crossed, right ankle resting on left knee, one arm across her stomach, the other at the hilt of her sword.

Lord Melbourne supposed that it was a position best suited for combat readiness. Or, at least, if he objected then that was the reason with which he would be supplied.

One could only thank God nobody could see them, he mused. For they were in the Yard Bed, deep in the gardens of the Palace, with mulberry bushes screening them from view and an order from the Queen that they should not be disturbed.

'You're still keeping something from her,' said Maggie.

'Am I?'

'Indeed you are, Prime Minister. You've neglected to mention those prophecies that speak of the Baal siring an heir, a human heir, bearing the bloodline of Baal, and that this child is destined to rule the empire, and death and destruction will follow in his wake, and that child shall be the Antichrist. You didn't tell her all that, did you? Or perhaps you did and I missed it? Or maybe you thought it too minor a detail?'

'No, I did not tell her that,' agreed Melbourne.

'Was there any particular reason to keep it from her, Prime Minister?' said Maggie.

Melbourne did not answer at first, and they sat in silence, watching Victoria with her katana.

'All right, Your Majesty,' said John, who stood holding a branch as though it were a sword. 'Here I am, an old man with a twig and a weakness for whisky – attack me.'

'Attack you?' Victoria looked over at Maggie, who in return gave her an encouraging nod.

Victoria took a swipe at Brown with the sword, only for him to nimbly sidestep, grasp her sword hand at the hilt and place the stick at her neck.

They stood there.

He made a sound she guessed was aimed at approximating the noise her throat might make if sliced. He then followed it with a sound she assumed was meant to be that of her blood leaking from the imaginary wound. In all, he seemed to be rather enjoying this particular flight of fancy . . .

Annoyed, Victoria pulled away.

He tutor laughed. 'You have spent too much time at the theatre, Your Majesty,' he said, 'that might be how the actors wield their swords in Shakespeare but if you try that in real life, your opponent will skewer you. A katana isn't just an offensive weapon, it's a defensive one. Likely is, it will spend more time in battle employed protectively. That being the case you need to keep it close to your body . . .'

Back at the bench, Melbourne took a deep breath. 'Maggie,' he said, 'young John's vision was of seeing the bloodline of Baal ascend the throne, but the vision may be open to interpretation.'

'Go on.'

'What if his vision were not of the future, Maggie?' he said. 'What if John was seeing the past?'

'*Index finger and thumb,*' John Brown was shouting at the Queen, who was attempting to master defensive flicks of the katana.

'I'm not sure I follow you,' Prime Minister,' said Maggie carefully. 'If it's in the past, then the vision has not come to pass.'

'What if it has?' said Melbourne.

'Prime Minister, stop playing games with me and tell me straight. What the bloody hell are you talking about?'

'*Forward hand roll, backwards hand roll. No, no, your wrist should torque forwards, not backwards.*'

'Maybe the Baal ascended to the throne on the morning of 20 June 1837, because Conroy, not the Duke of Kent, is the Queen's father. Perhaps this is what was discovered by Lady Flora Hastings and was the information she wanted relayed to the journalist.'

Maggie gasped.

'The dates add up, Maggie. Sir John was employed by the Duke. Victoria was born, the Duke died. Sir John could have had an affair with the Duchess. He could have killed the Duke. Perhaps those mischevous wags who implied that there was more to the Duchess's relationship with her comptroller than met the eye were on to something.'

There was silence for a moment and they watched Victoria

and John Brown, John Brown instructing his charge in the art of feinting, in this instance by transferring the katana from one had to the other:

'Watch your stance. Feet apart, if that drops you'll be missing your toes. Right – throw . . .'

'If that were the case,' said Maggie, 'then that lassie over there is no more the Queen of England than I am.'

'Quite,' said Melbourne, 'and what's more, the carrier of the bloodline of Baal.'

'Let's try a kata,' John Brown was saying.

'What's a kata?' asked the Queen.

'A kata? An attack choreography. Disorientates your enemies and puts them into a defensive position – oh, and it looks good.'

Victoria laughed, looking over at Maggie Brown and smiling, Maggie returning her smile with a wave.

'And if that was the case . . .' said Maggie.

'Exactly,' said Melbourne, 'We'd have to kill her. And not only would we have to kill her, but also her children.'

XXXIV

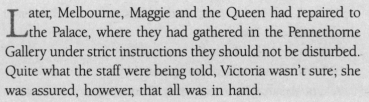

Later, Melbourne, Maggie and the Queen had repaired to the Palace, where they had gathered in the Pennethorne Gallery under strict instructions they should not be disturbed. Quite what the staff were being told, Victoria wasn't sure; she was assured, however, that all was in hand.

'We find that we are presented with a minor problem, and that is that Prince Albert is missing, yet this is not a fact we can afford to announce to the country. Moreover, you yourself, it is clear, are to be involved in the search to locate the Prince Consort, and thus may be absent from public life.'

'That is correct, Lord M,' said Victoria, and felt a twinge of something she preferred not to name. For this was something she herself had anticipated. She had, if she were honest with herself, rather hoped that none of those close to her would arrive at the same conclusion. The search for Albert could mean that she was neglecting her leadership of the country – or soon would be.

I must find Albert.

But my people need me.

But perhaps the people need Albert, she reasoned. Perhaps I need Albert in order to serve the people. Perhaps there was no right or wrong answer, and that she must follow her heart.

And her heart told her to go to him.

'What do you have in mind, Lord M?' she asked.

'Ma'am, I have taken the trouble of engaging the services of a stand-in for Your Majesty, a double if you like, the notion being that this lady can make public appearances in lieu of Your Majesty and when Your Majesty might be needed but is otherwise indisposed. Maggie, if you'd be so kind.'

Maggie made her way to the door, slouching rather as she did so.

'Posture, Maggie, poise,' the Prime Minister reminded her, sharply and Maggie turned, about to regale him with some colourful language of Anglo-Saxon origin when she remembered she was in the presence of the Queen and so instead curtsied, sarcastically.

'A stand-in?' echoed Victoria when she was gone.

'That's correct, ma'am.'

'A decoy?'

'Quite.'

The Queen resisted the impulse to laugh; in fact, found herself putting her hand to her mouth. 'Somebody will *pretend* to be me?'

'Indeed. And Albert also, ma'am.'

'Do you know what he would say, Lord M, if he were here?'

'No, Your Majesty?'

'I do believe he would tell you that you were quite mad. People pretending to be us. Why, whoever heard of such a thing?'

'Would it surprise Your Majesty to learn that there are already those who pretend to be Your Majesty and the Prince Consort.'

She started, drawing herself up. 'Really? For what purpose?'

'The purpose, ma'am, well, nominally of entertainment, though one supposes there may be those who use the look-alikes perhaps in order to improve their standing in society.'

'Lookalikes?'

'Yes, ma'am,' said Melbourne, just as there came a knock at the door and in walked Maggie Brown – ahead of a man and a woman who had self-evidently made a cursory attempt at appearing a little like the Queen and her consort.

Victoria's mouth dropped open.

'May I introduce Betty and Coventry Jones, ma'am,' said Melbourne, 'your stand-ins.'

Betty curtsied, Coventry inclined his head, the two of them murmuring a hello. Betty, noted Victoria, was rather more portly than she was, and shorter, and, she thought, though she disliked to think such unkind things, not quite so pretty, and perhaps her nose was a little sharper. Her hair was slightly lifeless, looked slightly greasy and wasn't well coiffed, she wore too much rouge on her cheeks, which were somewhat puffier then they should have been and her clothes were a shabby and looked a little small.

In short, she really is not much like me at all, thought Victoria. What should have been an experience akin to seeing one's reflection in a looking glass was more like opening *Punch* and seeing a particularly crude and unkind satirical cartoon.

And as for Albert. *Oh*. As with his fellow lookalike, Coventry had certainly made an effort, of sorts, and his hair was combed and parted correctly, his sideburns the length that Albert preferred. But his uniform bore signs of wear and tear, he looked to be thinning on top – even more thinning on top than Albert, that was – and again he was rounder than his counterpart.

In many ways, of course, she was glad. Not only for the confirmation that Albert was unique, but also because she was not sure how she would have coped to see a doppleganger, safe and well and standing in the home of the real thing, when the real thing was lost.

'Albert doesn't smile like that, Mr Jones,' she told him, not unkindly, 'he is not a smiler, my Albert, he is as likely to laugh as he is to smile, and when he's doing neither his mouth is set, like so.' She made the correct face.

'Yes, ma'am,' said Coventry.

'I beg your pardon?'

'Begging Your Majesty's pardon, I said.'

'Yes, I heard what you said, it was the *way* in which you said it. It was not quite . . . Albert speaks in a very considered and precise manner, you see, and with a pronounced German accent.'

'Yes, ma'am,' said Coventry, in what she dearly hoped was not an attempt at the diction she had been describing.

'Otherwise,' she said, placing a smile upon her face (and doing this with no small difficulty given the bewildering mix of emotions she felt, not least of which was a burning indignation that *anybody* could *possibly* think these two people actually looked like she and Albert), 'the likeness is really quite uncanny. Why,' she said, addressing Betty, 'it's like looking in a mirror. You do this as some kind of a . . . job, do you?'

'No, Your Majesty,' said Betty, whose voice, Victoria was unsurprised to learn, sounded not at all like hers, 'during the day we work hard in the clothing factory. By night and at the weekend we scrape together a few extra pennies with this as a sideline.'

'Ah,' I see, said Victoria, who had heard of the conditions at the clothing factories – that women sat in rags, stitching morning, noon and night; that their husbands heated irons and pressed the clothes in rooms choked with steam and dust.

'I see,' said Victoria. 'And what manner of functions do you attend in your capacity as lookalikes?'

'Well, ma'am,' said Betty, launching into what was, apparently, a well-rehearsed speech, 'we're often invited to parties thrown by the members of the new middle class, who think it a most entertaining distraction to have two members of Royalty present. We have also opened many fetes, appeared at numerous balls, and attended birthday parties as the surprise guests. We have been placed in the Royal box at the theatre and also, once or twice, appeared on stage as our namesakes.'

'Quite,' smiled Victoria. Her smile was now so strained it was beginning to hurt the muscles in her face. 'And you enjoy this work, do you?'

'Oh, most certainly, ma'am.' They both nodded enthusiastically. 'We're always made very welcome and well provided for. Often at fetes we're asked to judge the produce competitions. Why, I've had that much jam, you wouldn't believe!'

Oh, I can well believe, thought Victoria.

But she kept smiling.

'And are you called upon to *act* like Albert and I in these situations,' she asked, 'not just to look like us?'

'Oh, indeed, ma'am,' said Coventry.

'We have certain catchphrases they like us to say,' added Betty.

'Such as?' prompted Victoria.

'Oh, well, ma'am, I don't like to. Not with you standing in front me like this.'

'Oh you needn't worry, Mrs Jones,' interjected Melbourne, 'I'm sure Her Majesty would be interested.'

'Very well,' said Betty Jones, at which she drew herself up, pursed her lips very tightly, so that they resembled the puckered anus of a cat, and said, in a strangulated tone, 'We are *not* amused.'

She looked at Victoria, smiling sheepishly.

Victoria looked at her.

Then at Melbourne.

'Do I say that?' she said.

'I think it has been known, ma'am,' replied the Prime Minister. 'I believe you were once quoted in letters as having said it in response to a ribald aside made by one of the grooms-in-waiting.'

'Was I? But I like ribald jokes, as you well know.'

'Indeed, ma'am, but I do believe in that instance you were speaking for the ladies around you, in the event that they might have been scandalised by the unsavoury humour, hence your use of "we", which was not in this instance a case of you employing the majestic plural, though it seems to have been interpreted by wider society in this manner. Hence Betty employing it as a catchphrase.'

'I see,' said Victoria, 'and the people are associating this phrase with me, even though when I uttered the words, I meant them in a completely different sense?'

'That would appear to be the case, ma'am. It would seem that it is an example of you being quoted out of context, ma'am.'

'I see. Perhaps you could see to it that something is placed in *The Times*, clarifying this position?'

'I shall certainly do my best, Your Majesty,' said Melbourne, who, of course, had no intention of doing anything of the sort.

Victoria turned her attention back to Betty and Coventry, who smiled a little nervously, fearing they might have given offence, Coventry biting his lip.

'It's quite all right,' said Victoria, hoping to put them at their ease, 'it can be unusual sometimes, seeing how one is perceived.'

Then: 'Lord Melbourne?' she said, still smiling.

'Yes, Your Majesty.'

'Might I have a word in private?'

'Certainly, Your Majesty. Maggie . . .'

Maggie Brown came forward to direct Betty and Coventry from the room. Victoria waited until they had gone before letting the smile slip from her face.

'Lord Melbourne,' she said, 'neither of these two people, though very charming as they no doubt are, bear the slightest resemblance to myself or to Albert. They do not speak like Albert and me, they do not dress in a similar fashion to Albert and me, they do not have our poise or posture. In short, they are nothing whatsoever like Albert and me.'

Melbourne sighed. 'I agree that they may be a little . . . raw in their present state, but Your Majesty might remember that they are commoners. With the greatest respect, Your Majesty has lived her entire life with staff on hand to advise on matters of elegance and dress and manners and elocution. Betty and Coventry have merely admired from afar. I'm sure Your Majesty has heard the old saying that imitation is the sincerest form of flattery?'

'I'm sorry, Lord M, either we abandon this project, or find someone else,' said Victoria firmly. 'Would you be so kind as to bring Mr and Mrs Jones back into the gallery and I shall inform them that their services are not required.'

'Certainly, ma'am.'

Moments later, Betty and Coventry stood before her once more.

'Mr and Mrs Jones . . .' Victoria began. Coventry was staring at the polished floor of the Gallery, his hands clasped in front of him, red and raw hands, Victoria saw, worn by the steam of the factory; Betty, Victoria noticed for the first time, was trembling slightly.

The Queen paused. She looked over at Melbourne, who stood with his own hands behind his back, ready to help escort the pair of them from the Palace and back to their lives in the factory, earning extra pennies by doing poor impersonations of the Queen for people who probably thought them fit for little more than mockery . . .

'I think you would make fine stand-ins,' she said, all of a sudden, 'and would be more than happy to have you on the staff. Betty, I am placing you under the wing of the Duchess of Sutherland, Lady Harriet, who is most certainly one of the most beautiful and stylish ladies in the land and will be able to advise you on all matters of dress, maquillage, coiffure and etiquette . . .'

In response, Betty Jones' eyes had grown wider and wider and her mouth had slowly dropped open; Lord Melbourne, meanwhile, was exchanging an amazed look with Maggie Brown.

'. . . and you, Mr Jones,' she continued, 'I am placing you in the care of Lord Melbourne who will assign you a groom-in-waiting on whom you can rely for instruction in all matters relating to your proper comportment. The two of you shall live in rooms in the Palace.' She turned to Lord M. 'Can I rely upon you to see that these wishes are carried out, Lord Melbourne?'

'Yes, ma'am,' said the Prime Minister, coming forward.

'Good. Then as long as you are satisfied . . .' this Victoria directed towards Betty and Coventry, who both nodded enthusiastically, unable to believe their luck.

They were ushered from the gallery. The Queen turned to Melbourne, 'Lord M, I think I may have been powered by what is known as a second wind – and that it has just deserted me. I must take my leave.'

'Very good, Your Majesty,' he said, then added, 'I wonder, if having had some rest we might then reconvene, for then we have something we must show you.'

'Very well,' said the Queen, and with that, she called for the Duchess and together they left the room, Victoria adding, 'and Lord M?'

'Yes, Your Majesty?'

'You will see to it that Mr and Mrs Jones are well looked after, won't you?'

'Certainly, ma'am.'

They watched her leave.

'Wouldn't it be ironic, Maggie,' said Lord Melbourne, 'if she, who is such a fine monarch for England, turned out not be England's monarch after all, don't you think?'

Maggie looked at Melbourne. 'I don't think so, no,' she said, frowning. 'I don't think it is our place to think in such a fashion, Prime Minister – but simply to do our duty.'

XXXV

It was noticed, at the House that day, that Lord Montague Tales had several strands of long blond hair protruding from his mouth.

The effect, it was observed later, privately in the offices and corridors of the houses of Parliament, on the balcony on which members stood, drinking port and spitting into the black, stinking Thames, was really rather hypnotic.

For, as he spoke, the hair seemed to float, as though defying gravity, as though suspended, buffeted by his words (which were against reform – lately Sir Montague had been, in a surprising *volte face* from his previous position, vociferous against the implementation of the Factory Bill) and when he moved to address all sections of the house, members were treated to the sight of more hair. All subsequently agreed that Sir Montague really did have an awful lot of hair emerging from his mouth, with most coming to the conclusion that he had no doubt been in the company of a young lady shortly before arriving at the house; indeed, perhaps had even smuggled the woman into one of the rooms, there to avail himself of her, pausing only long enough to register his views against those measures being proposed making sure that women and children should not work long hours in the factories, and that all accidental deaths should be reported to the surgeon, and that factories should be washed with lime every fourteen months.

Melbourne stood up, speaking against a set of proposed amendments to the act. 'I am saddened,' he began, 'to learn of the right honourable gentleman's change of heart on this issue . . .'

Behind him sat the Whig MPs Granger and Tennant, each of whom had felt sleepy following a long and entertaining lunch, but were enlivened at seeing Sir Montague Tales' mouthful of hair and were even more alert now that it was the Prime Minister's turn to speak, for they liked to have a wager on the amount of times the Prime Minister would employ his favoured phrase, which was, 'Why not leave it alone?'

'I say more than three,' growled Granger.

'Indeed, sir, indeed, he may well do,' managed Tennant, behind a gutful of trapped gas. 'Normal terms and conditions apply, I trust?'

'Absolutely, sir, absolutely,' agreed Granger.

'Yes,' said Tennant, showing Granger the guinea wager he held, Granger doing the same in return, 'I think he rather hopes his phrase will be part of his legacy.'

'I do declare Melbourne will not be happy otherwise,' added Granger. 'In private he speaks of his fond wish that one day a city might be named in his honour.'

'Do you think so? Queen's Toady-on-Sea?'

Tennant coughed to disguise a guffaw.

'Perhaps he already has had a town named after him: Crawley.'

The two men's shoulders shook with mirth.

In the Strangers' Gallery, looking down upon the assembled parties from high above, sat Quimby and Perkins, Perkins wearing his scarf as was customary. They had the Strangers'

Gallery to themselves so Quimby had suggested his man-servant remove his sock and shoe to give the leg some air.

'What do you think, sir?' said Perkins.

'Of our government's touching regard for the plight of women and children in the factories, or the progress of our revenant?'

He looked down upon Sir Montague Tales as he spoke. Monty had regained his seat, still with those gold slivers of hair in his mouth – his mouth which, Quimby saw now, chewed slightly, as though of its own accord; in his eyes a faraway look. What did that hair mean, exactly? That he had been entertaining a young lady? Or eating one?

What's more, there were other members of Parliament of his acquaintance, who had also, recently been guests at Pembridge Villas, and they, too, sat glassy-eyed.

Quimby wasn't sure. He wasn't sure at all . . .

And his mind went back to the workhouse at the Old Nichol Rookery. Sir John Conroy's blade flashing. Little rhythmic arcs of red.

Now Quimby stood and scuttled to the end of the bench, motioning to Perkins to remain seated.

'Caught short,' he said, and darted up the couple of steps to the exit, which took him out of the House, and there on to a main corridor, darkened by oak panelling. Along it he found a toilet, so discreet as to be virtually a secret door, and let himself inside. There were two cubicles, and for a moment he stood, marvelling at this latest innovation, before stepping in, dropping his trousers and pants, retrieving from his jacket a hip flask containing one or two nips of whisky and allowing his sphincter to relax . . .

'These sitting toilets are a wonderful idea, don't you think, Quimby?

'Christ.' Quimby jumped a mile, his hip flask shaking in his hand and droplets of the precious fluid wasted. 'Christ, where are you?' he demanded of the voice.

'Why, in the cubicle next to you,' said Sir John Conroy, 'look up.'

Quimby did so, to see a hand waving at him over the top of the partition.

'Hmph,' he said, 'what do you want anyway?'

'To know how our plan progresses, obviously,' said Conroy. 'Time is of the essence, is it not. Do we yet have enough members of Parliament in our thrall to constitute a majority?'

'Very soon we will have, yes,' said Quimby, 'in a matter of hours, in fact.'

'And each of the revenants will submit to your will?'

'Oh, yes, absolutely,' lied Quimby, to whom the issue of obedience ran a distant second to those concerns involving the zombies' hunger for flesh.

'Good,' said Conroy, 'that is good.'

'May I ask,' said Quimby, 'for what reason you require these MPs to do our bidding?'

'No, Quimby, you may not. Your task is merely to see to it that we have enough revenants available to do our bidding, in which capacity you are so far performing admirably, it would seem. Now, I bid you farewell. Be seeing you, Quimby.'

Quimby hoped not; he dearly wished for nothing more than to never see Sir John Conroy ever again.

'Don't forget to wash your hands, Quimby,' said Conroy and Quimby heard the door open and close.

He thought about Sir Montague Tales and the mouth of hair. And he thought about the little rhythmic arcs of red.

He defecated.

Meanwhile, in the house, Melbourne bellowed, 'Why not leave it alone?' as he finished his speech, thumping the dispatch box in order to make his point and taking his seat.

A guinea passed from Lord Granger to Lord Tennant.

'Just the three on this occasion, sir,' said Granger, 'your prediction wins the day.'

'Well, then, what say I use my winnings to buy us a jug in the members' bar later?'

'A most tempting offer I must refuse sir,' said Granger, 'for I have a dinner date with Lord Quimby at Notting Hill this very evening – and his Lordship has promised to lay on some entertainment of a most *promising* nature.'

XXXVI

'Careful, Your Majesty,' said Melbourne, walking ahead of the Queen and holding his torch high, in order to give them as much light as possible.

The Prime Minister led the way, Maggie Brown at the rear. In the middle was the Queen, wearing her sword as instructed by Maggie. 'It's Protektorate business, ma'am,' she'd said, handing her a scarf with which to hide her face, a three-cornered hat to pull down low over her eyes, 'the tower is well guarded by the Yeomen Warders as you know, and they are accustomed to coming and going of a clandestine nature, but even so, they are not privy to information regarding the demonic threat.'

Melbourne had ushered them past the Beefeaters at the gates, Victoria with her head down, and into the castle complex, on to a courtyard, hurrying across it to one of the towers. Here they had taken up torches, then gone inside and began descending stone steps, the air becoming dank and cloying around them as they went further and further underground.

'Soon we will pass through into Lanthorn Tower,' said the Prime Minister. 'Your Majesty will recall that it was severely damaged in the fire of 1774. It is believed, in fact, that it was irreparably damaged, and now lies abandoned,' he continued, as they reached the bottom of the steps, 'but in fact that is not quite the case; instead, we have simply allowed the majority to believe this to be so, in order that we may use it for our purposes.'

'And what are they?' asked Victoria, as Melbourne paused before opening a door at the foot of the steps.

'It is used for interrogation,' he said.

They were now deep within the black depths of the Tower of London, far underground. Victoria, aware of a sudden sense of depth, instinctively looked up and what she saw was tower stretching high, high above them – from the depths where they stood, to way above ground level, and she experienced a moment of severe disorientation, quite unable at first to make sense of what she saw, which was that the fire had completely gutted Lanthorn Tower but the walls still stood, so that it was as if a giant hand had reached in and dragged out its insides.

Flickering torches lit the giddying expanse of stone, casting shadows on smoke-blackened walls. Towards the top were windows, and through them Victoria could see the grey of night. Looking closer she realised that strange angular shapes she had seen on the walls were in fact stone steps, suspended there, that must once have provided the access to different levels of the tower, destroyed in the fire. In places there were at intervals were the remains of picture frames, charred and rotting, but still, incredibly clinging to the walls, defying the years.

For some moments she was transfixed by the dimensions of the room in which she found herself and was listening to the sound of the ravens from way above her in the rafters. So much so that she quite forgot what Melbourne had said.

Then, however, she remembered.

Melbourne had already made his way down a secondary flight of steps to the main floor area of the Tower, which opened out before them, a huge expanse of stone interrupted by thick stone pillars that had once supported a ceiling, so that they now looked like a collection of tree trunks, shorn of leaves and branches.

Now Victoria followed him, and as she came into the area she saw something else, apart from the pillars: that it was studded with apparatus. Brown, rusty, spiked contraptions.

'Torture?' she said.

'Such an ugly word, ma'am,' protested Melbourne, 'I prefer to call it coercive questioning.'

'It's torture,' repeated Victoria.

'In any circumstance,' Melbourne said, discomfited, 'it really is used only in the cases of the highest of treason, and then only for the extraction of information which might be vital for reasons of state security.'

'I'm afraid there's no point in being squeamish about it, Your Majesty,' said Maggie Brown, 'call it a fact of war.'

'I'm sorry,' said Victoria, 'I think there is every reason to be squeamish about it. Lord Melbourne, all this . . . equipment? Is this all torture apparatus?'

'I'm afraid so, Your Majesty,' said Melbourne.

'This? What's this?' She indicated the item nearest to her: a tiny wooden box, with a door and a padlock hanging from it.

'This they call Little Ease, ma'am,' said Melbourne, 'it is intended to imprison a man, who would be in agonies, unable to move even a muscle.'

'It's barbaric,' said Victoria.

'We are in full agreement,' said Melbourne, his hands spread, 'you must believe that we in no way take this lightly.'

'These?' asked the Queen.

Two of the pillars were supplemented with manacles driven into a staple at their head. They were used to hang a man so that his feet might not touch the ground, explained Melbourne.

'And this, Your Majesty,' he said when she pointed out an evil-looking metal contraption, 'is the Scavenger's Daughter, invented by Sir William Skeffington in the reign of King Henry VIII.'

He indicated metal rings at its base, 'the feet go here and the arms go in here, and it compresses the body, like so, inflicting a great deal of pain by forcing the blood from the head.'

Victoria was aghast, but already striding forward, towards a large cabinet-like object that stood against the upright pillar. It was fashioned roughly after the shape of a human being. In fact, thought Victoria, it reminded her of one of the Russian dolls she had had as a child. A giant life-sized version. It had a door, which was half open.

And then she saw the spikes.

'Ah, yes. That, Your Majesty,' said Melbourne, 'is the iron maiden.'

Horribly fascinated, she moved forward to grant the instrument a closer inspection. Its insides were indeed studded with spikes, including the interior of the door, which Melbourne opened.

'The unfortunate victim is placed inside and the door closed, slowly,' he explained, 'the placing of these spikes might at first appear random, but in fact they are carefully positioned in order that they might pierce the body in those places that are painful, but not fatal.'

Victoria shook her head. But still hadn't finished, asking

about a malevolent-looking parody of a seat, an inquisitional chair, which was a seat covered in spikes on to the which the victim would be forced. It might also be heated, she was told, in order to induce an especially exquisite pain.

Then there was the Spanish Donkey, an upturned wedge of metal, resembling a large knife edge. The victim would be forced to straddle it, as though riding the eponymous ass, and weights attached to his legs until the wedge began to slice through his body.

There was a knee splitter, a skull splitter, a tongue tearer and a breast ripper; there was 'the pear' which would be inserted into the body through the anus or vagina and expanded to cause severe internal mutilation and a slow, agonisingly painful death; there was the Judas chair, an upturned spike on to which victims would be slowly lowered and there was the saw which would be applied between the legs of a man hung upside down so that the blood moved away from those parts being sawed, and the torture could continue for longer.

'How often is this chamber used?' asked the Queen.

'In my fifteen years serving with the Proketorate, I have been here but a handful of occasions,' said Maggie Brown, in what Victoria supposed was meant to be a reassuring voice.

'Then that is a handful too many,' she snapped, 'and what's more it is a handful enough! Some of the prophecies you have spoken of? Were they indeed prophecies, or were they the confessions of those forced to endure pain beyond belief; who would no doubt have said anything if it meant that pain would be at an end?'

Melbourne and Maggie Brown shared a look. 'A mixture of

both, ma'am,' said Maggie sheepishly, and Victoria glared at her, for she knew there was more to it than that.

'I forbid it,' said Victoria. 'I order that this equipment be destroyed at once, and that a curtain be drawn over this, which shames us – it shames us because we are English, the civilisers of the world, and this – this, Lord Melbourne, is assuredly not the work of civilised people.'

Lord Melbourne looked awkward. He passed a careful hand over his hair, then placed his hands behind his back to address the Queen. 'Sometimes, ma'am, our only recourse is to this form of coercive interrogation; that which takes place down here, unpalatable as it no doubt is, may save the lives of thousands in the fight against the forces of darkness.'

'And Your Majesty,' said Maggie, 'use of these methods is rare, but it is even more rare for it to be used against mortals. Those who feel the bite of the apparatus in this dungeon are demons not human; they who wish nothing upon the human race but death and destruction. They who would gladly torture you and call it entertainment.'

'Do they feel pain, these demons you torture?' demanded Victoria.

'Well, yes, ma'am,' said Melbourne, 'I'm afraid to say that's rather the—'

'Then it is barbarism, pure and simple. You would not see an animal suffer in this way. No, Melbourne, this is my final decision. Nobody – nothing – will be tortured in my name. Is that clear?'

'Even if torture means we can find Albert?'

Victoria's shoulders slumped. Of course. She should have known. Caught up in her own shock and horror and indignation she had not stopped to wonder why she might have been led to this ghastly chamber.

Melbourne walked over to a door inset to the wall at one side and pulled it open.

Victoria heard the machine first. Something heavy which was nevertheless moving easily on what, from their sound on the floor, sounded like wooden rollers. This device was wheeled into the central area of the tower by Hicks and Vasquez and consisted of a platform on wheels, on which were mounted two wooden shapes that looked much like wedges of cheese, hinged so that they might be made to move further and further apart.

Tied to the machine was a man dressed in the clothes and wig of a footman, his clothes, she saw, were torn and tattered. He was tied with rope, his hands to the top half of the machine, feet at the bottom.

'Is this what I think it is?' asked Victoria, flatly.

'Yes, ma'am, it's the rack. At least, a variation upon it,' said Melbourne.

The prisoner tied to the rack moaned, his eyes fluttering.

'And this man?' she said, knowing the answer.

'This is the driver of the first carriage, ma'am.'

Now he opened his eyes and looked directly at her, and smiled.

'Hello, Your Majesty,' he said.

Victoria ignored him. 'This is him in human form, is it?'

'Indeed,' said Maggie Brown. 'Arcadian, transform yourself.'

'No,' said the Arcadian, 'I don't think I will, if you don't mind.'

'Listen, sonny,' said Maggie, 'don't get bloody smart with me. A dog on a rack better watch his mouth, is my advice.'

'You won't use it.'

'Aye, who says so?'

The Arcadian grinned.

'She does.'

Maggie and Melbourne looked at Victoria, who experienced a second moment of sick realisation. Suddenly she knew why she had been brought here. Not to give her an induction into the secret practices of the Protektorate, but for another reason altogether.

'You need my consent,' she said.

'It's the law,' said Melbourne. 'Torture may only be applied in instances of over-riding need, and then only with the permission of the serving monarch.'

'We who serve the dark one need no authorisation to apply torture,' chuckled the Arcadian. 'That authorisation is simply assumed.'

'This, demon,' said Victoria, her voice raised and echoing in the cavernous space, 'is why we are superior to you.'

The Arcadian looked down at himself.

'But only just,' he said.

'Not only just, no.' She directed her next comment at Brown and Melbourne. 'I forbid this. Kindly cut this man down.'

'Ma'am,' said Maggie Brown, 'it gives none of us any pleasure. But sometimes in certain instances you need to adopt the tactics of your enemies in order to beat them.'

'The tactics of our enemies?' Victoria looked sharply at Maggie. 'What do you mean? Do you mean they could be torturing Albert?'

'Oh, they won't be torturing Albert,' said the Arcadian.

'Be quiet, sonny,' said Maggie Brown, 'or you see that wheel? I might just accidentally trip and give it a spin, know what I mean?' She turned to the Queen. 'Your Majesty, this beastie here knows where he was to take the Prince that night. We've asked him nicely and he won't tell us. We'd like your permission to ask him not so nicely.'

She motioned to Hicks, who moved to the rack and grasped the wheel.

'Tell us,' said Victoria, moving forward to stand in front of the Arcadian. 'Tell us what we need to know and I won't let them hurt you. You have my word.'

The Arcadian seemed to flex and change. Showing her the wolf within. 'In return you offer me – what?'

'Your freedom – *if* the information turns out to be correct.'

'They won't allow it,' said the Arcadian, turning his head to indicate Melbourne and Maggie Brown, who said nothing in reply.

'They have no choice if I command it.'

'I think not. It matters not anyway, for I would be killed by my peers on grounds of my treachery and failure.'

'We can protect you,' said the Queen quickly. 'We can do that, can't we, Lord M?'

'He'd be found by his own people, ma'am – and killed,' said Maggie. 'His best chance is to tell us the whereabouts of the Prince and in return we can promise that his death will be mercifully swift.'

Shadows danced and flickered on wall. From high above them was the sound of the birds, moving about the tower.

The Queen looked at him. She implored him with her eyes. 'We don't have to do this,' she said. 'It doesn't have to be this way.'

The Arcadian shook his head no.

Hicks tensed at the wheel of the rack.

'*Please*,' said Victoria.

Then, the Arcadian tensed, sniffing the air, craning his head to look upwards.

The ravens in the tower were silent.

And all hell broke loose.

XXXVII

High above them was a sound.

An explosion.

Glass raining down on them.

Victoria, twisting away, her hands to her face, protecting her eyes, heard a *thwump-thwump* sound, something dropping to the ground around them. Bags of something. She smelt paraffin.

'Your Majesty,' shouted Maggie, and Victoria, bent over, saw the Demon Hunter running, glass showering down upon her. At the same time there was the noise of something unfurling and suddenly all around them were ropes, dropping from above. Then another noise, a zipping sound.

'Arcadians,' screamed Vasquez, taking aim into the roof, then ducking as the bags that had been dropped burst into flames.

Victoria rolled to safety, scrambling to her feet and drawing the katana.

Feet apart. Watch your stance.

The other members of the Protektorate had done the same, all diving away from the flames.

In the middle of the floor, the paraffin bags were alight, forming a dense circle of fire, within which hung the ropes, like tendrils. As she watched, wolves were abseiling down them, descending head first, then flipping to land on their feet and fanning out to meet the Protektors in battle.

Those that avoided Vasquez's arrows, that is, which zinged overhead, bodies thumping to the floor before one of the raiders found Vasquez and she was forced to sheath her bow and draw her sword, fighting at close quarters now, the wolves pushing the Protektors further out, away from the blazing circle.

Inside which was the rack.

Victoria saw the Arcadian tied to it, struggling, desperate to escape. Instantly he transformed from man to wolf but still could not escape its bonds. Its eyes were distended and bloodshot; it knew death was close, and it let out a howl, to which the other Arcadians responded, so that for a moment the noise in the tower was deafening.

Then one of the assassins turned to the prisoner, its claws raised ready to strike, teeth bared, snarling.

'Your Majesty,' came the cry from behind her – Vasquez, who had found space to use her bow – and Victoria threw herself to the side.

The raider's claws flashed, but it was keeling over, an arrow in its back. The Arcadian on the rack, granted a reprieve, redoubled its efforts to free itself, when suddenly more cable was dropping, more invaders descending. A rope that hung in front of the prisoner jerked and pulled and then there was another wolf, descending head first, holding on with its hind paws. In its front paws it aimed a pistol, the prisoner in its sights.

Victoria had seen the line tug and tweak and had anticipated what was going to happen. She flung herself forward, crossing the fiery barrier created by the paraffin bags and thumping into the rack platform shoulder first, shoving it out of the way, just as . . .

Crack.

The pistol discharged, the bullet thumping into the far wall. The prisoner was screaming as the platform rolled backwards fast, travelling to the rim of the fiery circle, flames licking at the wood.

Victoria controlled her forward roll, coming to her feet, ducking her head to see the abseiling Arcadian, still upside down, struggling to reload his pistol for a second shot at the prisoner. She sprang sideways, slashing out with the katana and cutting the rope, the Arcadian dropping in a heap to the ground, and in a flash she was upon it, her boot to its chest, striking downwards with the sword and spearing it.

She heard her own battle cry as she executed the wolf; the whole move, pure instinct.

Meanwhile the other Protektorate were in combat, battling around and through the flames. Vasquez had again drawn her sword and was trading blows with one of the raiders; Maggie and two more were dancing and ducking, Maggie's sword flashing, sparks flying as it met their claws.

'Run,' she screamed to Melbourne, 'run for the guards!'

But as the Prime Minister made a dash for the door, one of those wolves attacking Maggie Brown was able to strike out, sending him sprawling to the floor, where he lay, unmoving.

Another, meanwhile, had found Hicks, and as the other battles raged around them, the two of them warily skirting one another, moving away from the circle of fire. Hicks had recognised this one from their encounter on the wagonette. The Arcadian had got the better of him that time. Not again.

'You remember me,' said Hicks.

The Arcadian grinned. 'Ah,' it snarled, 'it was your friend, wasn't it, that I ate in the maze?'

'My best friend.' Hicks shot forward, going into a crouch and thrusting with his sword, but the wolf parried and there was a great clash of steel against the talons of the Arcadian. For a second the wolf was exposed and Hicks' weapon struck, grazing the flank of the beast, which ducked and twisted, its paw going to the wound.

It brought the paw, dripping with blood, to its mouth, its tongue flicking to the droplets of blood.

'I ate his insides,' it told Hicks, smiling. 'He was still alive while I ate him.'

Hicks shouted in anger, came forward again, swinging with the sword, only now it was he who exposed himself and the wolf moved inside.

Striking with its claws. Into the chest of Hicks.

'*Hicks*,' screamed Maggie Brown, seeing the Protektor hit. One of the two wolves with whom she had been duelling lay dead, and the other was to follow shortly, but in that instant her attention was diverted and her assailant was able to land a blow, which sent her flying back, her head bouncing off the stone floor. Vasquez, meanwhile was being pushed back towards the ring of fire, the flames licking at her back. Her sword skills were lacking; Brown was always telling her, 'practise, girl, practise,' and oh how she wished she'd listened. Before her the wolf's claws whirled and flashed. She grunted and gasped, trying to hold it off, feeling the heat at her back.

Hicks moaning, sinking to the ground. The Arcadian, moving over him.

Lifting his chin.

Slashing his throat.

'Hicks,' screamed Maggie Brown, seeing the Protektor's

neck fountaining blood, his hands at it as he fell face forward to the stone, legs kicking, blood spraying. She leapt to her feet, slicing horizontally with the sword and swiping the advancing Arcadian's legs from beneath it. It screamed in agony, legs buckling and dumping it to the floor where it lay, Maggie jumping across it, chopping backwards with her broadsword as she did so, the wolf's howl of pain cut short as its head came free of his neck.

Not that Maggie saw, for she was already racing across the floor to the lead Arcadian, sword swinging.

They came together. A second Arcadian joined the fray and once again she fought two opponents, but fury lent her the edge, she knew, and she thought of John Brown telling her, *Use that fury, Maggie – use it against them, never let them use it against you*. She bent and swept up Hicks' sword, one in each hand now.

Block and parry. Block and parry.

Over towards the centre of the room Victoria was doing battle with another of the invaders that came at her claws out. She darted around it, but it was fast and came at her again, she only just managing to ward it off with the katana. She felt something at her back, when the wolf shot forward, with a fearsome howl.

Victoria moved but the wolf checked its progress, not to be fooled by the Queen's feint.

Which was just as she'd planned. For she knew what it was that she had felt at her back. It was the iron maiden, and as she dodged, she pulled the door of it open, simultaneously using it as a shield and weapon.

The wolf hit it with a yell, impaling itself on the spikes with a scream, then kicking uselessly as Victoria heaved the door shut, blood already dripping thickly from the inside of the torture device, as though strained through a colander.

Meanwhile, the Arcadian fighting Vasquez landed a blow, drawing blood from her face, making her scream and sending her flying backwards.

The Queen saw. '*Vasquez.*' And just as the archer dropped back into the flames, Victoria snatched at her, grasping her around the waist, pulling her to safety and at the same time kicking out high and catching the advancing Arcadian on the chin, knocking it off balance and giving her and Vasquez a moment's breathing space. Then, as Vasquez knelt, her hands at her bleeding face, the Arcadian leapt through the flames and into the centre of the circle, its paws raised and ready to spear the archer.

It met the Queen's katana instead and had a second's moment of sick realisation and horror as it slid down the steel, leaving a red slick on the metal.

Victoria didn't pause, dashing over to the flaming rack on which the prisoner still struggled, howling and terrified of being roasted alive. Now, though, was another danger. An Arcadian, moving towards it.

Victoria reached the platform first, coming to it from behind and with a wrench had it moving, jumping aboard and directing it into the path of the wolf. The sudden mass of the rack bearing down upon it, the beast was caught by surprise, had time only to let out a howl of shock and throw up its arms. Then it disappeared beneath the wheels of the rack, howling in pain, the platform thumping over it, and Victoria rotating and sweeping downwards with the katana, delivering the *coup de grâce*.

More ropes dropped from the ceiling.

'Vasquez, above,' warned Victoria, but the archer was ahead of her and was on one knee, her bow pointing towards the rafters, letting off two arrows in quick succession, a body thumping to the ground beside her. She notched another, saw a second wolf in her sights, coming down the line fast – pointing a pistol at her.

Crack.

Vasquez was just in time to roll to the side, her momentum taking her the wrong side of the circle but notching an arrow anyway, aiming blind through the flames and letting off three in short succession, hoping to catch the last raider.

Where was it? Where was it?

'Tell me,' the Queen had screamed, still aboard the coasting rack platform as it shot through the fire and across the floor, away from the centre.

'Release me,' squealed the Arcadian from the other side, still straining at the ropes.

'Tell me where he is!' demanded Victoria. She brought the platform to a stop and jumped from it, the rear of it now almost entirely engulfed by flames. Darting to the front she held her sword ready to slice through the Arcadian's bonds.

'Tell me and you shall have your freedom,' she promised.

'Do I have your word?' it asked.

'You have it.'

She raised the katana, ready.

'Then you will find him . . .' began the wolf.

Too late, from the corner of her eye, she saw it. A wolf, bursting from inside the circle of fire, Vasquez's arrows zinging around it. It was moving fast, and held one of the abseil lines, and as she watched it flicked the line so that it caught the top of a tall stone pillar, the sudden snag yanking the wolf up and around so that it was swinging towards them, leading with its hind claws. Instantly she moved to protect herself.

But the Arcadian was not aiming to attack her. At the last second she saw its intent and there was no action she could take to stop it. The Arcadian landed with both its paws on the rack wheel – the wheel used to open the rack and stretch its unlucky victim – and span it.

The prisoner had time for one scream of agony and it was torn apart, all four limbs ripped from its body, which slid, writhing from the device, the wolf's eyes rolling backwards in its head. The raider on the wheel threw back its snout in triumphant howl, grinned, drawing back its lips to growl at Victoria. At the same time an arrow thumped into its flank, then another, and Victoria was running it through with the katana just as Vasquez arrived, her nose wrinkling in disgust at the sight of the dismembered Arcadian.

'No,' screamed Victoria, 'no,' and she was running to the torso, which still jerked and writhed, bending to it.

'Where is he?' she screamed. 'Where is he?'

She felt the last breath of the Arcadian on her cheek.

Then, from across the way: '*Vasquez.*'

Maggie had been fighting two-sworded. Easily she fended off the wolves, her arms moving in a blur, the sound of the steel ringing in the room.

'I'm going to kill your pal first,' said Maggie Brown as they battled, addressing the lead wolf, 'I'm going to open its throat and watch it bleed. And then I'm going to kill you. I'm going to slit you navel to neck and the last thing you see will be me, watching your guts drop to the floor.'

And in one movement she crouched and span, slashing the first wolf's legs from beneath it and, as part of the same movement, opening its throat on the upswing. It sank to the stone, noiselessly.

Maggie Brown didn't like to make idle threats.

Which was the conclusion at which the lead Arcadian arrived, and hearing the howl of victory from across the way, seeing that the mission was accomplished, it ran. Maggie, regaining her feet, had raced after it, but was a second too slow to stop it bursting through the flame circle, grabbing an abseil line and beginning to shimmy, fast, towards the ceiling.

'Vasquez,' she screamed now.

But was too late. The wolf, strong and very fast on the line, had already reached the top.

It scrambled through a window then stopped. For a second just its snout was visible.

'I'll see you again, Protektor,' it taunted her.

'Aye, well you can join the fuckin' queue,' bawled Maggie Brown, but the Arcadian was gone.

XXXVIII

When Victoria had first seen the interior of the Protektors' carriage she had been amazed.

For on the outside, it looked like any other Royal coach: a Clarence, built to seat six, bearing the correct livery and crests. Inside, however, it could not have been more different. The large cushioned seats she was used to had been stripped out to make space for the Protektors' equipment, which, it seemed, mainly consisted of weaponry.

'Is this the Quartermaster's doing?' she had asked, on that first occasion.

'Yes, ma'am, we call it Bess. She runs faster and lighter than the usual model of Clarence, but is armoured against penetrating weapons, and will stop a bullet, and these windows? The Quartermaster developed a lacquer which, when applied to glass allows people to look out, but not in . . .'

It was Hicks who had told her all of that, fair bursting with pride.

It was Hicks, who on the journey out to the tower, had been driving; now Vasquez sat in the driver's seat and inside, the carriage felt empty.

They travelled in silence: the Queen, Melbourne and Maggie Brown.

Victoria unstrapped the katana sheath and hung it up, next to the spinsaw and short sword. She wished she'd had them all now – that she had taken all of them into the tower with her. Maybe the extra weaponry would have helped.

Or maybe not.

But whatever had happened in there, they hadn't been expecting that. None of them had. She put her elbows to her knees and placed her head in her hands. She grieved for Hicks and Hudson; she yearned for Albert.

They had cleared up. Opening the iron maiden, the dead wolf inside swung out on the door, pinned to it by the spikes, its blood having pooled to the floor. They dragged the corpse to the centre of the room, then done the same with the other dead Arcadians, taking them to where the paraffin fire still burned, where they formed a makeshift funeral pyre.

Vasquez had stood, a faraway look in her eyes, disconsolately feeding the limbs of the dismembered prisoner into the flames, Maggie having already tossed its torso on to the fire. Melbourne, meanwhile, had taken the body of Hicks by the arms and was dragging it over to the pyre.

'No,' commanded Maggie Brown, 'I'm not putting my boy on there – not with them.' And so they had fashioned a suitable plinth for Hicks, using part of the platform from the rack which all of them had lifted on to the fire, so that he could be given the appropriate send-off

When they had paid their respects, Victoria indicated the torture equipment. 'Lord Melbourne,' she said, 'I want you to see to it that this apparatus is destroyed. You will never torture a prisoner again as long as I am monarch, is that clear?'

'Yes, ma'am, if that is your wish.'

'You may be assured that it is,' she said.

She looked at Maggie Brown, about to say something but then thought better of it.

And then, they had taken their leave.

'How,' said Maggie in the carriage, breaking the silence and gloom that had hung over them since leaving the tower, 'how could they have known? You,' she was addressing the Prime Minister, 'you said the Tower was the last place they would look and that in any case Lanthorn was a secret. Even if they came to the fortress in search of their prey they should not have known about Lanthorn, but they knew exactly where we were. How could they?'

'They're demons, Maggie,' said Melbourne, who was nursing his banged head, 'we don't even know the half of what they're capable of.'

'Oh, really?' snapped Brown, her voice growing louder, 'then why has it never happened before? In case you haven't been keeping up on current events, Prime Minister, we just got our arses kicked in one of the most secure buildings in the country. We just lost another Protektor, a good man. We *lost* a prisoner . . .'

'*I know*,' bellowed Melbourne in return, 'I know exactly what we have lost, thank you very much.'

'I'll tell you what we have lost,' said the Queen. She was pulling on her hat, ready to arrange a scarf over her face. When they arrived at the Palace, they would gain entrance via a door known only to a few, and from there make their way to the Queen's apartments, but even so, she couldn't risk being seen by one of the staff, not in the state she was in now, bloodied and bruised from the battle, her skirts black with smoke. 'We have lost our last hope of finding Albert.'

Melbourne and Maggie shared a look. The carriage shook and rattled around them.

'We will find him,' said Melbourne.

'How, exactly?' asked Victoria. 'What scheme have you up your sleeve to locate my missing husband?'

'I have yet to formulate a strategy,' admitted the Prime Minister, 'certainly we may, with the very greatest reluctance, have to consider going public with the issue.'

'Go public?'

'To the police and newspapers, ma'am. In the absence of any concrete leads it may be the only option available to us.'

The Queen suppressed a shudder, staring out of the window. 'Then it would turn into a circus,' she said.

'Possibly, ma'am.'

'And he would be lost for ever.'

'No, Your Majesty,' said Melbourne, 'you are not to cast down all hope. For we will find him, I am sure of it.'

'Lord Melbourne,' she said and her voice betrayed the great exasperation and impotence she felt (*She: the Queen of England. Helpless!*), 'please don't tell me what you think I wish to hear. You say we'll find him. Find him where?'

Melbourne spread his hands. 'If we only knew, ma'am.'

'Why has there been no news? Why no ransom demand? No attempt made to capitalise upon his disappearance?'

'We can only guess, ma'am.'

'And what might that guess be?' she snapped.

'Ma'am?'

'Am I to believe that they may be torturing Albert right now?'

Melbourne swallowed.

'Don't be about to lie to me, Prime Minister,' barked the Queen, warningly.

'It is, of course, possible, ma'am, yes, despite what the Arcadian told us.'

'They are not so squeamish as we, it seems,' murmured Maggie Brown, and Victoria saw Melbourne wince.

'What did you say?' she demanded of Maggie.

'Nothing, Your Majesty,' said Brown truculently, her lips tightly pursed.

'No, pray tell,' pressed Victoria, 'if you have something to say, please tell the whole carriage.'

Maggie looked at her with flinty eyes. 'I merely said that perhaps our enemies are less squeamish than we are when it comes to torture.'

'Or less civilised?'

'Maybe so . . . But perhaps we could have found out where Albert had been taken if we'd just cut straight to the chase instead of holding a public inquiry into the rights and wrongs of torturing a deviant.'

'Maggie . . .' chastised Melbourne.

'In fact,' continued Brown, warming to her theme, 'perhaps we would never have lost the Prince in the first place if you'd let Vasquez take the shot in the maze.'

'She could have hit Albert.'

Maggie snorted. 'That girl could take the eye out of a wasp. She would not have missed. And anyway, I gave the order. I don't give an order like that lightly, Your Majesty. She would not have missed.'

'It was in the heat of the moment,' said the Queen, a little mollified, 'I had not time to think.'

'Aye,' retorted Maggie Brown, darkly, 'perhaps you acted out of instinct.'

'*Maggie*,' snapped the Prime Minister.

'I beg your pardon?' said the Queen, but she did not get an answer, for the carriage, which had some moments ago, crunched on to the gravel of Buckingham Palace, now stopped, and the door had been opened, and there stood John Brown.

'Your Majesty,' he said, to the Queen, bowing his head, 'Prime Minister, Maggie.' He looked about the interior of the carriage. 'You are missing a member?'

'Don't ask, John,' said Maggie sadly.

John cast his eyes downwards a moment, his sorrow evident, then said, 'I have messages, Maggie. Prime Minister,' he addressed Melbourne, 'a carriage is awaiting to take you to a secure location until the danger has passed, for the news that reaches us is of an uprising that has occurred at the House of Commons – something, Maggie, that may require our skills . . .'

XXXIX

Quimby had sat nervously in the Strangers' Gallery of the House, watching the members discussing the Factory Bill yet again, talk of which had caused a great tumult. Many of those members who in the past had talked so passionately in favour of reform seemed to have changed their position on the issue, and this had created great confusion and clamour amongst those present.

'They appear to be bending to our will, sir,' said Perkins, who sat next to him, his shoe and sock off, in order to give his leg some air.

Quimby worried at a nail and bit his lip.

'Perkins,' he said, 'the question of whether or not they do our bidding is irrelevant when placed alongside the larger issue that concerns me.'

'And that is, sir?'

Quimby looked at his manservant, who noted that his master's face bore its worry – that he looked drawn and tired.

'Their appetite, Perkins,' he said, his voice strained. 'What the bloody hell are we going to do if they get hungry?'

'We've no evidence they've acquired a need for human flesh, sir.'

'We've no evidence they haven't, either,' hissed Quimby. 'How long have they been in here debating this thing anyway?'

Indeed, the debate, which had begun in the middle of the afternoon, had gone on.

And on.

And on.

The reason for its length, of course, was that each of Quimby's revenants, numbering fifteen in all, had stood up to give a speech opposing the act. Quimby had not asked them to. Over the past few days, he had entertained up to five ministers a day, with invitations for meetings, tea, drinks, lunch and dinner. On more than one occasion, Perkins and Egg had been carrying the body of an MP to the basement, ready for the resurrection, when the next guest had been knocking on the door. Each zombie had been released back in the wild bearing instructions that they must represent Quimby's interest at all times and these – supplied to him by Conroy, of course – had included opposing the Factory Bill; indeed any reforming measures. Being MPs – even MPs who were, in the strict medical sense of the word anyway, dead – they had seized the opportunity to vocalise their changed sentiments at length.

All of them.

Each of whom had been greeted by either derision or angry shouts of disbelief regarding their change of mind, depending on which side of the House it was doing the shouting.

Every single one gave a lengthy speech, which was followed by what felt like hours of mutinous discord, which on each occasion only abated after much banging of a gavel by the progressively more red-faced speaker.

Now, it was almost midnight.

And they had not eaten.

Good Lord, how long could they last without it? Along with his instructions regarding their new constituency of one,

Quimby had informed them that eating human flesh was wrong and on no account were they to do it, deliberately phrasing the instruction in a jocular manner, in an attempt not to implant an idea in their head which would not otherwise have been there.

What if it had, though? What if him saying that had induced in them a *subconscious* need for human flesh?

'How long would you be able to go without eating, Perkins?' he asked.

'Normally just a few hours, sir.'

'What if I had specifically told you not to?'

'Then longer, sir.'

'Indefinitely?'

'Oh no, sir, I'd need to eat eventually, I'm afraid.'

'And it would have to be human flesh, would it?'

'Oh yes, sir, nothing else quite hits the spot.'

Quimby stared down into the House where Lord Granger sat with Lord Tennant, the latter enthusiastically feeding himself from a plate resting on his lap, that was piled high with chicken drumsticks. As Quimby watched, Tennant shoved a chicken drumstick into his mouth, his face slick with grease, then picked up another drumstick and offered it to Granger.

Who refused.

Granger, that fat pig, who had never been known to refuse food, especially if it was free. Over on the other side of the house, Sir Montague Tales sat with a glassy-eyed expression. Another of Quimby's revenants sat with his head jerking about in a manner resembling that of a bird.

A hungry bird.

This was bad, thought Quimby, very bad, and he was suddenly struck with the need to defecate.

'Keep an eye on them, Perkins,' he commanded, 'I shall return presently.'

He found the toilet as before, settled onto the wooden seat, retrieved his hip flask . . .

'Quimby.'

'Christ!'

Quimby leapt what felt like several feet from the box of the toilet. 'Christ,' he repeated, 'are you trying to bloody kill me?'

'I cannot be held accountable for your nervous disposition, Quimby,' said Conroy. 'I hope your state of mind has nothing to do with our arrangement, which continues to proceed as planned, I trust?'

Quimby took a large drink of whisky before answering, his hand shaking as he did so.

'It does,' he managed between gasps as the liquid lit a fire in his throat.

'Excellent,' purred Conroy, 'excellent. Then last night's resurrection went as planned?'

Quimby finished the hip flask. 'It did, it did,' he gasped.

'Then we have our majority?'

'Yes,' said Quimby, holding on to the wall of the cubicle for support.

Somebody banged at the door.

'I think you had better tell him, Quimby,' whispered Conroy.

'It's busy,' shouted Quimby.

The door rattled.

'It's busy,' repeated Quimby.

The rattling stopped.

'And they do our bidding?'

'They do,' said Quimby.

'Then this stage of the operation is complete.'

'And what now?' said Quimby, 'is our business concluded?'

'Oh no, my Lord, not by a long way yet.'

The door began rattling again. Then there was something thumping against it, as though the person on the other side was putting their shoulder to it.

'What the blazes?' said Quimby. He was standing up, pulling his trousers from around his ankles and stepping out of the tiny cubicle to meet Conroy, the two of them pressed up against each other in the toilet.

Quimby, who was nearest the door, turned, so that his back was to Conroy, the two of them looking, for a moment, as though they were trying to press forward in order to gain a better view at the races.

The door continued to thump.

Quimby reached for the bolt, drew it aside and pushed open the door.

It swung on hinges that squeaked, and for a second Quimby thought that the mystery door thumper had gone, and he allowed himself a moment of relief, mentally chiding his over-active imagination, for a moment – though he would never have admitted it – he thought that it might be . . .

The zombie moved across the door frame.

It was Sir Beaumont Grantham, Quimby saw, not recognising the man at first, for his hair and clothes were in a state of disarray, and his mouth and chin were slick with gore. In one hand he held part of an entrail and as they watched, horrified, he brought it to his mouth, took a bite and began to chew, ruminatively.

Then he started to growl.

'Oh dear,' said Quimby.

XL

Inside the House, Tennant had been greatly enjoying his meal of chicken legs that his man had been kind enough to provide for him. Next to him, Granger had refused even a bite of the feast, which was most unlike him. Even when Tennant had waved the greasy but fragrant fowl limb beneath his nose, Granger had merely looked irritated and waved it away.

Yet the right honourable MP for – wherever, Tennant couldn't recall the exact location of Granger's constituency, somewhere in the north, he thought – was quite clearly hungry.

This being evident by the manner in which he had begun to drool.

For, yes, there was no escaping the fact – really no getting away from it at all – that Granger was salivating. Quite copious amounts of it, too. It dangled and dropped from his lips, great strings of it hanging from his chin.

'Sir,' said Tennant, leaning over, 'I think perhaps you may be experiencing either the pleasant recall of a most gratifying sexual encounter, or you are quite famished, for I must warn you – you are drooling, sir.'

Granger's eyes had taken on a strange faraway look. His head jerked a little, making the strings of saliva hanging from his chin dance.

'I say, sir, perhaps a hankie?' said Tennant, who reached into the pocket of his waistcoat for one, trying to pass it to

Granger, who remained in the same state: drooling, his head jerking this way and that.

It really was most . . .

And then Tennant noticed something else. For it was not just Granger to have adopted this unusual manner. Across the house he saw other right honourable members for constituencies he'd never heard of, doing the same as Granger.

'I say, what the bloody hell is going on?' he said, which were the last words of Lord Tennant, unless his screams were to be counted. Because as it dawned on him that all was not well in the house tonight, he felt a searing pain in his shoulder and twisted his head to see that Sir Roger Blossom, the right honourable member for somewhere near Wales, had leaned forward on the bench and bitten Tennant, his hands on Tennant's shoulder, as though he were addressing the consumption of a particularly large pork chop.

Tennant heard a tearing sound. He saw Blossom straighten. In his mouth was a piece of red, glistening meat that still had the cloth of Tennant's waistcoat attached. He tried to stand, screaming, but next to him Granger had risen and pushed him back to the bench. From behind, Blossom grabbed him again and sank his teeth into the other shoulder, pinning him there as Granger reached and tore open his clothes, then raised his fist and rammed it into Tennant's stomach.

Tennant coughed a geyser of blood and food as Granger sank his hand into the stomach cavity and brought out a handful of gleaming red matter, complete with bits of undigested chicken drumstick.

And he had begun to feast.

The other revenants needed no further invitation.

It was dinnertime at the House.

XLI

The revenant lurched into the tiny room, snarling and reaching for Quimby, who cowered back, pushing into Sir John Conroy who stared terrified over his shoulder.

'I say, Grantham,' said Quimby, 'you might have waited for the toilet, you know. Really, this is most irregular.'

From behind Grantham came the sounds of a great commotion. Screaming and running feet. Somewhere a shot was fired.

'Don't need the toilet, Quimby,' said Grantham, 'at least not yet. Just need to eat.'

'Ah, well I hear the food is most passable in the members' . . .'

But Grantham was shaking his head no.

'Want to eat you, Quimby,' he said. 'Got to eat human flesh, you know that.'

'You *know* this?' repeated Conroy, from behind him. He sounded most unhappy, his voice cold. Quimby tried to recall when he last heard Conroy speak in such a fashion. Then remembered: it was at the workhouse in Old Nichol Rookery, moments after he had torn McKenzie's tongue from his mouth . . .

'Of course he knows,' said Grantham. He reached out one hand. Disgustingly, the entrail still dangled from his fingers. 'He made me, he knows. We're all the same, all of us. They say Sir Charles Hubbard has eaten his family. What have you done to us, Quimby, to make us slaves to this hunger?'

'We're working on it,' said Quimby, holding his hands before him. Grantham was inching forward, the blood dripped from his chin. 'We're working on a refinement of the potion that will cure you. *Cure you*, do you hear me?'

'You won't be working on any refinement, Quimby,' grinned Grantham, 'the only working you'll be doing is through my lower intestine, before I shit you out and you join the rest of the ordure in the streets.'

'Er, Quimby,' said Conroy from behind. 'Your revenant seems to have behavioural issues. Perhaps you would like to remind him whom it is he serves?'

'Quite,' said Quimby, attempting to draw himself up. 'Now look here, Grantham, you do as I tell you, is that clear? And I insist that you stand aside and allow us to exit the toilet, do I make myself understood?'

Grantham rocked back on his heels slightly. His out-stretched hand wavered. There was a moment when, beyond all reasonable expectation, things having taken the turn they had, Quimby wondered if Grantham might be about to obey; that he would simply look confused, scratch his head then shamble off and perhaps find one of the support staff to eat.

But he did no such thing. He grinned, bared his teeth so that Quimby could see particles of meat between them, and lunged forward.

Both Quimby and Conroy shouted out in shock, both huddled as far back into the room as was humanly possible – which was not very far at all.

The expected attack never came, however, for Perkins had escaped the carnage taking place in the main house in order to look for his Lordship, and what he had seen taking place in one of the new toilets, was Sir Beaumont Grantham – Sir Beaumont Grantham about to eat his master.

'Sorry sir,' he said, grabbing Grantham from behind and hauling him out of the tiny toilet, throwing him so that he slammed into the oak panelling on the opposite side of the corridor.

Grantham scrambled to his feet, declaiming, 'They're mine.'

'Sorry, sir, no,' said Perkins, 'and please I'd be most grateful if you might just stay where you are, sir; certainly if you would consider perhaps going elsewhere, as at the moment I am forced to assume your intention towards us are hostile.'

Grantham uttered a cry of rage and attacked, shrieking, *'They are mine!'*

From his trousers, Perkins pulled a sword and held it so that Grantham, flying across from the other side of the hall, simply impaled himself upon it.

But continued thrashing. Still pinned by the sword. But very much alive.

'Don't forget, Perkins,' prompted Quimby, coming forward, somewhat more intrepid now that his manservant, who not only boasted enhanced zombie strength but who had also the foresight to bring along a sword (*Perkins, I could kiss you!*) had arrived and effectively disabled their attacker.

'Come on, man – the head, the head.'

Perkins pushed Grantham further up the corridor, the undead MP pawing at the sword blade that speared him, cutting his hands to ribbons as he tried to manoeuvre himself off the blade.

Perkins waited until he had a bit of space to move, then in one swift movement withdrew the sword and used it to decapitate Grantham, whose face wore an expression of surprise and not a little frustration as his head bounced on the beautifully polished floorboards.

Quimby barely had time in which to gloat, make a show of relief and thank his lucky stars – or even thank Perkins, for that matter – when Conroy had taken hold of his upper arm and was hauling him back up the hall towards the entrance to the Strangers' Gallery

'Just what is going on, Quimby?' he barked. 'What is happening?' hauling the door open and shoving Quimby through, then following him.

The two of them stood at the top of the steps leading to the benches in which, until just recently, Quimby had been sitting, watching the usual rumpus of the house: the jeering and catcalling, the ribald jokes, the heckling and squabbling, bickering and backstabbing.

Now, though – now there was just killing, and gut-munching, and screaming and running.

Many of the right honourable members must have made good their escape before Quimby arrived on the scene, others had been clamouring for the door, which was beneath the Strangers' Gallery, so that Quimby, Conroy and Perkins had to descend the steps to the balcony and lean over the handrail to properly view the scene there.

It was of carnage. There had been a crush at the door, a pile of bodies blocked it almost to the top. Four of the revenants, having seen the opportunity for easy pickings had made their way over there and were attacking the writhing, screaming pile at random, tearing off limbs and ripping flesh from them with their teeth as though they were one of Tennant's drumsticks; plunging their faces into flesh and coming away with mouthfuls of red, dripping meat; unfurling strings of intestine, the bodies of the dead piling up at the doorway, further imprisoning the living.

Those right honourable members not caught up in the crush at the doorway were in the process either of cowering and screaming, or running and screaming, or being devoured and screaming or, in some rare instances fighting back against the remaining zombies who attacked at random, indiscriminately taking food where it could be found.

Then, as they watched, there was a movement at one of the members' galleries to their left. A door burst open and on to the gallery rushed three women. One, older, with wild, black hair; a second, much shorter, whose face was covered with a scarf and who wore a three-pointed hat so that she looked a little like a highwayman, and a third, who held a bow, and who was Quimby noticed, with a surge of feeling he had never before experienced, absolutely . . . *beautiful*.

For a second he was entranced by her, hypnotised by the flow of her limbs and the grace of her body as she ran to the edge of the gallery, raised her bow, notched an arrow, took aim and fired.

Then: '*Party's over*,' shouted the older woman, her accent Scottish, and she and the second were leaping down from the gallery balcony and onto the main floor, both immediately coming adrift, having failed to take into account the floor now being slick with gore. They regained their feet, the first woman immediately wielding the broadsword she held and slashing a revenant that had began lurching in her direction.

Oh – it was Sir Digby Chambers, Quimby noticed. Poor old Digby. Quimby had always quite liked him really; say what you like about him, but when he set his cap at something, he didn't stop until the job was done. Now he moved and lurched and his jaws moved as though unable to control his need for raw flesh – which, Quimby supposed, was exactly the case.

And instead of going down, however, Digby kept on advancing. Just as tenacious in death as he had been in life, he kept on coming. The warrior woman struck again, and again, taking off one of its arms, then the other.

'He won't go down,' shouted the woman in frustration.

The second woman was having the same difficulty. She fought with what looked like a sword in one hand and a most unusual spinning saw in the other, striking out at two opponents simultaneously, both of whom were rocked by mutilating injuries that should have felled them – though neither of whom fell.

'I've got the same problem here!' she yelled. Zombies from other parts of the house were aware of their presence now and were moving over. Bravely the two women stood their ground, chopping and slashing, sliding in the gore about their feet, unable to understand why their attacks had no effect.

'Arrows do not harm them,' shouted the archer, her accent of the South Americas, and before he could stop himself, Quimby was leaning over the handrail, cupping a hand to his mouth and calling to her, 'Go for the head, my dear. You must destroy the brain!'

She looked over at him. Their eyes met. He attempted a nonchalant smile, as though he were often to be found dispensing *bon mots* concerning the best way of killing zombies in the House of Commons.

'Go for the brain!' she called down to her two comrades.

The older of the two women heard, relaying the message to the shorter one. 'Your M—' she started, then stopped, 'Tora!'

The woman looked at her. 'Tora?'

The older woman shrugged. 'Just go for the brain, Tora, go for the brain.'

And Quimby basked for a moment.

Then, Conroy blindsided him and he was thrust between the benches, catching his head, the pain making him shout out. The next thing he knew Conroy was above him and his eyes were burning with anger and hatred as he snarled, 'You're going to die for this, Quimby.'

'Sorry, sir,' came the voice from above them both, and once again Perkins was saving his master's skin, hauling Conroy from him. Sadly for Perkins, Conroy was no Sir Beaumont Grantham, and he twisted in Perkins' grasp, shouting, 'Unhand me, gimp,' and kicking out with his left foot at what he knew to be Perkins' weak spot: the leg. Sugar's leg.

Which snapped and tore free with a crunch, depositing Perkins to the floor. Conroy turned, ready to finish the job on Quimby.

'Don't you ever call him a gimp again,' said Quimby and used every ounce of pugilistic experience he had ever acquired at Harrow, then at Oxford, to deliver an uppercut.

His pugilistic experience at these establishments, however, bordered on the non-existent. And rather than sending Conroy crashing back into the benches as had been his intention, he hardly even rocked the man. Instead, he heard the bones in his hand crunch and was crippled by a searing pain that began at his fingertips and raced up his arm to the elbow.

In an instant Conroy was upon him. In his hand was a knife. But as he moved across the gallery about to strike there came a call from the main floor below.

'*Conroy.*'

And Conroy, stopped, looked in the direction of the voice.

'Christ,' he said, and whirled, his cloak fanning out around him. 'We will meet again, Quimby,' he called as he hurried back along the benches to the gangway, taking the steps two at a time towards the door. 'Very, very soon. And when we do,' he said pausing as he reached the top, 'you will die suffering and begging for mercy and you will *rue the day* we ever met.'

And then he was gone.

What do you mean, 'will' rue the day? thought Quimby, nursing his hurting hand and crabbing along the benches to check upon Perkins. 'Will' rue it? I already rue the day we met – matter of fact I've been rueing the day we met since the bloody day we met.

XLII

Maggie Brown gingerly made her way across the floor of the House of Commons, looking for all the world as though she were a farm girl, negotiating a particular muddy field. Only it wasn't mud that caused her to slip and slide and be constantly in danger of losing her footing and falling, it was blood and guts. Everywhere was strewn the bodies of MPs, the majority in the most grotesque states of mutilation. It was simple to tell victim corpse from attacker cadaver: those of the revenants were headless, or boasted several arrows in their skulls; the remainder were missing limbs or had portions of their bodies missing or had been split like pea pods to be stripped of the meat from inside. Everywhere, though, whatever the manner of their death, were dead MPs and those were soon to be dead, who lay moaning in pain – and every now and then the air was torn by a high-pitched scream.

One thing was for certain, Soho was going to be quiet for a while.

Because this was a right bloody mess. She put her hands to her face, wiping from it some of the offal that had accumulated during the combat. Literally, a right bloody mess.

'Your Ma—' she said, 'I mean, Tora, did you . . .'

She stopped mid-question and was looking around.

'Vasquez,' she said, 'where is she? Where's the – you know who?'

Vasquez had stood and was peering over the balcony. 'I don't know, Maggie. Is she not with you?'

'No, she's not bloody with me,' Maggie was looking with a greater urgency now, darting around the main floor of the Commons, sifting through piles of butchery in case Victoria was trapped beneath bodies, and tossing limbs aside as though she were hunting through a pile of clothes in search of a shirt to wear.

'Oh, bloody hell,' she said, 'Tora!'

'She shouted something, Maggie, I recall,' said Vasquez from above her, 'that was the last I remember of her.'

'I don't believe this,' said Maggie, skating over to another corner of the room. 'Tora!' she called, 'Tora! Tora! I don't *believe* this, we've bloody lost her. So much for bloody protecting her, we've gone and bloody lost her. What was it you heard her shout, lassie?'

'Maggie,' said Vasquez, 'in the heat of battle I paid it little mind, but I think what she called was Conroy.'

Maggie stopped.

'Conroy?'

'Yes, Maggie,' said Vasquez, shame-faced.

'He was here then,' said Maggie, 'She saw him. Oh my God, girl, she's gone after him. Quick,' she was already racing to the door, dragging corpses from the doorway to allow her through. 'There's nothing to be gained by staying here. We don't want to be answering the peelers' awkward questions. Let's get back. I *cannot believe* we've bloody lost her . . .'

At Melbourne House in Piccadilly, Lord Melbourne sat with a glass of whisky, allowing his eyes to close as he, finally, after what had been days of little or no sleep, relaxed.

Secure location, he thought. *To remain there until the danger had passed.* And the carriage had returned him home.

Where could possibly be more secure than that?

He heard the sound of her coming into the room.

'You know,' he said to her, 'I thought I had lost you to Lord Byron, all those years ago.'

'Darling,' chided Lady Caroline, who settled on the sofa beside him. 'I want no more talk of George. That's all in the past now. You know that. I'm back, my love. Back with you.'

He opened his eyes to see her. She sat with one leg pulled up beneath her bottom. He liked it when she sat in that position. She reached and touched his hair, brushing his fringe from his eyes, and in response he relaxed even further into the soft welcome of the sofa, the comforting embrace of home and of the attentions of his beloved Caroline. (Who had returned – after all those long years. Put that in your pipe and smoke it, Mr *Don* bloody *Juan*!)

For a moment or so the only sound in the room was the crackle of the fire that Caroline had laid. She'd sent the staff home, she said, so that they had the house to themselves. It was because she wanted to spoil him, she said. Because he'd been working so hard lately.

'Come on, William,' she chided him, laughing, 'don't fall asleep on me just yet. I want to know all about what you've been doing.'

'Well,' he said, 'we moved the prisoner to Lanthorn, just as you suggested, my darling, and after the usual business of the day we took the Queen there to see the prisoner, but I'm afraid there was an attack.'

'Oh dear,' cooed Caroline, fingers still playing with his hair. 'Was the prisoner killed during this invasion?'

'Torn limb from limb,' said Melbourne, a note of pride in his voice.

'Oh, good.'

'Yes, I thought you would be pleased, my darling. I thought it might earn me a kiss . . .'

But there was no kiss forthcoming.

'I hope you stayed well clear of any action,' she said simply, in reply.

'I had your words running through my mind, my darling,' he smiled, 'though unfortunately I sustained a knock to the head.'

'Oh, my love,' she purred, 'where? Show me where.'

He took her hand and guided it to the back of his head where he had a bump like a half-egg. She stroked it, for a moment, then dug her fingers into it, giggling a little as she did so.

'Ow,' he pulled away, pained.

'Oh, I couldn't resist it,' she smiled.

'There always was a sadistic side to you, Caroline,' he said, rubbing the back of his head, 'but I do believe it's been even more pronounced since you came back to me.'

'It's what you love about me,' she said softly, into his ear, and he supposed that she was correct, and once again he closed his eyes.

'You do deserve a kiss, after all,' she said and she felt her lips brush his cheek and enjoyed the sensation of it; the tingle it left when she withdrew.

'Another,' he asked, his voice dreamy and faraway, and she kissed him again, and Lord Melbourne thought that he had found true happiness at this house here in Piccadilly, and that if her were to die now, well he shouldn't much mind . . .

'*William*,' she shouted, into his ear.

He shot upright.

'Don't fall asleep now, dear,' she said, her voice back to its usual volume, 'for there is more work to be done.'

'More?'

'Yes, you see, I know where the Prince is being held.'

'You do?'

'Darling, why, of course, I do. Caroline knows everything.'

'Yes – yes, of course, dear,' he said, smiling. Of course she did. When the Prince had gone missing, why hadn't he simply asked Caroline where he was being held? Or was that before she returned? All of a sudden he couldn't remember.

Caroline . . .

When had she . . . ?

How had she . . . ?

'Ssh,' whispered Caroline into his ear, noting that he had tensed and that his head was jerking like that of a passenger who has awoken from a nap on the omnibus and fears he may have missed his stop. 'Ssh,' she repeated, calming him, 'ssh.'

And he relaxed once more.

'Everything will be all right,' she murmured, her lips brushing his ear as she spoke. 'We just have one more thing we need to do.'

'Yes, Caroline,' he said, feeling light-headed, dizzy even.

'We need to send Maggie Brown to the Prince. We need to send her to the workhouse in the Old Nichol Rookery. So that she can fetch the Prince. Can you see to it that she gets the message? And that she goes alone?'

The thought nagged at him. He didn't want Mrs Brown hurt, did he? No, not Maggie Brown. She's on our side, isn't she? He thought she was. He wasn't sure. Caroline would know, of course. Yes, that was right. Caroline would know.

'We're not going to hurt her, are we?' he asked Caroline. 'We don't want to hurt Maggie Brown, do we?'

'No, of course not, silly,' said Caroline, 'of course not. Now run along now, with your message.'

An hour or so later, Melbourne reappeared. Caroline sat on the sofa still, as before, and he took a seat beside her.

'Is it done?' she asked. 'Is the message dispatched to Maggie Brown?'

'Yes, my darling.'

'Good,' said the succubus, who smiled at him, before extending one long pointed talon, and jamming it deep into Lord Melbourne's heart.

XLIII

The members of the Bethnal Green Baptist Ladies' Prayer Association, as they bumped and rattled along in the unprecedented number of *four* carriages in convoy, were most excited at the prospect of their impending visit to that famous institution, Bethlem Royal Hospital.

Or, as the asylum was perhaps better known: Bedlam.

Or . . . as some in the carriages were wont to describe it, in the name of inducing their fellow prayer association members to even greater heights of anticipation: 'the place where the lunatics are kept'.

The reason for this tremendous sense of expectation was that the Bethnal Green Baptist Ladies' Prayer Association had close (though, for obvious denominational reasons, unofficial) links with the Crouch End Catholic Ladies' Prayer Association, whose members had recently conducted a visit to Bedlam for reasons of education and a greater understanding of the hardships endured by others. Those attending on that occasion had, ashen-faced, regaled their friends with the horrors they had witnessed. They had spoken of the great trauma of the visit; the horrifying sights they had been forced to endure such as were almost impossible to relate – *impossible*. For those sights as they had seen, as they were led along the corridors of the asylum and been permitted to peer in through the barred windows of the cells had been the most uncommonly, ungodly, profane and depraved sights, such as would stay with them for the rest of their days.

So had said the members of the Crouch End Catholic Ladies' Prayer Association.

Without hesitation, the Bethnal Green Baptist Ladies' Prayer Association had booked their own visit.

Thus, the excitement in their carriage was palpable as they travelled from Whitechapel and made their way across London Bridge into Southwark, and as they approached the imposing building at St George's Fields, the ladies gathered at the windows of the carriage to ooh and aah at the asylum.

Or . . .

'The *Hospital*, ladies.'

They were constantly reminded of this fact by Mrs Audrey Wetherspoon, the group leader, who had arranged the visit and was slightly suspicious of some of those attending, believing that they might be motivated by reasons of prurience and voyeurism and an unhealthy interest in witnessing depravity and perversion, rather than education. This trip, despite taking place during night-time, in less than sociable hours, had been over-subscribed, attracting far greater interest than other trips. Arriving at the *rendezvous* that night, wearing bonnets and Sunday best had been a great many faces she did not recognise, friends and family, so she was told, who were keen for the edification of the visit.

Though not keen enough on edification, obviously, to attend either the weekly prayer meetings, or, indeed the Baptist Church itself.

'It *is* a hospital,' she insisted to those in her carriage, the mood dampening instantly. 'In this day and age it really is rather impolite to refer to the mentally ill as *lunatics*. These people are not *lunatics*, so kindly do not refer to them as such. I believe the polite term these days is *retards*, a derivation of retarded, which encompasses those who are mentally ill.'

Those ladies she was travelling with murmured 'retards' in a bid to show that they had been paying attention, although each of them secretly wished she were travelling in one of the other carriages.

Then they were craning to see once more as the structure of Bedlam hove into view. In front of it were perfectly mani-cured lawns, only just visible in the moonlight; trees, like sentries posted around their outer edge. The lawns were split by an approach road, into which their carriages turned, so that the asylum was now ahead of them, wide – as far as the eye could see either side – and tall, too. It towered above them, a vast, monolithic edifice behind a high perimeter wall, interrupted only by the wrought iron of the main gates.

There were more oohs and ahs, plus one or two private regrets all of a sudden. Visiting at night had seemed like such a good idea in the cold light of day but none of the ladies had expected the building to look quite so dark and fearsome in the flesh.

As they rattled along the approach road, they heard the wheels of a Hansom cab that passed them at great speed, driven by a man in a top hat, whose cloak fluttered behind him as he thundered up the road. They were able to see the cab come to a halt before the main steps of the building, and the driver drop down, one hand steadying his top hat, then taking up a cane and hurrying from the cab to the steps, not even stopping to tether the horses, flying up the steps and disappearing from view.

Goodness, thought the ladies of the Bethnal Green Baptist Ladies' Prayer Association collectively. They had yet to arrive at the asylum – or 'hospital' – and already there were exciting events to behold.

Their own carriages came to the forecourt, where the Hansom carriage remained, and the ladies descended to be greeted by a member of staff who bowed and bid them gather into a group so that he might introduce himself, which they did.

He was no ordinary member of staff.

He held a flaming torch, even though there was ample light provide by the many gas lamps in the forecourt, and was dressed in the gaudy outfit of a ringmaster, and addressed them just as though he were one: 'Ladies,' he bellowed, 'only the very hardiest souls should consider themselves of suffi-cient mettle to pass through the doors of the legendary palace of woe . . . *Bedlam.*'

He grinned, revealing blackened teeth, and the ladies clasped one another in terror, thrilled and titillated by the ringmaster's build up.

'For medical science,' he continued, 'has no explanation for the strange, terrible, most unnaturally freakish and deviant sights you are to witness and to behold within Bedlam's feared and legendary walls. Some say the poor unfortunates imprisoned here are victims of mother nature's macabre sense of humour, twisted in the head, compelled by their sickness to commit ghastly acts; others that their brains have been infected by devils.'

The ladies gasped.

'Indeed,' said the ringmaster, 'which means I must warn you, ladies, to stick very close to me at all times. Do nothing unless I say it may be done. Touch nothing unless I say so. Am I understood?'

Indeed. The ladies nodded.

'Then let us go.'

As the party trooped up the steps to the entrance, the ring-master asked them if they 'liked the threads' and they agreed that they did, and that the suit was most pleasing to the eye.

Although, in fact they were thinking that they cared very little for the attire of the man.

'And the little introductory speech?' said the ringmaster, 'it wasn't too much was it? You didn't think I was overdoing it a little? This is really quite a new thing for us, you see, ladies, just a way of optimising our assets in the evening, making a little money on the side, know what I mean?'

It was most colourful, agreed the ladies, who in fact wanted to move swiftly on to the section of the visit where they were able to behold the retards in action.

Now they had arrived in a large hall.

'Here we are in what we call the central administration area,' said the ringmaster, 'which divides the male and female quarters. You didn't think we'd have men and women living together did you, madam?' he said, winking lascivi-ously at Mrs Patricia Parsons and Mrs Pamela Player, who each turned a deep shade of red and decided immediately to report the man for his vulgarity. 'The passageways there lead to the smaller wards, wherein the patients are placed depending on the nature – and the severity – of their illness.'

At the word 'severity' the ladies of the Bethnal Green Baptist Ladies' Prayer Association drew breath, thinking that now they would be exposed to those manner of horrors that their colleagues in the Crouch End Catholic Ladies' Prayer Association had described.

How disappointed they were, then, when the ringmaster said, 'However, the seriously disturbed are not kept on this floor,' and went on to tell them how the women were involved in cooking, cleaning and sewing, 'for the purpose of their recovery these pursuits are considered most beneficial' winked the ringmaster, fingering his costume. While, the men, he explained were also involved in carrying out worthwhile tasks; indeed the wards were light and airy, and furnished with pictures . . .

The ladies continued to follow him, trying their best to hide the sense of anti-climax that was beginning to descend upon the group.

Then, the ringmaster turned to them and said, 'Ladies, I hope you are ready for this. Because in order that we may witness the madness first-hand we need to travel *below floors*.'

A collective gasp.

The ringmaster still held his torch, and he now raised it, significantly, opening a large wooden door and indicating the way down a flight of grey stone steps.

At the bottom the ladies assembled. Here the atmosphere was markedly different from the level above, which had been much like that of a hospital – a 'usual' hospital, that was – perhaps even one that was a little more modern and progressive and better-equipped than was normal.

Down here, however, the air was stale and dank. In the air a foul scent. And instead of the wards as above, furnished with home comforts, here there were simply cells lining both sides of the corridor.

'Careful, ladies, the inmates are prone to fling faeces – or worse.'

'What could possibly be worse than faeces?' asked one. There was much murmuring and shaking of heads as the women puzzled over the conundrum.

One of the ladies towards the front of the group screamed as an inmate threw himself at the bars of his cell, screaming.

'These are the hopeless cases, ladies. Those poor unfortunates cast aside by society. Their only benefit to mankind is to serve as *experimental subjects*.'

There was much shocked gasping and placing of hands to throats.

'What is behind that door?' asked Mrs Audrey Wetherspoon, pointing at a heavy oak door at the end of the hallway.

'That, ladies,' said the ringmaster, 'is an underground entrance to the State Criminal Lunatic asylum, the most dread section of Bedlam.'

The ladies all moved towards the door, assuming it was next on the itinerary.

'Oh no, ladies,' demurred the ringmaster, 'there are some sections of Bedlam that are simply too horrific to show.'

The ladies pretended to look relieved.

Then: 'Oh my God,' shrieked one of the prayer group, recoiling from a cell door, having been peering through the opening.

'I can't look, I can't look,' she screeched, craning to get a better look at the other ladies.

'Ah yes, the patient we call the Bishop. He *pleasures himself* constantly – *constantly*,' shouted the ringmaster hysterically, and those prayer group members not already crowding around the doorway now rushed over, only Mrs Audrey Wetherspoon and one other woman she didn't recognise were immune. The other woman, who had the appearance of a pauper, and was nursing a chill perhaps, had her coat done up tight around her throat. She wore a somewhat manly hat, too, and it was pulled down low over her eyes, which, now Mrs Wetherspoon saw, were darting this way and that. Looking in particular towards the door that led to the State Criminal Lunatic asylum.

'A man. *Pleasuring himself,*' gasped Mrs Wilmslow, who had physically hauled several of her prayer group colleagues out of the way in order to verify that this was indeed the case, and Mrs Wetherspoon sighed, knowing exactly what was coming.

'Mrs Wilmslow,' came the cry, as Mrs Wilmslow executed her usual trick whenever attention was in danger of leaving her alone for too long – and fainted.

'Oh,' she cried feebly on the floor, and several of the ladies bent down to help her, fanning at her face and offering words of encouragement. Those ladies remaining at the cell door suddenly, to a woman, placed their hands to their mouths.

'*He has reached completion,*' shrieked the ringmaster.

And in an instant the ladies of the Bethnal Green Baptist Ladies' Prayer Association were scattering – dispersing at speed from the door as they discovered exactly what it was that might be flung, that was worse than faeces.

For her part, Mrs Audrey Wetherspoon stood aghast, feeling a mixture of emotions, among them shock, outright disgust, a little shame and, if she was honest with herself, not a little amusement. She turned, seeking out the second woman who had held back, in order that she might, perhaps, share her amusement and caught sight of her at the door to the State Criminal Lunatic asylum. For a second the two women's eyes met, and Mrs Audrey Wetherspoon was about to call out, for surely this woman was about to place herself in danger, but something made her stop herself.

The woman gave a short nod of the head in thanks, and was gone.

XLIV

'I'm to go to a workhouse in the Old Nichol Rookery, there to meet the Prime Minister and a squadron of men,' said Maggie. 'There, he believes, the Prince is being held.'

Vasquez stood from the table in the cottage where she had been sitting, fidgety and frustrated at their inactivity as the Protektorate debated its next move.

This, at least, was something. Some action they could take, and Vasquez gladly snatched up her bow and quiver, ready for the journey to the rookery.

'No,' said Maggie Brown, 'Melbourne suggests you remain with the Queen.'

'The Queen is not *here*,' protested Vasquez.

'The only two places we can predict her to be are here or at the Rookery,' said Maggie. 'I'll be there, you'll be here should she turn up.'

And with that she pulled on her armour, back to her normal clothes now and glad of it, buckling on her broadsword, tying back her long, black hair.

'Maggie,' said John Brown.

He stepped forward and stopped her mid-tie, her hands at the back of her head as she tried to secure her hair, and he put his hands to her shoulders.

'What is it?' she said, but couldn't meet his eye.

'You know what,' he said. 'Something doesn't feel right about all of this. It's too convenient. Too well-timed.'

'Aye,' she sighed, 'it doesn't feel right. But nothing ever does, John.'

'It could be a trap,' he said.

She shrugged. 'It wouldn't be the first time the Baal have tried to catch Maggie Brown and not lived long enough to regret it.'

'They've never gone this far before,' he said, 'first the Prince, now possibly the Queen.'

'I'll be fine, John,' she said, after a moment of reflection during which she seemed to consider her options, 'I promise, I'll be fine.'

She reached and kissed him then took his arms away and made for the exit, climbing the few steps to the door, opened it and turned.

'Maggie,' said John.

'Yes, my love?'

'Block and parry,' he said, 'block and parry.'

She grinned and the door slammed behind her. There was a moment's pause and then the sound of horse's hooves, Henstridge and Maggie leaving, bound for Old Nichol.

John Brown sighed and sat down heavily. He placed his hands on the table in front of him and his head drooped slightly. He took deep breaths. He thought of Maggie.

And that she might be riding into a trap.

'Father,' said young John Brown, who sat opposite him, 'will she be all right?'

John Brown raised his head and grinned at their little boy. 'Your mother? Aye, she'll be fine. She's the redoubtable Maggie Brown, of course she'll be all right.'

There came a knock at the door.

'Oh thank God she's seen sense,' said John Brown in a rush, standing from his seat.

But Vasquez stopped him with a hand, her hand to the hilt of her sword.

'What is the code word?' she demanded.

'*What*?' came the voice. It was not a voice any of them recognised, and they tensed, Vasquez drawing her sword.

'What bloody code word?' came the voice, then: 'Perkins, did the Prime Minister say anything about a code word?'

'No, sir,' came a second voice.

'Er, I'm afraid we haven't been given one.'

'Then what is your business here?'

'We come from the Prime Minister, Lord Melbourne, about whom, I'm afraid, we have some rather bad news. But just before he . . . Well, before the event the bad news concerns, he gave us a message to give to a Mrs Maggie Brown . . . I say, I recognise that voice. You're not the archer from the House of Commons, are you? We met earlier. You might recall, I was the one with the advice on how to kill the zombies . . .'

But Vasquez had already dashed up the steps, yanked open the door and had her sword to Quimby's throat.

'What was the message?' she demanded to know.

'He said to tell her that it's a trap,' said Quimby, 'that she's walking into a trap.'

By Christ, thought Quimby, the blade at his neck, staring into Vasquez's beautiful, black and angry eyes, but the day was looking up. Talk about every cloud being the bearer of silver lining.

Up to that point, of course, things had been going

spectacularly badly. He and Perkins had hurried out of the Commons, only narrowly avoiding detention by the peelers who were arriving at the scene in great numbers and who would most certainly have wanted to speak to Quimby and Perkins, especially given their state, which was that of bedraggled troops returning from battle: Perkins was hopping on one leg and was leaning heavily on Quimby as they staggered slowly away from the Houses of Parliament, Quimby moaning and swearing every step of the way. Their progress made even more arduous thanks to the difficulty Perkins was having in holding on to Quimby as well as keeping the limb out of sight in his topcoat. He'd already torn off the shoe in order to make the limb less unwieldy and Sugar's toes were constantly beneath his nose or tickling at his chin – a sight that was not lost on Quimby, needless to say.

But made it they had, and after helping Perkins into the driving seat, an operation that was far less strenuous than helping him to walk, Quimby had clambered into the cab and stuck his head out of the window as the cab rumbled on, shouting to be heard over the noise of the wheels.

'What am I to do, Perkins?' he called up.

'I don't know, sir.'

'I'm dead, Perkins, dead,' shouted Quimby, his hand at his top hat, 'either by the hand of Conroy or at the gallows. What am I to do, man?'

'Might I suggest, sir,' called Perkins over his shoulder, 'that a possible shift in strategy is in order?'

'What do you have in mind, man?'

'That we switch sides, sir.'

Quimby thought about this for a moment, the wind in his face. 'That's not a bad idea, Perkins,' he said. 'Not a bad idea at all. And I know just the man to see. Change direction at once and take us to Piccadilly, to the home of Lord Melbourne. If we can't catch him there, we'll try the Reform. At least we know he won't be at the House.'

Thus, not long later, Quimby's Hansom pulled up outside the pillars of Melbourne House on Piccadilly, where his Lordship saw a woman – a quite beautiful woman, actually – leaving from the side gate, saying something to the driver of her own cab and jumping in.

'Did you see her, Perkins?' said Quimby, thinking that the Prime Minister was obviously up to his tricks again. He always had been a dark horse, that one. And he looked down his nose at Quimby! The cheek of the man!

He grabbed the toolbox from the well of the carriage, then went to help Perkins climb down from the cab, the two of them getting back into the carriage and closing the curtains.

Ever since the unfortunate incident in Pall Mall, the pair of them had carried a few tools with them, a sort of emergency repair kit to be used should Perkins' leg come adrift again. Now Perkins pulled the leg from beneath his coat and handed it to Quimby, who brought it to his nose to sniff.

'Don't you think it's incredible that it doesn't decompose, Perkins?' he said.

'It is, sir,' said Perkins, who had rolled his trouser leg up to the thigh and was now hunting the box for the wooden staples and a hammer.

'In many ways this leg represents our most successful experiment, don't you think?' he said, passing the limb to Perkins, who began to affix it, hammering expertly away.

'Well, yes, sir,' said Perkins, who finished his hammering,

and the two men admired his handiwork for a moment, before letting themselves out of the carriage.

Nobody answered the main doors of Melbourne House, so the pair of them decided to investigate the side door, which they found open.

'What do you think, Perkins?' said Quimby. 'Should we go in?'

'Perhaps we should write the Prime Minister a letter, sir?'

'Write him a letter? Don't be ridiculous, man. No, we'll go in. If he's here then all well and good – what we have to tell him justifies the intrusion. If he isn't, then no harm done. You first.'

Perkins led them along a hallway where they heard a noise, that of a quiet moaning sound that appeared to be emanating from the parlour into which they crept.

There on the sofa sat the Prime Minister. He could have been asleep but for the dark, spreading stain of blood at his chest.

'Melbourne,' shouted Quimby, and he moved over quickly to the sofa, thumping down beside Melbourne, who stirred a little, his eyes fluttering open, seeing Quimby.

'Oh God,' moaned the Prime Minister, 'I'm in hell.'

'No, you're not, Melbourne,' said Quimby quickly, 'you're in Piccadilly. What on earth happened to you, man?'

He motioned to Perkins, who reached to unbutton the Prime Minister's shirt so that he might tend the wound.

'Caroline,' croaked Melbourne, 'she . . .'

'Caroline? She's been dead ten years or more man, what's up with you?'

'No, not Caroline . . .' the Prime Minister was woozy. A droplet of blood escaped his lips and began running down his chin. Then he seemed to remember something and his head jerked, sending both Quimby and Perkins scrambling to their feet in surprise. '*No*,' shouted the Prime Minister, 'not Caroline. It was her. It was the succubus. Oh God! Oh God what have I done, oh Sweet Jesus please forgive me!'

'Forgive you for what, Melbourne?' asked Quimby. 'What have you done, man?'

Melbourne turned and grabbed him. When he spoke his lips pulled back to reveal bloodied teeth. Perkins had by now uncovered the wound and it oozed blood.

But now Melbourne had grabbed him, wanting to speak and he pulled Quimby in close. 'Maggie Brown,' he said, 'you must save Maggie Brown.'

'Who is Maggie Brown?' asked Quimby.

'The Queen's . . . the Queen's Protektor.'

The Queen. Of course. That was why they were here.

'We bring news of the Queen, Prime Minister,' said Quimby. 'We know of a plot hatched by her mother's private secretary.'

'Then find Maggie Brown,' managed the Prime Minister.

'Where, man?' said Quimby. 'Where do we go?'

Melbourne told them.

Then, with a last gasp of pain, the Prime Minister died.

Shortly afterwards, they had left, bound for Windsor.

XLV

Maggie Brown tethered Henstridge outside the workhouse and waited. There was no sign of Melbourne, nor of any soldiers; around her just the usual dirt and hubbub of the slum, upraised palms that she waved away. She waited.

When still no one appeared, she went to the workhouse door, stepping over those who slept or sat slumped around the doorway and knocked, wondering if she had the right place. Or, worse, if it was just as John had warned, and it was a trap. Presently, there was the sound of bolts being drawn back and the door was opened by an old crone.

'Hello?' said Maggie. She peered inside over the woman's shoulder, one hand at her sword, feet slightly apart and braced. 'Do you have men here, from the government?'

'Oh yes, dear,' said the crone, as though such a thing were a regular occurrence. 'Mr Melbourne and his men. They in the back room waiting for you now. They said you should go through. Just follow the hall down.'

Maggie stepped cautiously inside. The workhouse was eerily silent.

'This way, dear, follow me,' said the crone and she hobbled slowly down the hall. Behind her, Maggie drew her sword, every sense alert. Not liking this. Not liking it one bit, but drawn to the room, for what other choice was there? Flight?

No. Because that wasn't her way. Whatever was in the room, she would meet it.

She was Maggie Brown.

And now the old woman had reached the door and she opened it in order to allow Maggie to step through. She crouched a little, drawing a dagger with which to lead, her broadsword held low and behind her. Then she moved, slowly into the room, using the open door as cover on her left side, defending to the right.

Inside was dark, the only light coming from a single filthy window; on the floor the glow of something, a gas lamp at its lowest flame, which as she crouched, every nerve-ending screaming at her, was turned up by a figure, leaning from a chair.

Which straightened.

'The redoubtable Maggie Brown,' said the Arcadian, grinning at her. 'I told you we'd meet again.'

From behind Maggie the door slammed.

'So did I,' said the old crone at her back.

Except, of course, Maggie realised as she span around – it wasn't the old crone at all, it was the succubus.

XLVI

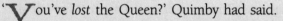

'You've *lost* the Queen?' Quimby had said.

'She went after Conroy,' snapped Vasquez.

She and Quimby had discovered much in common in their short time together, though none of it, sadly, as far as Quimby was concerned anyway, of much romantic currency. Not unless he counted the fact that they shared a nemesis in Sir John Conroy and had a vested interest in keeping the Queen alive.

'If she went after Conroy, then perhaps she's with him.'

'That is very clever-clever of you,' she said (he loved the way she used the language. As though she had learnt it but found it a little too prosaic for her tastes), 'but we don't know where Conroy is, do we?'

Quimby thought. What had Conroy told him? That he was moving his centre of operations. To the second abode he had spoken of, presumably, the one that was so noisy it was like . . .

Of course.

'Bedlam,' said Quimby.

'What?' said Vasquez, who looked most suspicious.

'Bedlam,' repeated Quimby, 'He's at the hospital: Bethlem. At least, that's where he might be. That's where I think he is.'

He smiled and he felt ridiculously happy to help, as though all of his other problems were as nothing compared to the pleasure he got from being with this archer – Vasquez. Oh, sweet, sweet, Vasquez. His joy was almost complete as she grabbed him by the top of the arm and dragged him towards Bess, Perkins limping along behind them.

'Get in,' she commanded, but Quimby preferred to sit beside her on the driver's plate. She frowned at him but shook the reins and they took off at high speed.

'If I'm right,' shouted Quimby, 'and the Queen is at Bethlem, can I perhaps count on your support when it comes to answering for my crimes? I am rather hoping that my good deeds will go some way to absolving me, you see. And perhaps when this is all over, the two of us could . . .'

'Your good deeds?' scoffed Vasquez. God, her hair looked beautiful in the half-light. The moon, sinking in the sky now, made it shine, and it was all he could do not to reach out and touch it. 'What good deeds is that you speak of?'

'By leading you to the Queen.'

'What about all the dead MPs? Are they one of your good deeds?'

Nobody will miss a few MPs, he thought, but opted not to say it. Contrition was the order of the day, he had decided. That and a willingness to atone for his crimes. If he could appear instrumental in the daring rescue of the monarch, he thought, then perhaps . . .

'You might escape the hangman, I suppose,' said Vasquez, sounding as though she were not especially bothered either way. 'The Queen may instruct the judge to be lenient, as you did try to make amends.'

'Well, that's something . . .'

'Maybe you will even escape deportation.'

Quimby gulped. 'Yes.'

'And perhaps simply be left to rot in jail?'

'Yes,' said Quimby, who by now, and despite even the presence of the beautiful Vasquez, was wondering about the wisdom of this latest strategy. Especially as it had the potential to deliver him straight into the jaws of Conroy.

Too late now.

The carriage thundered on. Bedlam in sight.

Maggie screamed in pain. She twisted away from the succubus and distantly heard her own blood splash to the floor and knew that she was hurt. She'd moved fast at least – and had been able to deflect the blow a little – deflect it from her throat anyway – but it had left her off balance and the succubus had struck again, hard and into Maggie's flank. Now Maggie knew she only had the armour to thank for the fact that she was still standing.

But she was only just standing. The bitch's talons had cut deep and she could feel the blood leaking from her.

Stupid Maggie, she thought. Stupid arrogant Maggie: *'I'm Maggie Brown.'* You think like that and you're dead is what you are. She took up a stance, trying to catch her breath. There was no lock on the inside of the door so she had a chance of escape if she could make her way over to it. She might not make it to the front door of the workhouse but she had more chance of taking them in the hallway. They'd have to come at her one at a time; they couldn't do what they were doing now, which was to come at her together.

The wolf was grinning, having stood up from the chair. Fuck him, though, she thought. They all knew the Arcadian alone was no match for her. The succubus, though. She was another matter. The succubus and the Arcadian together. Now she had a real fight on her hands.

A fight she wasn't sure she could win.

The succubus came at her fast and she worked hard to parry, but the wolf did what she'd half-expected it to do; as she was defending herself against the succubus attack, it moved in and slashed, then darted away from her broadsword. The sally over, succubus and wolf moved away, readying themselves for a second attack.

So it was to be that way, eh, she thought. Death of a thousand cuts. Wear her down until she was too exhausted to continue.

Not if she took the battle to them.

And she pounced forward, feinting to the left, then going right, wrong-footing the succubus and striking out at the Arcadian instead.

But she was slow. God, way too slow. From loss of blood, perhaps; the exhaustion; when was the last time she had slept? Either way she seemed to move like she was wading through molasses and the Arcadian danced out of reach, leaving her slicing at the air with her broadsword, only just able to pivot and return to the standing position before the two deviants were able to launch a counter-attack.

Once again, they faced each other.

'You're getting old, Maggie Brown,' taunted the succubus.

'You're getting slow,' added the wolf.

She felt it. She felt old and slow.

'How many of us have you killed over the years, Maggie Brown?' asked the succubus.

'Not enough,' grinned Maggie, wiping blood from her mouth with her sleeve. 'Not nearly enough . . .'

She lunged. The succubus dodged and slashed, catching Maggie on the shoulder, another wound oozing blood.

'You have killed the last of us, Protektor,' said the Arcadian as they resumed their positions. Maggie bristled at the way it paced the room as though it were in control. That mangy dog, that cowardly cur.

'Just you and me,' she told the Arcadian, spitting, 'and I'd take you apart.'

'Unfortunately for you, though, Protektor,' it laughed, 'it's not just you and me, is it?'

Maggie came forward, trying to find a way in. The wolf dodged and slashed, catching her on the arm, both of her arms now torn to shreds; at the same time the succubus kicked and she felt a rib go, then was staggering back, losing breath. God, the rib hadn't punctured a lung, had it? Please Lord, no. Her hand went to her chest and she winced at the pain there.

The succubus threw back her head and laughed. She felt strong, Maggie Brown knew, and confident. And what happens when you get confident, Maggie? You make mistakes . . .

'Which reminds me,' said the wolf, 'it has been most remiss of me not to ask after Mr Brown. It did reach my ears that the once-great Royal Protektor had hung up his boots. That he lost his nerve.' He pulled a mock sad face. 'Say it isn't so . . .'

Yes, thought Maggie. He lost his nerve. For months he had woken up screaming from the nightmares of his castration at the hands of the Arcadians. Months. He'd started drinking soon after. He'd never really stopped.

The succubus laughed once more. When she did it, Maggie noticed, her eyes closed a little. She relinquished concentration.

And the Arcadian. He was arrogant and sloppy and preening. He was too stupid to be vigilant.

There was a chance.

Maggie was outnumbered and hurt and every second that passed made her slower.

But there was a chance.

'Don't you talk about him,' snarled Maggie. 'Don't you talk about him.'

'Oh, is that a sore point?' said the wolf, who sniggered, 'From what I heard, it would have been a very sore point indeed.'

The succubus threw back her head and laughed; the wolf was grooming itself proudly in the aftermath of its joke.

It was her chance.

Maggie Brown attacked. She stepped forward, swinging down and kicking out, taking the Arcadian's leg from beneath it so that it hit the deck with a yowl of pain while at the same time, Maggie, at full stretch, threw herself out, stabbing with the broadsword and catching the succubus off guard.

Except she did not. She was too slow, her moves telegraphed, and though the wolf hit the deck, the succubus danced out of reach. Now Maggie was hitting the floor even as the succubus put her hands to the stone and kicked back, catching Maggie in the face as she tried to scramble to her feet, sending her rolling back, only just able to raise the broadsword and fend off a second attack.

She pushed herself to her feet, barely able to stand, trying to catch her breath. Blood now flowed freely from her face. The kick had broken her nose, she thought. She tried to raise her sword but found she couldn't – her hand, wet with blood, slipped on the handle. She dropped the dagger, tried to lift the sword two-handed now.

(John had always told her: 'Broadsword's too heavy Maggie, it's a two-handed weapon,' but she'd always laughed it off because she was Maggie Brown and she wielded a broadsword, because she was Maggie Brown.

Stupid . . . Arrogant . . .)

She took a grip on her sword, still bent over, her hair hanging over her face, blood and sweat dripping to the stone.

And with a last great effort she managed to raise the sword.

The succubus stepped forward and came to within an inch of Maggie's sword point. Maggie followed her with the sword, needing to wipe the blood from her eyes but unable to do so – until she took a swipe just to try and push the succubus back, so that she could wipe her face, and God she was going to die for want of being able to wipe the blood from her eyes and that was no way to die. No way at all.

Blindly she swung, and the succubus laughed and dodged out of the way. Then Maggie felt claws open her arm and heard the clang of steel upon stone as her sword fell from her bloody fingers and the strength deserted her legs and she sank to her knees. She felt the succubus take hold of her chin and raise her head, tilting it back to expose her throat, and behind the succubus she saw him.

John.

The image of him tinted a hazy red

'You came for me,' she whispered.

'Aye, Maggie,' he said.

The succubus span.

John Brown disembowelled her with a flick of the wrist. The wolf made for the door but John Brown stopped it, thrust the sword into its groin and opened it to the nape of his neck, just as Maggie had once promised to do.

Then, John Brown, grim-faced, sheathed his sword, picked up his unconscious wife and left the workhouse.

XLVII

The Queen stepped through the door that led to the criminal asylum and breathed a sigh of relief. She pulled down the mask that covered her face and breathed in, thankful at last for a lungful of air not contaminated by the fabric, for it was filthy.

And no wonder. Victoria had not, of late, been travelling in the manner to which she was accustomed. After all, she was more used to being transported *inside* a carriage – rather than underneath one.

Doing battle with the zombies at the House, her eye had been caught by the sight of three men in the Strangers' Gallery, one of whom looked like . . . a zombie had reached for her and she sprang away, then turned to it, hacking out with the spinsaw, which was already coated with blood. Go for the brain, Maggie had shouted, and Victoria had put her weapons to good use, the saw splitting skin and skull with ease, ripping into the matter beneath and felling revenants. Another came at her from the side and she stabbed out with the short sword, skewering it at the shoulder then slicing, first backhand with the spinsaw, the MP's scalp sliding from his braincase to reveal the white, blood-streaked cranium beneath; then, forehand – the second strike opening the skull and ploughing into the grey jelly of the brain. The zombie's eyes rolled up and it fell.

Moving into space, Victoria glanced up once more and – *yes*, there he was. He wore a top hat, but his ponytail gave him away. Before she could stop herself she had called out his name.

'Conroy.'

Upon the balcony he had straightened, looking down in the House and seen her. Did he recognise her? Even with the hat and mask? She wasn't sure. And not that it mattered, because Conroy was already making his way out of the gallery, and she knew she couldn't lose him.

She started for the door. Then, in her way, was a man she recognised, Sir Lucius Fulci, the right honourable member for she-wasn't-sure-where, but she had met him once at a gala ball and he had seemed most pleasant and, she recalled, had made a pledge, to always be an ally for her.

Now, however, he wanted to eat her.

'I'm thinking of having you for dinner,' he grinned and lurched forwards, his hands outstretched. Instinctively she ducked beneath his arms, striking up with the shortsword and stabbing him at the sternum. But the move left her beneath his legs and as she tried to pull herself away her boots slipped on the wet floor and she felt her legs go from beneath her, dumping her to the ground.

Sir Lucius Fulci was upon her before she could move, pinning her with his weight, her arms trapped. Then he was on top of her, like an ardent but inexperienced lover, bearing down on her, his face filling her vision. It shone. Saliva dripped from his mouth on to her cheek. With an effort she pulled one of her hands free from beneath him, the one that held the spinsaw, but the blade, trapped beneath their two bodies had ceased spinning. Fulci bearing down on her, she reached and flicked it on his body then with a burst of strength pushed up, giving her just the opening she needed to ram the spinning saw into his forehead, her face spattered with blood and cerebral matter as she performed a makeshift frontal lobotomy upon him.

His limbs were still jerking as she pushed him off, desperate not to lose Conroy, and darted to the pile of bodies blocking the doorway, which reached almost to the top of the frame.

But left a gap just big enough for one person to pass through.

As long as that person was small.

Without breaking stride, the Queen leapt on to the screaming, writhing pile of bodies, reached the top in one bound and was diving forward, arms outflung, the dive taking her through the gap, to the other side where she rolled down the other side of the carcass mountain to land in the corridor. She didn't stop, dashing straight through the main entrance hall and to the steps outside. There she saw Conroy, hurrying towards his carriage, and she prayed he would not glance behind him as she ran across the gravel in his wake.

He didn't. In a great hurry, he tossed his cane to the driver's plate of his hansom cab, then dashed to untether the horses.

Victoria reached the carriage a moment later. For a second her mind refused to comprehend everything that was taking place: she was the Queen of England; she was standing in Westminster in the early hours of the morning, with her face covered in zombie blood.

And now – now she was dropping to one knee and looking beneath the carriage, studying the axle.

And now she was climbing beneath it.

And hanging on . . .

The journey was mercifully brief. Any longer and her muscles would simply have given up. Her arms were on fire by the time they reached their destination and when the carriage stopped she literally dropped from the axle, landing face down in a puddle.

For a second she lay there, feeling the cool water on her face and enjoying the sensation, strangely. And briefly she wondered how long she might remain that way before she simply drowned and none of these worries would exist any more. There would just be . . . peace . . .

No.

With a cry, she pulled her face from the water, bringing her hands to her face and rubbing her eyes, then splashing more water upon herself to wash the blood from her. She heard the crunch of running feet on gravel and looked to her left, seeing the feet and legs of Conroy as he went towards a large building.

A building that, when she pulled herself from the underside of the carriage and took it all in, she saw was Bedlam.

Another carriage arrived and she hid, listening to the ladies disembark, hearing them chatter and formulating a plan. From one of their carriages she was able to take a cloak. Then, seeing her moment, she joined them, all the time seeking out signs of Conroy.

Then, at the door to the criminal asylum, she had gone with her instinct and detached herself from the group.

Now she walked carefully along the corridor. This led to a second door, which she opened, moving through.

Now she was in a hallway similar to the one in which she had left the Bethnal Green Baptist Ladies' Prayer Association members, lined with cells either side. Except this one was – though it hardly seemed possible – even more fearful and foreboding than the last. Noiselessly she moved to the first cell door and peered through the bars. Inside a woman sat on the floor, dressed in rags, pulling at her hair. In the next cell a man sat on the stone, wide awake and regarded her with cruel unseeing eyes. Down his face coursed droplets of blood from where a barbaric-looking steel device had been bolted onto his head. In the next cell a man whose hair had been shaved sat on a straw-covered bench, restrained by a harness and chained to a pipe, which steamed. His head turned to regard her and for a second she stared at him piteously.

'*Bitch*,' he hissed, grinning as she recoiled.

In the next a man sat chewing at his own lip, which oozed blood. He looked at her and, with his fingers to his mouth, poked out his tongue in a grotesque, bloody parody of a sexual act.

Then she heard a voice. It was coming from one of the cells halfway down the corridor.

It came from further up the corridor and she hurried past more cells towards it.

'I am the nephew of the great Egyptian God Osiris,' it said, 'and nobody will believe me, either.'

'Yes,' came a reply, in a voice Victoria recognised immediately, 'but I really *am* Prince Albert.'

'Albert!'

She rushed to the cell door, pressed her face to the bars and there he was. He sat on a bench in the cold, grey cell, his hands secured behind his back, and at the sound of his name, his head jerked to where she stood, though a chain which ran from his hands to a pipe in the cell prevented him from taking more than one step.

'Victoria,' he said. He was wearing the same clothes as he was the night he had been taken; his moustache had been supplemented by stubble. Otherwise, he looked well.

(And her mind flashed back to the wolf on the rack, which had said, 'Oh, they won't be torturing Albert . . .')

Even so, she asked him, 'Are you all right, my darling? Have they hurt you?'

'I am fine,' he smiled, 'all my scars are from the pain of our separation.'

'Albert,' she blushed, 'I do believe your incarceration has robbed you of none of your charm.' Then, 'Where is he? Where is Conroy?'

The Prince shook his head. 'He will be back soon. He was here with talk of leaving. Presumably he has gone to make preparations and will return.'

'Then there is no time to lose.'

She bent to the padlock, took a step back, drew her sword and brought it down, shearing the lock from the door, which she pulled open, and there was Albert, at last, and she ran to him, clasping him to her. With no time to luxuriate in the reconciliation, though, she pulled away so that she might inspect his manacles.

'I'm going to have to cut it, Albert.'

She stepped behind him and raised the sword.

Then stopped.

'Albert,' she said in a small voice, 'why did they take you?'

'I beg your pardon, my love?'

Louder, she said, 'Why has Conroy brought you here? Is it connected with what you were about to tell me that night?'

'Yes,' he said. His shoulders dropped a little. 'They took me because I was going to tell you.'

'Tell me what?'

'The truth.'

'What is the truth?' she hardly dared ask.

'That I am not all I seem to be,' he said, 'and that neither are you.'

She felt Conroy behind her a second before he spoke . . .

'Well, every marriage has its secrets.'

. . . and was already wheeling around, bringing up the katana. Steel clashed with such ferocity that Conroy was driven out into the passage, but not enough to daze him and he was able to meet Victoria as she emerged from the cell, immediately raining attacks down on her, stepping forward and pushing her back. Inwardly, she cursed her inexperience. What had John Brown told her? Never lead with your heart, lead with your head – always the head. And what had she done?

Now she'd been driven back and Conroy stood between her and Albert.

She parried, stopping his attack and dancing back a little to gain some space, the two of them now facing each other in the corridor.

Conroy took up position, his rapier out in front of him and his arm behind in a fencing position. He grinned. 'Do I see the dim light of realisation in your eyes at last, Your Majesty?' he said.

She shook her head no – not wanting to believe it.

'It's true,' he said, 'you are the seed of demons. But then, I believe you already knew that, didn't you?'

She shook her head again.

'Oh, I think you did. Your speed. Your instincts. I saw how ruthless you were in battle, Victoria, and these are all the qualities of your demonic side, qualities you should embrace but do not – because like Prince Albert you resist your true nature.'

'No,' she said.

'Oh yes, Victoria. As a mere mortal, I envy you. You're a half-breed. Half-demon, half-mortal. As is your blushing bridegroom. The two of you paired by your loving parents, placed together like dogs, in order to breed a male heir to the Baal. One who will sit on the throne of England.'

She could not take it all in, struggled with her words. 'My father—' she started, attempting to make sense of it.

'Your father was a human,' said Conroy. 'They needed his lineage, Victoria, nothing more. From his loins came you, the half-breed. They required a male heir, of course, but your mother was unable to conceive another. She wears the shame of it still.'

'My mother . . . inhuman?'

Her sword wavered in front of her and she tried to steady it.

'Yes. As with Albert's father and your Uncle Leopold, she is a descendant of Baal. She was once a very powerful demon, though much reduced now, of course.'

'And you serve them?'

'Yes.'

'For what reason?'

Her voice faltered as she spoke.

'So when the Heir ascends to the throne I will be right at his side, of course.'

'You would have an eighteen-year wait,' said Victoria, her head still reeling.

'The blink of an eye for a demon.'

'But you are—'

'Not for much longer. My services come with a price – and my price is to be granted inhumanity. Not a half-breed like you, but stronger. A demon. As powerful as the Baal. Only, I will have control of the throne, so even *more* powerful.'

'*No*,' she sprang, launching an attack. For a moment they fought, his rapier nicking her arm, drawing blood and eliciting from her a yelp of pain. In return she jabbed, wounding him at the flank and he snarled in surprise, his fingers going to the wound and coming away wet with blood.

She smiled.

'You see that, Your Majesty,' said Conroy. He held up his fingers. 'These skills are not your human skills; *these* are what make you a demon.'

The clash of the steel had been deafening in the corridor, and those prisoners who were able to had come to the bars of their cells, their hands to the bars, rattling the doors, and Victoria saw wide, insane eyes and bared teeth.

'Look how readily they embrace that evil within themselves,' said Conroy over the din. 'If only you could have done the same – your name might have been legendary within the ranks of the Baal. As it is you are merely its sow.'

He swung his rapier from side to side, in one action slicing off padlocks that secured the doors to cells on either side of him. Then took a step forward and did the same with two more.

As he did so, Victoria saw her opening and thrust forward.

'They do not embrace it,' she cried, and there was a great clash of steel as they traded blows, 'it is forced upon them.'

He fended her off then launched his counter attack. She

dodged, feinted, tossing the katana from one hand to the other then spinning to come at him from the other side, but he anticipated the attack and was able to sidestep.

They faced off. She heard a creaking sound and saw one of the doors Conroy had unlocked swing open, as though the cell's occupant could not believe the turn of events.

Conroy swung – left, right – shearing the locks from two more cells now.

'And it is forced upon *you*,' he cried, coming to her now, their swords meeting. 'You have demon blood. It is your nature – it is your instinct, your destiny. You are a servant of the darkness.'

'*No*,' she insisted. 'It only becomes my destiny if I allow it to be so. I once made a pledge, Conroy,' she said fiercely, 'and I have no intention of breaking it.'

'Oh, really?' he said in return, smiling. 'Not even now that you have discovered your mother is an inhuman, that your beloved a half-breed. Has nothing changed? Surely now you are ready to accept your true self?'

'I have accepted my true self,' she said. 'I am the Queen. Nothing changes that, Conroy – only that I now know the truth. And will use it to bury you.'

His smile faltered a little and she used his uncertainty to attack. She made a little ground as they fought, but then Conroy was bearing down on her once again, pushing her back. She was fast, and already a skilled swordswoman, but she was exhausted, and he was strong, and it was all she could do to hold him at bay.

'In that case, Victoria, though it pains me,' he smirked, 'we shall have to say our goodbyes.'

'What do you mean?' she said.

'Behind you is a door—'

'There is no door,' she snapped. There had been just a wall, marking the end of the corridor. Towards which she was now backing.

'No, Victoria, there is a door, look.'

She gave him a withering look as though to say, *Nice try*, but he held up his hands and put his sword behind his back, indicating that she should use the opportunity to look.

She did so, and indeed there was a door – one that had not previously been there, she was sure of it. At first she thought it was a stout wooden door, much like any other, but as she watched, it seemed to shimmer.

'What is it, Conroy?'

'The gateway to the second circle of Hell, Victoria, from which nobody returns.'

'And where is the first?'

'Well, you're standing in it, my dear. Where else do you think we would bring those who need corrupting. Those such as Albert – and yourself. You and he have proved too strong, my dear. I'm afraid there is nothing to be done but to send you – *to Hell*.'

He swiped at two more padlocks. Behind him she saw more doors open and inmates began to appear in the corridor. She saw crazed smiles, their heads darting about. Looking in their direction, but also back to the entrance door – to where Albert was chained in his cell.

'Albert,' she called, '*Albert*.'

She felt wetness on her cheek and realised she was being spat upon. For a second she caught the eyes of the culprit, a man screaming obscenities at her. In the same instant she saw into another cell where a man sat with his trousers about his ankles. He had a cat with him in the cell and was holding it by the neck, kissing it open-mouthed.

'Ah, good evening,' came a voice from another cell, this of a gentleman, and she glimpsed him briefly. He wore a suit and was well dressed. 'Perhaps you would consider letting me out of here,' he said, smiling pleasantly at her. 'Perhaps you would let me out of here so that I can *eat your cunt*.'

She gasped.

Then Conroy was coming forward, pushing her back. For a second he backed off, sheared off two more cell door locks. Then, with a shout, thrust forward again, and as she defended a lunge, he brought his elbow up, smashing her on the cheek and sending her sprawling, stunned, to the stone floor, her sword clattering away from her, the doorway now right behind her.

Distantly, she was aware of Conroy moving towards her. Her sword was kicked even further away from her; she heard it skitter away back down the passage. Then he was standing over her, and she felt fingers at her weapons belt, taking it. Then that, too, was tossed away.

He bent and hauled her to her knees, holding her by the lapels of her coat. Her head lolled, her eyes were half-closed; she was barely conscious.

'It is a shame, Victoria,' he said, 'you should have been a fabled figure in the annals of Hell, instead you are its next victim.'

'No,' she said. Her eyes snapped open and flashed red, and for a second he had a glimpse of the demon within, 'you are.'

Finding the reserves of strength she knew were there, she twisted, pulling him off his feet and to the floor.

He shouted in terror and surprise as he hit the stone then Victoria was throwing herself forward, pushing him into the shimmering doorway. One of his legs disappeared into it, breaking the image as though it was the surface of water, and as it did so, his eyes widened in pain and horror. Suddenly his whole body jerked and he slid on the ground, his other leg going in the portal.

He threw out his hands, grabbing hers, so that she, too, was yanked forwards to the door. Lying on her stomach now she yelled in pain as his grip tightened and he was, slowly, pulled into the inferno.

But pulling her with him.

She, her feet scrabbling and unable to make purchase.

Their eyes locked; his, huge with pain, his lips drawn back as he snarled, 'It is . . .' he tried to say. 'It is . . . *agony*.'

He began to scream. Still he gripped her. To try and pull himself free or her in with him, she wasn't sure. Either way—

He was going to drag her in with him.

She kicked and doubled up, bringing her legs forward so that her boots went to the wall by the side of the portal, and at least now she had some leverage. But Conroy was refusing to let go. With a wrench she managed to free one of her arms and for a second he floundered, but then he clutched her other arm with two hands, his grip like iron and still screaming, more of his lower body disappearing into the portal.

Behind her the lunatics screamed and howled, the noise of it cacophonous. And she heard Albert, too, from his cell, screaming her name. They would be upon him. She felt the heat from behind the door.

Braced against the wall, but moving inch by inch towards the door she threw her head back, seeing the inmates in the corridor. Most, she saw, her making their way to the entrance door – in the direction of Albert – two had begun to shuffle in her direction. One of them was the man with the cat, which now hung limp and dead from his hand, and he was eyeing up her . . .

Weapons belt. In it, her spinsaw. With her free hand she grabbed for it.

It lay just out of reach of her fingertips.

The cat man started to move with more urgency.

She braced her feet. She summoned her strength. And with a shout she pulled, able to gain an inch and getting her fingers to the belt – *just* – then snatching it from the grasp of the cat man who had gone to his knees to try and take it, and who now let out a howl of denial.

From the belt Victoria seized her spinsaw, flicking it to start.

It didn't.

Conroy saw what was about to happen. He redoubled his efforts. She felt herself pulled towards the portal. Felt the searing heat of it. Tried the spinsaw again.

It took, and was spinning now, and grimacing she reached forward and used it to amputate Conroy's hands. First one, her face spayed with gore; then the other, until at last his arm tore free and with a last anguished scream, he was sucked into the inferno.

In the same instant the cat man was upon her, screaming obscenities and grabbing her face as though about to try and kiss her, but instead she pushed the spinsaw into his face and he was falling back, grey brain matter sliding down his face.

'Victoria,' came a scream.

Albert.

Victoria was already on her feet, dashing along the passageway to Albert's cell, evading a second inmate, then a third.

Her sword? Where was her sword?

She stood for a moment, looking for it. Inmates gathered about her. One of the men had pulled down his trousers and was tumescent, pushing out his hips at her. Another, a woman, was laughing maniacally, blood dripping from her chin, reaching for her.

Then she saw movement at the door to Albert's cell and saw the Prince emerge. He was held hostage by the well-dressed man, who was marching him to the door.

But inmates crowded in on her. She screamed, slashing indiscriminately with the spinsaw, frantic to free herself and reach him – desperate not to lose him again. Now was aware of the door opening, Albert and the maniac moving through it.

At last the inmates fell away and she pushed herself off the wall onto which she had backed and shoulder-barged one of them out of the way, making for the door, certain that Albert and his captor would be through it by now and praying the man was simply too unhinged to think of locking it.

Except, they had not passed through. They stood still in the doorway.

On the other side of the door stood Vasquez. She was with two men that Victoria recognised from the Commons. Her bow was drawn and she was aiming at Albert and the psychopath, who looked nervously from Vasquez to the Queen.

'Your Majesty?' said Vasquez.

'Do you have a clear shot?' said Victoria.

The maniac shrank behind Albert.

'Negative,' replied Vasquez.

There was a second of stillness.

'Take the shot,' said Victoria.

The katana hit the floor and the psychopath was reeling back, an arrow in his eye, falling and releasing the Prince who sprang out of his grasp – and into Victoria's arms.

Moments later, she closed the door on the scenes of carnage in the asylum, glancing to the far end, where the portal appeared no longer. Then they made their way out of Bethlem and past the ladies of the Bethnal Green Baptist Ladies' Prayer Association, gathered together in readiness for their journey home, who, with eyes wide in shock, watched the group make its way to a carriage. All the ladies were as one fascinated by the exotic-looking archer, the upper class-gentleman who seemed to be trying unsuccessfully to ingratiate himself with the exotic-looking archer, the shambling manservant, and in particular by the couple who walked ahead of them: a distinguished-looking gentleman, who bore more than a passing resemblance to Prince Albert, and a short woman, covered head to toe in blood, who, were it not for the fact that she was covered in blood, was smiling broadly and was carrying a very large sword, might well have passed for the Queen of England herself, Queen Victoria.

XLVIII

Later that morning
Buckingham Palace

It was the early hours of the morning in the stableyard at Buckingham Palace. A mist hung about the ground and the breath of the footmen clouded before them as they carried trunks to the Clarence – a specially selected carriage with no Royal crest or markings upon it – and secured them to its roof, lashing them there with rope. With the job done the footmen gathered a few feet away, looking awkward and confused, unsure what to make of this most unprecedented event and wondering if they should perhaps alert one of the ladies-in-waiting, or the Lord Steward. Instead, all had been roused individually from their beds by the Prince, who required their aid, because, he said, he, the Queen and children were leaving – alone.

The two children were asleep on the seats, and Victoria made sure they were warm and comfortable, and she arranged sheets so that they could not roll out of their makeshift beds, then closed the carriage door, and climbed up to the driver's plate to join Albert, who sat there, holding the reins. They looked towards the footmen who stood quite unable to comprehend what they were seeing, and Albert touched a hand to the rim of his hat in farewell, then shook the reins, the only sound in the early morning courtyard, that of the hooves upon the cobbles.

The carriage rattled along the approach road and Victoria twisted in her seat to look back at the Palace, stifling a sob as her home receded – knowing she would never return.

She closed her eyes and tried not to think of the future, for it was so black and uncertain. She and Albert had decided that they should travel abroad and that wherever it was they should go, it should be outside Europe. As far from England and Germany and Belgium as they could manage. Beside that they had no plans, other than to live and survive and to try and be happy.

As long as it meant that they had escaped. This was their chief concern. That they should take themselves, and more importantly their children, away from those manacles of destiny that had been forced upon them.

Presently, the carriage drew to a halt and the Queen awoke. For a moment she was disorientated, thinking they must have travelled miles and that Albert had arrived at a port, but when she rubbed her bleary eyes and stared around her, she saw the distinctive trees and shrubbery of the Palace. It felt as though she had been asleep for hours, lulled by the movement of Albert's arm and warmed by his body. In fact, they hadn't even left the gates.

'Victoria,' said Albert, and he was pointing ahead of them to where a woman sat on her horse.

In the dead silence and crisp cold of the morning, Victoria and Maggie Brown looked at one another. Maggie was sitting astride Henstridge.

Both doing what they believed to be right.

Both doing their duty.

'A word, Your Majesty,' said Maggie, and she indicated a spot off the highway, beneath a tree on the lawn. She jumped down from Henstridge at the same time, patting his flank. She put a hand to the hilt of her sword and strode to the spot.

'You're not going?' said Albert as Victoria went to climb down.

'Yes, I'm going,' she said.

She paused on the step. 'If anything happens, ride, Albert.'

'Victoria . . .'

'No. Just promise me that – that if anything happens, you'll just go.'

Albert looked over at Maggie Brown, who stared back. 'It's just the lassie I need to see,' she said, dispassionately.

Albert bridled. 'The lassie,' he hissed. 'Why, who on earth does she think she's talking to?'

'Albert,' snapped Victoria, 'we've just abdicated. When you've abdicated you stop worrying about how people address you.'

She jumped the last step to the ground, then walked around the back of the Clarence to meet Maggie Brown. On the way she bent down and retrieved from beneath the axle her katana sword, which she had stowed there earlier. She was dangling it over her shoulder as she appeared around the back of the Clarence, the hilt of it at her left armpit.

Maggie Brown saw, and smiled.

And now Victoria saw Maggie Brown properly. The cuts and bruises that adorned her face.

'You were going to leave, just like that?' said Maggie.

'I was worried about doing it any other way,' said Victoria. Both women kept their distance. 'I was worried this might happen, in fact.'

'Aye, of course,' said Maggie, ruefully.

Now the Protektor smiled sadly. 'When you spoke to your mother earlier, guess who was listening?'

'I thought as much,' smiled Victoria.

'You're a half-breed, ma'am,' said Maggie Brown, who sounded crestfallen, as though nothing had ever pained her more. 'The blood that you, your husband and your children carry is what I am sworn to destroy. I can't let you leave those gates.'

She drew her sword.

Victoria looked at her. The Protektor had been badly hurt in whatever battle she had been involved. Victoria could see bandages beneath her sleeves and she limped slightly when she walked.

But even so, could Victoria beat her in battle?

No, she didn't think so.

'I won't let you kill my children, Maggie,' she said, hoping that she sounded braver than she felt.'

She drew her sword.

'Aye,' said Maggie. 'I didn't think you would.'

She lifted her sword.

Then placed the point of it to the ground, took the hilt in two hands and knelt, bowing her head, like a knight of old.

'Maggie?' said Victoria.

Maggie Brown looked at her.

'Last night young John Brown had another of his visions,' she said. 'This one was of the same conflict. He saw great death and suffering once more. He saw men in iron hats, burning. He saw men dying in huge troughs cut into the ground. A war on a scale mankind has never seen, or so he said. Now, I have no way of knowing whether or not this war will ever take place, and if it does whether it happens because of you or despite you. And I have no idea of knowing whether his premonition will come true, or whether or not my actions will have any effect on whether it does, because until a moment ago even I didn't know what I was going to do. Whether I was going to put you and your family to the sword or tell you not to be so bloody stupid and get your arse back in that palace and start running the country.'

She paused.

'The fact is, Your Majesty, that whatever the blood that flows through your veins, your heart is good, and your country needs that now. Which is why I'm down on one knee in the freezing cold at God-knows-what hour of the morning. She straightened. 'Which is why I'm telling you to get your arse back in that palace and start running the country.'

Minutes later, Maggie Brown had galloped off and Albert and Victoria watched her go, Albert about to shake the reins and drive on.

Victoria stopped him, though, of course.

'Turn around, Albert,' she said. 'We're going home.'

XLIX

The same time
Pembridge Villas, Notting Hill

Quimby stepped quickly back from his gratifyingly weighty drapes and turned to the room, addressing Perkins and Egg.

'Christ,' he said, 'they're coming. The peelers are on their way!'

Perkins and Egg stared back at him, unmoved.

'A fine help the pair of you are,' shouted Quimby, pacing the room. He still had no idea whether or not his revenants submitted to his control. Worse, when he tried to gather from Perkins and Egg whether or not they were under his control – *they who should bloody know!* – neither were able to say.

So it was that as the peelers banged on his front door, he still had no idea and was sweating profusely as Perkins answered the door. A sign they would surely take as evidence of his guilt.

Oh Christ.

Oh God.

He heard the two officers ascend his stairs and walked out of the study on to the main hall, greeting them breezily. But their faces were grave, and as they walked to the library the officers explained that they needed to ask his Lordship some questions involving some rather delicate subjects, and that his Lordship might need to come to the station.

'Oh,' said Quimby, smiling sweatily, 'I'm sure that won't be necessary.'

He opened the door to the library and all three of the men walked in. A man was already in the library, and was sitting in a leather chair eating what the two policeman took to be breakfast from a plate on a side table.

'You see, my friend here will be able to vouch for me, whatever the circumstances, isn't that right?' Quimby indicated Lord Melbourne, who sat still eating. Quimby added, 'Isn't that right, Prime Minister?'

With great relish, the Prime Minister took a bite from something that looked like a large length of meat, and the juices glistened on his chin.

He looked at Quimby, and smiled.

A note on historical accuracy

Though I have of course played fast and loose with history, the main action of the book adheres as closely to the real-life events of Victoria's life as was humanly possible, given the demands of weaving in the fictional elements – though I have conflated some events and massaged certain timelines. Meanwhile, all anachronisms are intentional, even those that are not.